MURDER AT RAVENSWOOD HOUSE

LOUISE MARLEY

Storm

Ebook ISBN: 978-1-80508-381-8
Paperback ISBN: 978-1-80508-383-2

Cover design: Ghost
Cover images: Shutterstock

Published by Storm Publishing.
For further information, visit:
www.stormpublishing.co

ALSO BY LOUISE MARLEY

Murder at Raven's Edge

To Andy, Jodie and Luke,
with love

ONE

Raven's Edge after dark was an eerie place to be. The surrounding forest loomed closer, darker, nastier, and the cottages along the narrow high street huddled tighter together. When the air was cold and the sky was clear, a mist would curl in from the river and it was all too easy to see how a swirl of leaves could be spun into a tale of ghostly revenge, or the rattle of a slate falling from a roof be twisted into spectral hooves clattering over the cobblestones.

Milla Graham ran along the high street, ignoring the shadows that appeared to shift and twist behind her, and the echo of footsteps that might not have been hers. The moonlight had turned the wet paving stones to silver beneath her feet and effectively lit her way towards the path that led past the village pond, where (legend had it) the local witch had met her end over three hundred years ago.

Witch: A smart woman with a smart mouth.

Someone who didn't follow the rules.

Someone who didn't belong.

She'd always felt a great deal of empathy with that witch.

Far too pragmatic to believe in ghosts, she still hesitated before taking the path that led into the forest, switching on her phone torch as the ancient, gnarled branches closed over her head, blocking out the moonlight completely.

The further she walked, the narrower and darker the foot-path became. It had been a hot, wet summer and the track was overgrown with ferns and nettles almost as tall as her. The only sound was that of her boots scrunching through fallen leaves and broken twigs. How long had it been since anyone had walked this way?

It was too late to realise she should have brought her car, but with its personalised number plate it was far too distinctive, and she had no wish for anyone in the village to guess she was up to no good.

Leaving it parked outside the house of an ex-lover definitely qualified as 'up to no good'.

The important word to remember here was 'ex'.

She was *not* betraying Ben. She *loved* Ben. He knew that. But, in the four months they'd been together, she still hadn't got around to telling him there'd once been someone else.

Milla had met Lorcan in Glastonbury last year. She'd given up trying to inveigle her way into the music festival and had been sulkily exploring the village. He'd been a bespectacled geek that someone was half-heartedly attempting to rob. She'd chucked a potted geranium at the would-be attacker – and missed, as usual: her aim was appalling – but the other man had taken fright and fled.

'I need a stiff drink,' the geek had said. 'Can I get one for you?'

'You can buy me a cola,' she'd replied.

It wasn't as though she had anything else to do.

So they'd gone to the pub and chatted for hours, until a

flurry of notifications had made him pick up his phone and grimace.

'Sorry,' he'd sighed. 'I'm supposed to be on stage in thirty minutes. They seem a bit upset that I'm not there already.'

'Stage?' She'd regarded him blankly. 'You mean at the festival? You're a *musician*?'

'Didn't I say?'

'No!'

'Ah... Well, I'm a musician and I'm supposed to be performing in thirty minutes, so my manager is sending a car for me. Would you like to come too? They give us extra tickets for family and friends, but I don't have any family or friends, apart from my manager, and...' Lorcan picked up his phone again and winced. 'Yep, he's *really* unhappy with me. I've got to go. *Please* say you'll come too?'

She stared at him. What kind of person didn't have family or friends?

A very lonely one, as it turned out.

She'd gone to the festival and had the best time ever, writing a series of articles about her experience and selling it to a now-defunct music magazine – launching a whole new career out of one good deed.

They'd dated for a few months, but they were better as friends. He'd returned to his house in Provence and she'd ended up here in Raven's Edge, reuniting with her long-lost family and meeting Ben, whom she still hadn't got around to telling about Lorcan.

She'd never told Lorcan about meeting Ben either, having a horrible feeling that neither man would approve of the other.

Hence this moonlit trek through a dark, allegedly haunted forest.

Honestly, sometimes she made things so *difficult* for herself.

.   .   .

After twenty minutes' walk, the path widened into a single-track lane and the outline of a building emerged from the shadows. A medieval farmhouse, long and low, the refurbished stone gleaming pale in the moonlight, the roof bristling with new thatch. There were no lights, which was odd, and the windows were dark, empty and dead. It was the classic sign of an empty house and she felt that first twinge of unease. Was Lorcan at home? Did she have the right day? Did she have the right *house*?

She walked around to the front. There was a freshly nailed sign on the gate that said,

RAVENSWOOD HOUSE

Definitely the right place.

She pushed the gate open. A neatly clipped box hedge lined a path that ended at a sturdy wooden door. She switched off her phone, slid it into her pocket and knocked. There was a hollow echo from the other side and the door creaked open.

That was strange.

Careful to keep her feet on her side of the threshold, she leaned inside. 'Hey, Lorcan! I'm here!'

The house remained silent.

She knocked again, accidentally pushing the door further open.

'Lorcan! It's *me*! Where are you?'

It was unlike him to stand her up. She took out her phone and checked for missed calls or messages. There was only one, and that was from Ben, saying he'd be home around midnight and not to wait up. She replied to that and then, feeling incredibly guilty, sent one to Lorcan.

> Where are you?

While waiting for a response, she checked the other side of

the door. It had a modern lock rather than an over-sized iron key. If she pulled it shut, the door should lock itself and she could go home with a clear conscience.

But as she pulled the door towards her, a crash echoed from the back of the house.

What the *hell* was that?

Hesitating for not nearly long enough, Milla took a step over the threshold into the cavernous hall. 'Lorcan? Are you OK?'

Ignoring the unassailable fact that the house would hardly be in darkness if he were in residence, she switched on the light and walked across the hall into a low, wide passageway that seemed to pass through the centre of the house. The scent of fresh paint made her cough, a testament to the newness of the deep dark gold of the walls. Rather less attractive was the row of Victorian hunting trophies along each wall, their eyes watching her progress with glassy indifference.

She grimaced. Lorcan's taste in interior design had *not* improved.

A door on the left led into a large modern kitchen, with crockery in the glass-fronted cabinets and cutlery in the drawers. If she needed any more evidence that he'd moved in, the clock on the cooker was set to the correct time. For someone who never worked regular hours, Lorcan had always been particular about that.

Was he working now?

Strike that thought. The house was too quiet. Even when he wasn't strumming on his guitar, Lorcan played music wherever he went, creating endless playlists to soundtrack his life. She peeped into the sitting room on the other side of the passageway, but that was deserted too.

His guitars and extensive collection of vinyl records were here, but he wasn't.

She headed back to the entrance hall. He hadn't replied to

her message. He must have completely forgotten he'd invited her here, which was unflattering to say the least.

The hall was two storeys high, with a wooden staircase tucked into one corner; as she passed beneath the rafters, she heard a curious flapping sound.

She paused, one hand on the banister. 'Lorcan? Are you up there?'

Was that a movement on the landing? Should she investigate?

What if there was an intruder?

(An intruder other than her.)

'Hello?' she said, but not quite as loudly as before.

'Hello,' a voice replied.

Her breath hitched.

The voice had come from upstairs.

'Lorcan? Are you messing with me? Because I'm *really* not in the mood...'

No response.

'I'm telling you now, if you jump out at me, pretending to be a ghost, I will *not* be pleased.'

'Hello,' the little voice said again.

'I warned you!' She started up the staircase. Warped and crooked with age, it creaked with every step she took.

Halfway up, she heard a curious whispering and fluttering emanating from the dark void above her head.

I don't believe in ghosts.

Old houses often made strange noises; three months of living in her current home had proved that. Wood expanded and contracted with the rise and fall of temperature, nails loosened over time, air got into pipes—

Something shot past her head, knocking her off balance.

If she hadn't been grimly holding onto the banister, she'd have fallen to the bottom of the stairs.

She still wasn't sure why she hadn't screamed.

A blur of black circled towards her and this time she ducked, swearing softly as some kind of creature plunged past, wings beating once, twice...

A leisurely glide around the hall and it vanished into the darkness. She followed its path, squinting into the gloom. A bat? It would have to be a big bat! A large bird? An owl or a crow, or...

Or a raven.

Obviously.

The woods were full of them, hence the name of the village. The local witch had allegedly turned herself into a flock of them and been known as the Raven Queen ever since. An *unkindness* of ravens. It seemed appropriate, because the villagers had been trying to kill her at the time.

The raven landed on the banister behind her. It was *huge*, almost the size of a chicken, and now it was sidestepping towards her, tail fanned out for balance.

She took a wary step up.

The raven tilted its head, revealing a sharp, curved beak and one black beady eye trained directly on her.

Milla tried to think calm, relaxing thoughts.

OK, it was big, but it was a wild bird. It should be more afraid of her.

How had it got in?

She released her grip on the banister and took another step up.

The bird sidestepped again, head bobbing, as though performing some weird dance – the kind her Great-Uncle Fergal performed at parties when he wasn't even drunk – lowering its head and cocking it sideways again, as though to get a better look at her.

Was it Lorcan's *pet*? He'd never mentioned having one.

More to the point, was it plotting an attack? Her eyes as a tasty *hors d'oeuvre*?

Why couldn't Lorcan have owned a *budgie*?

'Hello,' it said.

It could *talk*? She didn't know ravens could *talk*!

She backed up a few more steps.

The raven followed her every move with interest but, at the very moment she thought herself safe, it gave a horrible gurgling croak and stretched its wings, ready for flight.

Milla fell up the last few steps and yanked open the nearest door, really hoping it wasn't a linen cupboard, slamming it behind her, half-expecting to hear the bird crash against the other side and see that wickedly sharp beak penetrate the centuries-old wood.

On the other side of the door, all was silent.

Somehow that made it worse.

She leant against the wall, hearing her breath coming in short, sharp gasps.

What was Lorcan *thinking* to allow a bird like that to have free range of his house? The wingspan must be easily four feet, and as for that beak...

When she saw Lorcan again, she was going to kill him!

She switched on the light. She appeared to be trapped in his bedroom. The window was open, presumably due to the paint fumes, although the thick brocade curtains hung motionless, despite the breeze whipping up the hill.

Maybe she could leave the house that way?

Lorcan's taste for Victorian Gothic was evident in the relentlessly aubergine walls and hangings draping the four-poster bed. A silver skull on a shelf bookended a stack of poetry books. Beside the bed was a bottle of his favourite Finlayson's Best Whisky. Picking it up by the neck, she held it up to the light, swilling around the liquid. Half empty. Not surprising. What was surprising was the packet of sleeping pills beside it. Why did he need those? They'd be enough to knock anyone out for hours, particularly when mixed with alcohol. Had he taken any tonight? Yet his bed didn't appear to have been slept in.

Should she be searching the house for his comatose body?

With Mr Beaky outside, waiting for the chance to feast on her soft parts?

Maybe not.

Lorcan Black was a grown man. He could take care of himself.

There was only one glass beside the bottle, so he hadn't had company. Not unusual. Lorcan always had trouble trusting people. The packet of sleeping tablets had a dispensary sticker from a French pharmacy but she knew he'd been living in Provence since last Christmas. There was a copy of Shelley's poems, a silver pendant containing the wing of a morpho butterfly and, if that wasn't Gothic enough, a large specimen jar at the very back, containing more bits of dead animal.

This farmhouse was turning out to be a regular house of horrors.

She sighed and bent to check it out, and immediately wished she hadn't.

The contents were fake.

They had to be.

It was a prop from a film.

Because anything else...

Was unthinkable.

TWO

Milla took a step back and stared at the jar as though hoping that if she stared hard enough, it might change into something else. That it was all a mistake. That it wasn't real. That it was just a trick of the light.

She swallowed hard. This really wasn't a good time to be sick.

Why wasn't she running for the hills?

Why did she feel so *calm*?

What should she do?

What should she do?

What should she *do*?

Call someone.

Who? The police? And have to explain why she was trespassing in someone else's house? She could guess how that would go down and it wouldn't end with her being tucked up in her own bed, especially if Lorcan had locked himself in a studio and didn't answer his phone for three days to corroborate her story.

Where are *you, Lorcan?*

Had something happened to him?

She tried phoning him. No answer.

Her thumb wavered over Ben's name in her contacts list but how could she drag him into this? She could see the flash of disappointment in his eyes as she tried to explain how she came to be trespassing in the house of her ex. An ex he hadn't even known about.

Why hadn't she told him?

When he learnt about the contents of that jar, he'd issue a warrant for Lorcan's arrest. He didn't know Lorcan like she did. He wouldn't believe Lorcan wasn't capable of hurting anyone. No one knew how sweet and kind-hearted he was behind the goth image. They saw the black Victorian clothes and the over-long hair, the black nail varnish and eyeliner, and immediately assumed the worst.

The scandal would ruin him. How could she let that happen, after all he'd done for her? Was this why the jar had been left here? Was someone trying to set him up for a fall? In which case, she definitely couldn't call Ben, because that would play right into their hands.

Which brought her neatly back to the start.

What should she do?

Call someone.

But if you couldn't call the good guys when you were in trouble, who did that leave?

Milla hit the search bar and typed:

Kieran Drake

And there he was.

Kieran Drake Investigations
Quay Street
Port Rell

As much as it pained her to admit it, Drake was the perfect person to help. He was a 'problem solver', a 'fixer'. Anything slightly dodgy and he'd do it – for a hefty fee – or a favour in return.

Four months ago, she'd discovered that her father had paid Drake to follow her around and report back, to ensure she was 'safe'. It had been done with the best intentions (someone had been trying to kill her at the time) but, as it had happened without her consent or knowledge, she wasn't ready to forgive either of them.

Now, however, she needed Drake's help.

She didn't have a choice.

Milla tapped on the phone number and waited for him to answer.

As she listened to it ring, she belatedly remembered it was well past 9.00 pm.

Who answered a work phone at 9.00 pm? Who even had it off mute—?

'Well, *hello*, Princess.'

He'd mistaken her for someone else? That was awkward.

'Drake?'

'You should know,' he said. 'You phoned me.'

'Who do you think this is?'

'Camilla Graham.'

'How...'

How did he *do* that? She didn't give her number out to many people and certainly not to the man who'd spent the last few years stalking her on behalf of her wealthy father.

'*Detective*, Princess. Clue's in the name. What can I do for you that your boyfriend can't help you with?'

She could actually hear him smirk.

'I need your help,' she said, hoping she sounded brisk and business-like.

'And you called *me*?' He laughed. 'It must be bad.'

Her eyes found the jar again.

Yes, it certainly was.

'After last summer, I think you owe me,' she said.

'Firstly, that's not the correct way to begin a negotiation, and secondly, as your father and I were trying to ensure you weren't murdered, *I think* we can call that debt cancelled.'

'OK, I'll pay you.'

He was silent for a moment and then, 'We'll call it a favour.'

Damn.

A favour for him to call in at a time and place of his choosing? Not a chance.

'I'd be happier paying you, Drake. Whatever it costs.'

'I'm sure you would, Princess, but that's not how I work. Where are you?'

'How well do you know Raven's Edge?'

He hesitated. 'I used to work there.'

There weren't that many places to work in Raven's Edge: a trio of cafés, a couple of pubs, numerous gift shops, the museum and the police station.

He didn't look like a barista or a historian. Had he been a *cop*?

'There's a farmhouse on the edge of the forest,' she began, wondering why it felt as though she were selling her soul. 'It's really old, with a thatched roof—'

'I know the one. Fell into ruin, recently renovated by a rock star with more money than sense.' He paused, and then whistled. 'I can see now why you didn't want to call your boyfriend. Have you been *bad*, Princess?'

'I am *not* sleeping with Lorcan Black. Let's get that clear *right* from the start. He's just a friend.'

'A very *good* friend,' Drake laughed again. He was enjoying this far too much. 'That only leaves one other thing,' he said.

'What?'

'You've killed him.'

That was far too close for comfort. She wondered how to explain but it seemed her silence had done the work for her.

'Camilla? Please tell me you don't want me to dispose of a body.'

'I don't want you to dispose of a body,' she said. 'Well, not a *whole* body...'

He swore, and then he swore again. 'You're serious, aren't you?'

'Can you help?' She heard her voice crack and despised herself. 'This is beyond my capability. Ben can't find out...' *It would kill him.*

'You know the routine,' Drake said. 'Wipe down everything you've touched and get the hell out of there.'

Up until then she'd felt completely composed. OK, it was an unnatural kind of composure, and probably some kind of shock, and maybe this would all hit her tomorrow, but the tone of his voice (harsh and abrupt) poked at that little sliver of panic her brain had been trying so hard to bury, and her heart crashed back into action, and suddenly she couldn't breathe.

'Camilla? *Milla!* If you can hear me, if you're still there, you need to leave. *Whatever* you've done, I'm sure your father – and Ben – would say the same.'

'I need your help, Drake.' Did she have to sound so pathetic?

'You'll get it. I'm on my way. Just get out of there.'

'I can't... you know, leave it here.'

Silence, then,

'Leave *what*?'

As she told him the grim details, a small dispassionate part of her thought of Ben, blissfully unaware of the mess she'd got herself into, *again*.

She should never have entered the house. She should never have agreed to meet Lorcan, and she should have told Ben about how much Lorcan had meant to her *weeks* ago because now she was forced to choose between them. And as much as she cared for Lorcan, like a *brother*, having to choose him over Ben was destroying her.

'The person who did that?' Drake was saying. 'The sick, twisted person who did that? They could still be there.'

Why did he have to put that idea in her head?

She remembered the strange noises, the crash...

Oh, no...

'You need to *go*,' he said.

He didn't have to say it twice.

She terminated the call, glancing towards the door that led into the rest of the house, where the creepy stuffed deer heads and devil bird waited for her.

To hell with *them*.

She ran to the open window, slinging one leg over the sill.

Wait... Was that a creak from the landing? She cast a glance over her shoulder.

No, only an old building settling down for the night.

If she kept telling herself that, maybe she'd believe it.

She slung the other leg over and pushed herself off the windowsill, dropping onto the soft soil below.

And if she heard a sound from the room she'd left, or half-glimpsed a shadowy movement as she fell, that might have been someone coming into the room to watch her run into the forest, she did *not* look back.

FIFTEEN YEARS PREVIOUSLY...

One of these days his parents would kill each other and he wasn't sure he'd lift a finger to stop them. He wouldn't even care who won. It would be totally worth it to enjoy the peace and quiet.

He maxed out the volume on his grandfather's ancient record player, but a crackly Eddie Cochran was no match for his mother in full rant. So he switched it off and rolled off the bed as the entire farmhouse reverberated to the slam of the back door.

Exit his father, down the pub for poker night. So that meant—

'Darling, you won't believe what the bastard's said this time...'

Less than five seconds for his mother to be on the phone to her latest conquest for phone sex, or real sex, or whatever. Just so long as he didn't have to hang around to listen to it.

He shoved open the bedroom window, slid over the sill and down the drainpipe, landing softly in the backyard.

His father had taken the Mondeo, leaving only the beat-up Land Rover abandoned beneath the chestnut trees, the bonnet already covered in withered brown leaves and conker shells. If he pulled the seat hard forward he'd be able to reach the pedals, and there should be enough fuel left to get him to the village for the carnival.

He yanked open the door, flipped down the visor on the driver's side and held out his hand to catch the keys.

Nothing but a shower of dirt and woodlice.

In disbelief he bent to check the footwell and under the seat, and then heard his mother's bitter laugh behind him.

'Where do you think you're going? Back inside, right now. I don't need another snooty busybody telling me my kid's running feral.'

He stood slowly. His mother was standing on the back doorstep, silhouetted in the light from the kitchen, still holding the phone to her ear with one hand. In the other she dangled the keys to the Land Rover, before stepping back into the kitchen and slamming the door.

He used his boot to kick the Land Rover door shut, not caring that he'd left a dent in it, and then kicked the tyre for good measure. Sure, it was only a twenty-minute walk to the village through the forest, but who wanted to walk when they could ride?

Ride...

He swivelled slowly, turning his attention towards the unlit stable block.

And smiled.

THREE

October 28th

Raven's Edge was never going to be the kind of cute English village that would look good on a Christmas card, liberally sprinkled with glitter, but its inherent spookiness meant it was an extremely popular place to visit during the week before Halloween. There was the story of the witch who turned herself into one hundred ravens – the records were oddly precise about that – a highwayman seeking revenge on the man who'd sent him to the gallows, and the ghostly Cavaliers that allegedly haunted the surrounding forest.

The entire village had gone all out with their seasonal decorations this year. Old broomsticks were propped against doorways and cauldrons had been left beside garden gates, ready to be filled with chocolates and sweets for later in the week.

It was 8.45 am and DS Harriet March was due at work in fifteen minutes – hardly unachievable, because the police station was only a few doors down from her apartment over the florist, Foxglove & Hemlock. The owners had decorated their window for Halloween, with swathes of black netting and trailing cobwebs, huge bouquets of orange lilies, roses and alstroemeria, tied with wide black ribbons, and Gothic posies of Black Baccara roses arranged in white pumpkins.

Between Foxglove & Hemlock and the police station was a tiny, lopsided café called The Crooked Broomstick. So named, the legend said, because it had been built in a day, thereby tricking the devil into being unable to claim the mason's soul.

Harriet suspected this story had been created by an inept builder to explain his shoddy workmanship, but the café was a huge attraction for the tourists, the cookies were divine and so was the man who baked them – Misha Sokolov, whom she'd crushed on since they were in the same class at school.

Every morning there would be a long queue snaking out of the door, and today was no exception. Harriet tagged onto the end. She'd got into the habit of calling into The Crooked Broomstick each morning for coffee and a cookie straight from the oven. Not *breakfast*, obviously, because who had cookies for breakfast?

'Cookies for breakfast *again*,' a voice murmured into her ear and she turned to see DC Asheem Chopra behind her. With his shiny black hair, sensuous dark eyes and cheekbones you could peel a rosy-red apple on, all the other women in the village thought he was wonderful – but then they didn't have to work with him.

'Of course not,' she lied. 'This is elevenses.'

'Even though you'll be eating them at nineses?'

She glared at him. 'Maybe leave the jokes to Sam?'

He grinned unrepentantly. 'With the size of this queue, you know it'd be quicker to go to The Witch's Brew.'

Harriet surreptitiously counted the people in front of her. She recognised several of her colleagues at the police station. Ash was right, but she would never admit it.

'Shall we go?' Ash nodded down the high street. 'It's only a five-minute walk.'

For his long legs, maybe. For her it would be more like ten.

'Don't forget the five minutes to walk back,' she said.

'It's still quicker than hanging around in this queue. I'll see you later!'

'Don't be late. Ben's off today and I'm in charge.'

He laughed as he strolled off down the road.

That was the problem with working with people who'd known you since kindergarten. They never took you seriously.

As the queue moved forward by just one person, she wondered if Kat Davenport, the owner of The Witch's Brew, would be baking the same peanut butter cookies her aunt had always made at this time of year. Miss Lily would individually wrap each cookie in orange paper and tie them with green ribbon. They had been much prized by the local children – and their parents too.

Perhaps she should have gone with Ash. She could just eat a—

'Harriet?' Misha was watching her from the other side of the counter. 'What can I get you?'

There were people behind her but those in front had disappeared.

'Where did everyone go?'

He pointed to the clock on the wall. 'Don't you guys start work at nine?'

'It depends on the shift.'

'What would you like?' Misha asked patiently.

She could think of all kinds of answers to that question. The man ticked every box: ice-blue eyes, long blond hair, carefully tied back while he was working. He was a real-life Legolas – if Legolas had ever worn an apron with broomsticks on it.

'Harriet?'

'Sorry! A cappuccino and a – do you have anything new for Halloween?'

The queue behind groaned.

Misha's mouth twitched and he pointed to the board behind him. 'Well, in the cookie selection we have pumpkin cheesecake (that's *my* favourite), pumpkin and chocolate chip, *spiced* pumpkin and chocolate chip, pumpkin and oatmeal—'

Aware that the queue was becoming restless, Harriet quickly interrupted. 'I think I'll have a pecan and maple syrup and... maybe a pumpkin and chocolate chip – No, a *spiced* pumpkin and chocolate chip.'

He dropped two into the brown paper bag printed with the café's logo. 'Extra chocolate sprinkles on the cappuccino?'

He remembered!

Although she had been here every day this week...

'I'll take that as a "yes",' he said and smiled.

Was there some kind of etiquette for asking a barista out for coffee?

'Will you be going to the firework display on Halloween?' she said.

'Sure. Are you?' He took her money and handed her back the change.

'Actually—' Harriet began, before being barged out of the way by the man behind, who then barked out,

'Spice latte and three pumpkin and chocolate chip cookies, and hurry up. I've been waiting forever.'

He glared at Harriet who was very tempted to whip out her warrant card and charge him with something. Interfering with official police business? That might work... but would *not* go down well with the boss.

She sighed and scooped up her order. 'Thanks, Misha.' Maybe she'd try again tomorrow.

The police station was only a few doors down from The Crooked Broomstick. It was a low stone building with a sagging tile roof, and had once been the courthouse. Someone had draped a fake spider's web from the outside light, and the same someone (probably Dakota) had covered the downstairs windowsills with small pumpkins and squashes in a variety of colours. It was incredibly pretty, although DCI Cameron might not think so. Luckily he wasn't due to visit until well after Halloween.

She slunk through the front door because it was quicker than walking around to the back and readied her most charming smile for the civilian receptionist, but he merely rolled his eyes and buzzed her through.

'Better get a move-on, March. DCI Cameron is upstairs.'

What was *he* doing here? She broke into a sprint but as she approached their offices, she recognised the smooth voice of DCI Douglas Cameron giving what sounded like the morning briefing – and it wasn't even 9.00 am! Didn't he trust her to do the job when Ben was away?

She tried to sidle unobtrusively around the door and into her usual seat by the window.

DCI Cameron glanced up from his notes. The man must have the hearing of a bat.

'Good morning, DS March. Kind of you to join us.'

'Sorry, I'm late.' Even though she wasn't.

He waved one hand irritably. 'Your arrival is timely. I need someone to track down DI Taylor. He's not answering his phone. You know him best. Where is he likely to be?'

DCI Cameron was notorious for his sarcasm but sometimes it could be hard to tell when he was joking.

She glanced at DC Sam King, but he just shrugged.

Everyone knew Ben Taylor spent every free moment with Milla Graham since they'd met last summer, and Harriet was about to inform the DCI of this when she realised Sam was imperceptibly shaking his head.

Something was up.

She went for neutral. 'DI Taylor's on leave, sir. He's probably switched his phone off.'

'His leave has been cancelled. A woman has been found murdered at Meg's Pond.'

Meg's Pond? She frowned. That was right next to The Witch's Brew – where Ash had been headed this morning. Had something *happened* to him?

She turned to Sam. 'Where's Ash?'

'Where do you think?' Sam said. 'Ash called into The Witch's Brew this morning for a latte and chocolate muffin – and walked straight into a crime scene.'

FOUR

When Detective Inspector Ben Taylor awoke it was to the sound of breaking glass. Even without opening his eyes he knew Milla was still asleep beside him, star-fishing, one leg tangled between his, her lashes dark against her brown cheeks, her long black hair splayed across both her own pillow and his, as usual.

Another clatter and a shower of small pebbles appeared out of nowhere, dancing over the sun-dappled floorboards. He rolled out of bed, taking care where he placed his feet, and padded over to the broken window. Milla's curtains were the semi-transparent kind that fluttered romantically when the windows were open but hardly met their job description. He yanked them back and dodged another volley of stones.

Waiting on the cobblestones below was his sergeant, Harriet March. The early morning sun caught on her short blonde curls and created an undeserved halo effect.

'Sorry about the window!' she said, not looking remotely sorry. 'I couldn't think how else to wake you.'

Couldn't she?

He carefully swept the broken glass along the sill with the side of his hand and pushed open the window.

'Go away,' he said. 'I'm on leave.'

'Not anymore!'

Did she have to sound so cheerful? And loud?

'How did you even know where to find me?'

Not that it was hard to work out. If he wasn't at the station or in his own cottage, he'd be with Milla. Their relationship wasn't exactly a secret.

'You do know there's this useful invention called "a telephone"?' he said.

'Yes, and you should try switching yours on occasionally.'

Guiltily, he remembered swiping his phone to mute before falling asleep last night. He glanced back at the bed and the woman who lay asleep in it. The woman whose house it was, and with whom he had intended to spend the day, and he sighed. His first decent leave for three months and—

The curtains of the house on the other side of the alley were yanked apart and a woman in her sixties, with hair like a dandelion clock, did a very bad imitation of being surprised to see him.

'Well, *hello*, Detective Inspector!' she said in a deceptively deep, purring voice. 'Isn't it a lovely day?'

Fliss Merriweather: owner of the New Age shop next door to Milla, along with her sister Elvira (real name: Evelyn). They'd lived their entire lives in the village and knew everything there was to know about everybody.

And now they knew rather too much about him.

'Good morning, Fliss,' he said politely. 'It certainly is.'

In the background, Ben could hear Elvira asking irritably, 'What is it, Fliss? Who are you talking to? Oh, goodness! Really? Leave the poor man *alone*...'

Fliss winked in a very unsubtle way before drawing back the curtains.

Ben sighed. Why couldn't Milla have kept her mother's old house, the exquisitely pretty Rose Cottage – surrounded by fields and trees, and bordered by the river, with no neighbours for miles. Why move to the centre of Raven's Edge and gossip central? Was it for the company? Although, apart from him and her family, did she have any friends?

Didn't that just break his heart?

He glanced back at the bed. The rumpled white bedsheets had not quite rucked down far enough for him to see much more than one brown shoulder and the curve of her breast.

He sighed again.

'Hello?' a voice called from the street. 'I'm still here!'

He leant out of the window. 'Your timing, as usual, DS March, is impeccable.'

Harriet merely smirked.

'Fine,' he said. 'I'll be right down.'

He closed the window and had another tussle with the fluttering curtains, before scooping up the pile of clothes he'd been wearing last night – a grey T-shirt and faded jeans – and pulled them on.

He wrote a note for Milla:

Window broken
Will fix when I return.

Then picked up his coat and left.

Harriet was waiting for him on the other side of Milla's front door. She barely gave him time to exit the house and close the door behind him before she was striding off down the narrow alleyway and onto the high street. For a little thing she certainly moved fast.

Instead of turning in the direction of the police station, Harriet took a left and headed out of the village.

He caught her up. 'Where are we going?'

She gave him a sideways glance, clocked the scruffy jeans

and anorak he was wearing rather than his usual suit, but thankfully said nothing more than, 'Meg's Pond.'

Everyone knew of Meg's Pond.

To the tourists, it was the place where a supposed witch had been drowned three hundred years ago, but to the locals it was something more sinister. Ten years ago, a car with four teenagers had taken the bend too quickly and the vehicle had ended up in the pond. There had been no survivors. The local people had taken a collection, built a memorial and planted flowers in remembrance – irises and primroses – but the shadow of the tragedy still hung over the place.

'Another accident?' he said.

'No, not this time.' Harriet had lived her entire life in Raven's Edge, so she knew to which accident he referred.

'You sound very sure?'

'It wasn't hard to deduce because—' She was forced to break off as they approached a crowd loitering on the pavement, craning to see between the trees surrounding the pond. 'Bloody hell, you can't keep anything secret in a place like this.'

The press hadn't arrived, but Ben knew it wouldn't be long before they did. He had to turn sideways to squeeze through the mob but had no intention of dicing with death by stepping out onto the road. By the time unwary motorists reacted to the change in speed limit to account for the curve in the road, it was usually too late. At least he was in jeans and blended in with everyone else. Nothing said 'detective' like a man in a suit at a crime scene.

The pond was to one side of an ancient dwelling-place once known as Raven's Cottage, and the former home of Margaret Lawrence, the seventeenth-century healer known as Magik Meg. Now a popular café and second-hand bookshop called The Witch's Brew, the cottage was almost as famous for the scarlet Virginia creeper that covered it at this time of year as it was for the gingerbread muffins and peanut butter cookies baked by the owner, Kat Davenport.

The herb garden, unfortunately now a customer car park, was usually packed with cars, but today police and forensic vehicles were jammed between the crooked trees, bumper-to-bumper. A uniformed officer stood beside the path to the pond, but he recognised Ben and Harriet as they approached. When Harriet asked about protective clothes he waved them on.

'There's another cordon and you won't be allowed into that,' he said. 'Forensics are still working the scene.'

Ben realised Harriet hadn't briefed him when he saw the sunlight sparkling on the water in front of him and enough police and forensic officers milling around to recognise a serious incident. A tent had been set up, to minimise the view of the crime scene from the road, and to help the pathologist work undisturbed. One flap had been pinned back, but there were too many people in front of it for him to see inside.

'What the hell happened here?'

'Didn't I say? A woman's been murdered.' Harriet stopped in front of the barrier tape. 'DCI Cameron asked for you to attend. I only found out myself half an hour ago. Half an hour which I mostly spent tracking you down. Ash was on the scene first, I'll let him explain the gory details.'

Gory?

DC Asheem Chopra was deep in conversation with the Crime Scene Manager in front of the tent. Ben shifted impatiently, feeling his trainers sinking into the mud. He knew better than to duck beneath the tape. He wasn't suited up and the CSIs were still working – photographing the scene and taking samples.

Then one CSI moved and he saw the victim for the first time. A woman, as Harriet had said, lying on the edge of the pond. She was wearing a distinctive 50s-inspired party dress, the frothy red petticoats now squashed into the mud. On her feet were ballet-style pumps, and as for her—

Hold on…

'Where's her… head?'

The CSI nearest to Ben turned to give him her full attention.

'I can see why they made you Inspector,' she said, 'and don't you dare throw up on my crime scene.'

Ben, feeling his hackles rise instinctively, had the idea that the Crime Scene Manager would disagree with exactly whose crime scene it was, but knew better than to argue with his ex-wife in public. She usually won.

'Hello, Caroline. What do you have for me?'

She raised her eyes heavenwards. 'A dead body?'

Why did she always feel she had to get one over on him? He could already sense the others picking up on their mutual antagonism, but it was too early to fight and too macabre a scene.

'That's why I'm here,' he said, watching as the victim's hands and feet were sealed in plastic bags before she was zipped into a body bag.

He shivered as the zip passed the space where the head should be. No matter how many crime scenes he attended, he'd never been able to completely harden himself to the horrible things humans could do to each other.

'To answer your question, the head is missing.'

Deciding not to dwell on the implications of that, he asked, 'Do we know who she is?'

'Isn't that your job?'

OK, he'd walked into that. 'It helps if I have the odd clue to go on.'

'Female, white, well over twenty but no more than forty years of age, about five four…' Caroline rattled off. 'The head appears to have been removed with a surgical saw.'

That didn't reassure him. It meant the murder was likely to

have been premeditated but not necessarily carried out by a medical professional. One could obtain anything from the internet.

'How long has the victim been dead?'

'That is... a bit of a puzzler. More than twelve hours, as livor mortis has already set in and the blood has pooled along her back, but she appears to have been kept somewhere cool.'

It got better and better.

'I'll let you know more, along with the cause of death, as soon as we've done the post-mortem,' Caroline said. 'Could be a while. We've had a busy week.'

In Raven's Edge?

'How about "beheaded"?' Harriet muttered, unfortunately within earshot.

Caroline turned her pale blue gaze on his sergeant and any trace of good humour vanished. 'Does it not occur to you that the victim could have already been dead? Never make assumptions.'

'Good point,' Harriet conceded.

'I could certainly *guess*,' Caroline said, 'although it would hardly be professional. I'm sure you've already noticed that there's very little blood here at the scene.'

'Does that mean—?'

'Dismemberment took place elsewhere,' Caroline said.

'Thank you,' Harriet said, very nearly sounding like she meant it.

As they walked away, Ben bent his head to whisper in his sergeant's ear, 'Please don't bait the pathologist.'

'She started it.'

'Harriet.'

'Excuse me?' Caroline called after them, and from her tone it was obvious she'd heard the exchange. 'There is one item of interest that might prove useful to your investigation?'

'Yes?'

Ben really wished he and Harriet hadn't spoken in unison or quite so eagerly.

'The labelling on her clothing is predominantly American.'

'She's American?' Harriet repeated, 'That's going to slow everything down.'

'Perhaps she bought her clothing online?' Ben said before Caroline could suggest it, and then she really would be doing his job. 'Better organise the house-to-house enquiries, see if anyone knows anything.'

'Without a description? The victim could be a tourist. She could be *anyone*.'

'White female, between twenty and forty, five foot four, possibly American,' Ben said. 'Dressed distinctively – those clothes of hers certainly make a statement. Is she a fan of vintage fashion? 50s music? A retro lifestyle? Assign teams to go house-to-house, check for any surveillance footage, visit the local hotels and B&Bs in case she was a guest—'

'I do know how to conduct an investigation.' Harriet waved at Ash and Dakota to join them. 'I'm a detective sergeant and everything.'

Ben hid a smile.

Ash had already dumped the female CSM he'd been half-heartedly chatting up and sauntered over, ducking beneath the barrier tape and gracefully shedding his protective clothing as he did so, leaving someone else to pick it up.

If I'd tried that, Ben thought, I'd have fallen flat on my face in the mud.

Dakota, however, had paused on the path and was peering through the trees, back towards the village.

'Dakota!' Harriet snapped.

With obvious reluctance, Dakota ducked beneath the tape to join them. She was a stunning blue-eyed blonde who often gave the impression she was on another planet, but her intuition was usually faultless.

'Did you hear that?' Dakota said.

'Hear what?' Ben could hear nothing more than the occasional murmur between the CSIs as they got on with their work and, slightly louder, the crowd gathered beyond the trees, chattering excitedly amongst themselves.

'Could you be a little more specific?' Harriet sighed.

'I heard a scream,' Dakota said. 'It came from the village. I was wondering if it meant...' She trailed off, leaving them to fill in the blanks.

Someone had found the head...

They were waiting beneath the trees on the path that led to the witch's pool. Three boys the same age as him, who looked like him, who had the same last name as him. His brothers in everything except birth.

Like him, they wore black. Unlike him, they were in costume; their blond hair a contrast with the cloaks they wore, their eyes hidden by narrow masks bought from one of the many gift shops in the village.

He knew he'd forgotten something.

'You're late, Will,' Drew said. He was the eldest, the coolest – certainly the bossiest – and therefore their leader. 'You missed the carnival parade.'

Will leant forward to pat the horse. 'I had a problem with my transport.'

'And your costume?'

He shrugged.

Drew cursed proficiently, at odds with his angelic appearance. He pulled the three-cornered hat from his own head and frisbeed it towards Will, not bothering to check if he caught it.

'Why can't you ever do as you're told?'

Will was forced to reach up out of the saddle, barely hooking the hat with his fingers before resentfully jamming it onto his head.

Already skittish, the horse reared up, its head narrowly missing his nose. As it lashed out with its hooves, the only one who didn't scuttle out the way was Drew. He grabbed hold of the horse's bridle, calming it down with a gentle touch and softly spoken words, before glaring at Will.

'Save the drama until we have an audience.'

FIVE

As soon as Milla heard her front door click shut she was out of bed and into the bathroom, stepping straight under the shower and turning it on full blast to wash away the sweat and the grime – and the guilt, on so many levels. Guilt at what she'd done last night, guilt at lying to Ben, and guilt that she was pleased he'd been called away early so she wouldn't have to lie again.

She switched on her music, turning it up even louder than usual, making it impossible to think, to feel, to brood; distorting the sound and causing the glass door to vibrate along with the beat. She dressed in practical jeans and T-shirt, slinging on a hoodie before leaving the house, having no appetite for breakfast. How could she, after what she'd seen last night?

It was late October and the air held a noticeable chill. There was a crowd gathering at the other end of the village, which was odd, considering it wasn't even 9.00 am and the shops weren't open. Maybe there was some kind of event on? She started her car and headed in the opposite direction, remembering to slow down enough not to bump over the humpback bridge. She'd already lost a wing mirror and had owned the Peugeot 208 for less than three months.

Kieran Drake rented an office overlooking the harbour at Port Rell, above an expensive, slightly old-fashioned clothing store called Anya's: Port Rell. There was a branch in Raven's Edge too, but Milla had never stepped foot in either of them and didn't intend to. This week, the window display had a nautical theme: all cropped trousers, Breton striped tops and navy deck shoes. Cruise-wear, presumably, since this was the UK and autumn started in August. OK, maybe she'd like a pair of those deck shoes, but today she was more interested in the door to the left of the window. The one with the brass plate that said:

Kieran Drake Investigations

This early in the morning she half-expected the door to be locked, but it opened easily and she went up the stairs into a very modern reception room, all white paint and chrome, and empty save for a large white desk and a filing cabinet. Interestingly, there were no chairs for waiting visitors.

Maybe Drake didn't have visitors? Or maybe not the kind who were willing to be seen visiting him?

Milla deliberately coughed. Drake's sixty-something secretary, Esme Merriweather, who had the kind of determined expression more usually seen on a teacher trying to corral a class of eight-year-olds, barely glanced up from her laptop. Esme was the sister of Elvira and Fliss, Milla's neighbours who owned the New Age shop in Raven's Edge called Practically Magic. Looking at Esme, no one would ever guess they were related. Unlike Fliss's mad curls, Esme's grey hair was a neat, on-trend pixie cut, and she wore a smart black dress, rather than the multitude of trailing chiffon scarfs and bangles Fliss favoured.

'He's not in,' Esme told Milla in her distinctive, Bette Davislike voice. 'His office is locked up. You'll have to come back later.'

Like she'd never heard *that* before.

'Are you sure? Let me check that for you.' Milla leant on the door that had Drake's name on it and it swung open. 'Well, will you look at that?'

Esme's fingers, which had been moving swiftly across the keyboard, ceased abruptly, her wintery gaze fixing on Milla. 'Mr Drake is extremely busy.'

'I'm sure he'll make an exception for me,' Milla said, 'so I'll have a flat white with plenty of sugar. If we're longer than ten minutes, send in biscuits because one of us will need rescuing.'

Even Milla wasn't brave enough to hang around waiting for Esme's response to that. She slipped through the door and closed it firmly behind her, turning towards Drake's desk and trying to settle that prickle of unease she always felt when she was in the same room as him. She knew why. He was so unpredictable he set her on edge.

As usual, Drake had his feet up on his desk, his favourite red Chucks dropping dirt everywhere, but there was no sign of his laptop. He cradled a mug of black coffee against his chest as though it were his first-born, and his eyes were closed – until the door shut with an audible 'click'.

'9.15?' He opened one eye to glare at her. 'Really?'

Milla walked past several perfectly adequate chairs to perch on the edge of his desk.

'Don't get comfortable.' He swung his feet to the floor and pushed himself upright. 'I had enough of you and the *Hammer House of Horror* last night.'

She was surprised at how rough he looked. That was to say, he always looked rough – as though he were the picture in the attic and there was a model-perfect clone whooping it up elsewhere. He obviously hadn't been home; his clothes were the same ones he'd been wearing last night and absolutely filthy.

Being this close to him, she could also smell a distinct odour of damp soil. A graveyard?

Well, that *would* be a good place to hide a body...

'I thought you dealt with this kind of thing all the time?' she said.

'Er, no. *Cleaning* a crime scene was a whole new experience for me.'

That she found hard to believe.

'What did you do with the... erm...?' She pointed to her head, unable to say the word out loud.

'It's safe.'

'Good. I want the murderer brought to justice.'

He winced. 'A bit late for that, Princess, because we've completely sterilised the crime scene. I hope your new guy was worth it?'

She hadn't given Lorcan much thought. Last night had been mainly about finding the poor victim and ensuring she didn't end up the same way.

'Lorcan is a long-time ex,' she said. 'He was kind to me when I was down on my luck. Now it's my turn to help him. He can be a bit juvenile sometimes, but he's not capable of murder.'

'Anyone, given the right circumstances, is capable of murder.'

'He once fainted after a blood test.'

'Looks like he's over that now.'

How could Drake be so flippant? Was this his way of dealing with stress?

It was a bit late to realise the only thing she knew about him was that he was a private detective and a 'fixer' for her father.

Had she done a deal with the devil?

'We need to talk,' she said. 'Properly, without trying to score points off each other.'

'Now you sound like *my* ex. No, we don't need to talk. I want to forget it ever happened and you should too.'

'If you think I could forget what I found last night...'
Because 'nightmare' barely covered it.

'*Goodbye*, Princess.' Drake closed his eyes and leant back in
his chair, the front legs tipping off the ground.

Milla placed her foot on the seat, bringing him back down
with a crash. 'I have a lot of questions.'

He glared at her. 'I don't care.'

'You do know I'm capable of making a real nuisance of
myself?'

'I did you a *favour*.'

'I offered to pay!'

'Are you sure you can afford me?' His smile flickered in a
way she really didn't like. He leant on the table, giving her his
full attention, and now she had it, she wasn't sure she wanted it.

'Why were *you* there, Princess? You're dating our local law
enforcement officer. Does he know you're paying after-dark
visits to other men?'

Did he have to make it sound so *seedy*?

'Lorcan and I are ancient history; Ben knows that.' No, he
didn't, and she had no intention of telling him just yet. It was a
complication she didn't need. 'Lorcan and I haven't seen each
other since Christmas. He told me he was moving to Raven's
Edge, and invited me to see his new house. He's very proud
of it.'

'In the middle of the night?'

'More like nine o'clock in the evening. Lorcan is a musician.
He works through the night and sleeps during the day.'

'He was expecting you?'

Did Drake *have* to sound so disbelieving?

'Yes – and I have the texts to prove it.'

'The texts could be from anyone.'

Another reason she hadn't called the police. Who would
believe she was friends with Lorcan Black?

Drake sighed. 'Has Lorcan been in touch with you?'

'Not yet, but if Lorcan had found the jar, he would have called the police himself.'

'Unless he had something to hide or he was the one who left it there.'

'Obviously, but I thought we'd already agreed—' She broke off, narrowing her eyes. 'What aren't you telling me?'

'There was no *body*, Milla. After you'd left, my team went all over that house, including the grounds and the outbuildings.' Drake indicated his filthy clothes. 'We found nothing. No body, no weapon, no blood. Whatever happened to that poor girl, she wasn't killed in that house. The liquid in the jar was a preservative. Her death was planned, in advance, by someone with too much imagination.'

'When did Lorcan come home?'

'He didn't. I left someone watching the house but he hasn't shown his face.'

'Do you think he panicked? Headed to the airport and back to France? Does he have a car? Was it still there?'

'Two cars and one motorbike. Stored in the outbuildings.'

None of this made any sense. 'Don't you think this is strange?'

'All musicians are strange.'

There was something in the tone of his voice.

'You think he killed her,' she said slowly, 'and that's why you're not busting a gut trying to find him.'

'Why should I want to find him? It's not my job.'

'You want me to go to the police? Tell them everything?'

'Everything?' Drake repeated. He might even have rolled his eyes.

'I have nothing to hide.'

'Sure. You're going to explain why you had a meeting with your ex-boyfriend at his house at nine o'clock in the evening? How you think he might have killed a woman but you decided to call a friend, and not even the "friend" who's a detective inspector? You're going to tell them how you interfered with a crime scene and facilitated a clear-up? Basically, how you're a fully paid-up accessory to a murder? Even you can't lie your way out of that one, Princess. And now you've dragged me into it.' He put his head in his hands, muttering, 'I must be *insane...*'

What should she say? She'd always assumed Drake dealt with whatever life threw at him in the same way he dealt with everything else – with cold, ruthless efficiency – but what if he'd been as affected by what they'd found last night as her?

Now she'd helped to conceal a murder, destroyed evidence, *destroyed a crime scene.*

Ben would be appalled.

Ben could never find out.

Drake raised his head. 'Still believe Lorcan is innocent?'

'I *know* he's innocent.' There was something in Drake's expression. 'You do too. Why were you keen to help me last night? We're not friends. I'm nothing to you. I keep offering you money but you don't seem much interested in it.'

'Yeah, look at me: a sucker for a damsel in distress.'

That was Ben's failing too, but Drake was a world away from Ben.

'Yes, and you rescue kittens, help little old ladies across the road, and used to be a boy scout. What do you know, Drake? What is it you're not telling me?'

He regarded her speculatively and then sighed. 'Something was going to happen last night, I knew that much. I'd had a tip-off. When Lorcan turned up at The Drop, all bright-eyed and bushy-tailed, looking for a girl or a fight, we arranged for a little something to be added to his drink. The idea was, he would stagger home and sleep it off before he could get into any trouble. We'd even drive him, if necessary.'

'You *knew* this would happen?'

'Not *this*! Someone had been asking questions around the village, about who he was and when he'd be moving into the old farmhouse. You can't do up a wreck like that and expect no one to notice.'

'Journalists? He's had a lot of trouble in the past with the paparazzi.'

'The questions weren't the kind of thing a journalist would ask. Some kind of scam was in play. The last our girl saw of your guy, he was staggering out the door, his arm around a pretty brunette.'

'You thought he was about to be set up?' It was so far-fetched, it was almost believable. 'OK... Where is he now?'

He shrugged. 'With the pretty brunette?'

Nice to see he took his work seriously. 'Who's your client?'

'What client?'

'The one who asked you to "drop a little something" into Lorcan's drink to keep him out of trouble!'

'No idea what you're on about. Amazing imagination you've got there, Princess.'

This wasn't the first time Drake had flat out denied something he'd previously admitted, so this time she'd come prepared.

She took out her phone, tapped on 'gallery' and held it up. The first image was a still of the specimen jar, the next a grainy video of the arrival of Drake and his team at the farmhouse, all wearing coveralls, along with Drake's voice distinctly explaining what they were going to find, and how the client was expecting them to take care of everything.

He stared at it, disbelief evident on his face. 'I told you to leave – for your own safety! And you hung around to *film* me, to *blackmail* me?'

'You don't have the best track record! I wanted proof of what happened.'

'The whole point of last night was to bury the bloody truth!'

He made a grab for the phone but she shoved it back into her pocket and took a couple of steps back.

'Tell me you don't think I'm daft enough to have the only copy on this phone.'

'You've saved it to the *Cloud*?' He dropped back into his seat. 'You're *dafter* than I thought. *Anyone* could get access to that!'

'Who hired you?' she repeated.

'I have no idea what you're talking about.'

'Those photos implicate you. It proves you were there.'

'What are you going to do with them? Show them to the police? Show them to your boyfriend, who's blithely unaware of where you spent last night? Go ahead. By the way, you still owe me that favour.'

'Where's Lorcan?'

He laughed. 'No idea. Hopefully, sleeping off a night of debauchery and unaware someone wants to frame him for murder. If he's with someone, maybe they can give him an alibi.'

'*If* he's with someone else. *If* whatever you put into his drink is still in his system.'

'The stuff I use doesn't hang around.'

'The stuff— What on earth did you *give* him? He's already taking extra-strength sleeping pills! The guy could be unconscious in a ditch!'

'Then you'd better find him.'

'You're going to be absolutely *no* help, obviously. Your client needs to ask for his money back – or was that all about "favours" too?' Milla slid off the table and slung her satchel over her shoulder. 'Consider my debt void. I'll sort this out by myself, but I'm telling you this. If I find something that connects you to that woman's death, I *will* be back.'

'I look forward to seeing you.' He leant back in his chair, clomped his feet back onto the desk and closed his eyes. 'I always enjoy our little chats.'

SIX

Ben looked at Ash, who languidly shrugged a shoulder. 'I didn't hear a scream.'

Neither had anyone else. One team of CSIs were still working around the pond, others were beginning to pack up their equipment, walking back and forth along the path to where their vehicles were parked, forced to step awkwardly around the four detectives. Ben was struck by the almost reverent silence of the scene. Despite the chatter from the road-side, surely a scream would have been heard immediately?

Although the sunshine had burned away most of the early morning mist, it lingered in patches, particularly around the pond. The surrounding forest was so thick it was like existing in another world. An 'other' world. No wonder Raven's Edge was a magnet for tourists seeking to be thrilled by the Gothic chill factor.

The murderer could be watching them at this very moment. The woods would need to be searched. There was a track that led straight through to the clifftop road but it would be an impossibly wide area to cover. Perhaps with police dogs? Ben dismissed that idea as soon as he thought of it. These woods were crisscrossed by a maze of pathways used by tourists, walkers and dog owners. The murderer was long gone, of that he was certain. Why linger and risk being caught?

Only Harriet was blunt enough to come right out and say, 'You must have imagined it.'

Dakota gave every intention of arguing, senior officer or not, but Ash interrupted.

'Maybe you heard kids playing? Mucking about?'

Unappreciative of his attempt at tact, Dakota frowned. 'Maybe someone's found… something?'

'There'd be more screaming,' Harriet said, practical as ever.

Realising Harriet was about to add, 'We don't have time for this', and not wanting to correct her in front of a junior officer, Ben made his decision.

'You finish here,' he told Dakota, cutting off her immediate protest. 'You two,' he indicated Harriet and Ash, 'are with me.'

Dakota was the better officer – Ash was far too laid-back – but Ben couldn't bear to listen to her and Harriet sniping at each other any longer.

As they walked along the woodland path to the road, his thoughts strayed back to the victim. Who was she? What was she doing here? Why had she been killed in such a brutal, violent way? What kind of person could do that to another?

The crowd standing on the pavement were far too interested in the prospect of seeing a real live dead body being carried out of the woods to pay much attention to anything happening in the village behind them. Harriet shoved her way through, without bothering to be polite. Ash took his time, apologising with his usual indolent charm. Ben hurried him along, hoping his own motivation wasn't desperation to escape the scene behind him. By the time he'd cleared the crowd and rounded the bend in the road, Harriet and Ash were already standing on the edge of The Square.

Ben couldn't help glancing towards Milla's house, the last in a line of four half-timbered cottages that bordered the south side. Although her curtains were drawn, her car was no longer parked in the alley to the side of the house. He frowned. She'd got up and dressed very quickly. Hadn't she been asleep when he'd left?

Vaguely he heard Harriet muttering, 'This is a *complete* waste of time—' just as a beautiful redhead shot out of the churchyard opposite and ran smack into Ash, who roused himself sufficiently to elegantly catch her before she sprawled headlong into the gutter.

Carefully, Ash set the woman back on her feet. She seemed reluctant to let him go, digging long pale fingers into his biceps despite his polite attempt to extricate himself.

'Are you OK, ma'am?' Ash asked.

She stared at him wild-eyed as though she wasn't seeing him at all.

'Ma'am?'

'There's a man inside the church, covered in blood!'

Ben's eyes met Ash's over the top of her head and saw him mouth the word '*Hell…*'

He placed himself in the woman's line of vision. 'I'm Detective Inspector Ben Taylor. Can you tell me, did this man have a weapon of any kind? A large knife? Anything like that?'

'A *knife?*' Her expression turned to one of horror, her voice becoming higher. 'Why would he have a knife? It's a *church!*'

Because I'm looking for a murderer and I thought I'd found one.

He tried again, careful to keep his tone calm and unhurried. 'Is the man injured?'

'He might be. I found him lying on top of one of the tombs. I think he's dead. How did he end up like that? Did he fall? There's nowhere to fall from. I don't understand how this could have happened!'

'Did you try to revive him or attempt first aid?'

This was Harriet, naturally. Ben could have pointed out that the woman's wool coat was spotless. It was unlikely she'd been anywhere near the unfortunate man.

'He's covered in *blood*.' The woman hung tighter onto Ash. 'It was like a horror film. I'm not a doctor. I didn't know what to do. I thought the best thing would be to fetch help.'

Ben asked, 'Is there anyone else inside the church?'

'Only me. I'm responsible for arranging the flowers. I'd finished but had a bunch of chrysanthemums left over. I thought I'd put them in a vase in the old chapel. That's when I saw him lying there, dead.'

'Thank you,' Ben said. 'Now, could I ask you to wait in the police station while we look into this? It's just across the road. You see it? Good. Go to the front counter and ask for DC Sam King.'

He turned back to Ash. 'Call an ambulance, call back-up, contact Sam to let him know what's going on and keep an eye on the door in case someone leaves in a hurry.'

He ducked through the lych-gate and started down the path.

Harriet scrambled after him. 'What about waiting for that back-up?'

'A lovely thought, but no time.'

'What if he sneaks out the back?'

'We've lost him.'

'He could be a killer!'

'Or another victim. Whoever he is, he needs medical help.'

Harriet muttered something beneath her breath, which sounded a lot like, 'We could be walking into a trap.'

Ben came to a halt beside the church, placing one finger to his lips in warning before heading through the base of a square tower and into the nave. He half-thought Harriet would stay outside but, after a short pause, he heard her follow him quietly down the stone steps. The effort it must have taken her not to stomp.

After the bright sunshine, the church was dark and ominously silent. It appeared empty but he'd been caught like that before. He moved silently down one of the side aisles, hoping the stone pillars would afford him some kind of cover. Ahead was the chancel and, to the right, a separate chapel built for one of the important local families.

Now confident the rest of the church was empty, he leant against the wall and peered into the chapel, horribly conscious that he had no way of defending himself if anyone should launch an attack.

He indicated to Harriet that he was going inside.

She raised her eyebrows but for once refrained from telling him he was an idiot.

That he already knew.

The chapel was empty too.

Empty, save for the man lying on top of the tomb.

Either unconscious or sleeping, he wasn't dead. His chest rose rhythmically and his breathing appeared normal. His T-shirt, however, was soaked in fresh blood.

Ben stepped forward to check the man's pulse, holding his fingers against the carotid artery. Strong, regular—

'That's a lot of blood.' Harriet appeared beside him, her voice echoing around the still, silent chapel. 'How is he even alive?'

'It's not his blood. Look at the colour of his skin. If he'd lost that much blood, his skin would be grey and feel clammy. There're no tears, rips or holes in his clothing to indicate trauma. Even his breathing's steady. This man is in perfect health.'

As though in confirmation, the man on the tomb emitted a loud snore.

'He's the murderer?'

Ben's gut instinct was telling him that wasn't right either but he patted the unconscious man down, checking for a weapon, concealed or otherwise. He found nothing but that didn't mean there hadn't been one. There were plenty of places to hide a large knife (or 'surgical saw', if Caroline was correct) between here and the village pond, not to mention the church itself. The route would need to be searched, and that would take time, manpower, a huge chunk of the budget...

Harriet dug in her bag for a pack of wipes, extracted a couple of sheets and handed them over to Ben. He hadn't even noticed he now had blood on his hands.

'Why is he unconscious?' she asked.

Ben cleaned his hands and then wondered what to do with the used sheet. 'I would suggest collapse from an excess of alcohol – his breath smells terrible – but I'm not a doctor.'

He remembered the girl by the pond and sincerely hoped this wasn't some kind of twisted murder-suicide, but the man's pulse had seemed fine. Ben hadn't checked it properly though.

Where were the paramedics?

'Another victim?' Harriet suggested, holding out a small plastic bag for the wipe, before returning it to her handbag.

He wondered what else she kept in there, and then decided he'd rather not know.

'No apparent injuries,' Ben reminded her. Nothing to connect the man to the girl in the pond either, apart from the blood on his T-shirt. Too much blood. There were no splatter patterns; the blood had completely soaked through. Yet there was no blood on the tiled floor and very little on the tomb itself. The man didn't even have blood on his hands. Was it some kind of prank? It was in very poor taste, if that were so. Why go to so much trouble? And what of the girl by the pond? None of this made any sense.

'I'm missing something,' he said, not realising he'd spoken out loud until Harriet rolled her eyes and said,

'Yes...'

At least she didn't state the obvious.

'Do you recognise him?' he asked. Harriet had always lived in the village, whereas he'd left to spend eight years in the Met. 'Is he local?'

She gave the man another once over. 'No, I don't think so. He must be a tourist. Although, there is *something* familiar about... Oh, no...'

Whatever name Harriet was about to say, it wasn't going to be good.

'I know this sounds very unlikely, and I can't imagine what he's doing here, but he looks an awful lot like Lorcan Black. You know, the singer? Actually, you probably don't know,' she added under her breath, 'with all the golden oldies you listen to.' She stared again at the body on the tomb, as though she could hardly believe it herself. 'Trust me,' she said, 'he's very well-known. If we handle this badly, or arrest... the wrong person, that's *all* our careers down the drain.'

Will sat on the low stone wall that surrounded the churchyard and watched the kids his age prowl around the village in packs, giving lip service to the lie that was trick-or-treat.

Lots of treats, zero tricks.

His lip curled. Rebellion with a safety net.

Drew had turned up with an old Luger pistol that their grandfather had brought back from the war as a souvenir; it didn't even work, and the most he'd done with it so far was brandish it about shouting 'Stand and deliver!' Will could have had more fun with the nerds at the school disco. At least there would have been burgers and chips.

An enthusiastic crunch snapped his attention right back. The horse, apparently bored of chomping its way through the grass verge, was now tearing though the bag of treats he'd liberated from an eight-year-old dressed as Magik Meg.

Will swore, accidentally kicking the sweets into the gutter, and hauling the horse back to his side when it showed every sign of following after the forbidden treats.

Drew laughed, effortlessly leaning out of reach as Will swiped a punch in his direction.

When he tried to do it again, Greg caught his fist and shoved a can of beer into it. 'Get over it,' he said. 'You're too old for trick-or-treating anyway.'

'I don't care,' Will said, chucking it right back. 'I'm off.'

'Whatever.' Drew drained the dregs from his own can before swooping up Will's and cracking it open. 'Run along home to Mummy.'

'Who said I was going home? Unlike some people, I know how to have a good time.'

Drew's laughter followed him along the road.

SEVEN

When Milla yanked open the door into reception she came face-to-face with Esme Merriweather on the other side, her hand raised as though about to knock. For a second they glared at each other, before politeness forced the other woman to step aside.

'Goodbye, Miss Graham.'

Now? When something important had obviously happened? Milla thought not.

'Don't mind me,' she said. 'Pretend I'm not here.'

Esme remained silent, looking towards the man who paid her wages.

Drake opened one eye, not bothering to hide his irritation. 'Let me guess, Chapter Two in the *All-New Adventures of Lorcan Black*? That man is becoming such a pain in the arse.'

When Esme moved to close the door on her, Milla stuck her foot in the gap. It looked cool when people did it in the movies. Who'd have thought it could be so painful?

'Ow,' she said pointedly, muttering, 'Don't even try it,' when Esme went for another attempt.

One would think little old ladies were above smirking, but apparently not.

'Out with it, Esme,' Drake said. 'It's impossible to keep anything from Miss Graham. She's determined to ferret out all our dirty little secrets.'

'Lorcan Black has been found unconscious inside the church at Raven's Edge,' Esme said, in her sharp, no-nonsense way. 'The police have taken him into custody.'

Milla bit her lip. So much for running to Lorcan's rescue, but at least he'd been found and was safe.

Drake sighed. 'Don't leave out the best bit, Esme.'

'He was covered in blood.'

'His own or someone else's?'

'Our informant couldn't tell us,' Esme said, 'but the body of a woman has been found on the edge of Meg's Pond. The head is missing.'

Milla felt sick.

'I wonder where that could be.' He turned his attention to Milla. 'You have *terrible* taste in men, you do know that?'

'And *you* were being paid to keep him out of trouble!'

'Still think he's innocent?'

'*Yes!*'

'Your prerogative. Keep me updated,' he added to Esme, before closing his eyes and swinging his feet back onto the table.

Milla watched his chair rock back precariously and hoped he'd fall flat on his back but unfortunately she didn't have the time to wait for it to happen. She followed Esme into the reception area and slammed the door behind her. It didn't make her feel any better.

Was there any point rushing off? Lorcan was past her help. She had to have faith in the police's ability to find him innocent.

Although someone seemed really keen to have it proved otherwise.

Esme returned to her shiny white desk, doing her best to

ignore Milla, perhaps in the hope that she'd go away. Flipping her laptop open, Esme's fingers moved too fast across the keyboard for Milla to catch her password, even when she tilted her head sideways for a better view.

The movement caught Esme's attention and her eyes narrowed. 'May I help you?'

Milla summoned her most flirtatious smile and perched on the edge of the desk.

One frosty glare from Esme and she found herself sliding off again. 'I suppose it's no good asking you who Drake's favourite client is?'

Hopefully the same one who had paid for last night's job. That would be a start, wouldn't it? Follow the money. If she couldn't discover who had it in for Lorcan, maybe she'd find out who wanted him saved – and how they had known he was going to be in trouble in the first place.

The look Esme gave her was pitying. 'Goodbye, Miss Graham.'

The woman was a tough nut to crack; Milla had to give her that.

'Goodbye, Miss Merriweather,' she said.

For now.

Twenty minutes later and Milla was parked outside her house as though she'd never left. The tourists were lingering on the other side of the alley outside Practically Magic, taking selfies by the crystal balls and tarot cards in the window, and posing beside the stone tablet set in the wall. The one that said,

Margaret Lawrence
(aka 'Magik Meg' and 'the Raven Queen')
tried for witchcraft near this spot
15th December 1696

Even though Meg had actually been tried for witchcraft at the old courthouse – now the police station.

Raven's Edge was busier than usual. Why had she not noticed that?

And then remembered that she *had* noticed when she'd left her house this morning – all those crowds of people at the other end of the village – and promptly ignored them.

She'd make a terrible cop.

Speaking of which, one thing that *was* noticeable was the uniformed police officer lurking in the shadow of the lych-gate opposite. Behind him, blue and white tape fluttered in the breeze.

It was a pity she hadn't known Lorcan was in the church when she'd shot off to his rescue this morning. She could have helped him.

Really? What could she have done? Called Drake to help clean another crime scene? How very proactive of her. Plus, last night's activities were probably a one-time offer.

Was Lorcan guilty of murder? No, she refused to believe the man she knew could have committed such a horrible crime.

Why not? Everyone had secrets. What was that expression? Something about the quiet ones always being the worst? The media continually underestimated Lorcan, judging him by his brooding stage persona, but she'd hardly have called him quiet. He could be as extroverted as her when he put his mind to it. Maybe that was why they'd split up. Too alike.

Would he have done the same for her?

Ben would have, her conscience helpfully chipped in.

Ben, to whom she'd lied by omission.

Milla slid out of her car before her conscience could point out all her other character flaws, or the police officer noticed she was staring at him dreamily and got quite the wrong idea.

Was Lorcan still inside the church? More likely, he was being interviewed at the police station. It would be a good opportunity to have a snoop around before the media turned up, and they *would* turn up, she was sure of that. A famous singer, found unconscious in a church covered in blood? The headlines could write themselves. She hoped he had a good solicitor.

She locked her car and headed into the village florist, Foxglove & Hemlock, just two doors down from her own house. It was a gorgeous shop in a big old Elizabethan house, with silver galvanised buckets lined up on the cobblestones outside. With Halloween a matter of days away, many of the ready-made bouquets on display were themed accordingly, with an abundance of orange lilies and gerbera, teamed with mini sunflowers and hot pink dahlias. Milla was tempted to buy one for herself.

When she emerged, five minutes later, with a sweet posy of white roses, tied with a white satin ribbon, the police officer was still standing in front of the lych-gate and made no attempt to move out of her way at her approach, even when she was right in front of him, clutching the roses to her chest like an anxious bridesmaid.

'Is the church closed?' she asked. 'I wanted to put these flowers on my father's grave.'

She crossed her fingers behind her back. Her father was alive and well, spending an extra week in Frankfurt following the Book Fair – planned with the sole purpose of missing the masquerade ball his mother was hosting for Halloween.

The police officer's expression remained impassive. 'I can't let anyone through. I'm sorry.'

Milla pointed to the little stone wall surrounding the churchyard. 'You know, I could climb over the wall?'

'Please don't.'

'His grave is right there. I'll be really quick.'

'No. I'm sorry.'

'What if I came back later?'

He sighed in a long-suffering way. 'You're certainly welcome to try.'

If she'd really wanted to, she could have taken one of the paths through the woods and scrambled over the back wall of the churchyard. But she didn't want the destruction of crime scenes to become a habit, so she returned home and put the flowers in water, made herself a coffee and settled down in the seat beside the window to watch and wait.

It took a good couple of hours before a succession of CSIs trooped down the church path and onto The Square where their vehicles were parked. They stripped off their coveralls, loaded their equipment and drove off.

Milla waited until her second coffee had gone cold, but the uniformed officer didn't move from his position in front of the lych-gate.

If she wanted to see inside the church, she was going to have to be creative.

The wall that surrounded the churchyard was about a metre and a half high and was built of the same stone as the church, but more roughly cobbled together. Trying not to scuff through the fallen leaves and draw attention, Milla picked a spot behind a cluster of particularly large Victorian monuments, threw the posy over first and then attempted to follow.

It wasn't as easy as she'd thought. The stones in the wall were loose and crumbling. She scratched the leather of her favourite boots and wrenched her wrist. The ground on the other side was uneven, due to neglected and broken gravestones half-hidden by long grass and brambles. Soon she had a wrenched ankle to match the wrist.

The side entrance to the church could be seen from the road but was unguarded and unlocked. It led through a Victorian extension, encompassing toilets and the vestry. She emerged into the north aisle and immediately spotted one of Ben's team, DC Asheem Chopra, in the nave talking with a man about the same age. The man was dressed entirely in black save for a white tab at his neck – the new vicar, presumably. Milla had never met him, but her neighbour, Fliss Merriweather, always got very fluttery when she talked about him.

Careful to keep hidden behind the stone pillars, Milla tiptoed towards the chapel where Lorcan had been found. It was easily identifiable because someone had blocked the entrance with a couple of brass posts linked by thick blue rope, and then wound police barrier tape around it.

As if that would keep her out. She leant over the rope and peered into the chapel, standing on one foot to gain a few more centimetres, curling her fingers around the stone archway to balance herself—

'Hello,' a soft voice said, right into her ear.

She shrieked and let go of the arch. Only someone grabbing the top of her arm and pulling her back prevented her from pitching headfirst over the barrier and cracking her head on the flagstones.

'Damn!' she snapped, yanking free and turning to face her rescuer. 'You sure scared the hell out of—' before spotting he was wearing a white clerical collar.

EIGHT

As far as Harriet was concerned, Lorcan being covered in blood was damning evidence of his guilt, but Ben reminded her that they should exercise patience. A doctor had to be called, to ensure Lorcan was fit for interview; the CSI team had to be recalled; Lorcan's clothing taken for analysis, alternative clothing found, and specimens obtained for DNA and toxicology, and all the rest. Somehow, they had to transport him from the church to the police station without alerting the press to the rather delicious exclusive that the local rock star was likely to be charged with murder.

Throughout all this, Lorcan amiably agreed to everything suggested to him. Did that mean he *was* guilty, or that he expected to be found guilty whatever the true circumstances? Or that he was still groggy from whatever had knocked him out in the first place? Harriet had expected a little more resistance – certainly a demand to see an expensive solicitor, accompanied by the usual, 'Don't you know who I am?' Yet apart from a request to use the toilet, and another for a mug of strong coffee, there had been nothing.

Maybe it was some kind of reverse psychology? DCI

Cameron was heavily into psychological profiling. Harriet's opinion was that if you caught someone covered in blood after a murder, it wasn't hard to work out who did it.

Why did he have to choose *their* village for his murder spree?

Once Lorcan was declared medically fit, he was brought into the interview suite, incongruously dressed in white coveralls rather than the urban goth clothes he'd been found in. Perhaps it was the clothing, but Harriet's first thought was how insignificant Lorcan seemed. She was disappointed. If they'd passed in the street, she wouldn't have paid him a second glance. Although tall and lean, his distinctive black hair must be dyed that colour because a clear inch of blond roots was visible.

She started the interview slowly, having no wish to antagonise him before it became necessary. She switched on the audio and video recording, using the screen on the desk, and ran through the legal stuff, introducing herself and Ben, and then read Lorcan the caution again. Throughout it all, Lorcan slumped in his chair, slightly dazed.

Was he high?

DCI Cameron thought that a person's body language revealed as much about them, more so, than anything they said.

Harriet felt that kind of thing was too easy to fake.

With that thought, she noticed a chunk of hair had fallen across Lorcan's face, grazing one sharp cheekbone, and he hadn't bothered to push it away. Creating a barrier? Something to hide behind? Perhaps not as confident and relaxed as he'd like to appear?

Who cared?

Harriet began with a question she already knew the answer to.

(Number One in the *Idiot's Guide to Interviewing Suspects*.)

'Mr Black, I understand you've recently moved to Raven's Edge?'

Lorcan slowly inclined his head.

She thumbed in the direction of the monitor. 'Can you answer the question out loud? For the record?'

'Yes,' Lorcan said, looking up at the camera, a mocking edge to his voice. 'I've recently moved here.'

'When was that exactly?'

'Yesterday morning, around ten.' He sighed, anticipating the next question. 'Yes, I do have witnesses to corroborate that: builders, removal men, cleaners. Can I go now?'

Her eyes narrowed. Was that supposed to make her throw up her hands and say, 'I'm so sorry we've wasted your time, Mr Black. Please, feel free to leave. Oh, and don't forget to sue us for wrongful arrest on your way out.'

She knew Lorcan had an alibi – the team employed by the removal company he'd used had already been contacted, thanks to Dakota's attention to detail. She also knew it took less than twenty minutes to walk from the rear of the farmhouse and through the forest to Meg's Pond, because Sam had timed it for her earlier. *And* they knew Lorcan had two cars and a motorbike at his disposal, because they'd already been spotted in an outbuilding. Each one of those vehicles was going to be checked for minute evidence, along with the farmhouse, Lorcan's clothes, and whatever they'd scraped from beneath his fingernails.

It was going to be a very long, *very* expensive day but this had to be done right or the press would have a field day. When they'd finished, they'd know more about Lorcan than his significant other or even his mother.

She asked the question that was most on her mind. 'Why choose Raven's Edge? What was it about our village that appealed to you?'

His mouth lifted in a wry smile. 'I wanted to get on with

writing my new album in a quiet village in the middle of nowhere, where no one knew me and no one would bother me.'

'It must be hard to be famous.'

Ben kicked her under the table.

It was clear Lorcan wasn't quite sure how to take her.

'It's not so bad,' he said, 'up until today, anyway. I'm doing a job I love. I'm always grateful for that.'

She let the silence linger, then asked something else she already knew the answer to. 'When did you arrive in England?'

'The day before yesterday.'

'From where?'

'Nice, via British Airways. I spent the night at a friend's house in Surrey, and then drove here. I checked everything was OK with the removal company, and then I walked through the woods and into the village for dinner. Weirdly, that's the last thing I remember.'

'Walking?'

'Dinner.'

'Which pub did you go to?'

'The one by the bridge. You know, where they chucked the witch into the gorge and she turned into a bunch of ravens? Is it still called The Drop?'

Harriet frowned. How would Lorcan know that? Raven's Edge was famous for its witch, but most people assumed that she'd drowned in the pond that was named after her.

To lull Lorcan into a false sense of security, 'What did you order?'

'Steak and chips, and a cola. I'm sure the staff will vouch for that.'

'A cola?' She let her disbelief show.

'And *maybe* a sip of Finlayson's.'

'Only the one?' She'd be out-sarcasming DCI Cameron at this rate.

'Yes, I'm sure the bar staff will vouch for that too.'

'You had one sip of whisky,' she said, 'and yet you remember nothing more?'

'That's right.'

'No idea how you came to be lying on a tomb, unconscious and covered in someone else's blood?'

Lorcan grimaced. 'No.'

A better woman might have been able to resist politely enquiring, 'Has this happened before?'

Lorcan's response was equally polite. 'Not outside of a photo shoot.'

Harriet had already seen the cover of his first solo album, showing Lorcan in pseudo-Victorian clothes lying on an ancient table tomb with his eyes closed, holding a crimson rose so dark it was almost black, with a spreading bloodstain over his heart.

Coincidence?

No detective believed in coincidence.

The press were going to think Christmas had come early and even Harriet was beginning to believe their murderer was sitting right in front of them, practically gift-wrapped.

Maybe it was a little too convenient...

Harriet flipped through her notes. According to Lorcan's own website he'd been born in England but had lived in New York City since his teens, and then France. It explained why his accent was resolutely English. There was no mention of exactly where in England he was from though. Raven's Edge? One of the surrounding villages: Calahurst, Port Rell, perhaps even Norchester? He seemed to know a lot about the local witch, but he could have found it out online.

She glanced up. Lorcan's attention had wandered to the window and the autumn leaves drifting down outside. There was nothing familiar in his features. Had he attended the same school as her, like Sam, Dakota and Ash? Possibly, but Lorcan was a couple of years older so they wouldn't have been in the same class, or even the same year.

Lorcan's attention flipped back, catching her staring at him, and he winked.

She gritted her teeth. 'Does anyone else reside at the farmhouse with you?'

'No.'

'Staff?'

'My manager's arranging for a housekeeper/cook but she wasn't due to start work until next week and is not going to live-in. I came here to get *away* from people.'

'No one other than the bar staff who can vouch for you?'

'I remember a girl...' He had the air of someone clutching at straws. 'She came over to chat to me. I don't think she even knew who I was, so that was nice. Maybe if you find her, she'll know what happened.'

If she didn't sell her story first. Was Lorcan really that naive?

Harriet sighed. 'What was her name?'

'I don't remember.'

How did she know that was coming?

'What did she look like?'

Lorcan hesitated, and then, 'White, shoulder-length brown hair, big blue eyes...'

Like a good chunk of the female population.

'Nice figure...'

Harriet rolled her eyes. 'What was she wearing?'

'I don't... Is it important?'

Harriet thought of the girl lying beside the pond, dressed for a party in her vintage red dress. 'Yes.'

'Jeans and a T-shirt, I think.'

'What colour T-shirt?'

Lorcan attempted a casual shrug but the look in his eyes was panicked. 'Black, white... I can't remember.'

Despite herself, Harriet began to feel some sympathy for him. If his memory loss was genuine, it would be unnerving.

She slid out a sheet of paper from the folder, a sketch she'd drawn of a red 50s-style dress. Contrary to the plainness of the clothes she wore for work, she was heavily into fashion. She'd spent a lot of time copying all the details of the dress from the crime scene photographs.

'Do you recognise this dress?' she asked Lorcan.

'No. I'm sorry, I can tell it's important, but I don't think I've ever seen it before.'

'The girl at the pub wasn't wearing anything like this?'

'I would have remembered. She'd have been out of place. Everyone was dressed casually.'

Ben took out photos of the crime scene, the ones with the victim, but cropped to only show her from the shoulders down.

'A woman has been found dead in the village,' he said, laying the photos out on the table. Harriet glanced at him in surprise. He didn't usually share this kind of information so early in the interview process. Presumably he'd decided to speed things up. 'Do you recognise her?'

'No,' Lorcan said.

'Not the girl you saw last night?'

'I don't know.' Lorcan's hands were clenching and unclenching in his lap. 'You've cropped the photo. It's hard to tell without a head.'

Harriet winced.

She asked Lorcan to reel off his entire itinerary from the day before once again, while she went through her notes. Lorcan's personal website gave his place of birth rather vaguely as 'England', though he now lived in America. His stepfather had been a musician in an indie band that had had minor success in the late noughties, although Harriet had never heard of them. Lorcan cited his stepfather in several interviews as being a huge influence on his life and choice of career. Since Lorcan's split from a boy band five years ago, his stepfather had become his manager.

They must have a very close relationship.

Dakota had printed off photos from Lorcan's website. There were lots of black and white shots of him posing moodily beside ruined manors and mausoleums, and on the edge of bleak moors and windy cliffs. For his first album, *Deadly Sin*, his face had been heavily disguised with skull-like make-up. For the second, *The Raven King*, he wore a feathered bird mask, the kind often seen at Venetian carnivals. That was the one that had won several awards and had been his most successful. His third album, set in a *Terminator*-style dystopian future, had bombed.

He should have stuck to Gothic, Harriet thought.

Lorcan had now finished reeling off every little thing he remembered from the night before and sat back, slightly more relaxed, presumably expecting praise for being a good boy. When Harriet attempted to clarify a few points, he even attempted a mild flirtation.

She shot him down very quickly. 'I don't think you realise how much trouble you're in, Mr Black.'

'I'm going to need that solicitor, aren't I?'

Rueful, little-boy-lost looks didn't work on Harriet either.

'I think that would be for the best,' she said.

'I'll call my manager. He organises that kind of thing for me. Although he's probably on a plane right now...'

'We can give you a list of local solicitors. You're welcome to choose any one of them.'

Was Lorcan really this helpless or was it an act? What else did his manager do for him? Tie his shoelaces?

More to the point, how often did he need the services of the legal profession?

Still, before said solicitor arrived to overly complicate things...

'As you're aware, you've been arrested on suspicion of murder,' Harriet said. 'Under Section 18 of the Police and

Criminal Evidence Act, we'd like to execute a search of your house, the grounds and any outbuildings.'

Even though they'd already had a prowl around the grounds and a sneak peek into said outbuildings.

'Go ahead,' Lorcan shrugged. 'I've nothing to hide.'

Funny how often guilty people said that.

Did he think he'd hidden the evidence so well it wouldn't be found?

'Thank you,' Ben said. Harriet, having zero patience, was already gathering the paperwork together. 'It would be preferable if you could let us have the keys, to save damaging the property on entry, that kind of thing?'

'Sure,' Lorcan said, and moved to pat his pockets. The expression on his face, when he remembered he was wearing coveralls, was comical. 'I think you have those already.'

'We do,' Ben said smoothly, 'but we like to ask permission.'

'Oh, OK. No problem. If you could leave everything as you found it though? That would be good. And be particularly careful of my studio. It's not so much the guitars or the equipment, as my notebooks. That's my life in there, man. All my songs.'

Harriet tried to keep her expression neutral.

At least they'd learnt one more thing.

Despite his bad boy image, Lorcan had never had his home searched by the police.

Not for the first time, Will cursed his luck at growing up in a tiny village where everyone knew everyone and there was never an opportunity for trouble. He couldn't even go in the pub because his Uncle Charlie ran it.

Heading out of the village, Will passed the stone gateposts to the old manor house, now the village museum. Pausing only to throw the reins over one, he walked down the path.

'What are you up to?' grumbled a familiar voice.

His cousin Benedict emerged from the dark and ambled up the path behind him.

'What do you care?'

'I don't, but I lost the draw to decide who was going to be your babysitter.'

'I don't need a babysitter!'

Benedict didn't even bother to reply, shooting a doubtful look at the manor instead. It loomed out of the mist like something from a horror film.

'Why are we here?' he asked.

'Why not?'

Benedict raised a blond eyebrow. 'It's a museum? Hardly your thing!'

'Are you sure about that?' Will shoved open the heavy wooden door and stepped into the gloomy hallway, grinning as he saw the ragged pennants and rusting armour that he remembered from all his school trips over the years – along with the rows of pistols, axes, and swords arranged in elegant swirls and circles across its panelled walls. 'Because this looks like an armoury to me.'

NINE

With his riot of red-gold curls, white freckled skin, and *very* blue eyes (the kind of eyes a romantic novelist would have you drown in), the man standing in front of Milla could have stepped out of a Renaissance painting. Only a slightly battered nose stopped him from being too pretty.

'Hi, I'm David,' he said, 'or "the Reverend Griffiths" if you want to be formal.'

He looked like a David. It must have been those eyes: the clear, cerulean blue that implied honesty, integrity, reliability…

Milla didn't trust him an inch.

But Grandma McKenzie had always been strict on good manners, so even though she didn't give him her name, Milla still held out her hand. 'Good to meet you, David!'

He shook it politely. 'I'm sorry, our church is temporarily closed.'

'I'm not a tourist.' She too could imply honesty and integrity with a direct gaze. She held up the bunch of white roses, now sadly tattered. 'I'm helping with the flowers.'

'That's very kind of you.' He leant forward, presumably to prevent the acoustics of the church taking his words and running off with them for Ash to overhear. 'However, you might like to know that my sister Rose does the flowers and is very territorial.'

Bother.

'Obviously I'm not your sister...'

He quirked a brow. Those heroic good looks must be such a hit with his lady parishioners.

'I'm not a reporter either.'

The corner of his mouth hitched up. 'That had not crossed my mind,' he said. 'I'd assumed you were a concerned citizen.'

His educated accent and natural good humour reminded her of Ben. 'You mean, you're too polite to say "nosy".' She held up the flowers again. 'Maybe I can find a nice grave for these on my way out.'

The hitch turned into a smile. 'Everyone is welcome here.'

'You're being very kind, so I'll be honest with you.' Honesty often disarmed hostility, not that this guy was showing any sign of hostility: quite the opposite. 'Lorcan – the man who was found here – is one of my friends. He's in a lot of trouble. I'm here to see how I can help him.'

David's smile faded, his expression turning wary. 'I can't let you into the chapel. The investigation is still ongoing. And yes, I appreciate that you want to help your friend, but that kind of thing is best left to the experts.'

'I know this is a crime scene, but I thought the police had finished? I saw their vehicles driving away.'

'They have requested we keep this part of the church closed for a little while longer while they continue with their enquiries.' He indicated Ash still sitting in a central pew, oblivious to their conversation or even her presence, scrolling through his phone. 'I'm sure you understand?'

'I certainly wouldn't want to do anything to jeopardise the investigation.'

Big, fat lie.

She lifted her phone. 'Could I take a photograph instead?'

He frowned. 'Why?'

'Uh, crime scene? It might help, you never know.'

'It's not for me to say.' His voice was beginning to sound strained. 'Perhaps if you spoke to the officer-in-charge?' He indicated Ash, who was now snorting over a cat video.

If Ash was in charge, then heaven help them all.

The *real* power was Ben's boss, DCI Doug Cameron, or Ben himself – *if* he'd been made Senior Investigating Officer – and she could imagine how *that* conversation would go.

She dismissed David's advice with, 'In my experience, the police aren't great at sharing,' and turned her attention to the chapel on the other side of the rope. It was a funny place. Like another church in miniature, complete with an altar and pews, as well as the large tombs. 'This chapel is fascinating. What can you tell me about it?'

He hesitated. 'Do you want to know the history?'

'Sure, why not?' A little background information could come in useful. Was there a reason Lorcan had been found in a church and on that particular tomb?

It would be awkward to come right out and ask that though.

David reached past her, taking a booklet from a stack of them on a nearby table. 'This will answer all your questions.'

She glanced down. On the cover was a drawing of the church in black ink. Above it was written: *The History of St Francis's Church, Raven's Edge.*

She was losing her touch. 'Thanks...'

'That'll be £3.50, please.'

A fellow hustler. There was more to the Vicar of St Francis than mere eye candy.

'OK...' She dug around in the pocket of her jeans, hoping for some loose change. 'In aid of the bell tower?'

It had appeared quite sturdy to her.

'Laptops for the Sunday School,' he said.

Didn't that make her feel like the biggest idiot?

'I look forward to reading it,' she said.

When she was really bored.

She dropped a shoal of silver into the honesty box. 'As I'm already here, perhaps you could give me an overview?' Without pausing long enough for him to decline, she pointed to the sign on the wall. 'The Buckley Chapel? Presumably built and paid for by a family called Buckley?'

'That's right. They lived at the manor house – Buckley Hall. It's now the village museum.'

She knew the museum, although she'd never been inside. It was a seventeenth-century manor house in the centre of the village, built on the edge of the main road in the days before rich people decided they needed extensive gardens to show off their wealth.

'Are the Buckleys buried here? I can only see three tombs.' There were also some large plaques on the wall. Maybe the Buckley family's vast wealth had dwindled with each generation?

She leant over the barrier, wondering if she could sneak in a few photos—

He moved to stand next to her, blocking her view.

David Griffiths was annoyingly savvy for a vicar.

'These are only the monuments,' he said. 'Interment takes place in the vault.' He pointed to their feet.

How very Gothic, but her attention had been caught by the tomb in front of them. The marble had yellowed with age, there was a long inscription written along the top, and what appeared to be a design of flowers and trees carved around the sides. It was too far away to read, and was stained with brown paint.

Except that probably wasn't paint.

Her imagination began to fill in the gaps of what had happened here a couple of hours earlier, sadistically adding a flashback to last night for a grand finale. She swallowed, her mouth suddenly dry. How did the emergency services deal with scenes like this every day?

She took a deep breath, and then another, aware David was coolly waiting for her next question.

It would be a bit inconvenient to throw up; even worse to faint.

To distract him, she waved her hand in the direction of the grandest tomb of all, built into the opposite wall.

'How about that one? He looks important.'

Set in a highly-decorated alcove was the effigy of a rather handsome gentleman, standing beside a lady who had a sour expression – as though life had been a disappointment to her, and that she hardly expected the afterlife to be any different.

'That is Sir John Buckley and his wife Elizabeth,' David said. 'Elizabeth was the daughter of a wealthy merchant and it was her money that paid for the remodelling of the Hall, the renovation of the church, and the addition of this chapel.'

It didn't appear as though Elizabeth's wealth had brought her much happiness. Even Sir John had a resigned look about him; as well he might, if he'd been married to her.

Feeling light-headed, Milla leant against the table, as casually as she could make it. This couldn't be due to squeamishness. When was the last time she'd eaten?

David frowned. 'Are you all right?'

'Oh, I'm fine! Just... um... a blood sugar thing.'

'Are you diabetic?'

'No, I forgot to have breakfast.'

Why was he rummaging through his pockets?

He brought out a KitKat. 'Here, have this.'

'That's not your lunch, is it?'

'Not quite.'

He thought she was joking but there had been several days in her not so distant past when a chocolate bar had been breakfast, lunch and tea. There was no point in explaining. It would make him feel bad and she was beginning to like the Reverend David Griffiths.

'Thank you,' she said, taking it from him, sliding off the wrapper and biting into it. It was slightly squishy, from being in his pocket, but tasted good.

Note to self: stop skipping meals.

'I'd really love to know about that old tomb in the corner,' – she waved the KitKat in that direction – 'the guy wearing the armour, with the dog by his feet? At least, I assume it's a dog?'

'That would be Sir Gregory Stortford. He's credited for building the church in the fourteenth century, although the tower dates back to Saxon times. We had to move him from the main church to keep him safe from damage.'

'He's missing a foot?'

'That would have happened during the Civil War, when the church was a barracks for Parliamentarian troops. Otherwise, he's looking pretty good for a seven-hundred-year-old, don't you think?'

Was the Reverend Griffiths *flirting* with her?

Men flirted with her all the time, but they weren't usually wearing clerical collars.

There was one tomb left, directly in front of them. Large and flat like a tabletop. The one with the pretty carvings of woodland scenes around the side.

The one with the blood.

The silence stretched out.

'Go on,' he sighed. 'Ask me. I know you want to.'

'It does seem plain compared to the others...'

'The carving is beautiful!'

The now-stained carving.

Neither of them mentioned that.

'I meant, less ostentatious,' she said. 'No statues. Whose tomb is it? Anyone famous?'

Anyone with a connection to Lorcan Black?

'That is the monument for Lady Miranda Stortford,' David
said.

Who?

His tone was far too bland.

She waited.

He was going to make her ask.

Probably in payment for the KitKat.

She waited a little bit longer but patience had never been
her strong point. 'OK, who was Lady Miranda Stortford?'

'Sister to the Earl of Stortford, Miranda married a man
named Sir Philip Elliott.'

Elliott. Ben's surname! One of them, anyway. Ben had been
born Benedict Taylor-Elliott but had dropped the Elliott part as
a teenager, wishing to dissociate himself from his father's dodgy
family. Understandable, but his relations couldn't be any worse
than hers. One of them had tried to kill her.

David was still talking. She forced herself to pay attention.

'They had a son, Matthew Elliott.'

'The highwayman?' At last they were getting somewhere.

She'd only lived in the village for four months but couldn't
fail to notice that Raven's Edge had built an entire industry
around its various legends. The village carnival would take
place in a matter of days and, according to Ben, there were
always lots of people dressed up as witches and highwaymen.

'Matthew Elliott and his partner, Jacob Lewis, worked the
road between Norchester and the coast,' David was saying.
'Robbing the rich to give to the poor, as the saying goes. Jacob
Lewis vanished sometime around the turn of the seventeenth
and eighteenth centuries. Supposedly, he sold his soul to the
devil. My belief is that he fled to the continent, or even America. Matthew Elliott was captured and sent to the gallows.
Every Halloween, his ghost rides through the village seeking
revenge against the magistrate who condemned him to die.'

'That's a good motivator.' Milla glanced again at the tomb

showing the man standing next to his sour-looking wife. 'Who was the magistrate? Sir John Buckley?'

'No, Matthew's uncle, the Earl of Stortford. The man whose name he engraved onto his sword.'

It was an entertaining story but, 'Matthew Elliott engraved his sword with the name of the man who killed him... *after* he was dead?'

David smiled. 'The sword exists; we know that much. For a long time it hung on the wall in the village museum. I remember seeing it there as a child – we had so many school trips to the place, you wouldn't believe. The sword clearly had the name "Stortford" inscribed down the centre of the blade but "Stortford", if you remember, was the name of Matthew's mother's family, so the sword could have been an heirloom.'

'It could have been a Victorian fake. Did anyone think to test it?'

'In those days we accepted things at face value. Plus, the technology to do that would have been expensive.'

'How about now?'

'Sadly, the sword disappeared about fifteen years ago.'

Milla's gaze wandered back towards the tomb. There was a clean patch in the middle of the stain, in roughly the shape of a man.

Lorcan.

If that had been his blood, surely there wouldn't have been such a clear outline? It would have been more... smudgy?

That wasn't a question she could ask David, concern for her well-being evident on his face. He was far too nice. Did he believe she was a friend of Lorcan?

Maybe, maybe not. He didn't seem to be a stereotypical naive vicar.

She went for a question that would be easier for him to answer.

'Did the ghost of Matthew Elliott ever get his revenge on the Earl of Stortford?'

'They found the body of the earl on the main route between Norchester and Port Rell. His coach was held up by highwaymen. His servants fled, terrified. When they finally returned with soldiers, the earl was lying in the mud. Dead.'

'Beheaded?'

'All the evidence implied he'd fallen from his horse and cracked his skull.'

'To be clear, *not* murdered due to revenge?'

'Only a boring but sadly all too common accident.'

One theory ruled out.

Not that she thought for one moment that the murdered woman found beside Meg's Pond had been killed by a vengeful ghost.

That would have been completely ridiculous.

TEN

Harriet parked on what would have been a grass verge if there had been any grass left on it, taking care to align her car with the row of CSI vehicles outside the farmhouse. Ben climbed out feeling faintly sick, as he always did when Harriet drove – not that he'd ever admit to it.

Meanwhile, Harriet jumped out eagerly, pausing only to politely hold the wooden gate open for him, but she was too busy teasing him for being a slowcoach to notice the letters carved into the wall beside her. Letters that began

E L L I

before the grey stone crumbled into nothing.

Inside his head, he filled in the missing letters. It gave him a strange feeling to see his own name written there – the name he pretended was no longer his. Was the house still known as 'the Elliott Farmhouse', the way some landmarks kept their names for centuries, even if no longer relevant?

A freshly painted sign, nailed to the gate, answered that question.

RAVENSWOOD HOUSE

How deliciously Gothic. Yet why had Lorcan had settled for this unassuming farmhouse, when he could have bought the large but equally dilapidated Graham mansion on the other side of the village, which wasn't in danger of going over the cliff and even came with its own tragic backstory?

Bored of holding the gate, Harriet muttered something like, 'I can't stand here all day' and let it swing shut, leaving Ben to catch the gate before it smacked into him.

A new gate and a new flagstone path, he noticed, yet the house gave him the same uneasy feeling. He'd never liked it. There was something inherently creepy about the place.

He always tried to avoid talking or even thinking about his father's family, even though everyone in Raven's Edge knew each branch of his family tree and exactly which twig he'd sprung from. But as soon as his team began digging into Lorcan's background, including the purchase of this farmhouse, Ben's own link to the property would be recalled.

As much as it pained him, he would have to remind them of the connection.

The sooner, the better.

'In one of those strange coincidences,' he said out loud, 'this house was once owned by my grandfather. I used to spend the school holidays here, while my parents were working. It's strange to be back.'

It was like dropping a stone into a well and waiting... waiting... waiting... until it hit the bottom.

Had Harriet heard him?

He was about to repeat himself when she stopped and slowly turned.

'*What* did you say?'

'This house was once owned by my grandfather?'

If Harriet wore spectacles, she'd be glaring over the top of them. 'You couldn't have mentioned this *earlier*? Like, before we left the station? So I could have done some research before I lost my signal?'

By 'research', he assumed she meant the internet.

He shrugged. 'I can tell you anything you need to know.'

'OK, did Lorcan buy the house from your grandfather?'

At least she hadn't taken out her notebook. 'No, my grandfather died twenty years ago. He left the house in equal shares to his three sons: Liam, Charlie (my father) and Anthony. Liam bought out Charlie and Anthony. I believe he had the idea to turn the place back into a riding school, as it was in my grandfather's time, but he went bankrupt and ran off to Ireland, presumably to escape his creditors. That's the last we heard of him. The house fell into ruin. No one wanted to take it on. I'd always assumed the bank seized it.'

'Any secret passages or dungeons?'

'It's a *farmhouse*, Harriet. There are not many places to hide a...' He broke off and grimaced. Head. Body. Surgical saw. Take your pick. He'd almost forgotten the reason they were here.

Harriet started up the path again. 'Luckily for us, we have the entire CSI department on call to help find it.'

Heaven knew what *that* was going to do to the budget.

Standing sentry outside the front door was a detective constable that Ben vaguely recognised from Calahurst Police Station. Pete Kershaw?

Harriet held up her warrant card with a flourish. 'DS Harriet March,' and then, as an afterthought, thumbed in Ben's direction. 'DI Taylor.'

DC Kershaw barely glanced at their IDs before tossing them coveralls from a box by his feet. 'Sign the sheet and go on in.'

'The main thing I remember about this house,' Ben said, once they were suited and booted, 'was that it was always freezing cold, even in summer, very draughty, and that my grandfather had filled it with horrible, moth-eaten taxidermy.'

'Nice,' Harriet said. The door was already open so she went on through. 'I suppose in those days there wasn't a local IKEA.'

He followed her inside, closing the door behind him. The entrance hall had very little natural light and was open to the rafters to accommodate a wooden staircase that might collapse into a heap of firewood with one unwary breath. Ben recognised the flagstones beneath his feet as original, hollowed from centuries of use. The stretch of wall above the panelling had been painted a horrible ochre colour but it was an improvement on the flaking, off-white plaster that he remembered from his childhood.

What would his grandfather have made of it?

A very reserved man, he'd have hated it.

What kind of person painted their walls *ochre*?

Harriet pointed up and smirked. 'What were you saying about taxidermy?'

He grimaced at the sight of the stag heads forming a guard of honour up the staircase, with more along the corridor towards the back of the house.

Of all the things for Lorcan to keep...

There was a solitary sideboard against the wall, the oak so dark it appeared black. He remembered this too, situated in exactly the same place. Uncle Liam must have sold the furniture at the same time as the house. Ben even remembered the slightly battered pewter bowl in the centre (now polished and holding six or seven oranges), along with the carved wooden candlestick and dusty stuffed raven. Although in his day, the raven had held the key to the stables in its beak.

Why would a man in his twenties want to surround himself with such old-fashioned things?

Ben reached out to stroke the raven's head. What had they

called it? His cousin Will had come up with the idea, a nod to a famous author.

Poe! That was it. The raven had been called Poe.

'Hello, Poe,' he said, stroking the raven's head.

The raven let out a loud croak and bit his finger.

Ben let out a curse before he could stop himself.

Harriet shrieked and flattened herself against the wall. 'I thought it was stuffed!'

'Me too.' He checked his fingertip, relieved to see it was still there. It hurt like hell, and even in the dim light he could see a little ball of blood welling up.

The raven, oblivious to the commotion it had caused, waddled off to the other end of the sideboard.

With a grin, Harriet handed Ben a tissue. 'I'm telling everyone you swore.'

He shrugged. 'I shall tell everyone you screamed.'

'I did not! It was an exclamation of surprise.'

'I think you'll find that's the definition of "screamed".'

The door behind them opened and the raven took off in fright, doing a circuit of the hall before disappearing into the darkness.

'Sorry, sir,' DC Kershaw said, presumably coming to see what the fuss was about. 'I should have warned you. We hoped that if we left the door open the bird might fly out, but we think it might be tame. It's not frightened of us at all. Stole my lunch right out of my hand.'

'If I had a beak like that,' Harriet said, 'I wouldn't be frightened of anyone either.'

Ben wrapped the tissue around his finger and peered into the rafters. He could see something moving about. *Was* the raven tame? Having a raven as a pet seemed like the kind of stunt an eccentric musician might pull, but it was illegal to keep wild birds as pets.

At least he could charge Lorcan with that, if nothing else.

From above their heads came a sinister frog-like croak.

'What was that?' Harriet whispered.

'Our new friend, the raven.'

'He's been quiet up until now,' DC Kershaw said, adding a little too cheerfully, 'Perhaps he likes you, sir?'

'Don't be ridic—'

As though on cue, there was a flapping sound and a rush of warm air, and all three of them instinctively ducked.

Not quickly enough.

Something heavy hit Ben's back, causing him to stagger against the sideboard. When he stood up, he had a raven on his shoulder.

Great.

Harriet could barely contain her glee. 'He *does* like you! Oh, that is so cute!' She whipped out her phone and took a photo. 'Why does he like you and not me? Not that I mind. I would completely freak if he landed on me.'

The raven put its head on one side, as though posing for the photo.

Ben was *never* going to live this down.

'OK, Poe, or whatever your name is, playtime is *over*.'

He jerked his shoulder, intending to send the raven back into the air.

The bird dug in its talons and stayed where it was.

At least his jacket had padded shoulders.

Harriet took another photo as the raven rubbed its beak against his ear, croaking softly.

The weight of the bird was making his shoulder ache. He tried gently pushing it off, but it snapped at his fingers.

Time to try something different. With his other hand, he took an orange from the bowl and held it out. The raven waddled down his arm towards it, hopping onto the sideboard as Ben dropped the orange back into the bowl.

'That was clever,' DC Kershaw said. 'How did you know to do that?'

'Most animals follow food.'

'I didn't know ravens liked oranges,' Harriet said. 'I thought their snack of choice would be small animals and roadkill.'

Ben pointed to the beak-sized holes in the oranges left in the bowl, although the raven now seemed more interested in tapping at its reflection.

'Only Lorcan Black would have a raven for a pet,' she sighed.

Ben supposed they should be grateful it wasn't a tiger.

After their encounter with the raven, the rest of their search was fairly anticlimactic.

The CSIs found nothing out of the ordinary. No signs of a struggle or an injury. No blood in any of the rooms. No weapons. No body parts.

Only Harriet seemed disappointed by this. Everyone else was tired and fed up.

The main point of interest was Lorcan's bedroom. Apart from the sitting room, that was the only place with personal possessions. As well as more taxidermy, there was a modern four-poster bed, a silver skull set in a little alcove, a half-drunk bottle of Finlayson's Best Whisky and a packet of extra-strength sleeping pills.

The CSI bagged up the pills and the booze, and dropped them into a crate. 'Nothing much here,' she said, 'or in the outbuildings. No weapon that would meet the description of the kind of thing you're looking for. The knives in the kitchen are all in place and spotless, as though they've recently done a hot wash in the dishwasher. We're taking them with us, but we don't think we're going to find anything useful. Wherever your guy killed the victim, we don't think it was here.'

Ben doubted the murderer was 'his guy' at all, but kept that to himself.

'The strangest thing of all? Apart from bird droppings and feathers, this house is immaculate.'

'We believe the owner's just moved in,' Ben said.

'No one's that clean. There'd be fingerprints from all the people who've been in and out of this house over the past few days – builders, decorators, removal operatives. We've found nothing apart from faint traces of bleach.'

'Perhaps the house was professionally cleaned before the owner took occupancy?'

'We're talking about a completely sterile environment, and that's sending up as many red flags as a blood splatter pattern.'

'Will you put that in your report?'

'To be honest, I don't know what to put in my report.'

'The victim *could* have been killed here?'

'I'd rather not commit to that. In theory, if someone was murdered in the way you've described, there should be something – there isn't. But the way the house has been thoroughly cleaned... Well, it's too clean and that confuses the issue.'

'The owner's hiding something?'

The CSI shrugged. 'That's not for me to say. I deal in facts. I'll write my report, we'll carry out tests on the items we've seized, and let you decide.'

'Thank you,' Ben said, because it was expected, but he was out of patience.

At every stage this investigation threw up more questions. Was an unseen enemy out to frame Lorcan or was he playing a very clever game?

As usual, Harriet had questions of her own. Ben left her to it and wandered over to the window, curious to see how much of the outside had been altered. There was now a formal garden between the house and the forest, whereas he remembered only a concrete yard containing a few broken-down vehicles. The stables and old carriage house were still there (they must be as old as the farmhouse and were downright sinister), presumably converted into a garage for Lorcan's cars and motorbike. A more modern building, set between the stables and the house, must be Lorcan's studio.

'I think that's everything,' he heard Harriet say. 'We'll let you finish up and look forward to receiving your report.'

Ben hid a smile at the CSI's bemusement at being so thoroughly dismissed, and turned away from the window. As he did so, something sparkled and caught his eye.

It took a moment to work out what it was. A knot in the wooden windowsill had cracked, creating a small hole where something silver and metallic had become jammed.

He should have asked the CSI to dig it out with gloves and tweezers and drop it into an evidence bag. Instead, he used his thumbnail to flip the thing onto the palm of his hand.

It was a little silver bottle: a charm perhaps? Beautifully detailed, it even had a label.

Ben knew that if he stuck it beneath a magnifying glass, that label would say 'Drink me'.

Harriet came over. 'What have you found?'

Trust her to not miss a trick.

'Nothing,' he said, turning sideways so she couldn't see him slide it into his pocket. 'Nothing at all.'

The entrance hall of Buckley Manor was large, square and central. A door to each other room was set in every wall, except for the one directly opposite, where there was a battered desk and an old-fashioned cash register. Laid out on the desk beside the cash register were an array of cheap souvenirs – pens, bookmarks, mugs, and such-like, all with the familiar village logo – a raven in flight. Behind the desk, an elderly man slumped in a chair. His eyes were closed and his mouth partly open. He was snoring.

Will didn't bother to glance in his direction. He scooped up one of the chairs and dropped it in front of the fireplace with a careless clatter. The chair had faded blue cord tied around each arm, with a cardboard sign that said 'Don't Touch'. Will pulled the sign off and tossed it onto the floor, climbing on the chair to reach for the sword hanging above the mantelpiece.

Benedict was beside him in seconds. 'What are you doing?'

'Nothing!' he sang out, and heaved the sword from its bracket. It was heavier than it looked. The edge of the blade clanged against the floor as he staggered beneath its weight.

Benedict lunged forward. Worried he might drop and damage the sword? Or more concerned about exactly what he planned to do with it?

The sense of power was heady. Will jumped down, slashing the air between them (he had to use both hands), before raising the sword to the light. The metal was dull and pitted, and there were long swirling scratches along each side. Some kind of engraving? A name? The light in here was too dim to see.

'Put it back.' This time there was a definite note of warning in Benedict's voice.

Will patted his cousin's shoulder. 'No worries, I'm only borrowing it.'

He laid the sword flat against his shoulder and set off for the entrance.

'You can't steal it!'

'Technically, it's mine.' He thumbed towards the plaque on the wall. The one that said:

Broadsword (c. 1650)
European (possibly Italian)
Believed to have belonged to:
Matthew Elliott
(Highwayman)
On loan from the Elliott family

Benedict stepped in front of him. 'By that reasoning it's mine too. So put it back!'

Will swung the sword down, feeling his wrist wrench with the effort. 'Make me, Benny-Boy.'

'Benedict Elliott? Is that you?'

That's what living in a tiny village got you. With their distinctive blond hair and green eyes, the Elliott family were far too easily recognisable.

They both froze but only Benedict was brave enough to turn around. Will carried on walking. He'd have liked to have broken into a run, but the sword was too long and heavy.

Benedict stuck his fingers into Will's collar and yanked him back, turning him to face their accuser.

'Yes, sir?' Benedict was as polite as ever.

'Valuable antique that,' the curator said. 'Not a toy.'

'Yes, sir.'

'Ensure you bring it back in one piece.'

Benedict didn't respond. Will nudged him, unable to resist a triumphant smirk.

It was short-lived.

'And William? William Elliott? Is that right?'

'Answer him.' Benedict gave Will a shove.

'Yeah?'

This earnt him a slap around the head from his cousin.

The curator merely grinned. 'Don't go chopping off any heads with it, eh lad?'

ELEVEN

Before returning to work, Ben and Harriet dropped into The Witch's Brew for a very late lunch. Harriet had her usual cappuccino (with extra chocolate sprinkles), Ben asked for a black coffee. They both ordered bacon and cheese paninis that arrived in super-quick time because Kat had seen the two of them arrive, arguing all the way across the car park, and knew they always ordered the same thing.

Harriet opened her panini and smothered her bacon in ketchup.

Ben tried not to judge.

On the way out, they took a latte and a gingerbread muffin to go.

The drive from the café to the station took less than a minute. Harriet dropped Ben off at the front, because sometimes it was hard to find a parking space. He headed upstairs to his office to check his messages, before making a call downstairs to request that Lorcan be returned to the interview suite.

'Hello, again,' Ben said, once Lorcan was sat in front of him. He was still wearing the white coveralls, the dark circles ringing his eyes now more prominent.

'Your eyes have changed colour,' Harriet said, sliding into the seat beside Ben, slightly out of breath.

Both men stared at her.

Harriet shrugged. 'I'm just saying! They were blue this morning, now they're green. Coloured contact lenses, right?'

'Er, yes,' Lorcan said. 'They were giving me grief. I should have asked you to pick up my specs when you were searching the farmhouse, but I can get them myself now I'm free to go.'

'Not quite,' Ben said.

'But you took my statement!'

'There are a few points we'd like you to expand upon but we're happy to wait for you to have a solicitor present.'

Lorcan began twisting his fingers together. 'I requested one but she hasn't turned up yet. How about my manager? Have you heard from him? He was already on a flight from JFK before this kicked off. He should have arrived by now.'

'Sorry, we've not heard anything. Would you like us to try again? Perhaps call someone else for you? A friend? A relative?'

Lorcan hesitated, and then put his head in his hands. 'There's no one. I guess this is my own fault for getting arrested in a foreign country.'

Again, Ben wondered why Lorcan had chosen to buy a farmhouse in a country where he had no ties. Was he running away from something?

'In the meantime,' Ben said, 'we thought you might appreciate this.'

Harriet took an orange paper bag from the table behind them and placed it in front of Lorcan. The smell of warm gingerbread wafted tantalisingly across the room.

Lorcan glanced between them and then cautiously reached for the bag, brightening perceptibly when he saw what was inside.

'Coffee and cake? Thanks!' He lifted out the latte and took

a hefty gulp. 'I needed that. I love coffee. The stuff from your machine tastes like—'

'Yes,' Ben said. 'We know.'

'I haven't had anything to eat since last night.' Lorcan turned his attention to the gingerbread muffin, peeling away the wrapper. 'My own fault. I turned my nose up at the sandwiches they brought me for lunch. Couldn't face them. I still felt sick.'

Ben exchanged glances with Harriet. They'd brought Lorcan the latte and gingerbread muffin in the hope he'd open up; now he wouldn't shut up.

Harriet slid her phone from her pocket, tapped the screen and turned it to show Lorcan. 'We met your raven when we went to your house this morning. He's so cute.'

Ben hoped she wasn't showing Lorcan the photo where the bird had been snuggled up on his shoulder.

'I love him.' Lorcan's face softened. 'I've called him Eddie.'

'After Edgar Allan Poe?' Ben asked. Were *all* ravens given a variation of this name?

'No, Eddie Cochran. My absolute hero. I learnt to play guitar listening to "Summertime Blues".'

'It's illegal to keep a wild bird as a pet.'

'Eddie's not a pet. He comes and goes as he pleases. I think he gets in through a hole in the gable. Basically, he thinks that it's his house and I'm the interloper, *and* he's a lot easier to talk to than most people.'

'A good listener?' Harriet suggested.

Lorcan grinned to show he'd got the joke. 'Sure.'

Harriet's own smile turned shark-like as she made a point of looking at her watch, and then at the rain now hammering against the window.

'Do you think the rain's held your solicitor up? Sometimes the road between us and Calahurst floods in bad weather.'

One time, Ben thought, sipping at his own coffee – out of the machine. One time.

'We could take you back to the cell to wait?' Harriet said. 'You can take your coffee with you. It would be a shame to let it go cold.'

'Nah, let's get it over with,' Lorcan said. 'I've got no secrets. If I had, they'd already be all over the internet, wouldn't they? Bastards. I hate the press. Have they heard that I've been arrested? I bet they're camped outside?'

For someone who professed not to like the press, he seemed quite cheerful at the prospect.

'We've not issued any statements,' Ben said.

(It didn't mean someone else hadn't though.)

'You want to make sure you've got the right guy, eh?'

That was rather too close to the truth.

Lorcan took another long drink from his coffee. 'This is *divine*. Did you say it came from one of the local coffee shops? I'll have to check it out.'

Did he think he was going to be leaving soon?

'It's on the way out of the village. A café called The Witch's Brew.'

'Is that place still going? Miss Lily used to make the most amazing peanut butter cookies.'

'Sadly, Miss Lily is no longer with us. Her niece owns the café now.'

'That's a shame. Miss Lily was a sweetheart.'

'You've visited Raven's Edge before?'

'You could say that!' Lorcan's green eyes crinkled with humour.

Ben saw a flash of something... familiar? Then it was gone.

I know you...

'Ben?' Harriet prompted, but at least she didn't kick him under the table. She turned to Lorcan. 'We've conducted a search of your property.'

'Did you find anything?' Lorcan asked politely.

A man secure in the knowledge that there was nothing at the farmhouse to find.

'It's a very interesting house. How old is it?'

'The sixteenth century or thereabouts.' Lorcan leant forward, now quite at ease. 'No one's really sure. I suppose I could have one of the beams dated but that only tells you how old the beams are, not the entire house. It could be standing on the site of a much older building. I'd love to know for sure.'

'Are you fond of archaeology?'

'Just history. I've never liked the idea of digging things up – too much work and all that dirt!'

How about burying things?

They should have dug up Lorcan's garden, but it was extensive. There was an old orchard beyond the outbuildings, plus the forest between the farmhouse and the village. Far too many places to hide a body – or a part of one. Where would they have started? He could imagine DCI Cameron's reaction if he'd requested cadaver dogs or ground-penetrating radar without good reason.

'Was that why you bought the farmhouse?' Ben asked. 'Because of its age?'

Lorcan laughed. 'I didn't buy the house. It's been in my family for years.'

For someone who'd been arrested on suspicion of murder, this man was enjoying himself far too much. They'd brought him coffee and now he thought they were the best of friends. Did he have so few real friends? No one had phoned the station to ask after him – family member, manager, girlfriend – which was incredibly sad, and also unusual for a man in the public eye. Even his solicitor couldn't be bothered to turn up on time.

Ben backtracked. 'You said you grew up in Raven's Edge but I'm struggling to remember a single family living in the village with the surname "Black".'

'Yes, in the farmhouse. I've already told you that.' Lorcan

flipped his gaze between the two of them. '"Lorcan Black" isn't the name I was born with. You do know that, right?'

A stage name?

Deep breath.

Stay *calm*.

'Since you were arrested, you've signed everything "Lorcan Black",' Ben said.

'It is my legal name but I was well out of it for the first couple of hours. If you'd told me to sign as Henry VIII, I probably would have!'

Ben rubbed his hand over his face, thinking of all the time they'd wasted.

Lorcan frowned. 'You have no idea who I am, do you, Benny-Boy?'

The only people to ever call him 'Benny' (which he *hated*) had been his father's family.

Were he and Lorcan *related*?

It got better and better.

Beside him, Harriet shifted in her chair, evidently dying to take over.

He should terminate the interview. Send Lorcan back to his cell and let him stew.

'Don't feel bad,' Lorcan was saying, finishing the ginger-bread muffin and licking his fingers. Was he deliberately trying to be antagonistic? 'It took me ages to recognise you too, with that beard, and it must have been a good fifteen years ago since I saw you – at the carnival, I think? It was only when your girl called you "Ben" that I twigged.'

Harriet fidgeted some more, outraged at being called 'your girl', but Ben was hardly paying attention. He'd always tried to have as little to do with his father's side of the family as possible. Mainly because he had so little in common with them; it hardly felt as though they were related. His grandfather had died before he'd really got to know him. He'd never got on with his father, and his uncles were far too intimidating to be approachable.

The little he did know? Uncle Liam had taken his wife and son to Ireland, whereas Uncle Anthony had two sons, Drew and Greg, and they all lived locally.

Had there been other uncles or aunts? More cousins?

Lorcan sighed. 'I'll take that as a "no".'

Wait...

The notes Harriet had given him said Lorcan's place of birth had been England but perhaps he'd moved to *Ireland* before heading to America with his mother after his father had abandoned them?

'Will Elliott?'

Lorcan grinned. 'That's me!'

Was it *possible*?

The age was right, but Will Elliott had been small, slight, and supremely irritating. A mischief-maker, an attention-seeking trickster, but Ben had last seen Will when he'd been eleven or twelve. People changed.

He grimaced at the cliché. As a detective, one of the first things he'd learnt was that people didn't change. A trickster could always be relied upon to be a trickster.

Was Lorcan trying to con him now? Had that scene at the local church been an elaborate publicity stunt?

And he'd walked right into it.

'If I checked all the records, the land registry, and so forth, there would be no record of a purchase of Ravenswood House?' Ben asked.

'My father inherited the house from my grandfather, and then bought out his brothers. It was always known as the Elliott Farmhouse.'

Ben turned to a fresh page on his notebook. 'Your father's name?'

'William Elliott, but everyone called him Liam. We had him

declared legally dead a couple of years ago. No great loss to anyone. We didn't even bother with a funeral or a grave. My grandfather's name was Terrence and before him there was another William. Would you like me to go on? I can quote our family tree back to the 1600s and a wealthy cloth merchant called Philip, who married into the Stortford family. I've always been mad for history.'

Our family tree.

'It *is* me,' Lorcan said. 'I'm Will – your cousin.'

If they had taken the time to research Lorcan thoroughly, beyond the obvious, behind the manufactured image, they could have worked this out for themselves. It wasn't Harriet's fault, it was his. He'd taken Lorcan's name at face value because he was well-known and they had been pressured for time. Now they looked like a couple of amateurs.

How could he have failed to recognise his own cousin?

He kept his expression neutral as he asked, 'Did you change your name legally?'

'Yes, I think it was to distance ourselves from what happened on the night of the carnival. Our surname became Black. Mum chose "Stella" and I picked "Lorcan". I thought it sounded cool. I couldn't tell you what name Dad picked, he didn't stay around for long enough. He left us as soon as we reached Dublin.'

Ben sighed and gathered up his notes. 'It's great to see you again, Will—'

'*Lorcan.*'

'But this complicates things. Because we're related, I will have to terminate this interview.' He gave the time and switched everything off. 'DS March, please arrange for Mr Black to be returned to custody. Hopefully his solicitor will turn up soon and you'll be able to continue the interview.'

'Can't we carry on? I really don't mind. I like you. I thought we were getting on?'

Ben didn't trust himself to speak.

Dropping the case file into the hands of a delighted Harriet, Ben left the room without waiting for her to follow, almost flattening Ash who'd been lingering in the corridor, waiting for the door to open.

'Not now,' he said, before Ash could get a word out.

The problem with Ash was that he always thought the word 'no' didn't apply to him.

'But—'

'Give me a minute, OK?'

He needed to process this. The victim's body had been left in Meg's Pond without her head. Lorcan had been found lying on the top of Miranda Elliott's grave – the mother of Matthew Elliott – a highwayman notorious for chopping the heads off his enemies. The legend might not be historically accurate, but that was hardly the point. Lorcan Black had no connection to Matthew Elliott, but Will was a direct descendant.

Connection made.

Meanwhile, he was guilty of trying to sweet-talk Lorcan without a solicitor, wanting to speed things up so that he could let him go – his *cousin* – because he was convinced of Lorcan's innocence, without a shred of evidence, because of a *hunch*, to enable him to concentrate on finding the 'real' murderer.

Could he have made more of a hash of things?

'Sir!' Ash was following him. 'DCI Cameron has arrived and he's waiting—'

'Tell the DCI I'll be up to brief him in about five minutes.'

Ash grimaced. They both knew Cameron wasn't big on patience.

'I'm not sure—'

'I need time to get my head around something.' Ben turned sideways to squeeze past a gaggle of women from Admin cluttering up the corridor, perhaps hoping to sneak a look at Lorcan when he was taken back to the cells.

Shoving open the next door, Ben almost walked into Sam coming from reception, escorting a glamorous redhead in a bright yellow skirt suit, and an older, decidedly grizzled gentleman, to whom the passing years had not been kind.

'Hi boss,' Sam said, adding quite unnecessarily, because Ben had already recognised the woman and his heart was sinking in anticipation, 'This is—'

The redhead gave Ben a toothy grin and stuck out her hand. 'Fabulous to meet you again, DI Taylor. I'm Olivia Greenwich-Fitzpatrick, Mr Black's solicitor, and this is his manager, Jonesy, fresh off the plane from New York City.'

'Fresh' hardly seemed the right word. The man resembled a reanimated corpse – deathly pale, with frizzy grey hair all over the place and some very dubious tattoos.

Jonesy grunted something belligerent, followed by, 'Where's my boy?' in an unexpected English accent. 'I called at the farmhouse and it's crawling with cops.'

Boy? By Ben's reckoning, Lorcan must be at least twenty-six years old.

Thankfully, Olivia talked straight over any unthinking retort he might have made.

'When does Mr Black's interview begin? I do hope you haven't started without me?'

TWELVE

It was strange to be standing on the other side of his desk.

DCI Doug Cameron was leant back in Ben's chair, his long brown fingers tapping idly at his laptop. He wasn't much older than Ben, mid-to-late thirties at the most. He wore his dark hair cropped close to his head and his beard shaped far more elegantly than Ben had ever managed to achieve with his own.

The two men had had a similar scholarship-funded Oxbridge education, followed by a fast-tracked promotion through the ranks, until Ben had stalled at inspector. Yet somehow DCI Cameron always managed to make Ben feel as though he had ink stains on his fingers and a shoelace not only undone but trailing in the dirt. Cameron seemed to like him, although scathing of Ben's hunches and gut feelings: 'You can get pills for that, Benedict.'

Telling Cameron that he suspected Lorcan was innocent, without a shred of evidence to back it up, was likely to result in a swift reassignment to somewhere deeply unpleasant, possibly Traffic.

'Sit,' Cameron muttered irritably, waving his free hand in the direction of the other chair. 'It's your office, after all.'

Ben sat, wishing he'd thought to bring his coffee upstairs.

There was already a single mug of black coffee on the desk, steaming gently, and a plate of what Harriet called 'visitors' biscuits'. Thankfully someone had made Cameron's coffee in a plain mug with the Constabulary crest on it, rather than one taken from the MIT's stash. Sam's mug, for example, had the Southampton Football Club logo on it, whereas Harriet's said *The Queen of Everything*.

Cameron slid the laptop to one side but didn't close it. 'A woman was found beside the village pond this morning with her head missing?'

'Yes.' Ben expanded on the details of the investigation to date as Cameron drank his coffee, his handsome face expressionless. 'Possible suspect found unconscious in the church, lying on a tomb, his clothes soaked in blood. No sign of any weapon. No sign of victim's missing head, despite exhaustive search.'

'I suppose it is only...' – Cameron checked his expensive watch – '...3.00 pm.'

Ben smiled tightly. He was never quite sure how to take the DCI's sarcasm.

'Again, from DS March's report,' Cameron continued, 'the suspect has been identified as Lorcan Black, a musician much given to posing on tombs and in churches, judging by the photos she forwarded to me.'

Harriet had been very quick off the mark.

'Don't make me wait for it,' Cameron said.

'Sir?'

'The big fat bow to tie everything up?'

'Lorcan Black's birth name is William Elliott and he was found on the tomb of Lady Miranda Elliott. She was the mother of a highwayman called Matthew Elliott, famous for chopping the heads off his victims.'

'Not the highwayman's actual grave?'

'No one knows where that is.'

'Perhaps the prison where he was executed?' Cameron took another sip of coffee but didn't reach for a biscuit, he never did. 'I've had an interesting telephone conversation with Caroline Warner, the pathologist.'

Caroline was also Ben's ex-wife, although everyone was careful to never mention that.

'She's done the post-mortem already?'

'Relax,' Cameron said, reading his mind. 'You've not missed anything. There's been no post-mortem. After Caroline's initial examination on site, the remains were taken to the mortuary at the hospital in Norchester, where one of her technicians recognised the body.'

'Without a head?' Now he sounded like Harriet.

'I believe the woman had a birthmark on the inside of her arm. Unusual enough for the APT to check the record against that of another he'd logged two days previously.'

'We have an ID?'

'We do. Two days ago, a lovelorn young lady by the name of Raquel Marsh attempted to blow up the house of her former fiancé – with him still in it.'

'I saw something about it on the news...' It had been out of his jurisdiction and not terrorist-related, so he hadn't paid the story much attention.

'I've no idea where Ms Marsh found the information to build a rather impressive incendiary device, but unfortunately, it didn't appear to cover how to detonate said bomb. When it exploded, far too early, it caused minimum damage to all life and property in the vicinity, with the exception of Ms Marsh herself.'

'The news report said one person was killed but they didn't give further details.'

'The curious thing was that Ms Marsh didn't have a mark on her – outwardly, that is. Caroline didn't have the chance to perform a forensic post-mortem before the body was stolen from the hospital mortuary.'

'*Stolen?*'

'It didn't walk out by itself, Benedict.'

'Then how...?'

'Again, an interesting story. To gain access to the mortuary one requires an ID card to swipe the machine at the entrance, although no record is kept to verify who goes in and out. In theory, an ID card could be stolen. Oh, and all the fridges have locks.'

'An inside job?'

'Undoubtedly, but Caroline says she can personally vouch for all her staff.'

He wasn't going to be caught bad-mouthing his ex-wife. 'Caroline is a good judge of character, but if you offer someone enough money...'

'Exactly.'

'So, the corpse of Raquel Marsh was stolen, dressed in retro clothes, and had its head removed before being transported from Norchester to Raven's Edge?'

'To be placed beside the village pond,' Cameron said. 'A pretty setting and popular tourist spot meant the remains would be found quickly. Planned down to the last detail, undoubtedly.'

'Vile.'

Cameron inclined his head. 'It's certainly very worrying. Caroline suggests – you know how she never likes to commit herself until she's done a full PM – that the corpse's head was removed while it was still at the mortuary. All the equipment required to effect the procedure is there. The body would have been dressed afterwards, because there was very little blood on the clothes or at the location where it was found.'

'Lorcan Black was covered in blood. His clothes were soaked, although he didn't have any on his hands.'

'A cursory check proved the blood wasn't the same type as either Black or Ms Marsh, a rather basic error if the perpetrator had intended for Black to take the blame. Caroline suggests the blood could have been stolen from the hospital at the same time as the body. They keep a store there for emergency transfusions, that kind of thing. Again, you need an ID card to gain access, and there's usually someone on duty...'

'We could be looking at two suspects?'

Cameron shrugged. Like Caroline, he didn't like to commit himself to theories without any evidence.

'Why would anyone go to this much trouble? It's like the plot from a book.'

Cameron's smile was wry. 'Remember that case we had, where the victim was lying on a bed of flowers and wearing an expensive designer gown?'

Not one he was likely to forget. The press had called it 'The Sleeping Beauty Murder'.

'The murderer was trying to send a message.'

'I'm worried this person is too.'

'No one's been murdered,' Ben said.

'Yet,' Cameron said, in his usual morbid way, 'and we can't rule out the importance of the tomb where Lorcan was found.'

'That would mean the perpetrator knows Lorcan's birth name and is familiar with the legend of the village's ghostly highwayman.'

'I've asked the DI at Norchester to investigate the theft of the body and the blood from the hospital. It should be straight-forward enough. We're talking about either an inside job or someone with enough disposable income to bribe a member of staff.'

Feeling disloyal, Ben said, 'The latter could apply to Black.'

'A publicity stunt?'

'If it's not Black, then the perpetrator might try again – with a different result.'

'Kill him, you mean?'

Ben nodded.

'Isn't the highwayman an ancestor of yours too?'

'I'm afraid I don't keep track of my relatives, alive or dead.' Another reason he'd completely failed to recognise Lorcan. 'There's a new curator at the local museum. Ellie something-or-other. Very keen. I'll arrange for someone to speak to her, ask her to check the records. Perhaps the vicar might know? I'm not sure who keeps the parish records.'

'Aren't these things available for anyone to search online? You know the kind of site: send in your DNA and find out if you're descended from Robert the Bruce.'

That was hardly reassuring.

'I'll be frank with you, Benedict. This case worries me. For someone to go to this much trouble, without being caught at any stage of the stunt, indicates an extremely clever, extremely devious mind. Yet some aspects are sloppy. If you're going to steal a corpse, why not steal a blood type that matches?'

'Unless they knew further tests would be made and the difference would have been spotted anyway?'

'A medical professional?'

'Perhaps someone with CSI experience, who would know the kind of tests likely to be carried out.'

'We're back to someone who works at the hospital,' Cameron said, 'but I don't understand what result they were hoping for. Frame young Black for a murder – which we know didn't happen. Just a prank? To threaten him? To draw official attention to him in some way so that some other misdemeanour comes to light? Or is the entire event a publicity stunt?'

'I don't believe it is a stunt,' Ben said. 'While it might have appealed to him as a teenager, I'm sure he'd realise that it'd backfire very quickly, particularly once the press got hold of it. His career would be destroyed.'

'Someone else on his behalf? Maliciously or otherwise?'

'The only person I can think of would be his manager, but he's only recently arrived in the UK – this very morning, in fact. We're currently verifying that. Again, he'd have nothing to gain by Lorcan being ruined. Plus, Lorcan doesn't have anything to promote. He said himself that he's working on a new album. Presumably that won't be released for another year.'

Cameron sighed heavily. 'Desecration of a corpse is a serious offence but you don't have the evidence to charge him with that either.'

Ben didn't have any evidence at all but didn't like to remind Cameron of the fact.

'Is there any point in keeping him here?' Cameron asked.

Lorcan hadn't even been under arrest for twelve hours and his solicitor was piling on the pressure to obtain his release.

'Probably not,' Ben admitted.

'You'll let him go?'

When had that become *his* decision?

'I suppose so.'

'It'll be interesting to see how this pans out.'

Was his boss suggesting putting Lorcan's life at risk to flush out a body snatcher?

'Sir?'

Cameron had already snapped his laptop shut and was getting to his feet. 'Put a tail on Black,' he said, 'and assign someone to watch his house.'

'You want to see what he does next?' That sounded incredibly risky.

Cameron smiled, in much the same way as Harriet had done earlier. Distinctly shark-like.

'Don't you?' he said.

Drew and Greg were still sitting on the wall of the churchyard, chucking stones at empty beer cans, but they had been joined by a couple of girls.

Will used the sword to slash the air in front of Drew. 'Stand and deliver!'

Drew raised an eyebrow. Greg snorted.

The girl on Drew's lap said, 'Who are you supposed to be, sweetie? Matthew Elliott?'

Sweetie!

Will plunged the sword into the grass directly between Drew's long legs. It slid in with barely a sound, unlike the girl, who screamed loudly.

Irritated, Drew shoved her off his lap.

'No I'm not Matthew Elliott,' Will said. 'I'm—'

'Seriously winding me up,' Drew said, yanking the sword from the mud. 'Where did you get this?'

Benedict sighed. 'The little brat robbed the museum.'

'You let him? You were supposed to be watching him!'

'I didn't have a lot of choice!'

'You're twice his size.'

'I was slightly thwarted by the curator saying it was completely fine for him to help himself to it because, you know, we're Elliotts.'

Drew used his cloak to wipe the mud from the blade and lifted it up to the light. 'Well, William Elliott, aren't you the bad boy?'

Greg, leaning over his brother's shoulder, saw the swirly writing along the side of the blade and whistled. 'Isn't that...?'

'Oh, yes,' Drew smiled. 'Matthew Elliott's famous broadsword.' He sliced through an unopened can on the ground, sending beer in a sparkling brown arc across the gravestones. He looked a lot cooler than Will, too, as though he actually knew what he was doing. 'The question is, what are we going to do with it?'

THIRTEEN

Milla had lost a charm from her bracelet.

The silver bottle that had 'Drink Me' written on it.

She wanted to scream. She wanted to throw something. If it broke, all the better.

Her father had commissioned the bracelet for her sixth birthday, when she'd been obsessed with *Alice in Wonderland*. Each charm alluded to something from the story: a pocket watch, a top hat, a key, and so on. Milla only took the bracelet off to sleep or shower. When she felt restless or upset, she found it comforting to tug gently on each of the charms in turn.

Now one had gone she felt physically sick. What if she never found it?

If Ben were here he would shrug and tell her to commission another charm. The jeweller was still in business and her father would have the original design.

She could tell Ben it was like losing a part of herself; that it wouldn't be the *same*. He'd be sympathetic but he wouldn't understand. He'd think she was being a drama queen.

What the hell was she going to do?

She retraced her steps: to the church, the graveyard, and

along the woodland path. That took the rest of the morning and a good chunk of the afternoon. After searching her house for the second time, she checked her car and then drove to the car park at Port Rell, walking to Drake's office, where she learnt that Drake had gone out and was not expected to return, and that Esme was closing up early.

By now Milla was shaking.

Esme could have said that she couldn't care less what Milla had lost, but the cow had to go the extra mile and suggest that anything of that size would have been sucked into the vacuum cleaner and thrown out with the trash.

Milla ground her teeth.

She even drove all the way out to Lorcan's farmhouse, but the police had beaten her to it and several of their forensic vehicles were parked outside.

Angry and upset, she returned home and was in the process of stuffing her face with a peanut butter sandwich when there was a waking-the-dead knock on her door.

Ben was on the other side, leaning against the door frame, eyes half-shut, as though he'd fallen asleep on his feet.

'You look dreadful,' she said. 'Come in.'

'Thank you!' He eyed the sandwich still in her hand. 'I was going to ask if you wanted to go out to dinner.'

That would certainly take her mind off the charm.

She dropped the sandwich into the bin and grabbed her satchel from the end of the banister.

'I'll take that as a "Yes",' he said.

Ben wanted to go to The Drop, which Milla had never much cared for, but he was so tired it would be mean to disagree. It was the most popular pub in the village and had been built by a local bishop in Elizabethan times, as accommodation for pilgrims. At this time of year there was no sign of the pretty wisteria that trailed around the door and windows, but there were stone troughs of cyclamen and heather that added a splash of colour against the whitewashed walls.

It was early, so the restaurant wasn't busy. They were shown to a table in a little alcove beside an original sixteenth-century wall painting that had been preserved behind glass. There were several of these paintings throughout the pub, mainly of angels and saints. Milla always felt she was being judged – and found lacking.

When the waitress came to take their drinks order, Ben asked for a beer, which was unusual. Like her, he barely drank alcohol.

'I used to live here,' he said, somewhat randomly. 'In an apartment upstairs – until my parents divorced. My dad ran the pub. It was owned by a brewery in those days and didn't look as smart as it does now. The wall paintings were only discovered after renovation.'

In the four months she'd known him, Ben had never spoken about his childhood. She'd assumed, like hers, it had not been happy. All she'd learnt was that he'd lived with his grandmother and mother in the little cottage on the road to Calahurst he'd inherited when his grandmother had died.

She wasn't sure how to respond.

She went with 'safe'.

'What was the apartment like?'

He shrugged. Was he already regretting his confidence?

'Radiators that didn't work, a roof that leaked, and windows that iced over in the winter because it was so cold. The brewery were too stingy to do repairs and my father couldn't afford to tackle them, even if he'd known how. He wasn't a very practical person.'

Had Ben's family struggled for money? He spoke so nicely, she'd imagined his background as upper-middle-class, the kind where he'd never wanted for anything. She knew he'd been to university, whereas she'd dropped out of school at sixteen. Did they have more in common than she'd realised?

He finished his beer and ordered another. The blonde waitress, all smiles, brought it over and took their food order.

Two beers?

'Bad day?' Milla asked.

He took a thirsty gulp before replying. 'Oh, yes.'

'I'm guessing you can't tell me about it?'

'Nope.'

When the waitress passed their table again, Milla waited for him to order a third but he didn't, just lapsed into a brooding silence. Should she say something? What? She could talk for England as a distraction technique, but when it involved real emotions...

She began tugging her way through her charms. Hat, teapot, toadstool... Usually comforting, this time it was a mistake. As soon as her fingers touched the empty link, she remembered that she'd lost one and was overwhelmed by that same sick panic.

'Enough about me,' Ben said.

She glanced up to find him watching her. Had he seen her playing with the bracelet? He knew what it meant to her.

'How about you?' he asked. 'I'm sorry I had to cancel my leave.'

'You can rebook it though?' As casually as possible, she moved her hands beneath the table before he spotted the missing charm. He would see it, she was sure of that, and then he'd want to know where she'd lost it.

'I will, when this is all over. What have you been up to?' His voice took on a teasing note. 'Are you helping your grandmother plan her masquerade ball?'

Only Granny Brianna would plan a party like a military operation. Milla was more of a 'Hey, I've got a couple of beers and a packet of peanuts. Do you fancy coming round?' kind of person.

'I'd forgotten about it,' she admitted, 'which is a really good excuse, so please don't remind me again.'

'OK... so how did you spend your day?'

Blackmailing the local private detective and checking out crime scenes with the vicar.

'Reading,' she said.

He raised an eyebrow. 'Anything interesting?'

'I have lots of interesting books,' and hadn't read a single one of them. Any moment now their food would arrive and the subject would be dropped. 'As you know, I bought the house with everything in it.'

'I thought at the time that was odd.'

'That I bought everything?'

'That someone would leave everything they owned behind.'

'Only a detective would think like that. Some people like a fresh start.'

She could almost pinpoint the moment where he remembered that when they'd first met, she'd only had one box of belongings to her name, kept stored in her car for a quick getaway.

'The house I bought was a holiday let,' she said, to fill the awkward silence. 'It was furnished with lots of nice things, which saved me the bother of having to buy any.'

The way he was staring at her, presumably that was the wrong answer.

Fortunately, before he could interrogate her further, their food arrived. Milla had ordered chicken burger and sweet potato fries; Ben, his favourite trout almondine and green beans. She was about to ask the waitress for mayonnaise to dunk her chips into, when Ben beat her to it.

'Could I ask you a question?'

'Sure,' the waitress said with a big smile, perhaps expecting to be asked where the toilets were for the tenth time that evening.

Ben was already reaching into his wallet for his warrant card.

The moment the waitress spotted it, she looked as though she'd really like to make a run for it.

The evening *had* taken an interesting turn.

Milla got comfortable and prepared for her chips to go cold.

'You're not in any trouble,' Ben said.

(A clear indication that yes, the waitress was in trouble.)

He handed her a photo. 'I want to know if you recognise this man? I believe he was here last night?'

The waitress's gaze flicked to the photo, then towards the bar and the woman standing behind it, watching them. She bit her lip.

'No,' she said.

Milla had seen toddlers lie with more skill.

'Are you sure?' Ben said. 'Look closely.'

More-or-less code for, *I can tell you're lying but I'm going to give you another chance.*

Was the waitress going to lose it? Sprint out the door with Ben in pursuit? That *would* be entertaining. However, it was usually Harriet that did the running. Milla didn't think she'd ever seen Ben move faster than a brisk walking pace.

The girl's hand was shaking as she held the photo.

Was she the one who'd slipped something into Lorcan's drink on behalf of Drake's mysterious client?

No. She was younger than Milla and unlikely to be high enough up the food chain to be trusted by Drake to complete the job.

Milla wondered what Ben would say if she admitted she knew more about his murder case than the poor waitress?

Actually, that didn't bear thinking about.

'Sorry, I've not seen him.' The waitress handed the photo back so quickly she almost threw it across the table.

Ben fumbled to catch it and they all watched the photo flutter to the floor.

Ben bent to pick it up.

'I'm sorry!' The waitress wrung her hands. 'I'm sorry!'

Spotting there was a problem, the woman behind the bar strode over to their table.

'Is everything OK with your meal, sir?' She was about Ben's age and the contrast between her dark wavy hair and deep blue eyes made the pale blonde waitress appear colourless by contrast. She also spoke super-quickly in a Dublin accent. 'I'm Sorcha, I'm the manager.'

Their original waitress faded away, relieved at being rescued.

Ben held out the photograph. 'I was asking your colleague if she remembered this gentleman visiting your establishment yesterday evening.'

Even after two beers, Ben spoke like the King of England.

'I remember him,' Sorcha said, but didn't take the photo or even give it more than a cursory glance. 'He ordered steak and chips but ate them at the bar, which we don't normally allow, but he was very friendly. Told some fine tall tales, some of which might even have been true. Said he was a musician, and that he'd moved here for some peace and quiet. I got the impression that he was lonely and that perhaps he'd regretted the move. He drank a couple of glasses of whisky over ice. When it was time for him to leave, he left a big tip.'

Sorcha was the one who'd spiked Lorcan's drink, Milla was sure of it. Nothing would happen on this woman's territory without her being very much aware of it.

'What time did the man leave?' Ben asked.

'Just before closing time. He made friends with a woman.

Dark hair, blue eyes, my height.' Sorcha smiled. 'Very much like me, but not me.'

Ben smiled back.

Did he *believe* her?

'The curious thing was,' Sorcha said, 'that even though he'd only had two drinks, it affected him very quickly. When he left, the woman was virtually keeping him upright. I did give a statement to one of your colleagues. A DC Lawrence, I think she said her name was? The same surname as Magik Meg. That's how I remember it. DC Lawrence downloaded a copy of the security footage too.'

Security footage? Milla took a good look around but could only see one camera from where she was sat, and it wasn't trained on the bar.

'Thank you,' Ben said.

Sorcha said something about being glad to help and returned to the bar.

Ben asked Milla if she thought the women had been lying.

It was nice to be asked but really? Could he not tell?

'The first one definitely was,' she said.

'I worked that out for myself,' he said wryly.

'Sorcha *seemed* to be telling the truth,' *but was lying by omission.*

'The security footage backs up her statement but, as I am sure you would have noticed, they only have two cameras, neither of which cover the bar area.'

What if the owner didn't want what was happening behind the bar recorded? This led to the question: who *was* the owner?

Ben was lost in his own thought process. 'To me, something seemed a little "off".'

'You think? That Lorcan only had two Finlayson's but could hardly walk?'

He glanced at her sharply. 'How did you know I was talking

about Lorcan Black – and that the whisky he drank was Finlayson's?'

Here was the opportunity she'd been waiting for – and dreading.

Why was it so hard to tell the truth?

'In answer to your first question...' The photograph lay on the table between them. She turned it to face him using one finger.

'He's that recognisable?'

'If you listen to anything other than golden oldies, yes.'

Ben winced. 'Harriet said the same thing.'

'Plus, I have a confession to make...'

He must have seen something in her expression. 'I'm not going to like it, am I?'

'I already know Lorcan Black and what brand of alcohol he likes. We met at Glastonbury eighteen months ago and saw each other for about six months after that. I even lived with him in France for a while, but we decided we were better off as friends.'

He stared at her as though he couldn't quite believe what she was saying.

(A given, when one lied all the time.)

'It's true,' she said. 'I can show you his text messages...'

Belatedly, she remembered the call she'd made – and the messages sent – from Lorcan's house the night she'd found that Victorian specimen jar.

'I believe you,' Ben said, a bit too quickly. 'It's just...'

'Unlikely?'

He smiled. 'I don't know what to think! Do you know any other celebrities? A member of the royal family perhaps? What other secrets are you keeping from me?'

'Er, just Lorcan.'

'That's a relief.' He raised his glass. 'The week I've had, I don't think I can take any more surprises.'

October 29th

As always, Ben slept like the dead.

It was not hard for Milla to slide from beneath his arm and out of her bed without waking him, even when she accidentally trod on the buckle of his belt and had to hop across the bare boards in an effort not to curse.

She kept her attention on him as she pulled on her jeans and T-shirt, a perfect lie at the ready, but his eyelids didn't flicker. He may have even snored. He lay in his default position, curled towards her. The arm that had been around her waist was now resting where she'd been, as though he were cuddling a ghost.

Wasn't that a cheery thought?

The moonlight spilled through the window, creating a pretty lattice pattern across the floor and lighting her way to the staircase. She hurried downstairs, not switching on the light here either, knowing it would illuminate the bedroom above. It had rained during the night, although the sky was now clear with a scattering of stars. She pulled her favourite black hoodie over her T-shirt and quietly closed and locked the front door behind her.

She needed to be quick but, more importantly, she needed to be silent. So she ignored her car and set off towards the witch's pond, and the path that led through the forest.

Ben rolled onto his side, reaching out to snuggle Milla against him, but his hand swiped air and his fingertips stroked cold bedsheets. Not the result he'd been hoping for. He sat up and stared at the bed in disbelief. It was the middle of the night! Where the hell was she?

Not in her bedroom, or her tiny bathroom that was little more than a cupboard, that was obvious. He would have been able to see a light shining through the inch-wide crack beneath the door.

Downstairs? Milla wasn't the type to be making hot chocolate if she couldn't sleep.

He slid out from beneath the duvet and padded towards the banister, leaning over to check the ground floor, but all was dark and silent. He called her name, softly at first, then louder.

Wherefore art thou, Milla?

He turned to check the bedroom. Her phone and keys were gone from the table beside her bed. Where could she have gone? Was she in some kind of trouble?

Without bothering to retrieve his clothes, he ran down to the empty sitting room. There was no light on in the kitchen either and the kettle was cold to the touch. There was a satchel abandoned on one of the armchairs, the contents spilling onto the floor, including her wallet, so that was something. He tried the front door. It was locked but not bolted, and he could still see her car through the front window.

Had she gone for a walk, at this late hour? To stretch her legs? To clear her head?

No. Everything Milla did had motivation and purpose.

And that was what worried him.

FOURTEEN

Milla cursed as she fell onto the solid oak floorboards of an ensuite bathroom. Both doors to Lorcan's farmhouse had been locked, but a quick shimmy up a drainpipe and through an open window, and here she was: flat on her back and surrounded by new and shiny.

This used to be easier.

When the farmhouse had been built, however many hundreds of years ago, this room must have been a bedroom. Now it was a luxurious bathroom with a free-standing bath and a huge walk-in shower. A few scattered toiletries and a big pile of fluffy towels were stacked on shelves, waiting for the return of their owner: but that wouldn't be for hours because Lorcan Black was safely locked up in the police station.

She pulled her phone from her pocket but, before she could switch on the torch, she saw a thin beam of light glowing around the door into the main bedroom.

A light that hadn't been on two minutes before.

A light left on and a window left open?

Bother.

Wasn't she the fool of the night?

There was no getting out of it. The noise she'd made falling through the window would have alerted him to her presence. She needed to let him know it was only her before he called the police. So she stood up and opened the door, knowing exactly who she was going to find on the other side.

And there he was, halfway through pulling a dark green shirt over the top of a plain black tee. He'd hardly changed since she'd last seen him. Lean and long-limbed, all crackling energy and intensely green eyes, but his black hair had an inch of blond roots and he'd swopped the dandy highwayman image for something so subtle he could have been there to install the plumbing. He was even wearing *spectacles*.

'Hi, Lorcan,' she said. Why *wasn't* he phoning the police? 'It's great to see you again.'

Too late, she realised she could have made a run for it and he'd have been none the wiser.

Lorcan Black was wearing ear buds.

'*Bloody hell!*' He sprang back, crashing against the four-poster bed. There was an audible 'crack' as his head hit the wood. He ripped out the ear buds. '*Milla?* Where the hell did you come from?'

'I knocked,' she said breezily, 'but the door was open, so I came in. I didn't think you'd mind?'

He stared at her as though he could hardly believe she was real, and then behind her, into the ensuite, as though it might be a portal to somewhere else. 'Uh, I did wonder if you might be in touch now after I stood you up.' He absent-mindedly rubbed the back of his head. 'But I thought you'd text.'

'Half the time I forget my phone does that.'

Not quite able to make eye contact (it wasn't often she was caught in the act), she looked around his bedroom. Her attention was immediately drawn to where the specimen jar had stood. Not only was it no longer in situ, there wasn't even a space to show where it had been.

'I'm so sorry I wasn't here the other night,' he said. 'It was the weirdest thing. I was arrested! Can you believe it?'

'Really?' Lying used to be easier too. 'How awful for you!'

'I've never been arrested before, so it was fun at first, but that soon wore off. Those cells are tiny! They thought I'd killed someone but must have realised their mistake because they let me go and here I am! It's great to see you again. I could do with some company. Do you want to call out for pizza? We could watch a movie?'

Milla thought of Ben lying asleep in her bedroom and the guilt felt like a shard of glass twisting inside her. What was she *doing* here? All this, *for a charm?*

'Um... It's a bit late?'

'Is it?' He picked up a bottle of Finlayson's and held it up. 'How about a drink instead? I was about to open this. The police seized the last one, along with my sleeping pills and a Victorian laboratory jar stuffed with hummingbirds. I have *no* idea what they're planning to do with those.'

'Hummingbirds?' Was that the same specimen jar that had...? She shook her head. She wasn't going to think about *that*.

'Stuffed hummingbirds,' he repeated, as though she didn't understand. 'A Victorian laboratory jar, stuffed with stuffed hummingbirds. Tiny little things,' – he indicated the size with his index finger and thumb – 'all posing on this little gold branch. Very cute.'

'Sounds gross.'

He looked vaguely insulted. 'They'd been dead a long time.'

'Doesn't make it any better!'

'You always were a soft-hearted little thing.' He waved the bottle again. 'Sure you don't want a drink?'

'I don't really drink alcohol.' Didn't he remember? 'Just birthdays, Christmas...' *Moments of severe stress.* Maybe she *should* have a glass?

'Oh yeah, I forgot. Why is that? Is it a religious thing?'

'Not really.' Neither of her parents had followed any particular faith. She'd had one Sikh grandparent, one Methodist, one Catholic, and one Church of England. Two had died before she was born but neither of the remainder had tried to foist their own beliefs onto her. 'Just habit, I guess. I've never liked that dreamy sensation of being out of control.'

'That's the best part. You're no fun.' Lorcan poured himself a generous measure, apparently not bothered about watering the Finlayson's down with ice either, and walked over to the window. It was the same one she'd climbed out of the last time she'd been here.

'It's really good to see a friendly face, Mills. I've missed you.'

Uh oh. She needed to put the brake on that right now.

'I'll always be your friend, Lorcan. You know that.'

He turned to face her, framed by the lights of Raven's Edge sparkling prettily through the forest like fireflies. 'That sounded like a "goodbye". What's up, Mills?'

It was the perfect moment to tell him about Ben.

She couldn't have wished for a better prompt.

Except...

'Of course it's not a "goodbye"! I was just wondering why you wanted to move here? I thought you were happy in France?'

He shrugged. 'It's not the same without you!'

Oh no... 'Lorcan...'

'Also, I remembered I owned a house here! What a coincidence, eh?'

She stared at him. 'You *remembered* you owned a house?'

Just how many did he own?

'It was a bit of a wreck but I've always liked it. It was my grandfather's. I thought you'd be pleased to see me? Have another friend in the village?'

'I am.'

There was that word again.

Friend.

She had the idea Lorcan would prefer something more.

'Why are you here now?' he asked.

She didn't even hesitate. 'I wanted to check you were OK and I know you like to sleep during the day.'

'True enough.' He took a sip of his drink. 'I was surprised when *you* said you'd bought a house in Raven's Edge.'

She'd met Ben…

'The village is cute and I have family here.'

'What are you doing? I heard the magazine you worked for folded. That was a shame. Have you found anything new?'

So he didn't know her dad was the Graham in Graham Media?

'Living a life of leisure,' she said flatly.

He laughed. 'You're serious? That sounds dull.'

That was entirely her problem. She'd gone from broke to rich overnight and was so *bored*. No money worries, no work, nothing but herself to think about. She should be grateful for her good fortune and devote herself to charity work, as Granny Brianna had suggested, not search for nefarious ways to distract herself.

Lorcan poured himself another generous measure. 'I've had a very bad day,' he said, in response to the disapproving expression on her face. 'I'll be completely honest with you. The police seem to think I've murdered this poor girl they found beside the village pond. I'll spare you the gruesome details, although you'll be able to read all about it tomorrow. For now, I want to drink myself into oblivion.' He raised the glass in a toast.

'That's very sad.'

She'd meant the girl that had been found murdered, but he said, 'Ain't it just. Put that in your next article about the glamorous life of a rock star.'

Now she *was* concerned. Lorcan had always considered himself a songwriter first, a performer second. Never a rock star. She'd not seen him this low before, but she owed her loyalty to

Ben, not to her ex. Agreeing to meet him again was a mistake. They should both move on.

'I'm sorry to have burst in on you like this,' she said, turning towards the door. 'I'll leave you to get some rest. It must have been very traumatic for you, being arrested like that.'

'No,' – he caught hold of her arm – 'please don't go. Don't leave me alone.'

She glanced at his hand, surprised, and he immediately let go.

'Sorry,' he said. 'I'd say I'm not usually such an idiot, but I guess you'd disagree.'

He really *had* hit rock bottom.

'What about your manager? Can't you call him?'

'Jonesy's basically a helicopter parent. I have to keep leaving entire countries behind me to create distance between us. Can't we be friends again? Like the old days? Purely platonic! I could do with a friend right now.'

He'd sensed weakness and she only had herself to blame.

'Why did you *really* move to Raven's Edge, Lorcan? Because I have the feeling there's something you're not telling me.'

He sighed. 'You're right, I haven't been completely straight with you. I grew up here. This is where I was born. In this actual room, probably. That's so weird...' he muttered, looking around him. 'My parents must have had in sex here – ew! – at least once, anyway. I never thought about that. You'd think I'd want to leave Raven's Edge behind me, and I thought I had too. Something keeps drawing me back. I've lived in Dublin, New York and Paris, and a little farmhouse in Provence, but it turns out there's no place like home.' He grimaced. 'Now I'm quoting from *The Wizard of Oz*. Shoot me.' He took another glug of alcohol.

She couldn't help smiling. 'I can see you've put your own

stamp on the place,' she said, nodding towards the silver skull and the fat white candles.

There was a glimmer of the mischievous grin she remembered.

'Wait until you see downstairs,' he said. 'Family motto: If it moves, shoot it.'

She'd already seen downstairs – the dark wood furniture and the mustard-coloured paint; the dead animals stuck on the wall and the live bird flying around the hall – and she'd rather not see it again.

'Sounds great,' she said.

'This house is isolated, that was another attraction. Too many people knew about the place in the south of France. Album #3 bombed. I went "dystopian" while everyone else did "chilled". I'm supposed to be writing my new one but it's not going well. I'm hoping I can work here without any disturbance. No one knows I'm here.' He grimaced. 'Well, they *didn't* know I was here but as soon as someone hears about my most recent adventure it'll be all over the news. Even the police seem to think someone is out to get me.' He broke off to sigh heavily.

'I think the stress of the last few hours is getting to you,' she said. Why did she sound so much like Granny Brianna? 'Let's go downstairs and have a nice mug of coffee and a catch-up.'

He grimaced. 'We can go downstairs, for sure, but I'm not going to be drinking coffee.' He picked up the bottle of Finlayson's and opened the door. 'After you.'

Milla hesitated, staring into the darkness of the upper hall, remembering the last time she'd been here.

'What's up?' he asked. 'Not afraid of ghosts, are you? Those creaks and groans you can hear are the sounds of a very old house settling down for the night.'

Ghosts were the very least of it.

Although, she could certainly hear something...

'Do you hear sirens?' she asked.

'You mean emergency vehicles?' He listened for a moment, and then nodded. 'What of it?'

'This is Raven's Edge. A sleepy little English village. We don't do sirens.'

'They're getting closer,' he said. 'There are no other houses along this road. It leads to the moors and there are quicker ways of getting there.'

There was a window on the landing, overlooking the front of the house, but Milla didn't need to look through it, because she could already see red and blue lights bouncing off the sloping ceiling.

She backed into the bedroom and quickly closed the door. 'Did you call the police?'

'Why? I've had enough of the bloody police for one day, thank you very much. I think I'm gonna let them call me next time.'

'How about a burglar alarm, something I might have set off inadvertently?'

'Not yet, although Jonesy says—'

'Jonesy's in the UK?'

'Yep.'

'Is he here now?'

'You know Jonesy. He booked himself into a five-star spa hotel in the next town. He's never liked slumming it.'

Milla zoned out. She hadn't liked Lorcan's manager when she'd met him the first time around and knew the feeling was mutual. As far as Jonesy was concerned, someone like her would never be good enough for his 'boy', mainly due to her not putting up with any bad behaviour just because Lorcan was famous.

'They must be here for me. Hell, doesn't *anyone* text first?' His lame attempt at a joke might have worked better if his voice hadn't cracked at the end.

'Something's happened...'

'You think?'

Had the police found the head?

Had Drake told them everything?

But no one knew she was here…

'I haven't *done* anything.' Lorcan dropped heavily onto the bed, his head in his hands. 'Why won't they believe me? It's a nightmare. They've only just let me go. I can't spend another night in a cell, Mills.'

As far as she knew, he hadn't spent a whole day in a cell, let alone a night.

'Call your solicitors,' she said. 'Let them sort you out. That's what you pay them for. In the meantime…' She ran over to the window and looked out. The garden appeared empty, as far as she could see in the moonlight, and the track leading into the forest seemed clear.

'What are you doing?'

She flung her leg over the windowsill. 'Sorry, got to be going.'

'Is there a reason you're not using the door?'

'I can't be found here. It'd be awkward for both of us. My new boyfriend…' – Oh hell, now she *had* to tell him! – 'He's the local police detective. I expect he's the one that interviewed you.'

Lorcan's green eyes turned unexpectedly icy. 'You're dating *Benedict Elliott*? *That* boy scout?'

She froze. How did Lorcan know Ben's birth name?

'I know him as Ben Taylor,' she said carefully.

'Yeah? Well he's my cousin, so I've known him a lot longer than you.'

Cousin?

She'd thought it couldn't get any worse.

'How long have you been seeing Benny-Boy?'

The police were about to come bursting through Lorcan's front door and *that* was what he was bothered about?

'I've really got to go. I'll be in touch,' she promised, swinging her other leg over the windowsill and dropping into the garden below.

'Milla!' he bellowed, appearing at the window. 'Come back, I need to talk to you!'

A car skidded to a halt on the road outside the front of the farmhouse, swiftly joined by another. No sirens now, only flashing lights. This was a rural area and the road would be deserted at this time of night, but this certainly wasn't a social call either.

She flipped up her hood and sprinted through the back garden, shoving open the gate and running onto the track that led into the forest. At every step she expected a police car to draw up behind her, or someone to grab her and haul her back.

Then *she'd* be the one spending the night in a cell.

As she reached the cover of the trees, and was enveloped in a comforting darkness with no sign of anyone following, she relaxed enough to slow to a walk, risking a glance back to the farmhouse to see what was going on.

At which point someone caught her around the waist, slapped a large hand over her mouth and yanked her into the bushes.

Michael Griffiths loved the Halloween Carnival and the way Raven's Edge embraced its heritage. It was good to see the kids dressing up and having fun.

Not his kids, mind you. Sure, they dressed up and they watched the carnival – but from the sitting room window because his wife thought trick-or-treat was begging, and Halloween was the work of the devil.

His kids refused to open the door to their friends, so the big bowl of sweets beside the front door was now his responsibility, while his wife and kids watched wholesome Disney films. Guess that was what he got for marrying the daughter of a vicar. One night of sin; fifteen years repenting.

He was sitting on the stairs, chatting on his phone (and absent-mindedly dipping into the trick-or-treat bowl), when he heard heavy footsteps on the cobblestones outside.

'I'll call you back,' he told the person on the other end of the line, as the door in front of him vibrated with a loud bang.

'All right, mate! I'm coming!' He slid the phone into his pocket. 'Impatient little brats.'

He opened the door to three highwaymen: each dressed completely in black, with tricorn hats, cloaks and eye masks. They would have looked impressive – if he hadn't opened the door to at least twenty highwaymen this evening already.

These kids were a lot taller than his earlier callers. Were they even kids? They had stubble...

Michael bent to reach for the bowl. 'Aren't you guys a little old for trick-or-treat?'

Only to receive a crack on the head that sent him reeling.

'What the—' He grabbed the newel post of the banister to steady himself.

Effectively lining himself up for the sucker punch that followed.

FIFTEEN

Milla was about to bite down hard when she heard a familiar voice.

'Milla, what the *hell* have you done?'

She relaxed and was immediately released.

'Ben?' She spun to face him. 'Why are you here?'

'To save your arse, apparently.' He nodded towards the farmhouse.

At least he didn't add, 'again'.

Silhouetted against the flashing blue and red lights on the road were several figures searching the garden with torches and shouting back and forth. They didn't sound happy.

'What are they looking for?'

'You.' He caught hold of her hand and pulled her back onto the track. 'We need to leave before one of them realises there's a path that leads directly into this forest. Fortunately, they don't seem to know the area very well.'

Milla allowed herself to be led, switching on her phone torch once they were further into the forest and out of sight. 'If Lorcan was released, why have the police come back to arrest him?'

'They're not here for him. We're working on a theory that someone is trying to frame Lorcan for murder. DCI Cameron asked me to arrange for someone to watch the house.'

She'd blundered into a stake-out? 'Oh, dear...'

'If it had been one of the local team, you'd already be cuffed and trying to explain yourself back at the station, but I'd called in help from Calahurst. Whoever it was must have been spooked enough to call for back-up rather than tackle you on their own.'

'Because I'm so scary.' She indicated her 5'2" frame.

'Be grateful. These days we never know if the person we're planning to arrest is going to have a gun or a knife.'

Abashed, she fell into step beside him.

He released her hand. It felt like punishment.

'What possessed you, Milla? Why do you feel you have a right to walk or climb into other people's property whenever you feel like it?'

She winced. He'd seen her do that?

'I usually try to make sure they're out first,' she said, but he didn't smile. 'Lorcan's an old friend. I heard he'd been released and I wanted to check he was OK. I didn't get any reply when I knocked on the door. I was worried.' She hesitated. 'He mentioned that you two are cousins. Why didn't you tell me that earlier?'

'There didn't seem to be a right moment.'

That was a lie, if ever she heard one. The perfect moment would have been while they were at The Drop, and she'd been telling him that she'd once dated Lorcan.

'Why are *you* here, Ben?' she sighed. 'You know, I was doing pretty well saving myself when you showed up.'

'I woke up and found you gone. I wanted to know what was so important to you that you'd leave the house in the middle of the night without telling me, without even taking your car. I was worried about you.'

He slept like the dead, but this one night he hadn't?

'I suppose that might seem a little bit suspicious, but Lorcan is a musician. He often works at night and sleeps during the day.'

For a moment he stared at her, and then, 'How stupid do you think I am, Milla? I'm a police detective. I can work out when you're lying. I usually let it go, but every time you lie it... kills something inside me.'

'This time I'm telling you the truth!'

'Really?' He stopped and fumbled in his pocket, bringing out something tiny that glinted on his palm. 'Because my guess is that you went back for this.'

'My charm!' She snatched it, holding it beneath her torch-light. 'It is! It's my charm!' She threw her arms around him and hugged him, hardly noticing that he'd stiffened. 'You found it! Where was it?'

'I found it on the windowsill of Lorcan's bedroom. If you were there tonight, trying to get it back, what were you doing on the night you lost it?'

Busted.

'The *first* time I'd agreed to meet Lorcan at the farmhouse but he wasn't in. He must have forgotten to lock the door, because it was swinging open. I thought I heard a noise, so I had a quick look around to check everything was OK, and that he hadn't had a break-in, and then I came home again. It was the night you were working late, remember? Didn't I tell you?'

'No,' he said. 'You didn't.'

'Oh, well, I thought it would be fun to meet up with an old friend but he had to cancel at short notice. *This* time, I was looking for the charm.' She stared at the little silver bottle in her palm. 'I can't believe you found it. I was so upset when I saw it had gone.'

'Why didn't you tell me you'd lost it?'

'I forgot.'

'You... forgot? That bracelet means the world to you, Milla. How could you "forget".'

'We've both been so busy...'

She trailed off, hating the pain she saw in those green eyes.

Why couldn't she tell him the truth?

Because Ben was all about following rules. He'd arrest Lorcan and then he'd arrest her for helping him. He'd hate doing so, but he'd still go ahead. 'No one is above the law', blah, blah, blah. She couldn't risk it. Take a gamble on losing her freedom – and Lorcan's – on Ben's ability to solve that woman's murder? No, thank you.

'I didn't want to bother you...' Now he'd think she was blaming *him*! 'I thought I'd be able to find it by retracing my steps.'

'Are you and Lorcan still together?'

'What? *What?* No! How can you think that?'

'Right now, I'm not sure what to think.'

'Lorcan and I split up months ago.' She stared at him in shock. 'I'm telling you the truth.'

'This time? What about next time?'

What was he saying?

'I might have this wrong,' she said carefully, 'but it sounds as though you don't trust me?'

'You're a liar, Milla! Sometimes it's fun: a cute personality quirk. Sometimes... it isn't. If one of those officers tonight had recognised either one of us, I'd like to have some kind of story to tell them. Preferably one that was true. Trust works both ways. Do you know how hurtful it is that you don't trust me? Why didn't you tell me you'd lost the charm? It was a simple enough thing to do. Even now, why do I get the feeling you're hiding something else from me? Something big. You're not that good a liar.'

Now he was just being insulting.

'Do you know how many laws I've broken since I met you?' he asked. 'I'm supposed to be the one upholding them.'

And that was *exactly* why she hadn't told him.

'You said you'd give me the freedom to be me,' she said miserably. 'You know everything about me, my entire life history, all those things I did before I met you. I haven't kept anything back. I've never had a normal life. I wouldn't know where to start. You know I struggle with being... I need to be free,' she repeated. 'I know it's your job to solve puzzles but I don't want you making that puzzle *me*. I don't need you checking up on me all the time. *What are you doing? Where are you going? Who are you seeing?* I don't...' – she reined in her anger – 'I don't deal well with that.'

'It makes you want to run,' he said softly. 'I know. Have I ever been like that? Treated you in that way? I don't want you to stop being "you", but when it causes a conflict of interest with my day job...'

'Sometimes I feel your "day job" is more important than me.'

'That's unfair.'

She knew that but she still hadn't been able to stop herself from saying it.

'I'm tired,' she said. 'Can we discuss this tomorrow when we're both more awake?'

He raised an eyebrow and she could almost see the words forming above his head like a speech bubble.

Running away?

'What did you and Lorcan talk about?' he asked. 'You were in his bedroom for a good ten minutes.'

Why was he so hooked up on *that*?

'His hummingbirds,' she replied. 'He was upset that the police had seized them.'

'*Hummingbirds?*'

'Stuffed ones, in a specimen jar,' although she knew what

had happened to the jar. 'Little birds, about this big.' She held up her finger and thumb, about three inches apart.

'I know what hummingbirds are,' he said irritably. 'I was present when the CSIs performed their search. I don't remember seeing a glass jar or any stuffed hummingbirds. The only things they took from his bedroom were a bottle of Finlayson's and some sleeping pills, because Lorcan suggested that he'd been sedated – and I shouldn't even be telling you that.' He rubbed his hand over his face. 'Has he told you anything else pertinent to the case?'

'No. Your mates were about to force their way in through the front door and I didn't feel like hanging around to explain what I was doing there.'

'No chance for you to catch up on old times?'

Why did he sound so calm?

'Not really, beyond the "Hey, how are you?"'

'Before you left via the window?'

'I know this is hard for you to believe, but sometimes the window is the most practical option.'

'Even if it's an upper-storey window?'

'It was less than eight feet from the ground! Raven's Edge, remember? Hobbit-sized houses.'

They'd reached Meg's Pond and the main road that led into the village. Ben, she noticed, did not look at the pond, even though it was ethereally beautiful in the moonlight. A tiny strip of fluttering blue and white tape around a tree branch was the only evidence of what had happened there this morning, along with the flattened grass and churned-up mud around the water's edge.

Ben politely held the gate open for her, but she stopped.

'Thank you for coming to my rescue,' she said, 'although I didn't need rescuing. I'll be OK from here. You can go home.'

'You're right,' he said. 'I should.'

Not what she'd expected him to say.

'I can't do this anymore,' he added.

For the first time since they'd left the farmhouse, she saw his face beneath the street lamp, and his bleak expression.

Oh, Ben...

You did that, a little voice said in her head.

'Ben?' She took a step towards him.

He took a step back and she didn't like that at all.

She was used to dealing with men who spilled out emotions all over the place, not one who kept his closely in check. Explosive rows and arguments: she could deal with those, easy-peasy, preferably in bed, but a complete withdrawal?

Was Ben suggesting that he wanted to shut her out of his life forever?

A break-up without the make-up?

This was alien to her.

It hurt.

What should she do?

Apologise?

She wasn't in the wrong!

OK, maybe she was. A little bit.

How dare he judge her like this?

Was it a huge surprise? They were such opposites in character and personality, even their core beliefs. It was bound to happen.

He was doing her a favour, letting her go before she became too attached.

She was already attached.

'Do you want to break up?' she asked him.

He could have said 'No'. He could have said 'Let's sleep on it; we'll talk tomorrow.'

Instead he said, 'I'm sorry, Milla.'

That was the worst of all.

'OK,' – she lifted her chin – 'if that's what you want. If you've left anything back at my house, I'll box it up and leave it at the front desk in the police station. You can post my key back through the letterbox.'

'Oh.'

Second thoughts?

'OK,' he said.

Maybe not.

'OK.' She walked through the gate he seemed to have forgotten he was still holding. 'Goodbye,' but she didn't look at him, just ran away, because apparently that was what she did.

Who would have thought it would have been so easy to walk away, knowing that she'd never see him again?

If only she hadn't bought a house practically next door to the police station.

SIXTEEN

Milla couldn't sleep. Not with her argument with Ben stuck on repeat. A freezing draught blasted through the broken window he'd promised he'd fix (how had he managed to break it anyway?), which, in turn, caused the curtains to billow back and forth in a very sinister way.

It was lucky she didn't believe in ghosts.

She pulled the duvet up to her nose. She was cold. The bedroom was too quiet. The bed was too big. She was too *alone*. She didn't like it. It was *wrong* that Ben wasn't lying here beside her.

Whose fault was that? snarked her conscience.

In her head, she reset the argument to the point where he'd said *I can't do this anymore* and she tried to imagine all the other things she could have said. Smarter things, wittier things, things that ended with Ben apologising profusely.

Did that make her feel better?

No.

Seriously, what was she? Five?

She was in the wrong. That was why it hurt so much. She had to deal with it. Apologise. Tell him everything.

Everything...?

He'd never forgive her.

She rolled out of bed and switched off her alarm, even though it wasn't due to go off for another thirty minutes. She messaged a local glazier to repair her window, telling them to get the key from Elvira Merriweather at Practically Magic, then switched on her music and stepped into the shower.

She had a lead that Ben knew nothing about. That client of Drake's who had been so keen to stop Lorcan getting into trouble they were willing to sedate him.

(Not sure why a cosy chat with Lorcan over a Finlayson's wouldn't have been a far more sensible alternative.)

The client must be someone that knew Lorcan. Someone from his past, who was aware he was back in Raven's Edge – not common knowledge. The obvious thing would be to ask Lorcan who this person could be. Except, all indicators were that this 'guardian angel' didn't want Lorcan to know of his intervention. Not surprising, the way events had played out. Between the three of them, hadn't the guardian angel, Drake, and herself, made everything worse?

In the meantime, what did she know? (1) The guardian angel was rich, because (2) they had the resources to hire Drake, whose dubious services didn't come cheap, except (major drawback) (3) Drake hated keeping any kind of records, especially to a 'cloud'.

Although...

Drake had to fill in tax returns, like everyone else. He'd mentioned that the first time they'd met, four months ago, when she'd discovered that he'd been spying on her for her father. She'd seen a copy of the invoice Drake had sent. It had said 'Services, as discussed', without providing any further details, but, at the time, the fact that her father had hired him was evidence enough.

Where did Drake keep these copy invoices? On his laptop?

Saved to a memory stick? Printed out the old-fashioned way, and hidden somewhere dark, depressing and damp, along with his immortal soul?

Or filed someplace really obvious, like that shiny white filing cabinet behind Esme's sleek designer desk?

Could it really be that easy?

She stepped out of the shower and switched off her music, dressing in her usual jeans, T-shirt and black hoodie. She plaited her long dark hair into one fat braid and tucked it into a logo-less baseball cap. When she left the house, she grabbed a banana from the fruit bowl and a bottle of water from the fridge. A healthy breakfast. Go her. Eating the banana while driving one-handed, not so good for her health, but she arrived in Port Rell unscathed and parked in the tourist car park beside the dive centre.

Drake's office was located halfway along the harbour road, in what had once been a substantial Georgian house. Most of the little gift shops on either side had once been fishermen's cottages and were painted in pretty pastel colours. This building, being a more austere slate grey, stood out.

Instead of walking alongside the harbour and in through Drake's front door, she had the idea to take the service road behind the various stores, where several vans and lorries were already making deliveries. It was chaotic, with people walking in and out of all the shops, carrying boxes or pushing porter trolleys.

The back entrance of Anya's: Port Rell was wide open. A twenty-something man, his hair dyed grey, took a box from the back of a small white van and walked inside. It was almost too easy. Milla grabbed another box with the same logo and followed him, keeping her head down as she walked through a small lobby and past a tiny kitchen. Not a single person challenged her.

She dumped the box outside the stock room and carried on

towards a staircase. She'd been operating without a coherent
plan at this point, relying on her usual mix of spontaneity,
charm and luck, but the bottom of the staircase was where good
fortune really kicked in.

A red break-glass call point.

It was *fate*.

She jabbed hard on the glass with her thumb. It broke and,
from somewhere behind her, a shrill alarm sounded. She waited
for the staff from the shop to swarm past, and then ran up the
stairs.

As she'd hoped, there was a small landing and a door. The
door was locked, unsurprisingly, but easy enough to pick.
Within seconds, she was standing on the threshold of Kieran
Drake Investigations, grinning at an empty office.

How long would it stay that way?

The first thing she did was lock the opposite door to stop
Drake and Esme coming back.

Did she have the time to carry out a thorough search,
including Drake's personal office?

No. It wouldn't take him long to figure out that the alarm
was false, and when he returned and discovered he'd been
locked out of his office…?

(Best not to think about that.)

There was one small filing cabinet behind Esme's desk. A
quick rattle of the top drawer ascertained it was locked, and the
lock was not easy to pick.

Bonus points to Drake.

The safest, most logical place to keep the key would be on
Esme's keyring, tucked into her bag, but when were people ever
logical?

She yanked out the top drawer of Esme's desk but found
only stationery. In the second drawer was more stationery, with
a small key on top, next to a Cadbury's Whole Nut bar – which
she slid into her pocket and refused to feel bad about.

As she'd guessed, the cabinet contained invoices and receipts neatly filed in green envelope folders and labelled with the client or company's name in alphabetical order. She cast a wary glance at the door, before flicking through each file in turn.

One labelled 'Elliott, Benedict' meant she hit pay dirt almost immediately. Drake had a file on Ben? When had *he* required Drake's services?

She pulled the file out, dropping it onto Esme's desk and flipping it open. Inside was a colour headshot, which looked remarkably like the one on Ben's warrant card, and a sheet of paper with handwritten notes about two meetings he'd had with Drake earlier in the year, one of which she'd been present for. No invoices, thank goodness, so at no time had Drake been working for Ben.

She photographed the pages anyway, careful to place everything back into the folder as she'd found it.

The next file, labelled 'Elliott, Drew', contained only the usual invoices stating: 'Services as discussed'.

The last file was labelled 'Elliott, William'.

Who the hell was he?

Inside was a photo of Lorcan staring right back at her, aiming for mean and moody in Victorian goth clothing and lots of black eyeliner.

Lorcan's real name was William Elliott? Why had he never told her?

Because it wasn't the kind of thing that came up in conversation?

The door rattled, making her jump, and Esme's silhouette appeared on the other side of the frosted glass.

Could Esme see her?

Maybe if she kept very still...

Esme muttered something and disappeared back down the stairs.

Milla dropped the file labelled 'Elliott, William' onto the desk and photographed everything as quickly as possible, hoping it was all in focus.

Something smashed against the door and she nearly dropped the phone.

Drake?

Had he *thrown* himself against it?

Would it hold?

She took another photo and turned the page, not caring whether he could see her outline through the glass. He was smart enough to have worked out what was happening, but hopefully not the person who was doing it.

Slam!

She lined up her phone with a hand that wasn't quite steady, took another photo and turned over the page.

Slam!

One more to go...

Slam!

She shoved the file back into the appropriate slot, slid the drawer shut and locked it, chucking the key back into the drawer. Top drawer or second drawer? Who cared? They knew she was here and what she was likely to be doing; the most important thing now was to get out.

It had gone very quiet on the other side of that door. Had Drake remembered the back entrance?

She tiptoed over but couldn't hear anything on the other side. Should she exit this way? It would be a quicker route to her car but what if Drake was waiting for her to do just that?

She unlocked the door anyway, running back across the room to where she'd come in. There was no sign of anyone on the staircase, only the sound of the staff below, flooding back inside, grumbling about having to stand about in the cold but, as she reached the street, she saw Drake limping towards her.

Had he seen her? She ducked back inside, into the kitchen,

flattening herself against the wall, holding her breath, straining to hear his footsteps as he moved quietly through the lobby and up the stairs.

He didn't appear to be in any hurry. Did he think he was going to catch her in the act?

Not daring to wait for him to reach the landing, she sprinted out of the store and then slowed to a walk to avoid attention. The service road was almost deserted and most of the delivery trucks had left. She'd timed her arrival perfectly. Her exit? Not so much.

There was the usual melee of tourists ambling alongside the harbour and she joined them, hoping to blend in until she could reach her car.

Drake was standing outside his office, scanning the road, first left, then right.

Checking her plait was tucked safely beneath her cap, she fell into step with a large group of students who were dressed almost identically to her. She couldn't have planned it better. The car park was only a few metres away. She could even see her car.

Her step lightened. Hard to believe, but she'd actually gotten away with—

A familiar figure appeared in front of her, ignoring the angry protest of the teenager he'd yanked out of the way.

Sharp features, dishevelled black hair, knowing smirk?

Oh, *hell*!

'Going somewhere, Princess?'

Michael awoke to silence but the last thing he remembered...

He sat upright and something wet and cold slid down the side of his face, and slapped onto the floor. He glanced down. A bag of frozen peas?

The last thing he remembered was a crack over the head and a punch to the jaw...

He touched the back of his head and found an egg-sized lump.

What the hell had happened?

A soft whimper made him glance up.

Lined up opposite him, on three chairs taken from the dining room, were his wife and children. Gags around their mouths, rope around their waists, eyes huge with terror.

'Hello, Sleeping Beauty!'

He turned his head, wincing at the pain and the bright light. It took a moment for his eyes to focus on the three tall figures opposite, each dressed as an eighteenth-century highwayman, complete with cloaks and tricorn hats.

What the...?

'Glad you could join us, Michael,' the same man spoke again. He had a local accent with a languid drawl. 'We have a little job we'd like you to do for us.'

'A job?' Michael was about to tell him exactly what he could do with his 'little job', and to get out of his house, when he realised the man was standing directly behind his son – one hand resting lightly on the child's shoulder – and the fight went right out of him. 'I'll do whatever you want.'

The other man grinned. 'And that, Michael Griffiths, is the right answer.'

SEVENTEEN

At some point Milla and Drake needed to have a long, painful conversation about the importance of communication and respecting boundaries, but she'd rather not have it now. As the student who Drake had yanked aside recovered enough to swing a punch, Drake was forced to step back to avoid it. His attention safely elsewhere, Milla slipped around the side of the group and sprinted towards the dive centre, knowing she'd never reach her car in time.

She ran through the double doors, which were automatic and opened with an elegant 'swoosh', pausing to orientate herself. Reception was painted in pretty shades of blue, an oasis of calm compared to the busy street outside. There were racks of swimwear and divewear in neon colours, a waiting area with a low table and stacks of diving and travel magazines, a hot drinks machine and a water cooler. The reception desk was straight in front of her but the corridor beside it was blocked by a turnstile, operated by the swipe of a membership card, because it led to toilets, changing rooms and a pool – she could smell the chlorine.

While she hesitated, she heard female voices coming from

the corridor. Drake was still standing on the pavement outside, hands on hips, searching the crowd. She'd certainly succeeded in holding him off for the moment, but those female voices were moving closer.

'I can do the beginners' classes, Lainey. I'm not an invalid.'

'I'm not arguing with you, Selma. You know full well that pregnant women aren't supposed to dive.'

'I'm not talking about *diving*, I'm talking about—'

The two women broke off and stared at Milla. The dark-haired one, who was not much taller than her, smiled uncertainly.

'Can I help you?'

'Hi, I—' Milla caught a movement outside and broke off. Drake was standing there, turning and scanning the road.

At any other time she might have enjoyed the expression of confusion on his face, but she backed slowly away from the window until partially hidden by the rack of swimwear. The window, which stretched all the way along the front of the building, had a tint to it. Would Drake be able to see her?

The dark-haired woman drew closer. 'Hi, I'm Lainey. I'm the owner. Can I help you?'

'I'm only looking,' Milla said, bending her knees slightly.

'At anything in particular?' Lainey followed her gaze. Her mouth tightened.

Drake turned towards the dive centre. Looked straight at it. Looked straight at Milla.

Had he seen her?

She dropped to her knees and heard the bell over the door signalling it had opened. All he had to do was walk around this rack and then he'd—

Why was the pregnant blonde pointing behind the desk?

'Can I help you?' Lainey said, and for a moment Milla thought she was talking to her, but then Lainey walked forwards, effectively blocking Drake's view.

The blonde woman was gesturing with more purpose. What—?

Oh, behind the desk!

Milla crawled around the curved desk and found a large space suitable for hiding.

The blonde, who was wearing a very tight pink dress, hoisted herself up onto a high stool and breathed a sigh of relief.

'Hello, I'm sorry to bother you,' she heard Drake say. 'I was wondering, have you seen my girlfriend by any chance? It's such a crush outside, we were separated and I can't get a signal on my phone. She's south Asian, about this high, and was wearing a black hoodie and baseball cap.'

It was so different to how he usually spoke: his accent softened, he used less slang – an accomplished actor playing the part of an anxious, middle-class tourist. In any other situation, Milla would have been impressed. Right now, she was worried the women would fall for it.

'We've been quiet today,' Lainey said. 'Selma, have you seen anyone come in?'

'We had that guy who wanted to book a couple's dive for his anniversary?' the blonde said.

'That was yesterday!'

'Sorry, pregnancy brain. Have you checked the boutiques? Some of them have sales on?'

Drake gave an exasperated sigh, quite out of character for the part he was playing. 'Never mind, thank you for all your help.' The bell rang and the door whooshed shut.

'I suppose at least he said "Thank you",' the blonde said, bending to peer beneath the desk. She had large blue eyes and a rosebud mouth, currently painted in a glittery pink lip-gloss. 'But you're well shot of him, honey.'

'Tell me about it,' Milla muttered, crawling out from beneath the desk.

'I'm Selma,' the blonde said, helping her up. 'I'm one of the diving instructors.'

Lainey coughed.

'Currently on maternity leave, and this is my boss, Lainey. Would you like to sign up to one of our classes? The first one's free!'

'Diving?'

'We *are* a dive centre,' Selma said kindly. 'We start small, in the pool, then move on to open water. There are lots of wrecks around here. Port Rell's famous for them.'

'It sounds interesting...'

'Please don't feel obliged,' Lainey said firmly. 'We're always happy to help a woman in distress.'

Ah... Now they thought she was a victim of domestic abuse.

'Drake's OK. We had a difference of opinion, that's all.'

'Drake? As in *Kieran* Drake? I've heard of him. He has an office down the street. The guy's a snake! Why are you dating *him*?'

'I'm not dating him. It's... complicated.'

Lainey wasn't impressed. 'You had an argument and had to hide until he calmed down?'

'It was totally my fault.'

'That's what they want you to say.'

'It's called "gas-lighting",' Selma said helpfully.

Poor Drake, she'd really landed him in it.

'If you feel you're in any danger, you must report him to the police. We can do it for you, if you like?'

'No, no! Nothing like that. Just a silly argument. I'm sure it'll blow over.'

Both women looked sceptical.

'Thank you for all your help,' – Milla began backing towards the door – 'but I really must be going.'

'Here, take this,' Selma handed her an advertising flyer.

'Thanks,' but as Milla turned, the door opened and she froze, assuming Drake had come back.

Instead, a tall blond man came inside, balancing a tray of takeaway coffee and a box of chocolate ring doughnuts.

'Selma, the bakery only had the chocolate doughnuts with the hazelnut sprinkles, not the pink ones I know you like—'

'*Ben?*'

The man glanced around and frowned. 'Who are you?'

It took a moment for her to register that he didn't have a beard. Whereas he and Ben had the same-shaped face, this man's features were more angular, giving him a harder look. His hair was very short but the green eyes were exactly the same. It was disconcerting.

'I'm Milla,' she said.

'Hi, Milla.' He placed the tray on the desk and handed the box of doughnuts to Selma, who ripped them open excitedly. 'My name's Greg Elliott. I think you've mistaken me for my cousin, Ben?'

'Another Elliott?' was out before she could stop it.

He looked amused. 'How many of us have you met?'

Milla ticked the names off on her fingers. 'Ben, Lorcan – aka William – and now you.'

'You almost have a complete set.' Greg shared out the coffees. 'I heard that Will had moved back into the Elliott Farmhouse but I haven't seen him since he was a kid. Ben likes to pretend he doesn't know me, even when we worked together at the Met.'

'You're a police officer?'

'Not anymore. I'm a diving instructor, working for my wife,' – he slid an arm around Lainey – 'and my sister-in-law, who's married to my brother Drew. It's a real family business. Selma's dad operates the dive boat.'

'Drew Elliott?' She'd never met him, but knew he was as

rich and powerful as her father. Not the kind of person to upset. Of all the buildings she had to walk into…

Greg frowned. 'Please don't believe everything you've heard about Drew. He's not—'

'Oh *do* believe it.' Selma winked and bit into one of the doughnuts. 'He's absolutely dreadful.'

Greg sighed. 'Not helping, Selma!'

If Selma could joke, maybe Drew wasn't so bad?

Sure, and lions were harmless pussycats.

'How do you know Ben and Will?' Greg asked.

'I've been seeing Ben for about four months. Lorcan and I are just good friends.' (She could hardly admit to sleeping with two cousins, one after the other.) 'We met through work. Ben never talks about his family. I only found out last night that his father used to run The Drop. Is there anything else I should know?'

Greg gave a short laugh that didn't have any humour in it. 'If Ben hasn't told you anything about us, then he doesn't *want* you to know. It's good to meet you, Milla, but I'm sure that if you've really been "seeing" my cousin for the past four months, then you know not to go digging around in his past. He won't like it.'

With that, Milla found herself back on the pavement, holding a glossy flyer and a chocolate ring doughnut, dropping hazelnuts into the gutter.

EIGHTEEN

Harriet skulked at the back of the murder investigation team office for the day's briefing, drinking her coffee and being careful to keep her head down, like everyone else, because Ben was in such an appallingly bad mood.

Was there anything more embarrassing than suffering a break-in at a property you were supposed to be staking out? OK, the detective constable he'd despatched had been from Calahurst and didn't know the area, but what could one DC do anyway? By the time back-up had arrived, the intruder was long gone and Lorcan Black was denying there'd ever been one.

Right...

Ben was now explaining that the intruder must be someone Lorcan knew but didn't want to bring to the attention of the police.

Everyone already had a solid theory as to this 'mystery intruder's' identity, and the reason behind Ben's foul mood, but no one was brave enough to call him out on it.

Not even Harriet.

She took another swig of coffee. In front of her, Sam King was surreptitiously eating a bacon bap he must have picked up at The Witch's Brew on the way in. The scent was tantalising. It was amazing no one else had said anything.

Maybe, like the 'mystery intruder', they thought it safer to keep their opinions to themselves.

It was a relief when Ben brought the briefing to an early close, announcing that he was going to pay a call on Lorcan Black's manager, who was booked into a spa hotel on the other side of Calahurst.

Surely this was low priority, when there was a whole bunch of other people they could be interviewing, not least Lorcan Black himself?

Still, hers was not to reason why, etc, etc. She drained her coffee and collected up her belongings.

'DC King?' Ben barked. 'You're with me.'

What? Wait, rewind…

It was lucky she'd swallowed that coffee or Sam would now be wearing it.

'Um, sir?'

Ben gave no indication that he'd heard her speak and walked out the door.

Sam shot her an apologetic glance and hurried after him.

What was *that* about?

In a moment the office was a mass of moving bodies and scraping chairs, jackets being shrugged on and bags being grabbed, but she caught up with Ben as he reached the stairs.

'Sir? What would you like me to do?'

He paused, one hand on the banister, while Sam waited awkwardly beside him, clearly wishing he were somewhere else.

'Pick something,' Ben shrugged. 'You're a sergeant. Isn't it time you chose and allocated your own tasks?'

'Well, yes—'

Now he was halfway down the stairs and she was talking to air.

Harriet returned to the office, in lieu of anywhere else to go. She and Ben had worked as a team since he'd arrived from the Met almost a year ago, and needed someone to show him around. At other stations in the county the sergeants would be more independent and have more responsibility, but Raven's Edge and Calahurst were small and old-fashioned, and this was the way they'd always done things.

So this felt remarkably like a punishment.

What had she *done*?

'Don't worry about it.' Dakota glanced up from her laptop. 'He's taken Sam because he knows Sam won't ask questions.'

'Isn't that the point of interviewing someone?' Honestly, sometimes Dakota was so away with the fairies it was amazing she'd ever got into the Force.

Harriet dumped her bag back on her desk – the much coveted one by the window – and went over to stare at the dry-wipe board where Ben had scribbled notes for the briefing. She should have paid more attention, because now it was obvious that her name wasn't on it.

Had everyone else noticed too?

The dry-wipe board began to blur in front of her.

Pick a task, pick a task...

How hard could it be?

Dakota came to stand beside her. 'The boss has had a row with Milla. Maybe they've split up?'

You didn't need to be a detective to work *that* out.

'What the boss gets up to outside work is his own business.'

'This is why he's left you behind. If you'd gone with him, you'd be asking if everything was OK and how you could help.'

'Of course I—' Harriet broke off.

Wouldn't?

Would.

Dakota was right. How many times had she teased Ben about being a grump, in the hope of getting him to snap out of it? Maybe he'd finally got fed up with being teased? He was her boss, after all, and she wasn't known for her subtlety.

As her brother would have said, 'You have the sensitivity of a brick, Harriet.'

She certainly wouldn't have asked Ben how she could *help*. He was responsible for sorting out his own problems, not inflicting them on everyone else.

Maybe she'd have said that too.

Dakota raised an enquiring eyebrow.

Harriet ignored her, turning back to the board. What was she doing? Oh, yes.

Pick a task...

Dakota's elegantly manicured hand appeared over her head and pointed to the postcard of a generic and historically inaccurate highwayman that someone (probably Sam) had stuck on the board for a joke.

'That could be fun,' she said.

Was she serious? 'The guy's been dead for three hundred years.'

'Still pertinent to the case.'

'How can I interview someone who's dead?'

'Go to the museum,' Dakota suggested. 'Maybe the curator can help? Lorcan was discovered lying on top of Miranda Elliott's grave. He's also descended from the Elliott family. How many people know that? Perhaps the next incident will take place at another location connected to our famous highwayman? It might give us a clue to the perpetrator's identity.'

'*Damn—*'

The words following that should have been 'you're good' but somehow they got stuck in her throat.

Sometimes, Dakota could be a little *too* good.

Harriet tugged out her phone. 'I don't need to go to the museum. I can do a search from right here.'

Dakota placed her hand over the screen. 'And receive a hundred different answers, none of which are correct?'

Now she sounded like Ben, but she had a point. If Harriet wanted to know more about Raven's Edge's famous highwayman, perhaps she should check out the museum. At least it would get her out of here.

She slung her bag over her shoulder and headed towards the door. 'If anyone needs me, tell them I'm following up a lead at the museum.'

Not something she thought she'd ever say.

'You're welcome,' was Dakota's cheerful reply.

She wasn't even being sarcastic.

No one was quite sure how old Buckley Manor was. According to legend, it had been built on the site of a Saxon hall at the same time as the church, but 1626 had been carved over the door, so that was the date everyone went with.

Harriet had visited the museum several times as a child, and immediately remembered the chill and general gloom of the place, not helped by the cracked panelling, rusting suits of armour and dusty display cabinets. The most impressive room was the large entrance hall, where there was an awe-inspiring display of Civil War weaponry, incongruously arranged in pretty spiral patterns across the walls. Until now, she'd never appreciated that anyone could walk in off the street and help themselves to a broadsword and a couple of pistols, and possibly a cannon ball while they were at it.

Perhaps she should have a word with the manager before she left.

'Five pounds, please.'

Beside the door was an ancient wooden desk with a woman sitting behind it, reading a very old, very large book. About the same age as Harriet, she had a definite 'librarian' thing going on:

a pink skirt suit accessorised with black-rimmed glasses and a messy bun, but at least the bun wasn't held in place with a pencil. Small mercies.

Harriet was about to flash her warrant card but the museum could probably do with the cash, so she handed over a fiver and received a raffle ticket in return. It had a 5 printed on it. Did that mean she was the fifth person that day? Week? *Year?*

'You go in that way,' the woman said, pointing ahead but still not looking up.

'Do you have anything on Matthew Elliott, the highwayman?'

'Loads of stuff on Magik Meg, aka "the Raven Queen". A huge display. Potion bottles, grimoire – *that* way.'

Again with the pointing.

'I'm not interested in Magik Meg.' Harriet dropped her warrant card onto the book. 'Could I see the manager, please?'

The woman gave an extravagant sigh, picked up the warrant card as though it were a dirty sock, and handed it back.

'That'd be me. Manager, curator, event-organiser, reception-ist, cleaner and child minder. Dog-sitting by prior arrangement, two weeks' notice in advance.'

Was that supposed to be a joke? Because Harriet *really* wasn't in the mood.

What would Ben do?

Breathe.

Smile.

Try again.

'Do you have many people ask about Matthew Elliott?'

'It's coming up to All Hallows' Eve. This is when his ghost stalks the village, seeking a violent and bloody revenge on all those who committed him to an excruciating death on the gallows. Mwah ha ha ha ha…'

Harriet said nothing but waited patiently. Another tip she'd learnt from Ben.

The curator sighed. 'We know very little about the man, other than he was born to the local gentry and became a highwayman after he fell out with one of his trustees, who was also his uncle, probably over a woman. It's usually a woman.'

'Did he leave a journal?' Harriet remembered all those films she'd seen where the entire case had been solved because someone had found an old diary.

'The man was an eighteenth-century farmer. All he was likely to be writing about was crop yields.'

'Highwayman, gentleman, and now farmer? Are you sure these are all the same person?'

'Entirely my point!'

Ben always made this look so easy.

'Let's start again. I'm Detective Sergeant Harriet March. I'm based at the police station down the road. You are...?'

'Ellie Garlick. Manager, curator, event-organiser.' She waved her hand. 'You know the rest.' Contemplative pause; slight increase in interest. 'Are you investigating the murder?'

Apparently the real truth about Raquel's death wasn't yet widely known.

'We are investigating recent events at Meg's Pond.' That covered everything relevant. 'So, back to Matthew Elliott. You must have *something* on him?'

The look she got in reply could have redefined 'scathing'. 'Some poor woman gets her head chopped off and immediately everyone decides it must be the ghost of Matthew Elliott returned from the dead, which would be impossible, not to mention the fact that he lived to be a ripe old age, wasn't sent to the gallows, and didn't chop *anyone's* head off with his trusty broadsword. Have you ever tried to chop someone's head off with a sword? Unless you're seven foot and built like a barn, and have sharpened the sword to the nth degree, it's impossible. *No one* bothers to do research. No wonder people believe everything they read on the internet. Pure laziness.'

'Which is why I've come to talk to you,' Harriet said, after a significant pause.

Ellie sighed. 'What, specifically, did you want to know?'

Specifically? *Anything* would be a start.

'Was Matthew Elliott a real person?'

'The parish records have a child by that name being baptised in 1670, the younger son of Sir Philip Elliott and his wife, Lady Miranda, who was the daughter of the Earl of Stortford.'

Now they were getting somewhere.

Harriet took out her notebook and wrote it down. 'Was he a highwayman?'

'The date and name ties in with that of a notorious highwayman who fell foul of the Earl of Stortford, and was believed to have been executed at Norchester Prison in 1697.'

'Believed?'

'The county museum has the original records for the prison at Norchester and there's no record of anyone of that name, or anything similar, being either imprisoned or executed in a twenty-year period on either side of that date.'

'But?'

There was *always* a 'but'.

'We have a will in our archives for a wealthy farmer and landowner by the name of Matthew Elliott, dated 1765, leaving everything to his only son, Philip Elliott.'

'He named his son after his father?'

'This is another indicator that it could be the same person.'

'Where's *his* grave?'

'No idea,' Ellie said. 'However, in his will he requested that he be buried in his private chapel.'

'He was a farmer, but he had his own *private chapel*?'

'If he was wealthy enough to own a large house with land and servants, it's entirely possible. Over the centuries, the house might have been downsized or even demolished.'

Downsized?

'Where was this house? Raven's Edge? Calahurst? Port Rell?'

That was the problem with the King's Forest District. It was chock-a-block with big old houses, in various states of repair, many already demolished to make way for housing estates.

Ellie cheerfully shrugged. 'No one knows. It just vanished.' She snapped her fingers. 'Like that. All reference to the house disappears around the mid-nineteenth century. Demolished, is my theory.'

But Harriet was already starting to get a very good idea of where it might be.

One of the men drove a small lorry around to the rear of Michael's house. Their leader gestured for him and his family to get into the back.

'Can't the kids stay here?' Michael asked. 'Why drag them into it?'

For leverage. To ensure he did as he was told. He wasn't a fool.

'On their own?' the leader mocked. 'What if something bad were to happen to them? Good try, Michael, but they'll be safer with us.'

The leader got into the front with the driver, while Michael was shoved into the back by the remaining man, landing on his face in a pile of sacking. He rolled over in time to see his kids being pushed into the lorry, their hands still tied.

'It's OK,' he said. 'If we do as they tell us, everything will be fine.'

David nodded tearfully. Michael's daughter still had her head buried against her mother. His wife regarded him coldly, as though this were entirely his fault.

Wasn't it? He'd taken this stupid job to secure their future. He'd moved them here, away from her family and friends. He'd done it all for them, given up on his own dreams, yet she'd never understood what it had cost him.

NINETEEN

Lorcan's manager, Jonesy, had booked himself into the presidential suite at a starkly modern spa hotel outside Calahurst. The gossip (via Dakota's friend, who worked in housekeeping) was that he'd flashed enough cash for the management to downgrade someone else to make room for him, which told Ben all he needed to know about both the hotel and Jonesy.

Sam had driven them there. He'd kept 1mph below the speed limit, took corners on all four wheels, stopped at traffic lights on amber, and parked, dead centre, in a marked bay beside the hotel entrance. While it was a relief not to stagger out of the car feeling as though he were going to hurl his breakfast into the bushes, something was missing.

Harriet.

They were directed to the bar without any need to show their warrant cards. Decorated in black slate and lots of glass, the bar had a stream flowing right through the centre, bubbling over large shiny black stones. The entire hotel reminded Ben of Hartfell, the strange glass and stone house owned by Milla's father. Perhaps it had been designed by the same architect?

Jonesy had been on a plane, mid-Atlantic, when Raquel's body had been taken from the hospital mortuary. It was a sterling alibi, which Dakota had confirmed with the airline. It didn't mean he wasn't still a person of interest. The logistics of this particular case meant it was unlikely to have been carried out by one person acting alone. Had Jonesy provided the cash to facilitate the stunt? He certainly seemed to have plenty of it.

When they walked in, Jonesy was tapping on his phone, slouched on a pile of pink cushions in a chair shaped like a giant plastic egg. He was in better spirits, which might have had something to do with the glass of Finlayson's on the table in front of him, even though it was only 11.00 am. His clothes were as rumpled as they'd been yesterday but possibly more expensive than they'd first appeared. His frizzy grey hair had been slicked down and tied back, and he had a multitude of tattoos, including a hissing snake on his neck.

Yesterday, Ben would have guessed Jonesy was in his mid-sixties. Today, despite the tinted glasses undoubtedly worn to conceal the bags beneath his eyes, Ben recalculated that he was likely a decade younger.

Jonesy stood up, as though delighted to see them. Was he trying to make a good impression? Why did he care? Did he realise he was under scrutiny? He even went for the two-handed handshake, which Ben had always thought a sure sign of shadiness.

Ben smiled briefly (what Harriet called his 'on/off' smile), and said, 'Thank you for agreeing to see us this morning, Mr... er...?'

Was 'Jonesy' derived from his surname or just a nickname?

Harriet would have known.

It was hard not to glance resentfully towards Sam, who shrugged apologetically.

Jonesy grinned, showing surprisingly good white teeth. 'Jones, mate. Caradoc Jones. You ever tried going through school being called "Caradoc"? Not recommended. It's always been Jonesy. Ironic, because my old man was trying to make up for Jones when he saddled me with Caradoc. Can I get you a drink, lads? Apologise for me being so impolite yesterday?'

Like Lorcan, it appeared Jonesy was a talker.

This could work in their favour. Once an interviewee got going, they'd happily spill all kinds of secrets. Unfortunately, they'd also often go off topic and any good intel could get lost in the waffle.

A waiter was hovering.

'That's kind, but no thank you.' Let a potential suspect buy him a drink? Inadvisable. As for that egg chair... Highly undignified, even if it didn't look brittle enough to snap with one touch. He dragged a more traditional-style chair across to the table with an ear-rending screech.

'I'd love an americano,' Sam said, dropping into the egg seat without a qualm, although he removed a couple of pale blue cushions first. 'Thank you, Mr Jones.'

'Good choice, lad.' Jonesy lifted his whisky. 'Best to stay off the good stuff, if you're working.'

Ben *really* wished he'd brought Harriet.

He took out his notebook and clicked his pen. Something else Harriet usually took care of.

'Mr Jones, I have an address here for you, in New York City.' He reeled it off. 'Is that correct?'

'Sure, that's one of them,' Jonesy smirked.

Did the man manage more than one act? He seemed to be doing very well out of Lorcan's 10%.

'Is that your main residence?'

'I guess so. I've never thought about it.'

Liar. 'You flew in from JFK to Gatwick yesterday?'

'First class, British Airways. Can't beat 'em.'

Yes, we know, you're rich. Now, how to ask: 'You don't sound very American?'

'You were born in the UK?'

The smirk turned into an outright grin. 'Well spotted, mate. What was it that gave me away?'

Ben gritted his teeth. 'Whereabouts?'

'London, but I've lived all over. My family was from Gwent, which is how I ended up with a name like Caradoc Jones.'

'What is your relationship to Mr Black?' He already knew the answer but was hoping Jonesy would elaborate.

The man didn't disappoint.

'I'm his manager but also his stepfather. I married his mum about thirteen years ago, lovely lady, but we lost her to cancer three years after that. Me and the lad have been together ever since. He doesn't have any other family, poor kid.'

Again, Ben felt that pinch of guilt, but if Liam hadn't run away to Ireland, Lorcan could have grown up in Raven's Edge, surrounded by his very extensive family.

And, like Ben and their cousin Greg, left as soon as he could.

That was the second time Jonesy had called the twenty-six-year-old Lorcan 'kid'.

Was he one of those parents unable to accept their child had grown up?

Ben turned to a fresh page in his notebook. 'Do you know of anyone who would wish Mr Black harm?'

Jonesy glowered but took his time answering, finishing his whisky and signalling for another, which arrived the same time as Sam's coffee.

Ben tried not to be distracted by Sam plopping three demerara sugar cubes into it.

'I could crack a joke, and say, "Sure, there're loads of guys out there, jealous as hell, desperate to see him fall." Truth is, he's a good kid and everyone likes him.' Jonesy took a slug of whisky. 'You reckon some bastard's trying to set him up for this girl's death?'

There was no point in denying it. 'That is one line of investigation.'

'Kill some poor girl, to set up my boy? That's sick.'

Ben didn't comment. Raquel hadn't been murdered but very few details regarding the case had been released to the public.

As though he could read his mind, Jonesy said, 'I've not seen anything in the press. Why are you keeping it quiet?'

'It's an ongoing investigation.'

The Press Office had made an official statement yesterday, to say a woman's body had been found, but no more than that. They couldn't release any more detailed information until they knew what they were dealing with. Something else would have to be said soon: the more gruesome elements of the story had already leaked out, and the police needed to be the ones controlling the narrative.

'You know something the rest of us don't?'

Ben refrained from saying, 'That's my job', and asked instead, 'Why did Mr Black move into the farmhouse?'

Jonesy shrugged. 'A right stupid idea, if you ask me, but it's his ancestral home, isn't it? He's always had a bit of an obsession with it, to tell you the truth. There's a lot of pressure in this business. I reckon he wanted to go back to being a kid, with no problems, no responsibilities. We love our childhoods, don't we? Get a nice rosy glow when we think of them, forget all that bad stuff. He'd tell me what it was like growing up here with his young cousins. I think there were four of them all together? They'd dress up for the carnival every year. It's a big thing around here. I told him the house would cost a fortune to put right, but he didn't care.'

A montage of Lorcan's album covers and photo shoots began to play at speed inside Ben's head. Castles, ravens, tombstones, the stark skull-like make-up and the feathered carnival masks.

It was starting to make a lot of sense.

'What else did Mr Black tell you about Raven's Edge?' Ben asked.

'Not a lot. It was the house he was obsessed with. An old farmhouse. Medieval. He had to have the stonework redone, the thatch, new windows, and it's a listed building too. Bloody money pit. Lucky it wasn't wattle and daub. I've not seen it yet. Only photos.'

'Where did you meet Mrs Elliott?'

He blinked. 'Who? If you mean his mum, she was Stella Black by then, her deadbeat husband long gone. Me and my mates were playing in a bar in Greenwich Village, she was staying with some friend-of-a-friend. We clicked. She and the kid moved in with me. Turned out he had a thing for music too.'

Who was it that had told him Jonesy had been in his own band before he began managing Lorcan? Harriet? He flipped back through his notes but couldn't find anything.

Had it been something she'd found on the internet?

'You mentioned playing in your own band?' He mentally crossed his fingers. 'Didn't you have some success in the noughties?'

Jonesy looked surprised. 'You're good,' he said. 'That's right. I love music but hate everything else that comes with fame. My mates were furious when I left the band, just when we were hitting the big time, but it wasn't for me. I'm more of a behind-the-scenes man.'

Strange, because Ben would have said he was the opposite.

'Not the frontman, then?'

'Heh heh. No.'

'You decided to manage Mr Black instead?'

'That kid has a huge talent. He was signed at eighteen but the record company put him together with a bunch of pretty boys without an original idea between them. I quickly got him out of that. He was doing all the work. Do you know, he taught himself guitar from listening to his granddad's old record player? Scratchy rock 'n' roll? He was writing songs at thirteen. Thirteen! If I hadn't taken over managing him, someone else would have – and taken advantage of the poor kid. Like me, he's only ever been about the music. He doesn't care about money or fame.'

Was that true? The little he remembered of Lorcan as a child was that he'd always been in some kind of trouble – with his teachers, with his parents, and getting into fights with other children. Joking, clowning, disrupting, annoying – a textbook definition of attention-seeking. Had he just needed someone to care about him enough to funnel that surplus energy?

'Was it the record company's idea to use the raven imagery for his branding?'

Jonesy sighed. '*That* is pure Lorcan. He's always been into myths and legends, the more gruesome and Gothic the better. He told me this story once, about an ancestor of his. A Robin Hood character, who had his revenge on his enemies by chopping their heads off. I still don't know if it really happened or was a story Lorcan found in a comic book. Have you heard of it?'

Ben put away his notebook. 'Yes, it's a local legend but has no basis in fact.'

'Pity,' Jonesy said. 'It's a good story.'

Ben couldn't tell if the man was joking.

TWENTY

Milla drove back to Raven's Edge and parked in her usual spot in the alleyway, half-expecting to find Drake leaning against her front door, his arms folded, a big scowl on his face. There was no point hiding. He knew where she lived. Although she'd have to talk to him sometime, she'd rather delay it until she fixed things with Ben. Would Drake's attitude towards her change once he found out she no longer enjoyed the protection of the local chief of police?

In the meantime, there was one thread in her investigation left untied.

Slinging her satchel over her shoulder, she headed off to the other end of the village, where The Drop crouched on the edge of the gorge, its black and white exterior stark against the red and gold autumn leaves.

The Drop didn't open until twelve (it said so on the door), and no one answered her knock. Hearing voices, she followed the sound into the backyard, where Sorcha was supervising a delivery of beer barrels, her long brown hair tied back in a no-nonsense ponytail and the sleeves of her blue plaid shirt rolled back to display pretty floral tattoos on her forearms. She was having an argument with one of the delivery drivers (even though he was twice her size), stabbing at a notebook and waving it under his nose.

Milla watched in admiration, although her unobtrusive approach failed the moment she kicked a discarded cola can. The delivery drivers eyed her dismissively. Sorcha didn't even glance over.

'We're not open,' she told Milla, 'and *you*,' she added to the delivery driver, 'can take that barrel inside and put that one back. I'm not paying for stuff I haven't ordered. Don't think you're going to get one over on me.'

The delivery driver muttered beneath his breath but did an about turn with his trolley, forcing Milla to step aside before she was flattened.

This time Sorcha did look up. 'Why are *you* still here?'

'I want the answer to one question and then I'll leave you in peace.'

Sorcha raised her eyes heavenwards but said, 'Which is?'

'Who owns The Drop?'

'How very dramatic of you.' Sorcha snapped her notebook shut. That, too, had a pretty floral cover. 'It's no secret. His name's over the front door. Didn't you spot it on your way past? Perhaps you need to brush up on your detective skills.' She signed for the delivery and ducked through the low door of the pub as the lorry started up and rumbled out of the yard, narrowly missing the corner of the bridge.

Irritated, Milla followed Sorcha inside. It took a moment for her eyes to adjust to the gloom, but she spotted Sorcha's ponytail swinging ahead of her as she marched into the main restaurant, and hurried after her.

'Why can't *you* tell me?'

'I'm not paid to answer silly pointless questions. I have a business to run, every minute counts, and you're wasting my time.' Sorcha stepped into an office behind the bar, crouched to unlock a safe, and took out a fat bag of cash.

'Your attitude's certainly changed from last night.'

'Last night you were with Detective Inspector Taylor.'

Ouch.

'I'm here on his behalf' was such a big fat lie Milla couldn't bring herself to utter it.

'Why should that make a difference?' she said, but knew the answer before the words were out of her mouth.

Drake.

She should have come here before breaking into his office. He knew she was investigating him and his clients. Now the drawbridge was up and the portcullis was about to come slamming down – on her head, if she wasn't careful.

Sorcha glared at her until she stepped sideways, allowing the other woman access to the bar.

'I have nothing to hide,' Sorcha said. 'The owner of The Drop, along with several other hospitality businesses in this area, is Drew Elliott.'

Did that honestly come as a surprise?

'Nothing happens on these premises without him being aware of it?'

Sorcha opened the till and began filling it with the cash from the bag. 'Drake said you'd be here, asking questions and playing at detective. You can't let it go, can you?'

Nothing happens on these premises without him being aware of it.

Why *wasn't* there a camera trained on the till?

Milla took another look at the beams. If she'd been responsible for placing a camera, she'd have put it right about... there. Subtle, not easily seen, but trained directly on the till, and that neatly answered her question.

Drilled into the plaster, almost invisible in the shadow of an oak beam, were four smooth holes where a camera must have been situated until very recently. Maybe even taken down the very night Lorcan had been in. Whoever had sedated him had known he was coming, had possibly even invited him here, because they'd planned everything in advance.

Except it hadn't gone to plan, had it? Lorcan had eaten his food at the bar because he was desperate for company. He'd fallen into conversation with a woman because he was super-friendly, loved flirting, and knew no one else in Raven's Edge. He'd happily left with her before the sedative had the chance to take effect. That was fast work on the part of the mystery woman. Milla didn't know which sedative had been used, but some only took twenty minutes to act.

Drew Elliott might have wanted to keep his young cousin out of trouble but had ended up landing him right in it, inadvertently smoothing the way for the person trying to frame him for murder. Removing the camera beforehand had also been counter-productive – now they'd never know who that woman was.

The murderer?

Milla moved to stand beneath the beam. Had Ben noted these holes last night?

Unlikely. He'd been looking for the existence of cameras, not their absence.

She'd spotted something he hadn't!

A tingle of pleasure shot through her.

Sorcha saw her smile, followed her gaze, and frowned.

'Congratulations,' she said. 'A clue for you to take back to your boyfriend. Do your worst. I have nothing to hide. The camera was removed because it developed a fault. I have a receipt from the repair shop. It's been fixed and it'll be re-installed tonight.'

'Why take down the mounting too?'

Sorcha's expression didn't change. 'In the meantime, our

mutual friend said to remind you of this: He knows where the bodies are buried.'

A popular phrase, often used as a joke.

It could mean anything.

Except Drake wasn't referring to a body. Not a whole one, anyway.

It was definitely time to leave.

She smiled at Sorcha. 'Thank you so much for your time. You've been very helpful.'

Sorcha smiled back. 'The pleasure was all mine.'

It was hard not to slam the door behind her. Last night she'd *liked* Sorcha but now she seemed like a completely different person. Had being with Ben (who everyone knew and respected) given her a protection that she hadn't been aware of? What would happen now they'd split? Four months hadn't been long enough to make friends of her own.

To be honest, she'd not tried very hard to fit in. After living out of her car for most of her adult life, she hadn't a clue how to go about it. Wasn't the onus on the existing residents to invite her to their book club or film night, or whatever people did in small rural villages like this?

Other than to murder each other.

She was no closer to solving the death of the poor woman who'd been found at Meg's Pond. She didn't even know her name. There'd been nothing on her news app this morning, which was odd. Usually the police would take any help they could get – posters up everywhere: *Did you see anything?* Appeals for information on radio and TV. Yet there had been complete silence.

Was there something about the woman's death they didn't want people to know?

Who could she ask? Not Ben, obviously, and his team were so loyal they were unlikely to betray his confidence.

Would Lorcan know anything? The police had released

him without charging him, but maybe they'd let something slip when they'd interrogated him?

She'd promised him another visit. What else did she have to do, other than help her grandmother plan the carnival and masquerade ball, both of which would run more smoothly without any input from her?

The police were still watching Lorcan's house, but she'd always enjoyed a challenge.

The quickest way to the farmhouse was through the forest and Milla had always felt at home there. She and her elder brother Mal had spent a large chunk of their childhood playing amongst the trees. King's Rest, the house she'd lived in until the age of six (when it had burnt down), was to the west of Raven's Edge. Hartfell, the modern house which had replaced it, was to the east. Lorcan's farmhouse was directly ahead, a twenty-minute walk from Meg's Pond.

Most of the houses in the King's Forest District were big and old. Some had been demolished, some were derelict, some had been turned into something else – a hotel or apartment block. Lorcan's house was the only farm – not surprising, because farms were usually surrounded by fields for crops or animals. This house was perched on the top of a slope with cliffs falling dramatically away in front of it and forest creeping up from every other side.

Could the farmhouse be older than the trees?

The path emerged from the forest, widening into a lane that led past an orchard and an extensive garden, bordered by a newly planted holly hedge that was about as tall as her shoulder. There was the garden gate she'd used before, or she could walk around to the front of the farmhouse, wave to whichever police officer who'd lucked out on stake-out duty, and knock on the main door.

But why break the habit of a lifetime?

She walked up to the back door, almost as wide as it was tall, scarred and pitted enough to be original. Tempting, but this time she knocked without trying the handle first.

No sign of Lorcan. Had he gone out?

She fidgeted a bit, pretended to admire the garden, and then knocked again.

Was he asleep? Drunk? Dead?

She tapped her foot.

Anyone would think he didn't want visitors.

Was he working? He'd mentioned a studio, but where was it?

At right angles to the house were two long, low buildings, the same height but with tiled roofs rather than thatch. The one nearest the house was new. Was that Lorcan's studio? She walked over and pressed her nose to the tinted glass door but couldn't see inside. The door was locked, as was the door to the building beside it, although she could see Lorcan's Porsche inside, parked next to a Harley-Davidson. He must have had them shipped from Paris. No sign of his other car though. No wonder the police officers guarding the house hadn't jumped out at her. They were too busy tailing Lorcan.

It was only as she retraced her steps through the garden and out of the gate that something caught her eye. Someone had come out of the farmhouse and was carefully closing and locking the kitchen door behind them, before walking across to the recording studio.

Was it Lorcan or one of his musician friends? Whoever it was, they were wearing something that looked very much like one of his stage costumes – a long black coat with breeches tucked into boots, their hair tied back like the hero of one of those Marina Grey historical romances left abandoned on her bookcase by the previous owner. Were they filming something?

Is that why he hadn't answered the door?

She shouted his name but he ignored her.

How could he? After all she'd done for him? She'd risked arrest and completely wrecked her relationship with Ben.

It hurt more than it should have. If he needed to work she'd have understood, but he could at least have said 'hello'.

She turned away, not bothering to watch him enter the studios.

As though picking up on her mood, the sun went in and by the time she walked back into the village, thick mist was rolling across the churchyard like a horror movie, and she could have sworn she heard a horse on the cobblestones behind her.

After twenty minutes, the lorry rocked to a stop and the doors at the back were wrenched open. One of the men lifted Michael's children out, another yanked out his wife.

Michael, meanwhile, suffered the indignity of being dragged out by his collar.

'Lead the way, Michael,' the leader of the highwaymen said.

Because here they were, standing outside the security depot where he was the manager. It was cleverly disguised as another anonymous building on an industrial estate outside Norchester. Only those watching closely might spot the trucks disappearing through those double doors at the back. Those small armoured trucks seen in every town and village, endlessly looping around the country and always ending up back here.

That was what the company did.

They moved other people's money.

TWENTY-ONE

On his return to Raven's Edge, Ben took out his phone to text Harriet – but what should he say? He'd allowed his personal life to seep into his work life. He'd treated her badly, *unprofessionally*, in front of colleagues. While he'd been correct in saying it was time she was assigned her own team, it was something that should have been said in private and with a good deal more kindness.

Yes, she occasionally overstepped her boundaries, treating him like another brother rather than a superior officer, and she never remembered to call him 'sir'. Yet she'd stopped him from making an idiot of himself when he'd first arrived from the Met, kept him appraised of the various political factions he'd never thought would exist in a rural police division, and updated him on everything that had happened in the tiny village he'd never wanted to live in again.

He was an arse.

He kept it brief.

Lunch. Catch-up. Witch's Brew.

She couldn't tell her boss to 'get lost', as much as she'd like to. She might pretend not to have received the text at all, but he was relying on her inherent nosiness.

Within seconds, his phone had pinged a response.

Fine.

Ben walked the short distance from the police station to The Witch's Brew. The sunlight warmed the scarlet Virginia creeper and glinted on the little lattice windows, and he could smell gingerbread before he'd rounded the curve in the road.

Instead of waiting for him at their usual table, Harriet was browsing the little second-hand bookstore adjoining the café.

Books being more important than space, the bookstore had a labyrinth of shelving curving around the crooked walls, bowed under the weight of books of every shape and size. The bookstore also had a cat: a Persian blue, fat and grey, currently asleep on the shelf reserved for Victorian poets.

It was here that Ben found Harriet, scratching the cat behind his ears and asking him about his day. The cat, stretched out in the sunshine, appeared to be asleep but when Ben approached, he lazily opened one yellow eye.

'Hello, Cat,' Ben said.

'His name is Mister Snuggles,' Harriet said.

'My commiserations,' he told the cat, who ignored him. Harriet picked up a pile of books from the floor and stood up. When she realised there wasn't room to walk around him, she went the other way, looping around to the checkout, letting her pile of books slide onto the counter, where the pale, skinny teenager on the other side began scanning them.

Ben followed. 'I'm sorry, Harriet.'

'Yes,' Harriet said, passing her debit card over the machine.

Was she talking to him or the boy?

Probably him.

'Would you like a bag?' the boy enquired politely.

'Thanks, Jay.'

The boy neatly packed the books into a large orange paper bag with 'The Witch's Brew' written on the side. He slipped in a receipt and held the bag out. Harriet took it, murmuring her thanks again, and then walked back into the café, towards 'their' table by the window. She stashed the bag on the stone windowsill.

'What did you buy?' Ben knew he shouldn't ask this question, but suspected the books were related to work. 'Anything good?'

'Local history. I thought they would come in useful for this case.'

'Don't forget to claim for them.'

'I don't mind. I thought I'd keep them afterwards. They'll be an excellent source of information about the village.'

Harriet had lived here forever; likewise, her family before her. What was it she needed to know about the village? It was almost as though she was baiting him to say, 'Who are you and what have you done with Harriet March?'

Fortunately, Kat bustled up with their bacon and cheese paninis.

They went into their usual routine. Ben handed Harriet the ketchup. She passed him her salad, but deliberately waited until he'd taken a too-big bite of his panini before saying,

'I know why you did it.'

Did what? With a mouth full of panini, he could hardly ask.

'You took Sam with you to interview Jonesy, to avoid me asking you awkward questions about why you were in such a foul mood.'

He hadn't been in a mood. A little quiet, perhaps. Thoughtful. It was to be expected with such an unusual case and—

'Yes, foul mood. Everyone noticed.'

He winced.

'All you had to do was say something like, "I've split up with my girlfriend but I don't want to talk about it" and no one would have said a thing. It's called "communication".'

That might work between female friends but the same hardly applied when one was the detective inspector of a murder investigation team, the majority of whom were men.

'Anyway, I've done lots of research on your ancestor, Matthew Elliott.'

What on earth for?

'I went to the museum and spoke to a very strange woman called Ellie Garlick. She's as grumpy as you, but that could be because she's been left to do everything over there – manager, curator, events-organiser, etc. Maybe the council don't have a big enough budget; the place looks like it's stuck in the nineties. Anyway, she gave me a potted life history of Matthew Elliott. It seems he was a real person, but the whole riding through the village at midnight on Halloween, chopping off people's heads, is pure invention.'

This was how she'd spent her morning?

'I suspect that the reason Lorcan was found on Matthew's mother's grave, is that no one seems to know where his grave is. I have my suspicions...' – she pointed to the bag of books – 'but we can talk about that later. Basically, I came to the same conclusion as you. Someone's trying to stitch Lorcan up. No idea why, but they seem to know his birth name and that he was born here. We need to interview him again, discover if he has any enemies now or in the past. The past bit is important, because this only started when he came back. The big question is, who did he upset fifteen years ago? You were there. Do you know?'

He swallowed valiantly. 'Lorcan was eleven years old. Anyone carrying on a feud that long, with a child—'

'Has a problem. Yes, I know. What do *you* remember from that time?'

She took a defiant bite out of her own panini.

He supposed his would now have to go cold.

'Will – Lorcan – was a normal kid. He was younger than me by four years and I only spent time with him when I had to. You know what children are like. Four years is a big gap when you're a teenager. Growing up in a small village, I didn't have much choice when it came to friends. The only other boys the same age as me were my cousins, Drew and Greg, who were a little bit older, but at that age I found them intimidating. Drew was bossy and liked to be in charge. Greg was one of those strong silent types, who'd stare at you until you backed down. I never got on with either of them.'

'The villain, the muscle, and the comic relief,' Harriet said. 'What were you?'

Ben tried to think back. In those days he'd spent a lot of time talking about rules. No wonder he became a police officer. So had Greg, ironically, considering what the rest of their family were like.

'They called me Benny-Boy-Scout,' he sighed, 'and if you ever tell anyone else that, I *will* have to kill you.'

'I'll take it to my grave.' She took a cheerful bite of her panini, casually waving her hand, indicating that he should go on with his story.

'I have nothing else to say. It was a normal childhood.' He paused at the unexpected panic as he tried to remember the details. Everyone at the station – in the village – knew his back-story. Why should he have to dredge it all up again? What use did it serve?

'You know what happened to my dad,' he said. 'I grew up a lot after that. My parents divorced, my mother changed our name to distance us from the scandal. Drew and Greg's parents divorced too. Greg went to live in Sheffield with his mother. She wanted Drew to go but he refused to leave Port Rell. He had to take over his father's nightclub business. He was only eighteen. It must have been so difficult for him, like being flung into a tank of sharks. I don't think I've really appreciated that until now. Will – *Lorcan* – moved to Ireland and we lost touch...'

One family wrecked by one stupid mistake.

'I already knew most of that. I meant, was there something else?'

'I don't think so.' He was finding it hard to remember. Trying to recall those days was like trying to see through fog. What was the matter with him?

'All the more reason to re-interview Lorcan,' Harriet said. At least she'd appeared to have forgiven him – for now. 'We're obviously missing something. Have we heard back from Norchester? Do they know who broke into the mortuary?'

'The records are inconclusive. They're about to start interviewing the staff.'

'Then we're stuck in limbo,' Harriet said. 'Waiting to see what this guy does next.'

DCI Cameron had said much the same thing. 'It's been less than forty-eight hours. We're doing well to have progressed this far.'

'That's still too long. We're dealing with a pathological narcissist, like last time.'

'You don't know that. You can't label people that way.'

She rolled her eyes. 'A self-important attention seeker, who thinks he's cleverer than we are, staging such a gruesome scene? What else would you call him? Aren't you at all concerned he'll strike again? We didn't fall for his stupid prank at the pond. He'll want to raise the stakes.'

That had already occurred to Ben. 'I have a team watching Lorcan's house. Someone's with him all the time.'

In response, Harriet hauled one of her new books out of the paper bag and crashed it down on the table. Evidently he was back in the doghouse again.

He read the title upside down. Elizabethan architecture? How was *that* going to help?

'Then let's hope Lorcan is his next target,' she said, and then proceeded to ignore him.

Ben bought Harriet another cappuccino as a peace offering, and left her making copious notes in one of her pink notebooks. He walked back to the station, first calling Norchester to see if they'd made any progress on those interviews – they hadn't. He offered to send one of his DCs, maybe tag along too, but they turned him down flat. He terminated the call, feeling disgruntled. If they didn't get a move on, he'd pull rank.

In the meantime, Milla's house was en route. He'd call in and apologise for last night – if she'd even answer her door.

The weather had turned cooler. Crisp brown leaves blew along beside his feet. He pulled up his collar, shivering. It was foggy, damp and trying to rain. If the weather didn't improve by the end of the week, the Halloween carnival would be a washout.

Strange how the mist was swirling in from the forest, even curling between the houses. He'd never seen anything like it. How had it come down so quickly? He could barely see the church.

It took a moment to register the strange hollow 'clop' behind him, because it was so out of place.

A *horse*? In the centre of the village?

He turned. Behind was nothing but eddying fog. It could have been dusk rather than the middle of the day. Where were all the cars? It was so quiet.

What was going on?

The sound of hooves hitting the tarmac grew louder. Slowly, steadily. Closer.

Could a rider from one of the local stables have got lost in the forest? It was easily done. The paths tracked back and forth between the ancient trees but there were few signposts to show the way.

A flash of red on the opposite pavement caught his attention. A middle-aged woman had paused to frown into the gloom.

Some distance ahead, he saw a couple of teenagers walk past Practically Magic.

'That's weird...' One gestured towards the fog. 'Where did that come from?'

Ben kept walking, faster now. The Square was in front of him and beyond that he could see the church's lych-gate. Milla's house would be directly opposite.

He crossed over the road and the familiar red brick building emerged from the mist. There was a light on in the sitting room. She was home.

The horse hooves were right behind.

He turned his head. A black horse trotted towards him, following the white line in the centre of the road. Its rider was dressed entirely in black. Later, he would recall other details – that they were wearing a long coat over breeches and boots, but curiously no hat. Right now all he could see was dark hair pulled back from an unnaturally pale face... Too pale... Sharp cheekbones emphasised black hollows where there should have been eyes.

A *skull*?

He blinked. Was he *hallucinating*?

Behind him, the teenagers whistled and catcalled.

'You're too early, mate!'

Early? Early for what?

Halloween!

It was a dress rehearsal for the carnival! All this talk of ghosts and highwaymen had addled his brain. The road had been closed to traffic, which was why it was so quiet.

But the council always notified the police of road closures...

He crossed the alleyway beside Milla's house, hearing the horse break into a canter.

It snagged his attention. One never forced a horse to canter over a hard surface – that was something he'd learnt from his grandfather. It could damage the soft part of a horse's hoof.

Cantering up and down the main street of the village, parade or not, was hardly safe for everyone else either.

He stepped into the road to remonstrate.

The rider drew a sword – a *sword*! – and swung it towards him.

A bloody sword!

Belatedly, Ben remembered to duck, falling back against the house as the sword thwacked into one of the oak beams above his head, missing him by centimetres. It hit so hard he felt a vibration.

A chunk of wood bounced off his shoulder and fell to his feet.

He stared at it, watched it roll into the gutter.

In the distance a woman screamed, motivating him to shove himself away from the house and stagger after the horse, but the rider had already yanked it around, the bit cutting cruelly into its mouth. The horse reared and, whether from shock or adrenalin, Ben felt as though he were seeing The Square through someone else's eyes.

Swirling mist, a churchyard, a highwayman...

It could have been a film set.

The woman was still screaming, drawing attention to herself.

The horse, unnerved, sidestepped, tossing its head. The rider merely stared at Ben, no expression on that sinister face.

Careful not to make any sudden moves, Ben took out his phone and called Harriet.

When she answered, he didn't give her chance to speak.

'Man, sword, The Square, back-up, *now!*'

The rider patted the horse's neck, soothing it, whispering something into its ear, not taking his eyes from Ben.

This was personal.

He got that message loud and clear.

The screaming abruptly stopped. Behind him a door slammed, but he couldn't risk taking his eyes from the rider.

His brain rattled through a variety of scenarios. How to catch the horse, how to unseat the rider, how to disarm him.

Disarm a man with a very big sword?

He couldn't think of a single situation where it wouldn't end badly.

The only advantage was that, as the rider was right-handed, the sword was now on the other side of the horse. If he wanted to have another go at Ben, he would have to swing around, which might give Ben a chance to grab the reins.

The rider dug in his heels, leant low against the horse's neck, and charged.

Ben slid around the corner of the house and into the alley.

This might have worked if he'd been in a gunfight, but the rider pulled up, then slowly and deliberately followed him.

They were both aware Ben had nowhere to go. The alley led to a dead end – a six-foot fence with the forest on the other side.

How the hell was he going to get out of this?

The rider smirked, urging the horse forward.

Ben fought the instinct to step back.

Grab the reins. Unseat the rider. Simple.

But how?

Maim the horse was the obvious answer but harming an animal was out of the question for him.

He took another step forward.

Grab the reins. Unseat the rider.

This was going to hurt...

A door opened to the side of him and he was yanked into warmth and light.

Milla slammed her front door shut and turned the key, swearing and cursing, turning the air a colour far beyond blue.

Beside her, pale and trembling, was the woman in the red coat. Next to her, the two teenagers, stunned into silence, all bravado gone. Milla had not only saved him, she'd saved them too.

Something slammed into the door, snapping his attention back.

It bowed, but by some miracle, held.

Milla leant forward and shoved home the bolts.

They all held their breath.

Waited.

Horse hooves echoed along the alley, quieter now, fading into silence.

Had he gone?

Ben sagged against the door, boneless with relief, only to have Milla smack his arm.

'What the hell, Ben? What the *hell*?'

TWENTY-TWO

'Were you *trying* to get yourself killed? Anyone else seeing a man brandishing a broadsword would run in the opposite direction, but not you. *You* have to confront him!' Milla smacked his arm again, and then threw her arms around him, burying a sob in his chest. 'I thought you were going to die, you bloody idiot!'

Ben had never seen Milla cry, not even when someone had once held a knife to her throat. His gut twisted to see her so upset. His arms went around her, intending to pull her close, but she shoved him away and he remembered he still hadn't apologised for last night.

'Milla,' he began, aware they had an attentive audience and that the timing was terrible.

She ignored him, scrubbing at her face with the sleeve of her hoodie.

He patted his pockets for a handkerchief but came up empty.

One of the teenagers stepped between them. 'I'm calling the police.'

Ben was sorely tempted to snap, 'Do whatever you want,' but Milla beat him to it.

'He *is* the police.'

The teenager regarded him doubtfully before tapping out treble 9.

Ben sighed. 'I've already called it in,' he said, but then blue lights were bouncing off the ceiling and someone with a deep, gravelly voice was shouting his name outside.

He unbolted the door. There was no sign of a horse or a highwayman, spiritual or corporeal, but lots of police officers in Kevlar vests clutching H&K carbines. Not an armed response vehicle, as he'd expected, but what appeared to be the entire Tactical Firearms Unit.

He'd called Harriet for back-up and she'd sent the cavalry.

Their leader, a broad-shouldered action-hero with a face that could have been carved from pure granite, came forward. Ben recognised Sergeant Rackham from a joint operation four months ago, when he'd faced down a man with a knife.

'I'm DI Taylor,' Ben said.

'I remember.' The other man inclined his head. 'I'm Rackham. You're lucky we got here so fast. We were on exercise in Calahurst. So, what have we got?' He smirked. 'A headless horseman?'

Ben was never going to live this down.

He pointed to the broad gash in Milla's door. 'A man dressed as a highwayman, riding a horse, attacked me with an authentic-looking broadsword.'

The sergeant's smirk dropped the moment he saw the huge chunk carved from Milla's door. He stepped back onto the main street to survey the road towards The Witch's Brew, and then in the direction of The Drop. The sinister fog had disappeared and the road was clear in both directions.

'Which way did he go?'

Ben flipped his thumb behind him.

They regarded the six-foot fence and thicket of trees growing right against it.

'OK...' the sergeant said. 'This was a good test of our response time, and you all seem fine, and this... er, headless highwayman appears to have gone—'

'He had a head,' the woman in red interrupted. She was standing on Milla's doorstep, still pale with shock. 'It was like a skull... White, with black hollows for eyes...'

'OK...' Sergeant Rackham said again.

'I caught him on video.' The teenager shoved his way through, holding up his phone. 'This is the guy. He was wearing face paint to make him look like a skeleton.'

Chilled, Ben remembered the skull-like make-up that Lorcan had worn for the cover of his first solo album: white, with black hollows on his cheeks and over his eyes.

Judging from the constant 'ping, ping, ping' the teenager had already shared the video with his friends.

Had this been the highwayman's intention all along? To create an event that could be shared and shared again, aimed at humiliating him?

Sergeant Rackham's attitude had turned from baffled amusement to cold hard determination. 'Civilians back in the house.' He stared at the fence. 'Down here, you say?'

'I know it seems unlikely...'

The sergeant was already striding down the alley and Ben had to run to catch up.

On the left was Milla's house, with a small courtyard garden behind it, entirely enclosed by a high brick wall. On the opposite side was Practically Magic, its much larger garden enclosed by the same green featheredge fence panels that were at the end of the alley.

What had not been apparent at a distance was that there was a gate in the fence.

Ben lifted the latch but the gate had been bolted from the other side.

Milla was beside him, even smaller and slighter against the

height and bulk of the TFU. 'Shall I ask Elvira or Fliss to unbolt it for you?'

'No,' Ben said. 'They should stay inside.'

'Where you should be, girl.' Sergeant Rackham aimed one hard kick at the gate, which cracked, splintered and flew open, but he barred Ben's way while two of his officers went through first.

'Clear,' one called back.

'My guess is the guy's long gone,' Sergeant Rackham said. 'Any idea what he wanted? Why did he pick on you? You're not in uniform.'

'I challenged him,' Ben said, but remembered the chilling way the man had stared him down.

This is personal.

What could he have done to arouse such animosity?

Yes, he was a police officer and he'd suffered the usual complaints from the public for just doing his job. He'd been spat on in the street, had bottles chucked at him, and been refused service at a restaurant because he'd arrested the owner's cousin for sexual harassment. His detractors didn't usually go to the trouble of dressing up in historical costume, jump on a horse, and threaten him with a sword, though.

That make-up... Was it to make him believe the rider was Lorcan? If it *was* Lorcan, why advertise the fact?

'I saw the video,' Sergeant Rackham said. 'The guy wanted to make a point.'

'He made it,' Ben said. Was he still out there, waiting to make it again?

Regardless of whether they thought the threat had been nullified for now, if the police weren't seen to act, they'd be torn apart by the press for putting the public in danger.

Were the public in danger? Was it egotistical of him to believe he was the target? Could it have been any police officer, in which case it would be considered a terrorist attack, or was someone out to embarrass him in the same way they'd tried to disgrace Lorcan?

Ben followed the TFU into the garden. He saw the hoof prints that had churned up the lawn, and the shrubs that had been flattened by something large barging between them. Unlike the alleyway, Elvira and Fliss's garden merged into the forest – the perfect route for a getaway.

The rider must have local knowledge, something else that pointed to Lorcan.

'Your call,' Sergeant Rackham said. 'We could attempt to track him but that's not our remit. You'd have more success with a dog.'

'I agree,' Ben said, 'and I'll put in a request for the Force helicopter.' That had thermal imaging, which would help track the horse and rider in the forest's thick foliage.

Sergeant Rackham grimaced. 'I'll let you tell the boss.'

He needed to preserve those hoof prints before the TFU trampled all over them, and check with the local riding and livery stables to see if any of them were missing a horse.

It would be a long day, and that bacon panini turned out to be the last thing he had to eat for the remainder of it.

With the help of a police dog named Creda (which meant 'Faith', according to the cheerful female handler), they tracked the horse a mile through the forest until it began to rain and the dog lost the scent. It was half-term and there were too many people about, including riders from the three local stables. The helicopter had the same problem. It was impossible to distinguish one rider from so many. Ditto the officers on the ground: all the rider had to do was swop his long black coat for an anorak, pull up the hood, and he'd look the same as everyone else.

DCI Cameron's voice sounded tighter and tighter with every negative update.

They made the local news, and then the footnotes of the

national news. The teenager's video clip was everywhere; *Ben* was everywhere, but fortunately out of reach of the TV cameras here in the forest, unlike the rest of his team who were centring their investigation on the village.

The reason for the lack of traffic during the highwayman's attack soon became clear. Two 'Road Closed' signs had been placed at either end of the high street. Simple, but effective. The fog had been created by a series of dry ice machines, already in place for the carnival. This was why the mist had appeared between the houses, rolling across the road in such a theatrical way.

Once darkness settled over the forest, the search was called off. The TFU and the Force helicopter had been called away to other, more important jobs. Police officers were patrolling the village on foot; police vehicles were covering all the main roads. There was nothing else they could do. DCI Cameron had already given a statement to the press. Harriet was due to give the joint agency debriefing later that evening. Ben couldn't face it. His head kept replaying the events of that afternoon. Could he have done anything differently? Grabbed the reins, certainly. At least they'd have been spared this search and stopped the panic from spreading.

Every time he closed his eyes he saw that sword swinging towards him.

He had no coat and was soaked and frozen. His head throbbed and his throat was sore, hopefully from the constant talking, shouting and issuing of orders rather than a virus. He didn't have time to get sick. He needed to catch this fool before he hurt someone.

As the rain eased off, Ben finally emerged from the trees. Black clouds scuttled across the sky, the moonlight revealed fields and a large expanse of sea. Instead of Meg's Pond, he was trudging along the muddy lane that led past the Elliott Farm-house and on towards the cliff road.

He should phone for a taxi, go home, shower and sleep, preferably for a week.

Instead, he pushed open the farmhouse garden gate as though hypnotised.

The farmhouse had stables. Why hadn't he remembered that? He could see them on the other side of the garden. They'd been built from stone at the same time as the farmhouse and recently renovated, but were not easily seen from the road, where he assumed the two officers assigned to watch Lorcan were camped in their car.

He should have knocked on Lorcan's door and announced his presence, but the house was in darkness. Had Lorcan gone out?

Ignoring that implication, he followed the path until the stables loomed out of the dark, giving him a strange sense of déjà vu. Even as a teenager he'd never liked them. He had no idea why. He'd never cared much for horses either.

One of the double doors was already slightly ajar. He pulled it open with his fingertips and slipped inside, still using his phone torch rather than groping around for a light switch, even though he knew there was one on the left-hand side of the door.

How had he remembered that after all these years?

What else did he recall?

There had been stabling for eight horses in this half of the building, with a carriage house on the other side, although his grandfather had used it to store the junk that wouldn't fit in his attic. Lorcan kept his cars and motorbike there now.

On this side, each partition gleamed with fresh black paint, but the stone floor was free of straw or any other sign that a horse had been kept here recently. Only an old broom remained, propped up beside the door.

Why did the stables still smell of horse? The only lingering scent should have been of paint.

This was the moment where he should have turned around and walked straight out, but as Milla had said, he was a bloody idiot.

He peered into the first stall.

It was empty.

Moonlight poured through the jalousie windows, emphasising the dark shadows in the corners where the light didn't quite reach, shadows that rippled as he walked towards the second stall, re-forming into a man sitting on an upturned barrel.

Ben blinked and the apparition vanished, but he couldn't erase that familiar feeling of panic. A hallucination caused by sheer exhaustion? Another memory? What was it about these stables that made him feel this way?

He took another step forward. The third stall was also empty.

Had he expected it to be different? OK, he knew horses didn't vanish but there were many other ways the highwayman could have evaded the police. There were three riding stables in the King's Forest District, not to mention the livery yard managed by his Uncle Anthony. Harriet and Sam had checked each one this afternoon. No one knew of a horse that matched his description, or had admitted to it.

Ben moved forward, his attention snagged by the darkest corner at the far end of the stables. He could swear he could hear the shadows breathe.

Another image snapped into his head.

That same man sitting on the barrel, leaning forward, his head down, utterly defeated. Three other men standing in front of him.

Ben heard a pistol shot.

But it came from *behind* him...

He spun, heart thudding. The stable door had flown open

in the wind, smashing against the wall. There had been no gunshot, only his over-active imagination.

Why couldn't he breathe?

Forcing his attention back to that corner, he carefully illuminated every crevice. There was nothing to see, apart from a large spider scuttling away from the light.

A shadow separated from the others, moving towards him at speed, arm raised...

There nothing to create that shadow in front of him, so it must be—

He turned in time to block a blow from the broomstick, which smashed painfully into his forearm but better that than his head.

The pain grounded him in reality.

When his assailant tried again, Ben grabbed his wrist, yanked him forward and head-butted him. A devious trick he'd learnt from Drake, who never obeyed any kind of martial art or boxing rule.

His assailant collapsed against the wall, holding a nose that now streamed blood.

'Ow! Damn, Benny-Boy! What did I ever do to you?'

Michael went in first. At this time of day there weren't many staff, only a couple of security guards and the night shift. The guards laughed and joked with Michael, surprised to see him here so late, greatly entertained that he'd brought a real live highwayman with him.

Was he on his way to a party? Trick-or-treat? Where was their candy?

The laughter and joking died when the other men appeared behind him. He could see it written on the guards' faces. What the hell was going on? Who were these guys?

Then one of the highwaymen took out a gun.

Was it real or fake? It made no difference. It had the desired effect.

'Damn,' one guard said, raising his hands, 'we don't get paid enough for this.'

'Quite right,' the leader of the highwaymen agreed, 'so take yourselves, and whoever else is inside the warehouse, upstairs to the meeting room.'

When the last member of staff had been rounded up, the leader turned to Michael. 'Lock them in the meeting room, ensure they have no access to a telephone or any other way to contact the outside world, and then come and find me. We should be ready to go.'

'No, that wasn't part of the plan.'

The highwayman rolled his eyes. 'Don't test me, Michael. You're going to lock your friends, family and colleagues in the meeting room, and we're going to collect the cash. Young David is going to help me. Aren't you, David?'

The boy regarded him uncertainly, eyes huge in his pale, freckled face.

'It's only lots of old paper money that no one else wants. Did you know they were going to burn it? We're not stealing, only repurposing. You're going to help.'

David shook his head. He was his mother's son, and not easily swayed by that argument.

Michael swallowed. 'Do as the man tells you, son,' he said. 'The sooner they get what they want, the sooner they'll let us go home.'

'Absolutely,' the leader said. 'Carry on, Michael. David and I'll return for you when we're finished.'

Michael started up the steps. His legs felt like lead. How the hell were they going to get out of this unscathed?

TWENTY-THREE

Ben shone the torch into the man's eyes. '*Lorcan?* What are you doing here?'

'What am *I* doing?' His cousin glared at him through streaming eyes, holding the hem of his T-shirt against a bloody nose. 'You're the one who broke into my stables!'

Ben held out his hand. Lorcan hesitated before taking it.

Ben hauled him up. 'I'm sorry. I didn't know it was you. I was looking for a horse.'

'Don't you need a warrant for that?'

'Section 18, remember?' Ben said, hoping he didn't.

'Not really.' Lorcan regarded him resentfully. 'Something about you being in suspicion of something? I thought I was in the clear?'

He pulled off his bloodstained T-shirt and used it to wipe his nose, leaving him in bright yellow jogging pants with no shoes – completely off-brand for a brooding rock star, but looking like any other twenty-something who might have been interrupted while slouched in front of the TV.

Ben moved forward to check the next two stalls.

Both were empty.

Lorcan returned the broomstick to the wall, before falling into step beside him. 'What are you doing?'

'Still looking for that horse.'

'It's the middle of the night!'

Ben held up his phone for Lorcan to see the time. 'It's 8.15, hardly the middle of the night, unless you're eighty.'

'For me it *is* the middle of the night. I've been having trouble sleeping since your friends went off with my pills. I had lunch with my manager – you interviewed him this morning and he wanted to compare notes – and then I came home and crashed out. You can check with your guys out front, if you don't believe me. I know they followed me to the hotel and back.'

Compare notes or synchronise stories?

How convenient that Lorcan and Jonesy could give each other an alibi.

'Those officers are there for your protection,' Ben said. 'Don't you watch the news?'

'I have an app for that. It sends me notifications of impending zombie apocalypses, wouldn't want to miss one of those.' Lorcan stopped talking, thankfully, because he was starting to give Ben a headache. 'Did something happen?'

'Other than a zombie apocalypse?' Ben brought up his own news app. There was nothing on the home page, so he swiped to the local news and there he was, starring in his own personal horror movie. He cringed inwardly but clicked 'play' and turned it around to show Lorcan, who grinned.

'Is that you? On TV? Why are you running...? *Damn!* Is that...? *Bloody hell!* Was that a *sword*?' He stared at Ben. 'You could have been killed!'

'Now you know why you need police protection.' Ben tucked the phone back into his pocket before his conscience made him check all those missed messages. 'Now you know why I'm looking for a horse.'

Lorcan frowned. '*That* horse?'

'Plus the rider.'

'You thought it was *me*?'

Ben sighed. 'He was dressed like you and he's wearing the same skull-like make-up you wore on your first album cover. What else was I supposed to think?'

'I don't know; that someone's trying to set me up? That it's kind of odd that your own cousin would want to kill you? The face paint is hell to get off, by the way. Soap and water, make-up remover, and whatever else they say on the packaging, I had dark circles around my eyes for days after shooting that cover. I looked permanently hungover.'

Ben remembered his daughter, Sophie, having her face painted as a fairy at the school Summer Fayre. Despite being 'water-based', that had taken a lot of scrubbing to get rid of too.

He lifted his torch to shine it at Lorcan, who swore volubly and put his hand up to shield his eyes.

No face paint.

'Are you deliberately trying to blind me?'

'I needed to check something.'

'Man, I'm your *cousin*!'

Most murder victims were known to their killers and a large percentage were related to them too. Tactfully, Ben didn't tell Lorcan that. Instead, he switched off the torch and headed towards the door.

Lorcan hurried after him. 'Are you going now?'

'Thank you for your help.'

'That's it? You turn up in the middle of the night—'

'Eight-fifteen.'

'...search my stables for no good reason—' He broke off as Ben sighed again, rather too heavily. 'Why don't you call a cab and come in for a drink while you wait for it. You look like you're about to fall over.'

Ben felt as though he was about to fall over too. How many miles had he walked today, zigzagging through the forest?

'I could give you a lift,' Lorcan said, 'unless you think I'll murder you on the way home and chuck your body in a ditch? Tell you what, why don't we invite one of those nice officers out front to chaperone you?'

Perhaps it *had* been a little anti-social to search Lorcan's stables without warning now he was (mostly) in the clear.

'I'd hate to put you to any trouble,' Ben said. 'Why don't we go into the house and you can murder me at your leisure?'

There was a pause as Lorcan stared at him. 'You're joking, right?'

Ben waved his hand to indicate that Lorcan should lead the way back to the house. He then took care to close the stable door properly, although there didn't seem to be a key.

'Are you sure you've not kept a horse in here recently?'

It certainly smelt like it.

'I haven't, but the house was abandoned for fifteen years. I have no idea what's been going on. The builders found all kinds of – well, you don't want to know what the builders found,' Lorcan said, before promptly telling him, 'Condoms, used condoms – I even found my hummingbirds chucked in here yesterday. No sign of the glass jar they were in though. People think they can trespass here all the time. They treat it like a dump.'

Hummingbirds?

'I get the idea' Ben said. 'When was the renovation work completed?'

'On the house or the stables?'

'Either.'

'The house was finished six weeks ago, the studio four weeks ago, the stables and carriage house two weeks ago. They were low priority.'

Two weeks for someone to move a horse in and then out

again, removing any trace that it had ever been there. What would be the point? If Ben was to be the victim, they couldn't have known he'd have been walking through the village at that exact time.

Except...

If they'd been watching his movements, they would have known he had lunch with Harriet in The Witch's Brew practically every day, although the timing did vary. Even Kat, the owner, started on their paninis the moment she saw them approach because they always ordered exactly the same thing. Their predictability had played right into the highwayman's hands.

Despite the relentless, freezing rain, Lorcan wouldn't let Ben inside until he'd taken off his muddy shoes.

'Original sixteenth-century oak floorboards, mate.' He looked doubtfully at Ben's soaked suit too, but compromised by spreading towels over the leather sofa before allowing him to sit down.

Any other day Ben might have found the contrast amusing between the defiant pre-teen from fifteen years ago and this house-proud fussiness.

Once they'd settled in front of the fire with mugs of steaming coffee – 'Use the coaster, Benny-Boy. Were you raised in a barn?' – Eddie the raven flew excitedly in from the hall, as though he'd been waiting for their arrival, hopping up onto Lorcan's shoulder and rubbing his beak against his ear.

'*Wild* bird?' Ben derided.

'I found the hole in the roof where he gets in. You can come upstairs and check, if you don't believe me.'

Ben didn't but was far too warm and comfortable to get up again. Besides, any wild animal became a 'pet' as soon as people began feeding them.

'When I first met Eddie, I thought he was stuffed,' he admitted. 'I stroked his head and he bit my finger.'

Lorcan laughed. 'I'm sure he's sorry now, aren't you, Eddie?' He stroked the raven's beak. The raven croaked ecstatically. 'We used to have a stuffed one in the old days, maybe that's why you were confused? It was on the sideboard in the hall and Granddad used to hang the key to the stables from its beak.'

'What happened to it?'

'A lot of things disappeared from the house after we abandoned it. All the electronic stuff, like the TV and microwave. The Aga was ripped out, but that was forty years old, so it didn't matter. Losing the original furniture was the killer but we were able to track down and buy most of it back because one of our ancestors had the family crest engraved on everything.'

'We have a *crest*?'

'A raven sitting on a bridge. Didn't you know?'

'I've never cared much for family history.'

'It's *fascinating*. I have a genealogy app on my phone; I play with it while waiting for a plane or during a sound check.'

Lorcan made 'waiting for a plane' sound like 'waiting for a bus'. How had Ben ended up with a cousin who was a famous singer? If someone had asked him to pick which of his three cousins would end up as a bone fide celebrity, he would have chosen Drew. Even at the age of eighteen, he'd been glamorous and cool, and destined for great things. Instead, Drew had taken over his father's failing businesses, turned them around and made a huge success out of them. Although, Ben realised with hindsight, it had probably nearly killed him. No wonder he was such a control freak.

'Why did you come back?' Ben asked. 'You could have lived anywhere.'

'I already have, but I was happiest here, running around with you, Drew and Greg. I know you didn't really want me, and most of the time you barely tolerated me, but it was fun – three older brothers to watch my back but not take me too seriously. I'm utterly fed up with people taking me seriously. No shared history, no in-jokes, no teasing. No one dares roast me in case Jonesy fires them. It's so boring you wouldn't believe.'

Boring? Being rich and famous? Not that he'd like that lifestyle – another reason he'd tried to hide behind the anonymous and very common 'Ben Taylor', so no one would make the connection with his father and uncles.

'Why did your parents leave Raven's Edge in the middle of the night and never come back?' he asked Lorcan.

'Why do you think? Dad wanted to avoid jail! Mum woke me at midnight and told me I had five minutes to pack because the police were on their way. I had to leave most of my stuff behind. I grabbed my guitar and a few clothes, and that was it. The only thing that stuck in my mind was how Mum kept promising to buy me anything I wanted if only I'd hurry up, because we had a boat to catch. I did wonder where the money was coming from. We'd never had much of it before then.'

'A boat?'

'The ferry. We drove through the night to Holyhead, caught the ferry to Dublin, and crashed at a crummy B&B once we got there. I remember that, because if we suddenly had so much money, why couldn't we have stayed in a fancy hotel?'

'The police would have been looking for your dad, even in Ireland. They would have been able to trace his movements via his passport.'

'After about a week Mum announced she'd had enough of him messing her about, so we caught the next flight to New York and stayed with some relation of hers in Greenwich Village.'

'She didn't consider returning to Raven's Edge?'

'Maybe she thought the police would assume she was guilty too?'

'No one stopped her leaving Ireland. Had you changed your names by that point?'

'I think so...'

Meaning there had not been enough time to make it legal. So how had Dina Elliott, a nurse practitioner from Raven's Edge, been able to obtain fake identity documents good enough to gain entry to the USA? They would have been very expensive, hard to come by and taken time to arrange. Something didn't add up.

He should ask Dakota to research it.

The other thing that had been bothering him was, 'How did you know your father had died?'

'We didn't but he vanished just before we left for America. Mum's theory was that Dad fell out with some criminal friends of his and they did away with him in such a way that his body would never be found. We hired a private detective a few years back, to try and find him. None of his friends had heard from him since that night, none of his bank cards had been used, or his phone. His passport showed him entering Ireland but nothing after that.

'Every now and then one of those true crime TV shows would dig everything up – about the robbery and his disappearance, and we thought it might end if he was declared dead. He'd written a will years ago, leaving everything to me. He had no money, only debts, which I paid off, even though I didn't have to. The only thing left was this house.'

Ben noticed the liberal use of 'we'. Jonesy again. Had the idea truly been a joint one?

'When I finally walked in through the front door,' Lorcan went on, 'even though the house was a wreck and there was no roof, it was as though I'd come home.'

Ben didn't feel that way at all. There was something chilling about this place. Something... sinister, lingering beneath the surface.

'Do you get along with your stepfather?'

'I must do; I made him my manager! He's a big character,

and can seem overpowering if you don't know him, but he treats me like the son he never had.'

Ben recalled how belligerent Jonesy had been when he'd arrived at the police station demanding to see his 'boy'. To an outsider, it appeared to be a rather claustrophobic kind of relationship.

'You're all right with that?' he asked.

'Compared to the indifference of my real parents? Yes!'

There were times when Lorcan appeared to be a lot younger than twenty-six. What would happen when he felt he'd outgrown Jonesy and wanted to move on to other relationships, professional and personal?

'Jonesy was so happy when Mum agreed to marry him,' Lorcan said. 'I was only a kid, but I could tell how sad and lonely he'd been on his own. He was thrilled to become part of our family. Mum died soon after and he could have abandoned me, but he didn't. He's always been a real father to me. I love him to bits. We're a perfect team.'

Ben didn't find this reassuring.

TWENTY-FOUR

October 30th

Milla woke to the smell of bacon cooking.

She opened her eyes and there was her bedroom ceiling, in the right place, above her head. So far, so good. In the old days, she'd never know quite where she'd wake up – living from day-to-day, sometimes sleeping in her car, sometimes in the spare room (or on the sofa) of casual friends. This morning she was lying on top of the duvet, wearing the clothes from the day before – ugh, but no big deal. Ben *wasn't* lying beside her, but she needed to get used to that, and—

She lurched up, swinging her feet to the floor.

Ben. The highwayman. The *sword*.

She'd fallen asleep. *How* could she have fallen asleep? He'd gone into the woods and not come back. *Anything* could have happened to him.

She scrolled through the notifications on her phone. Nothing, although he'd be lucky to get a signal in the middle of the forest. Sometimes she couldn't get one in her sitting room.

Surely he'd message her to let her know he was OK? He'd know she'd be worried.

Wouldn't he?

Or would he take note that her last words to him after their argument had been 'Goodbye'?

He must be OK. His boss had given an interview last night to say that, while they hadn't found the highwayman, there was no reason to believe the public were at risk. It was believed to be an isolated incident – 'a prank'.

Did people *believe* that rubbish?

Apparently, if it was on the news or in the papers, it was considered the truth.

The delicious scent of bacon intruded on her thoughts.

It was almost as if someone was in her kitchen, cooking breakfast.

Ben?

She rolled off the bed and leaned over the banister, but could see nothing, only a shadow moving around the kitchen.

'Ben? Is that you?'

She ran down the stairs, ending up in the centre of her kitchen, directly opposite the stove.

A man was frying bacon and eggs. He had his back to her, but his hair was black not blond.

Her brain couldn't process it.

Neither could her mouth, which immediately said: 'Ben?' again, even though she knew full well it wasn't.

'Morning, Princess.' He turned and grinned. 'How do you like your eggs?'

Not something she ever thought she'd hear Kieran Drake say.

'I'm guessing sunny side up,' he said, flipping them over, 'but by the way your mouth is hanging open, I expect you're not used to a man cooking for you. Hmm, I wonder what it was that attracted you to Detective Inspector Taylor, if not his cooking?'

Ben was intrinsically good and always did the right thing, qualities she hadn't often come across over the past few years.

Not that she planned to talk to Drake about her love life or current lack of it.

'How the hell did you get in?' If she hadn't left her phone upstairs, she could have been dialling 999.

'Not nice is it,' he said, 'finding a stranger making themselves at home in your personal space?'

'You broke into my house... to make a *point*?'

He held up one finger, then used a tea towel to take two plates from where he'd been warming them in her top oven and slid the bacon and eggs onto them, where they joined sausages, tomatoes, mushrooms – basically, a full English breakfast.

It was surreal.

'I did,' he agreed. 'I thought it showed a certain dramatic flair.'

Dramatic flair? The nerve of the man!

Was it any worse than what she'd done to him?

'You're crazy,' she said.

'I certainly am. Why else would I risk arrest on a murder charge to rescue your ungrateful arse in the middle of the night? Not to mention disposing of a body and destroying a crime scene.'

'Part of a body,' she said automatically, but he'd already turned his back on her to walk over to the bow window that overlooked the street, where there was a table and two chairs. He'd set out mats and cutlery, and there was a little vase with a single pink flower in the centre of the table. *That* she recognised from the rose climbing around the door to Practically Magic.

'Have I left anything out?' he said.

At first, she assumed he was talking about breakfast. There was even a jug of orange juice and a large cafetière of coffee on the table. She hadn't been aware she owned a cafetière, she drank so much of the takeaway stuff from The Witch's Brew.

Then she realised he was talking about everything he'd done for her the night she'd broken into Lorcan's farmhouse and found the specimen jar.

He wanted to play it that way?

Fine.

'You're still brooding about that?' She sat at the table and poured a glass of orange juice. Freshly pressed? Where had he *found* all this stuff? She didn't own an orange, let alone a presser. The only things in her fridge were a tub of margarine and a jar of peanut butter.

'I have *many* things to brood about,' he said, taking the seat opposite. He shook out a napkin and dropped it into his lap, an oddly incongruous gesture from a man who also appeared to have slept in his clothes. 'The very least of it? That you felt the need to break into my office and sneak a look at my clients' confidential files. Beyond the pale, Princess.'

'I didn't find out anything I didn't already know.' She kept her gaze down and concentrated on cutting up the food in front of her. Hopefully, gripping her knife and fork meant he couldn't see her hands were trembling. Fortunately she could still string a sentence together. '*Services as discussed?*'

He shrugged. 'My old dad was a great fan of never putting anything in writing. Hard to tell that to the taxman though.'

'You told me that the first time we met. It gave me the idea to check your files in the first place.'

He winced. 'Really?'

'I only wanted to find out the name of Lorcan's guardian angel.'

'Guardian angel? What does that mean?'

'You know him as "Drew Elliott".'

'He's Lorcan's cousin,' he said. 'Why shouldn't Drew help out a family member?'

'Exactly! Why couldn't you have told me that? It would have saved the bother of breaking into your office.'

'The *bother*?'

'It was very inconvenient.'

'*Inconvenient?* Esme isn't pleased with you either. I had to buy her another bar of chocolate as a peace offering.'

'My heart bleeds. You still haven't answered my question. Why keep Drew's involvement a secret?'

'It's called "confidentiality".' He said the word slowly. 'Maybe you've come across it occasionally? 'Along with "respect", "honour", "decency", "integrity"... Do *any* of these words mean anything to you?'

She ignored him, helping herself to a couple of slices of toast... from a *toast rack*? Had he found that in her cupboard too? Was it real silver? She resisted the temptation to turn it over to check for a hallmark.

'Where did you get all of this?' she indicated the food. 'It wasn't my fridge.'

'It certainly wasn't.' He shuddered. 'Have you *seen* the inside of your fridge? It's where good food goes to die. If you were a restaurant, you'd be closed down.'

'I have better things to do than housework.' Although, maybe it wouldn't hurt to waft a duster around occasionally, for the next time someone broke into her house.

'Evidently,' he said. 'I called in at the supermarket in Calahurst. It was on my way.'

'But *why*?'

'It got your attention.' There was that irritating grin again. 'I hoped you'd take it as the sign of a truce.' He took the remaining slices of toast and began buttering them. He was avoiding eye contact, in much the same way she'd done earlier. '*Did* it get your attention?'

'Sure, I'm shallow; ask anyone. I'm still waiting for the truth.'

'OK... This is how it goes. You want something from me, I want something from you. Maybe we can trade?'

'What on earth would you want—' She broke off. Surely he didn't mean…?

Drake rolled his eyes. 'Mind *out* of the gutter, Princess.'

She speared a sausage and defiantly bit off the end. 'Why do you keep calling me that?'

Because the way he said it, it didn't sound like an endearment.

'You can't work it out for yourself? OK, let me explain. You seem to believe you have a right to go wherever you want, do whatever you want, and take whatever you want, regardless of anyone else's feelings on the matter. It's extremely irritating.'

His words stung, especially as Ben had said the same thing.

'Pot, kettle, black?' she retorted.

'*This*,' he indicated the breakfast table and all the food on it, 'is me teaching you a lesson in a *nice* way. Doors have locks for a reason, Camilla. I'm amazed you've survived this long, to be honest. One day you're going to cross the wrong person.'

'Like Drew Elliott?'

'Stop obsessing about the guy. All he wanted was to protect his cousin. Family means everything to him.'

'Yes, about that. Why didn't Drew just *tell* Lorcan that someone was out to get him?'

'Because he didn't want to worry him? How should I know? I'm paid to do a job, not ask questions. Something you were happy enough to go along with the other night.'

'You *have* to keep bringing that up.'

'To get you up to speed, here comes favour number two. The woman whose body you found? She wasn't murdered. Her corpse was stolen from the mortuary. No motive, but now your boyfriend's been targeted, the police think someone has it in for the Elliott family.'

Her stomach swooped, as though she'd driven too fast over the village bridge.

'Ben's in danger?' Was that why she hadn't heard from him? 'Has something happened to him?'

He sighed. 'Did you ever search for 'Benedict Elliott' online? You know, like any normal woman?'

'Your idea of "normal" seems a bit skewed. I've never checked out any of my boyfriends. That would be unfair.'

'You have a strange set of values, Camilla. Breaking into houses? Completely fine. A basic safety precaution, to check your date's not a serial killer...'

'Get to the point. I know Ben's family are bad news. It's no secret. What did they do? Rob a bank?'

'Close,' Drake said. 'Ben's father, along with his uncles, robbed a security depot at gunpoint, with help from the manager. They got away with about £30 million.'

'Ben's father robbed *a security depot*? Was he caught?'

'Yes, and he died in prison. Drew's father, Anthony, spent many years in prison but was eventually released. Liam – Lorcan's father – escaped to Ireland with his share of the money. The rest of it was recovered.'

Yet Ben and his cousin Greg had become police officers.

'What happened to the depot manager?'

'Liam killed him.'

'I never knew any of this...'

No wonder Greg had refused to tell her about their family.

'Would it have made a difference?' Drake asked softly.

'Of course not! I don't care what Ben's family have done. It's him I—' She broke off. 'Why are you telling me this?'

'I have an aversion to being locked out of my own office. If you're that keen on breaking and entering, come work for me and do it legally.'

'Legally?' she scoffed.

'You'd be surprised.'

'Why on earth would I want to work for you? If I wanted to

stalk unfaithful spouses, I could do it myself. I could buy your detective agency four times over.'

'I'm sure you could, although it's not considered polite to say so. Since you brought the subject up, tell me something. You inherited all those millions but you moved *here*?'

'I like it here. It's convenient.'

'End of terrace, one bedroom? It's hardly Hartfell!'

Hartfell was the large modern house owned by her father. All stone, slate and obsidian glass, it brooded in the centre of a manmade lake and was surrounded by acres of topiary.

'This house is perfect for me. It's in the centre of the action, just how I like it, but not as manic as a city centre.' Anything larger and she'd be spending her entire day keeping it clean or hiring staff to do the job. She couldn't bear the thought of a stranger going through her things. The irony of *that* didn't escape her. 'I also bought a car,' she said, hating the note of defiance in her voice. Why did she need to justify herself to Drake?

'For the Graham family, that would be small change.'

'And some clothes...' She trailed off as his gaze swept her plain black T-shirt. She had six more just like it in her wardrobe, but in different colours.

He was right; she hadn't got the hang of her unexpected inheritance at all. She kept giving large chunks to the charities close to her heart, like the homeless and refugees, but the thing about Graham Media was that the stuff kept coming in.

'Now you have everything you've ever wanted, you're bored out of your mind,' he said. 'Admit it! Come and work for me. Twenty-four seven wall-to-wall excitement, and on Fridays, we have doughnuts.'

'Doing illegal stuff?'

'Nothing I do is illegal,' he said.

She didn't believe him for a second.

'You've made it quite plain that you despise my "values". Why are you so keen to employ me?'

The corner of his mouth hitched. 'You have the relevant skill set.'

She'd asked for that.

'I'll have to think about it,' she said.

'You owe me a favour.'

'No, I don't.'

'I heard you and the police officer broke up. Who will you call the next time you're in trouble?'

'I think you've outstayed your welcome.'

'Fair enough.' He put his knife and fork together and dropped the napkin back on the table. 'Think about what I said. I'm serious.'

'Thank you for breakfast,' she said, escorting him to the door. It was only polite after all. 'But why did you have to call so early?'

'You weren't my only errand in Raven's Edge. I had to make a delivery first. Two plump little birds, one hard little stone.'

A plump little bird?

'Goodbye, Drake,' she said firmly. 'You can consider us even.'

She closed the door in his face, and wondered who the other 'little bird' was.

The highwaymen called Michael by his name, laughed and joked with him, clapped him on the back, and generally treated him like one of them. The confusion on the faces of his co-workers turned to distrust and then to outright animosity.

It didn't take long for the lorry to be loaded with the crates of cash. Around £30 million sterling in used notes, wrapped in different-coloured plastic according to denomination. They could have taken twice as much, three times even, if only they'd had another lorry, something their leader was particularly bitter about.

When they'd finished, they locked David in the meeting room with the others, and signalled for Michael to come with them outside.

He should have made them force him because, as soon as he climbed into the lorry, he realised what he'd done.

'What about my family?'

'They'll be fine. When they realise we've gone, one of those security guys will raise the alarm.'

'What about me?'

The leader laughed. 'You're one of us!'

'That wasn't the plan!' Michael grabbed the other man's mask and yanked it off. 'What the hell were you thinking, Liam? Now everyone knows I was in on it.'

Liam shoved him away. 'We punched you and grabbed your family, as arranged. Wasn't that realistic enough for you?'

Michael remembered the fear on David's face and sank back against the seat. 'You didn't have to threaten my kid.'

'You can't have it both ways. Why should we take all the risks? This way we're equal.'

'Equal? No one saw your faces!'

'The police aren't stupid. They'll work out who we all are. Disappearing off to Spain will be a bit a clue too.'

'But I can never go back!'

'Why would you want to? You can do anything now, go

anywhere. You're always moaning about that wife of yours. Now you're free.'

Michael watched the forest zip past the window. 'I'll never be able to see my kids.'

'None of us will. That's what was agreed. We take the money and we go on the run. £5 million each. More, probably, once we count it. Isn't that worth it?'

Michael stared out of the window, keeping a tight lid on his cold rage. Never see his children again?

No amount of money was worth that.

TWENTY-FIVE

Ben woke with a pounding headache. One glance at the clock and he could see he'd overslept by two hours. When he switched on the television, DCI Cameron was on every news channel, chairing a news conference in response to the video of the highwayman.

'We do not believe there is any ongoing risk to the public,' he was saying. 'The incident appears to be a prank.'

A *prank*? Whenever Ben closed his eyes he saw that sword swinging towards him.

He popped two paracetamol out of a blister pack and chugged them down with a coffee, swallowing hard to ensure they didn't come back up again.

'The body of a woman found beside a pond in Raven's Edge two days ago was stolen from the local mortuary,' the DCI added, careful not to say which mortuary.

Ben knew he should sit down and pay attention, but switched the television off after hearing Cameron ask people not to panic.

A guaranteed way to ensure people panicked.

If his head hadn't hurt so much, Ben would have slapped it.

By the time he slunk into work, hoping that with the DCI on the case no one would notice his absence, the MIT office was almost empty. His own office was also empty, except for the remains of DCI Cameron's black coffee and a very large, medical cool box.

Ben wondered if he was hallucinating.

What the hell?

Was the cool box pertinent to the enquiry? Evidence of some kind?

What was it doing here?

He leant back into the main office. 'Where did this box come from?'

Ash shrugged. 'I think someone brought it up from downstairs. It was too big to fit in your post tray.'

'You know nothing about it, what it contains…?'

Ash continued to stare in that hopeful way he often had, as though expecting someone else to miraculously come up with an answer.

'Where's Harriet?' Ben sighed.

'With the DCI. You weren't here so—'

'Dakota? Sam?'

'Erm, enquiries?'

Ben glanced back at the box on his desk.

Ash got up and wandered over. 'Do you think it's a bomb? Should I evacuate the building?'

Had Ash slept through his training?

'It's not a bomb. There are no protruding wires, no strange noises…'

Ash caught on. 'There's no postage, so it must have been hand-delivered. They even spelt your name right.'

'There aren't many ways to go wrong with "Ben Taylor",' was out before he could stop it.

'The "y",' Ash said, 'perhaps "or" at the end?'

Ben opened his desk and took out his box of disposable

gloves, snapping on a pair before he could snap a retort back at Ash.

'Call DCI Cameron and let him know there's been a development, and get me Caroline Warner on the phone – the pathologist.'

'OK,' Ash said, still staring at the box. 'Why do you need a pathologist?'

A reasonable enough question. Ash hadn't spent five years married to one, or he'd have recognised the logo of the medical transportation company stamped on the side of the box, knew the work they did, and therefore what was likely to be inside.

The incident appears to be a prank.

'Wait a moment. I want to be sure...' Ben felt around the side, found the release – thankfully it wasn't locked – and steeled himself for what he knew would be inside.

Ash took a step closer.

Ben glanced up. 'How squeamish are you?'

Ash promptly took a step back.

'Good man.' Ben lifted the lid and found exactly what he'd expected, tightly squashed into a space meant to ship nothing much larger than biological samples. At least whoever had packed this had made an effort to preserve it. 'Hello, Raquel,' he said.

There was a soft thud as Ash hit the carpet.

Thirty minutes later and he'd been kicked out of his office by his ex-wife (bed, house, office: he was noticing a pattern) and a couple of CSIs had trooped in from the car park, too weary to make their usual 'Not you again' joke. DCI Cameron was delighted Raquel's missing remains had turned up with minimum effort on their part. The entire team crowded around a monitor in the hastily commandeered conference room to watch the security footage of the cool box being delivered to the police station, confirming the civilian receptionist's statement that it had arrived by motorcycle courier.

They watched the courier enter the station and walk through reception, which was fortunately empty, straight up to the counter.

He knew the layout: he'd been there before.

The receptionist asked him to take his helmet off. (There was no sound but the receptionist pointed to his head.) The courier ignored the first request, heaving the box up onto the counter. The second time he cupped his hand to his helmet, pretending he couldn't hear, before turning away – and saluting the camera.

He knew the camera was there. He thought he'd got one over on them.

There was less than ten seconds of footage. What else could they establish?

He'd been wearing black motorcycle leathers and a black helmet.

At no point did he take his helmet off.

Neither was it entirely clear he was a man. The courier could equally have been a woman.

Everyone looked at Ben, perhaps hoping for divine inspiration.

'Is it the same person?' the DCI asked.

'I don't think so. The person on the horse seemed thinner, despite the bulky coat, and took a malicious joy in trying to terrify me. This person appears taller, broader and more certain of himself. The way they walk...' Ben broke off, staring at the screen.

The walk.

It couldn't be...

Harriet leant forward eagerly. 'Do you recognise them?'

He kept his expression neutral. 'They're wearing a helmet, Harriet.'

'You can tell a lot about someone by the way they walk. Some actors start with the walk or the voice of a character, to help them get inside their head.' Harriet stared again at the screen. 'Are they walking with a limp?'

Yes.

'I don't think so,' he said, 'although it appears that way from the camera angle.'

'Are you sure?'

They all stared at the screen.

The DCI pressed 'play' on the remote for what seemed like the thousandth time.

It probably was.

'There!' Harriet tapped the screen. 'A slight limp.'

She was good, and it killed him to do it, but he shook his head. 'I can't see it.'

Harriet slumped back into her seat.

'They're not the same person,' he said. That was the truth. 'The one on the horse was deadly serious. It was no prank. Maybe it started as one, but when I was stood in front of him, he knew who I was.'

'Someone who doesn't like the police?' suggested Ash.

'Someone who doesn't like me.'

'Lorcan is your cousin,' Cameron said. 'There's every indication that this is a campaign against your family.'

'Yes.'

'How many Elliotts are there? You, Lorcan Black, Drew Elliott and... who was the fourth one?'

'Greg Elliott. Drew's brother. He works at the dive centre in Port Rell.'

'All sons of the men who carried out the robbery on that security depot?'

'Yes.' No matter what he pretended to himself, everyone in the village knew about his family; they had always known. It was why he'd joined the Met. He'd been sick of his family history defining him, of strangers assuming he was like his father and uncles, purely because his surname was Elliott.

'Send someone to interview them,' Cameron said.

'Drew won't talk to you.' The first thing Drew was likely to do was set the best and most expensive legal team onto them.

'He doesn't have a choice,' Cameron said. 'He's not the boss around here, I am. Any other living relatives?'

For a once prolific family, modern-day Elliotts were somewhat thin on the ground.

'Only my Uncle Anthony. He runs the Green Acres Livery Yard, although Drew owns it.' Drew owned everything.

'Stables, eh? Did we interview him?'

'Yes,' Harriet said. 'All his horses were accounted for and none matched the description DI Taylor gave us.'

'We should chat to him again,' Cameron said, stroking his beard. 'Two perpetrators. I've said that all along. The "Road Closed" signs at both entrances to the village, the smoke machines set off at exactly the right moment. Our mysterious highwayman needed help to set that up, not to mention that it would have been impossible to create those macabre scenes at the pond and the church without being spotted by a member of the public. Two perpetrators, that's what we're looking for and now we have them both on camera. Excellent work!'

DCI Cameron was obviously thrilled; everyone else, less so.

Ben knew they were thinking the same thing, but no one wanted to be the one to say it out loud.

Two suspects, as if one wasn't bad enough.

Except...

He looked again at the black-suited man frozen on the screen, mid cocky salute.

He'd recognise that self-confident swagger anywhere.

Kieran Drake.

How the hell had he become involved?

TWENTY-SIX

Milla left her phone on the sitting room table while she headed upstairs to shower and change into fresh clothes – another black T-shirt and jeans, so it was not like anyone would notice the difference – before returning to the kitchen for coffee. Her self-control didn't last until her second sip.

What was so bad about Ben's past that he'd changed his name in the hope others would forget it too?

Googling 'Elliott' with 'security depot' sent her back to the late noughties when Liam Elliott ran a riding school, his brother Charlie managed The Drop, and Anthony Elliott owned a nightclub in Norchester called The Crooked Cat. Outwardly successful, in reality each brother faced financial difficulties and, in Liam and Anthony's case, outright bankruptcy. For three middle-class, attractive, supposedly intelligent white men, who'd probably floated through life having everything handed to them on a plate, a heist must have seemed like a perfectly reasonable way to make some extra cash.

Idiots.

According to Charlie's testimony (published on a true crime website), the robbery had been Liam's idea, cooked up between him and his friend Michael Griffiths after a drunken night of poker. It had been Halloween, so they'd worn highwaymen costumes, already treating the heist as a game. Steal a bunch of banknotes marked for destruction, then back to the pub to celebrate. What could possibly...

Well, it had gone wrong. Horribly. Two brothers had been caught and Michael had ended up dead. Only Liam had escaped unscathed, along with his share of the cash.

Milla did a search on 'Michael Griffiths'. *The family man who betrayed everyone's trust*, screamed one newspaper headline, with the same few photos repeating down the page. A man in his late thirties, with red-gold curls, white freckled skin and very blue eyes, accompanied by a pretty blonde wife and two red-haired children, one of whom Milla recognised immediately, even as a teenager: the Reverend David Griffiths.

Ben wasn't the only respectable resident of Raven's Edge to have a skeleton stuffed away in his closet. If Michael Griffiths was the father of David, their highly regarded vicar would have an excellent motive to hate the Elliott family.

Had she cracked the case?

She stared through the window at the little church opposite. The warps and bubbles in the old glass gave the building a hazy, dreamlike quality. In the foreground, David was unloading cardboard boxes from the back of an estate car, pausing only to laugh and joke with the postman.

Did Ben know Michael Griffiths's son was working here in the village?

Sure he did. He had a whole team of detectives working for him, here and in Calahurst, so he must feel the relationship wasn't relevant. Yet the investigation had been knocked off-course by the appearance of that highwayman.

Had that been the intention? A classic distraction?

She watched David disappear through the lych-gate with one of the boxes. He'd left the boot of his car open, with another box on the pavement. Even in Raven's Edge that would be considered naive, but at least it meant he was coming back.

She scooped up her keys and her phone, belatedly remembering to lock her door behind her, before running across The Square.

She misjudged the distance between her and an oncoming car. There was a blare on its horn as a red VW swerved around her. She cursed loudly.

'Are you all right?' David had returned to his car without her noticing, concern evident on his face.

'Hello, vicar,' she said. 'You always seem to catch me swearing.'

'I won't judge.' He turned his attention back to the boxes.

She sauntered over, as though their meeting were coincidental, and kept the conversation going. 'You leave that to the guy in charge?'

'More of a "He that is without sin" and "cast the first stone" kind of thing.'

She glanced into the boot, almost imagining a corpse rolled up in black plastic, but there was only another cardboard box.

'Do you need any help?'

'I'm done. Parish magazines, hot off the press. I'm about to take these to the village store. £4.50, if you'd like one?'

'I've no cash on me,' she said. 'Sorry.'

On the other hand...

'I live over there,' she thumbed in the direction of her house. 'I could fetch my wallet?' When she'd got him alone, she could interrogate him about his deep, dark family secrets. Did his parishioners not know who his father was or, like the inhabitants of any typical English village, were they aware but too polite to say anything?

'Why not pay me the next time you see me?' He ripped open the box in the boot with his key and handed her a surprisingly slick, glossy magazine.

Let him get away? No chance.

'I'll be two seconds,' she said. 'I live right there. Literally.'

He frowned. 'Number 4? The house on the end?'

Why did that sound as though it were a bad thing?

'You're not going to tell me my house is haunted, are you?'

'No. At least, I don't think so. It wasn't when I... I used to live there, you see.'

That didn't make sense. She'd fallen in love with her house the moment she'd seen it. With its red brick, blackened beams and slightly lopsided appearance, it was cute and quirky but very, *very* small.

'Was it formerly the vicarage?'

'No, this was years ago. I lived there with my mother and sister, when I was about fourteen.'

'I bet the house has changed. When I bought the place it was a holiday let, but much of the original furniture is still there.'

'How interesting.'

His indifference was bordering on rudeness.

'Would you like to have a look around?'

A shadow crossed his face. 'It wasn't a happy time for me.'

His father's death? If only one parent had worked, there would have been a substantial drop in income, hence the move to a smaller house.

Milla remained silent. She'd done her best to plant the seed but sometimes it was better to let the mark believe a course of action was their idea.

He glanced again at the house. Curiosity won out.

'I suppose I have five minutes before my meeting with the parish council.'

'Excellent.' Milla set off across The Square before he could change his mind. As she unlocked her door, she hoped Fliss Merriweather wasn't watching through the window of Practically Magic and having quite the wrong idea. When Milla went inside and turned to make some throwaway comment to David, he was still waiting on the doorstep, like a vampire unable to cross the threshold. 'You *can* come in.'

She hoped she wasn't about to trigger some childhood trauma, but if his memories were that bad, how did he cope with working right opposite the house?

David stepped inside and took a wary look around. He dismissed the kitchen with a cursory glance, but seemed fascinated by the open staircase and old oak banister, reaching out to stroke the wood, smoothed shiny by four centuries of use.

'The number of times I slid down this,' he said.

Really? Because there wasn't a lot of space.

'Did you ever crack your head on the stove?'

'Never.' He walked on past and into the sitting room, staring around at the gnarly wooden bookcase filled with someone else's books, and the little red sofa pulled up in front of an equally tiny fireplace 'It's strange,' he said, 'but hardly anything has changed, even after all this time. Although I'm sure I remember two separate rooms?'

'I took down the partition wall,' she said. 'I suffer from claustrophobia, so although I love cosy, the rooms were too small for me. Upstairs is the same. One big bedroom with the staircase in the centre and a bathroom screened off at one end.'

'There were three bedrooms when I lived here. My sister and I had one each.'

Milla nodded but thought the family must have been incredibly cramped. When she'd removed the partitions, her architect had explained that the house had originally been built with only one room on each floor.

'You've mentioned your sister before. She arranges the flowers in the church?'

'Rose is very artistic. I thought she'd become a florist but instead she took a job at the hospital.'

Rose Griffiths, who arranged flowers in the church and tended the sick.

She sounded dreadful.

'She sounds like a very caring person,' Milla said.

David gave her a sharp glance, but was fortunately distracted by the table in the bow window. 'We carved our initials into that table! I don't think my mother ever realised we'd done it.'

Not such perfect children then. She hadn't noticed the initials either. The table was very old and had lots of scratches and grooves. Her brother Mal had suggested re-varnishing it if she was that attached to it, but Milla found the wear and tear comforting. The table belonged here more than she did.

'I remember the dining chairs,' David was saying, 'and also the bookcase. The sofa is new though.'

The sofa was one of the few items of furniture she'd bought herself. She'd gone on her own to a showroom in Norchester and, overwhelmed by choice, more-or-less ordered the first one she'd seen, paid for it with a wad of cash, much to the sales assistant's astonishment, and shot out, swearing never to do it again.

'Our sofa always felt too big,' he said. 'My parents had bought it for our old house around the corner, which was much larger.' He paused, realising how his words might be construed. 'I'm sorry, I didn't mean to imply—'

'It is a small house,' Milla agreed, 'but I like it that way. Would you like a cup of tea?'

She was turning into Granny Brianna. Whenever conversation became sticky, offer a pot of freshly brewed tea.

Maybe David hadn't heard her, because he moved over to the bookcase as though in a trance.

'I recognise some of these.' He flipped one out with his index finger. '*Frenchman's Creek*? I think this was my mother's. She loved Daphne du Maurier.'

'Would you like to take it for her? I wouldn't mind.' Milla hadn't had the time to read any of them but could hardly admit it. People would wonder what she did all day.

He shoved the book back onto the shelf. 'My mother died twelve years ago. We only lived here for a couple of years. When she became ill, we went to live with my grandfather in Norchester. He was the vicar at St Mary's and lived in a rambling Victorian house beside the church. We'd have moved there sooner but he'd cut her off when she married my father.'

'He came good in the end?'

'They made up before she died. My father...' David sighed. 'My father was a troubled soul, always wanting what he couldn't have. Moving here was supposed to be a fresh start for everyone. With hindsight, I suspect he'd been cheating on my mother. Their relationship had never been good, but it was distinctly frosty by the time we arrived in Raven's Edge.'

Did she dare risk asking?

'Was that for work?'

'Yes, he was hired as the manager for a security depot. It was a huge promotion for him, a fabulous opportunity, and, like everything else in his life, he completely blew it.'

Was he actually going to tell her? Without any prompting?

David ran his finger along the bookshelf and then back again. Back and forth... back and forth...

It was... disturbing.

Had she pushed him too far?

It was rather late to remember that she knew nothing about this man.

Was he even a real vicar? Maybe she should have researched him too?

Now she *knew* she'd been spending too much time with Drake.

She took a step back.

The door was right behind her...

The movement made David glance down and realise what he was doing. He shoved his hand into his pocket and turned around.

'It was a horrible time for all of us,' he said. 'My father fell in with some bad people. They found out where he worked – it was supposed to be a secret – and encouraged him to help them rob it, promising him a share of the money. So he did, and then they killed him.'

'K... killed him?' It was true? Ben's father was a murderer?

'One of them admitted it, said his brother had done it. Conveniently, that brother ran off with his share of the money and we have no idea where my father is buried, so we have no closure. Somewhere in the forest, the police told us. He might never be found.'

'How horrible for you.'

'My sister suffered night terrors for years afterwards. We were taken in the middle of the night, by a group of men wearing masks. She was only ten years old.'

'I am *so* sorry.'

'It was Halloween. They were wearing fancy-dress costumes – highwaymen, like the legend of Matthew Elliott. It made everything worse – gave the night a surreal, nightmare quality. I've hated this time of year ever since.'

What should she say? What should she do? She could hardly hand him a mug with a cheery, 'Here, have a cup of tea and everything will be all right.'

How many times could one say 'Sorry'?

He managed a wry smile. 'I've never hidden who I am and where I come from. Although I usually save the "My Father Was a Bank Robber, So Choose Your Friends Wisely" talk for the rebellious teenagers on my school visits. Standing here, in this house, brings everything back.'

Exactly as she'd planned, so why did she feel so bad about it?

'Ironically,' David said, 'the man who let us stay here was Anthony Elliott – one of the other robbers. It helped ease his conscience, I expect. He owned several rental properties that he signed over to his son when he entered prison, along with his other businesses, but he'd left instructions that we should be allowed to live here, rent-free, as long as we wanted. He thought he was being kind, but to my mother, it was an everyday reminder of how the Elliott family had ruined our lives.'

In Raven's Edge, the carnival was winding down. The pubs were full but the packs of trick-or-treaters had gone home with their overflowing bags of candy.

Drew grew bored with throwing stones at beer cans and went off to meet his mates in The Drop, carelessly abandoning their grandfather's broken Luger pistol on the church wall. Benedict sighed and stuck it into his pocket before Will could appropriate it. Drew was the only one legally old enough to drink, and there was no way Benedict could get away with sneaking into The Drop, because his father managed it.

Greg had disappeared some time ago, into the woods with a girl from school he'd fancied forever. Will was now completely drunk, which meant Benedict had to remain stone-cold sober, responsible now for both him and the horse.

Could his life get any better?

By encouraging Will to clamber up on the churchyard wall, he was able to shove him onto the horse's back. Fortunately the horse was happy enough with this, placidly plodding back through the village, oblivious to the drunken revellers in their capes and masks.

Miss Lily had decorated The Witch's Brew and the trees around Meg's Pond with hundreds of tiny white fairy lights. It was incredibly pretty but not remotely spooky. Benedict had the idea that the elderly Miss Lily didn't fully understand the concept of Halloween. The large cauldron outside her door, which had held her famous peanut butter cookies, wrapped up in orange tissue paper and tied with green paper ribbon, was now empty.

He and his cousins had taken at least three each.

He nudged the horse onto the path past the pond.

Why was he the one to always be saddled with Will? Why did everyone automatically assume he was the sensible one? He could hold his liquor better than any of them (a perk of living above a pub), he knew more curse words than Drew, but, just *once, he'd like to be the one who got the girl. He could under-stand the appeal of Drew's bad-boy glamour but what did girls see in Greg? He barely said more than two words in an entire day, so it wasn't his scintillating conversation.*

It was very unfair.

Will chose that moment to lean over the horse's neck to throw up, rudely interrupting a happy fantasy where the most popular girl in the school pushed Greg out of the way to get to Benedict.

Benedict sighed. The sooner he left Raven's Edge behind him, the better.

And he was never coming back.

TWENTY-SEVEN

Harriet wondered how Anthony Elliott would take a second police visit to his livery yard. He hadn't been pleased to see her and Sam yesterday, when they'd been checking every riding stable and livery yard for a distinctive black horse. He'd even accused the police of pursuing a vendetta against him.

If he felt like that, maybe he shouldn't have robbed a security depot in the first place.

The lane leading to Green Acres Livery Yard was longer than she remembered (probably because Sam was driving so *slowly*). They drove past a couple of paddocks and through a small copse, and then a large red-brick Victorian house was in front of them. Sam drove around to the huge modern complex behind it and parked his car well clear of any 'mud'.

Two women leaning against a wall watched them get out of the car and walk across the yard. Harriet let Sam do the introductions and wave his ID card about, but the women recognised them from the day before and politely explained that Anthony Elliott wasn't in.

Harriet didn't believe them for a moment, but then her default was never to believe anyone. 'We can wait.'

'Join the queue,' said a voice.

Harriet glanced round. Camilla Graham was sitting on a bench against the wall, her eyes closed, her face upturned to the weak October sunshine.

Harriet strode over. 'What are you doing here?'

Milla didn't bother to open her eyes. 'The same as you, I expect.'

'Which is?'

'Someone obviously has it in for the Elliott family. I thought I'd get Anthony's take on it.'

'Thank you for your interest, but we'll take it from here.'

'I have as much right to be here as you. It's a free country.'

'I'm a detective sergeant. I'm here legally. You, on the other hand, are trespassing.'

'I'm only trespassing if the owner says I am.' Milla opened her eyes. 'Here he comes now. Let's ask him.'

Harriet glanced towards the smart reception block but the sound of horses' hooves came from behind. Anthony Elliott, on the back of an enormous horse, walked through an open gate and into the yard. For one heart-stopping moment, she thought the horse would run her over, but at the last second Anthony swerved away, chuckling.

Bastard.

One of the stable hands immediately stepped up and took the reins while he dismounted. Harriet had to admit he was pretty spry for a fifty-seven-year-old. When he took off his hard hat and gave it to the stable hand, she could see he still had all his hair, with only a hint of grey. Was this what Ben would look like in thirty years' time?

Anthony stuck his riding crop into his boot and peeled off his gloves as he stalked towards her – very lord of the manor. She resisted the temptation to step back deferentially, and put her chin up instead. No one was going to intimidate *her*.

'I thought I answered all your questions yesterday, Detective Sergeant March?'

'I'm here on a personal matter, Mr Elliott. Perhaps we could talk inside?'

Well away from Milla who, typically, chose that moment to gracefully unfold from the bench and join them.

Anthony stared at her, confused. 'Little Milla?' His face curved into a smile. 'My goodness, it *is* you. Little Milla, all grown up!'

'Um, hi?' Milla said. 'Have we met before?'

'Your mother used to bring you to the Elliott Farmhouse for riding lessons. You look very like her, you know. Of course in those days the farmhouse was a riding stables, owned by my father, and was the biggest in the King's Forest District. All the local children went there.'

Harriet hadn't, but he was probably talking about rich kids.

Milla shook her head. 'I'm afraid I don't remember.'

'You'd have been about five or six? It was before the... Ah...'

Fire.

Milla had been six years old when her family home had burned down and her mother had been killed.

'Come inside,' Anthony said quickly, to cover his misstep. 'We can have a coffee and a catch-up.'

'That would be lovely.' Milla followed him across the yard. 'I did have something I wanted to discuss with you, and it would be better said in private.' She glanced back at Harriet as if to say, *Who's the trespasser now?* before following Anthony through the automatic doors and into reception.

Harriet ground her teeth. Seriously?

'Wait here,' she told Sam. 'Speak to the stable hands. See if you can find anything else out.'

'Will do,' he said.

Harriet hurried after Anthony. He led Milla through a palatial reception, more suited to a private healthcare clinic, and into a dining and recreation room that was presumably for the staff.

'What kind of coffee would you like?' he asked Milla.

'I'd love a flat white, thank you.'

'No problem.' He slid a mug into a fancy coffee machine, while Milla walked over to a black leather sofa and sat down. His easy smile vanished when he spotted Harriet had followed them. 'I've said all I'm going to say to *you*.'

'I'm sorry to hear that. You have a potential death threat against you and it's my duty to warn you.'

'A death threat?' Anthony threw his head back and laughed. 'Who'd want to kill me?'

Harriet bit down on the obvious retort and hoped Ben was making more progress interviewing Drew.

Actually, no she didn't. Why should she be the only one to suffer?

Anthony took another mug from the stack beside the machine and waved it in her direction. 'As there's no getting rid of you, how do you take your coffee?'

'However it comes.' She plonked herself on the sofa next to Milla. After a few minutes, Anthony placed a black coffee in front of her and took a chair opposite them. She'd seen him make his own and Milla's coffee with real cream. Harriet was used to people not liking the police but honestly, how petty. 'Thanks,' she said. 'That's a cool coffee machine you have.'

'It's more trouble than it's worth. People keep pinching the pods.' He pointed to the large bowl of little foil-covered containers beside the machine. The different colours meant different flavours, presumably.

'Was it expensive?'

'I suppose so.' Anthony's shrug was from a man who had little idea how much anything cost. 'It's mean-spirited, when anyone can come in here and help themselves to a drink as often as they like. What would be the point in stealing the pods? I shouldn't think many people can afford the machines to put them in.'

Which neatly answered that question. Had it not occurred to Anthony that the staff could be stealing his precious pods as a joke or to spite him? She bet his favourite flavour went first.

'Perhaps you should switch back to instant?' she suggested.

'Let them win? I don't think so. I had a camera installed.' He pointed in the vague direction of the ceiling. 'That'll catch them.'

She squinted up. The room was single storey and open to the rafters, but she couldn't see anything fixed to a beam.

'A *hidden* camera,' he added. 'I have an app-thing on my laptop to monitor it.'

'You know, you could have put up a sign to *say* you had a security camera and saved yourself the trouble. Legally, you should put up a sign anyway.'

It was the wrong thing to have said. Anthony immediately turned his back to concentrate on Milla.

Harriet sighed. Anthony Elliott was a man unused to being contradicted, apparently.

'What brings you to Green Acres?' he was now asking Milla. 'Are you looking for stabling or do you wish to resume riding lessons? We don't give them here but I can certainly recommend someone.'

'It's the strangest coincidence,' Milla smiled prettily, obviously well versed in dealing with men like him (Harriet tried not to roll her eyes), 'I've recently moved to Raven's Edge, and it turns out that you used to own my house!'

'Did I?' His avuncular expression slipped slightly. 'Which one? I owned several houses before I handed my portfolio over to my son.'

Translation: before I was sent to prison.

'Number 4, The Square,' Milla said.

'Yes, that one was a holiday let. Very popular, particularly during the school holidays, I'm surprised Drew sold it.'

'I happened to mention it to the local vicar, and he said he used to live there too.'

Anthony frowned. 'The Reverend Dickens? Are you sure? I thought he had one of those Victorian houses on the other side of the bridge?'

'The *new* vicar – the Reverend David Griffiths.'

Where on earth was Milla going with this?

The name evidently meant something to Anthony, because his lips tightened. 'My son warned me Brianna Graham's grand-daughter was a journalist—'

Milla laughed self-deprecatingly. 'I used to write reviews for a music magazine. I'm not sure that counts as journalism?'

'If you're digging for dirt, you can leave right now.'

'Not at all.' Milla was unfazed. 'David mentioned that you were kind to him and his family, letting them stay at the house for free. They were left in extreme poverty after his father's death. The life insurance company refused to pay out because Michael Griffiths's body was never found.'

Was David on their person of interest list? Harriet couldn't remember. Had anyone even interviewed him? She remembered Ben saying something about an alibi, but had any of the team checked it out? It would be super-embarrassing if Milla (of all people) had spotted something they'd missed.

'It made no difference to me,' – Anthony's tone was guarded – 'I was in prison.'

'Do you know how Michael died?'

Harriet winced. *Too clumsy...*

'I didn't kill him, if that's what you mean?' He stood abruptly, collecting up all three mugs of coffee including Harriet's, which was halfway to her mouth, and walked over to tip the contents down the sink.

Damn, that coffee had been really good.

'I can't tell you anything that's not already public record,' he said. 'You'll have to leave now. I'm a very busy man.'

Milla didn't move. 'Your brother Charlie said Michael was shot by Liam.'

Anthony stood at the sink, his back towards them. The only sign that he'd heard her was a slight stiffening of his shoulders.

'I know nothing about that,' he said, his voice cold and pinched. 'I didn't kill Michael and I don't believe Liam did either. Charlie was the one to volunteer that to the cops. Perhaps his solicitor had advised that it would help reduce his sentence. Not that it did him any good. He died a month before his release date, stupid idiot.'

'Do you believe Michael's still alive?'

'No, he loved his children.'

Anthony spoke without hesitation, so it was most likely true, or at least he believed it to be true. Harriet watched as he turned away from the sink, but his expression was hidden by the light streaming through the window behind him.

'Michael would never have abandoned his family willingly,' Anthony said. 'I'll tell you that for nothing. Charlie and I took our share of the money and went home. The police were already waiting for Charlie at The Drop. They arrived at my apartment later. Charlie blamed me for selling him out but why would I have done that? I've no idea who informed on us. I assumed it was Michael, but the police said he was dead. Only Liam managed to escape – to Ireland, with his wife and son. Maybe it was him. The police never did catch up with him. Whatever he did, that bastard always landed on his feet.'

'What, *exactly*, is going on here?'

Damn.

Drew Elliott stood in the doorway. Although she'd never met him, Harriet knew it had to be him. He was the image of Ben, for a start – if Ben shaved off his beard, spent all his free time being pampered at an exclusive health spa, and wore clothes that cost a month's salary.

Drew's attention fell on her. 'You're a cop,' he said.

Never mind how he could tell, she stood up quickly.

So did Milla. Smart girl. It would not be a good idea to annoy someone as wealthy and powerful as Drew.

'Mr Elliott,' Harriet said, as soothingly as she could manage, 'I believe Detective Inspector Taylor has already called on you today, to explain why we're visiting members of your family?'

He shrugged. 'No, he hasn't, but let me guess. You can't solve a crime, so you're going to charge one of us? Isn't that the way it always goes? Blame the Elliotts? No wonder Benny changed his name.'

Had Ben missed him?

'We're concerned about your safety, Mr Elliott. There's been an attempt to frame your cousin, Lorcan Black, for murdering a woman, and yesterday an attempt was made on the life of DI Taylor. You might have seen it on the news?'

'What's this?' Anthony frowned. 'I saw something on TV last night, about a man with a sword, but the police chief said it was a prank and nothing to worry about.'

Harriet ran through the events in reverse order, finishing with Lorcan being found on top of Lady Miranda's tomb, covered in blood.

The older man blanched. 'That wasn't on the news!'

'We were trying to keep the details quiet to avoid panic,' she said. 'We believe Lorcan – Will, as you call him – was the victim of some kind of stunt, but the stunts are becoming more vicious and there's a fear that someone might get hurt.'

'Is this true?' Anthony demanded of Drew. 'Someone did this to Will? Why wasn't I informed?'

'Why do you think I'm here?' Drew snapped back. 'As soon as we found out a threat had been made against Will, I put my people on it, but you know what he's like. So desperate for friendship he'll talk to anyone. He doesn't care who they are. How can I keep someone like that out of trouble?'

'I always felt sorry for that boy,' Anthony muttered. 'His parents were uncaring fools. People like that shouldn't be allowed to have children.'

'Is there anyone you feel might have a vendetta against your family?' Harriet asked.

'Vendetta?' Drew laughed. 'This isn't *The Godfather.*'

'It could be one of the staff at that security depot?' Anthony suggested. 'I believe one of the guards had a heart attack a few days later. He'd always had health problems though.'

Drew sighed. 'Let's not speculate in front of the nice police lady, eh Dad? We can discuss this later.'

Harriet knew when to quit. 'If you think of any relevant information, please get in touch.' She carefully placed one of her business cards on the table in front of her. She didn't risk handing it to either Anthony or Drew, in case they handed it right back. 'We won't take up any more of your time.'

As she left, she wondered if Milla might stay behind but the other woman seemed as eager to leave.

Harriet walked towards Sam's car, waiting until Milla was out of earshot, and then dialled Ben's number.

She gave him a quick update, finishing with, 'We really need to interview David Griffiths.'

'His name has come up before,' Ben said, 'and he has alibis for both incidents – he was officiating at a funeral in Calahurst yesterday – but it won't hurt to talk to him again. Ask him to come into the station for an interview with you and Sam.'

'Sure,' Harriet said. 'How did you get on with Drew Elliott?'

'I'm about to speak with him now,' Ben said.

'Oh, are you? OK, I'll see you later.'

Ben disconnected and Harriet slid her phone into her jacket, completely confused.

Because on the other side of the yard, Drew Elliott was leaning against the exterior wall, his arms folded, watching her intently.

TWENTY-EIGHT

Ben stood on the pavement outside Kieran Drake Investigations and looked up at the grey, Georgian house. He'd met Drake on three separate occasions. On two occasions he'd been beaten up – with minimum effort on Drake's part – which was why he couldn't quite bring himself to go inside.

As well as being a private detective, Drake was a fixer for wealthy, powerful men like Milla's father. So why deliberately poke a poisonous snake? He must be insane.

He should have brought his team with him and interviewed Drake properly. Agreed with Harriet that the man in their security footage had a limp, which would have been 'reasonable suspicion' to effect an arrest. He could have 'invited' Drake to attend the station, voluntarily, for interview. What he should *not* have done was arrive here unofficially and on his own.

Bloody idiot.

Knowing Drake and his love of surveillance (it was his job, after all) he must be already watching Ben and laughing his Converse trainers off.

Ben should leave. He should definitely leave.

No good would come of this. Drake would lie to his face or

set a highly paid solicitor on to him. He should drive back to the station while he still had his dignity.

Why was he still standing here?

'Excuse me? May I pass?'

'Of course.' Ben obediently stepped to one side. 'I'm sorry.'

'Thank you. Would you like to come upstairs for a coffee like a civilised person or would you prefer to stand there and brood?'

Damn.

'Hello, Mr Drake,' Ben said.

'Mr, eh? We are feeling formal today. Come up, have a coffee. Or a tea. You look like a tea drinker.'

What was *that* supposed to mean?

He followed Drake. He could hardly do anything else.

The man very subtly favoured his left leg. He'd once been a detective sergeant at Raven's Edge, a good six or seven years ago, but had been shot on duty, hence the limp, and invalided out. A regular hero, now working in the private sector doing heaven knew what, because Kieran Drake Investigations was definitely a front for something darker, Ben was sure of it.

'Morning, Esme,' Drake called to his secretary. 'I found this reprobate lurking on the pavement, so hold my calls and order in two coffees, please.'

'Yes, Mr Drake,' Esme said.

Reprobate? Drake looked like a tramp, brawled like a cage fighter, often talked like a teenager – and then used words like *reprobate*. Sometimes he could be remarkably helpful. Other times he was a complete pain in the arse. It was that constant shift that was so unnerving – like trying to get a grip on fog.

Drake waited until the door shut and then dropped into his chair, steepling his fingers as he glared at Ben.

Ben didn't need to have taken a body language course to know what *that* meant.

'What can I do for you this time, Detective Inspector? By my reckoning, you're all out of favours.'

Two could play at that game.

'Thank you for my present,' he said, sitting without being asked, leaning back and making himself comfortable – or look comfortable, at least.

Drake's scowl deepened. 'No idea what you're talking about. Is it your birthday? Many happy returns. I'd have sent out for cake and balloons if I'd known.'

Why did the man have to be so *irritating*?

'Raquel. Marsh's. Head,' Ben said. 'Gift-wrapped.' Or as near as.

Drake's expression didn't alter. 'Help me out here. Who is Raquel Marsh?'

No surprise or consternation that Ben had received a head in a box?

'Raquel's corpse was stolen from the mortuary at Norchester and desecrated. We found her body beside Meg's Pond on the 28th October. Today, the head was delivered to Raven's Edge Police Station in a medical box addressed to me.'

'Someone's been watching too many movies,' Drake drawled. 'Not sure why you've come to ask me about it, but I'm sure you have everything in hand.'

'We also have footage of you entering the police station and leaving said box on the counter.'

Checkmate.

Again, not a flicker of change in Drake's expression. 'Do you now? That was mighty careless of me.'

Had it been that easy?

'You admit it?'

A flash of irritation, then Drake's palm hit his desk. 'Of course I don't admit it! I have no idea what you're talking about. I've never done anything other than operate within the law, as you know very well. I'm tired of these baseless accusations. If you believe I'm guilty of something, then charge me with it.'

It was interesting to note how his accent became more refined when he was under pressure. Most people went the other way.

'Tell me where you found the head, Drake. If you didn't have anything to do with the stunt at Meg's Pond, are you helping someone else? Lorcan Black? He's Drew's cousin and Drew is one of your clients.'

'Lorcan's also your cousin, and is nothing confidential these days? Come in!' he shouted, in response to a knock.

Esme entered, carrying a tray with two coffees on it, apparently delivered from the local bakery rather than made by Esme herself, because the cups were cardboard and emblazoned with the familiar blue yacht logo.

'Black coffee for DI Taylor,' Esme said, placing it in front of him. 'Flat white for you, Mr Drake, and a box of iced doughnuts. I wasn't sure which flavour DI Taylor liked, so I bought a selection.'

'Thanks, Esme. I certainly need the caffeine. DI Taylor is being particularly trying this morning.'

Chilled, Ben stared at his own coffee. How did Esme (and by default, Drake) know how he took his coffee? What else did they know about him?

'Cheers,' Drake said, lifting his coffee. 'Doughnut? Watch out for the hazelnut ones, they stick in your teeth.'

Ben counted to ten inside his head.

'How did you become involved?' he asked, after Esme had left. 'This isn't you. It's too macabre. Give me a name and I'll leave you alone.'

'Or you'll make life difficult for me? You need to work on the calibre of your threats, Detective Inspector. You have to make it sound as if you mean it.'

'Someone has got it in for my family—'

'*Your* family?' The mocking note was back. 'Since when have you cared about any of the Elliotts? Half the time you pretend you're not even related.'

'Someone could get seriously hurt.'

Drake stared at him, silent.

'No smart comeback?' Ben taunted. 'Perhaps I'm finally getting through to you?'

'I can't help you,' Drake said, 'but I'll tell you this and you can owe me. While you're wasting time with me, the real perpetrator is planning his next move. He's having far too much fun to give it up and you're naively following his playbook. Didn't they teach you anything at police college? You put him on television! Pathological narcissists love that.'

'Not intentionally!'

'The only thing you did right was to play everything down, but now he'll want to up his game. You're right. Someone could end up getting killed. Give up on me, give up on Raquel, and concentrate on finding this highwayman. He's the one you really want.'

Drake was right, Ben reflected, as he walked back down the stairs to street level. They'd become too hung up on Raquel. It was the classic murder investigation technique: look at the life of the victim. As she hadn't been murdered, it wasn't applicable.

Drake never revealed his clients or his sources but he was an ex-detective sergeant and knew Ben could obtain a warrant and search his office. He must feel fairly confident Ben wouldn't find anything but he was certainly protecting someone. One of his clients? Or someone off-the-record, as a 'favour'?

The most logical person would be Lorcan, who had already been found covered in blood in the church, but one thing Ben still didn't understand was why Raquel's head had been removed in the first place. Not from her body – that was to draw attention to the similarities with the highwayman legend and the connection to the Elliott family. The logical place for the head to have been left would have been in the church beside Lorcan or somewhere in the farmhouse.

That was it!

He stopped to collect his thoughts, only for the person behind to cannon straight into him.

'Look where you're going, mate!'

'Sorry!' He stepped to one side and leant against the railing, leaving the tourists to flow along the harbour path unobstructed, while he tried to untangle each thread connected with the case. What if the highwayman had not hidden Raquel's head but left it in plain sight? Somewhere that would be easily found; an obvious location to be searched, nailing the coffin on Lorcan's guilt.

The farmhouse.

Discovering the head in a property owned by Lorcan would have been irrefutable evidence.

Who had access to the farmhouse, apart from Lorcan?

The estate agency, the removal company, the cleaners... and Milla.

'*What did you talk about? You were in his bedroom for a good ten minutes.*'

'*His hummingbirds. He was upset that the police had seized them.*'

'*Hummingbirds?*'

'*Stuffed ones, in a specimen jar. Little birds, about this big.*'

'*I know what hummingbirds are. I was present when the CSI performed their search. I don't remember seeing a glass jar or any stuffed hummingbirds.*'

Milla and Lorcan were old friends. What was the betting that she'd found the head inside an antique specimen jar – the one that had previously held Lorcan's beloved hummingbirds – at the farmhouse the night before Lorcan had been found on that grave. She'd panicked, understandably, wanting to protect her friend... and yet she'd called *Drake*?

Instead of him?

He was surprised at the depth of the pain that shot through him.

Why would she do that?

She didn't *trust* him and it wasn't hard to work out why. He was a police detective and she'd never had much faith in the police. She wanted to save Lorcan (and herself) from possible arrest. It was understandable, it really was.

Keep telling yourself that.

A seagull swooped low and snatched a bag of chips right out of a tourist's hand. The tourist cursed and waved his fist, and Ben realised he'd been gripping the harbour rail so hard that his knuckles were turning white. He released it and found flakes of paint were now stuck to his palms.

There was one other question.

Why had Drake agreed to help Milla?

A favour for her powerful father or for Milla herself?

And why was Drake so determined to keep her secret that he was willing to risk losing everything?

The Elliott Farmhouse was in darkness. Benedict led the horse, with Will slumped on its back, into the yard. A few years ago, when their grandfather had been alive, this yard had been a hectic place, busy with horses, grooms and stable hands. Then he'd died and Liam had bought the place from his brothers, with his usual swagger and boasts of how the stables would soon be the largest in the King's Forest District.

Curious how seldom these things go to plan.

There were other, more central riding stables, with owners who were popular and didn't over-charge, staff that were friendly, horses that weren't poorly trained and cruelly treated. Why visit the Elliotts? Loyal customers began to spend their money elsewhere.

Now the yard was empty, save for a broken-down Land Rover and a small white lorry with 'Removals' written along the side. Slates had blown from the stable roof and not been replaced, rotting conker shells littered the once pristine cobblestones, and weeds grew through the cracks and gaps. It was a sad and lonely place. Benedict's grandfather would have turned in his grave.

Benedict had never much liked his uncle, so he was pleased Liam's green Mondeo was not parked in its usual spot. None of the lights were on either. Were both of Will's parents out?

He tried the back door. It was unlocked but that was not unusual. There weren't many who were brave enough to rob an Elliott.

Tying the horse to a drainpipe, Benedict helped Will into the house. Usually, he'd see to the horse first (one of his grandfather's rules), but he had to ensure Will was OK. His cousin had stopped throwing up some time ago and appeared to be more sober. To be on the safe side, Benedict made him drink half a glass of water, and left him tucked up in bed, while Benedict returned down-stairs, watched by the glassy eyes of the stuffed stag heads, the creaks of the ancient floorboards the only sound.

This place gave him the chills.

The key to the stables was always left hanging from the beak of a stuffed raven on the sideboard in the hall.

Tonight, when Benedict swiped beneath the raven's beak, his hand came up empty.

The key had gone.

Someone had got there before him.

TWENTY-NINE

Milla arrived home from the livery yard to find a handwritten note from Granny Brianna, summoning her to a cocktail party at Hartfell to thank the Carnival Committee for their hard work. It was worded in an affectionate tone but with the distinct implication that the only acceptable reason to decline would be severe illness or death.

Perhaps she could encourage Ben to come with her, for moral support?

She dialled his number and he answered immediately.

'Hi, Ben!'

'Hello, Milla. How are you?'

His satnav was speaking in the background, so he must be driving. Did he have someone with him too? He sounded so... cool, so formal. It was unsettling.

'Granny Brianna has invited me to a cocktail party tonight,' she said. 'Would you like to come?'

Even the poor signal couldn't hide his heavy sigh. 'When were you going to tell me about the head?'

'Head? What head?'

Lying, even to Ben, was shockingly instinctive.

'The one you found at the Elliott Farmhouse,' he said. 'I'm theorising here, but it might have been in an old specimen jar?'

How the *hell* had he known that?

She stared at the phone in horror.

Then instinctively disconnected, heart pounding.

She'd cut Ben off!

Way to go to make it worse.

What must he be thinking?

That she was as guilty as hell.

Could she blame the poor signal?

Not really.

Did that mean he was going to arrest her? Was that why he'd sounded so odd?

That, and the fact he'd discovered she'd lied to him.

Was he driving here *right now*?

In which case, she really needed to leave.

If DI Taylor wanted to take her into police custody, he would have to find her first.

Hartfell was the Graham family's 'public' house, where they held meetings and parties; they rarely lived there. It was very modern, all symmetrical cubes of grey stone, slate and obsidian glass, and located in the centre of a man-made lake with only an elegant footbridge for access. Milla could hear the music as soon as she got out of her car and, despite the chill October evening, people were already spilling out onto the decking surrounding the house.

It was just as busy inside. Waiters moved deftly through the throng, carrying trays of strangely coloured cocktails, and the glass table in the dining room was covered in platters of bite-sized snacks. Her stomach rumbled. When was the last time she'd eaten?

She had one hand poised over a plate of miniature sandwiches when a familiar voice made her turn.

'Camilla, darling, I'm so pleased to see you!'

Milla froze and slowly turned. Brianna Graham was the
matriarch of the Graham family and, quite frankly, terrifying.
She was taller than Milla by nearly a foot, and wore her long
grey hair braided around her head like a crown. Despite her age
(seventy something? Milla had never liked to ask) it would be
easy to imagine Brianna defending Hartfell against siege, and
her influence over Raven's Edge was almost feudal. The strange
thing was, none of the villagers seemed to mind.

'Hi, Granny.'

'Where's that delightful young man of yours?'

'Ben? I'm hoping he'll be along later.'

She hoped he wouldn't. Arresting her in front of her grandmother wouldn't go well for any of them.

'Hmm... Well, I'm glad you could make it. I've hardly seen
you at all this week.' Her grandmother pressed a bowl-shaped
glass into her hand, giving her a sideways hug at the same time.
'Strawberry gin cocktail from your father's distillery. It's a
brand-new line. You must tell me what you think.'

They had a *distillery*?

Milla peered into the glass, clocking the strawberries, rasp-
berries... and what appeared to be dried rose petals on top.
'Would you prefer something polite or the honest truth?'

'The truth, darling, I expect nothing less.' Granny Brianna
turned to the man beside her. 'Have you met my granddaughter,
Camilla Graham?'

'I'm Milla.' She held out her hand, and then realised it was
David shaking it. 'Hello, again.' Standing beside him was a stunning redhead with very blue eyes. She looked like a movie star
in her 30s-inspired lavender dress. 'You must be David's sister,
Rose?'

They were so similar it was an easy deduction to make.

'Have a gin cocktail, Rose,' Granny Brianna said, swiping two more from a passing waiter. She handed Rose a tall glass of striped cream and purple liquid, with a sprig of lavender sticking out of the top. 'Lavender lemon, to match your beautiful dress.'

Rose took it, somewhat bemused. 'Thank you.'

'For you, dear vicar,' – Granny Brianna handed over a short, chunky glass – 'toffee and sour apple. Enjoy!' she said, before gliding away.

David's cocktail had apple slices on top, sprinkled with cinnamon. He regarded it dubiously.

'You don't have to drink it if you don't want to,' Milla told him.

'After the day I've had, I probably need it.' He raised it to his lips and took a tentative sip. 'Actually, it's not bad...' He promptly drained it.

'That did contain real gin. Two shots, I should think.'

'It was delicious.' He peered into the glass. 'Should I eat the apple too?'

'That's garnish, darling.' Rose removed the glass from his hand and handed it to a passing waitress. 'Have mine,' she said. 'I'm driving, so I can't drink.'

'There ought to be soft drinks...' Milla put her own glass down on the table, but was distracted by David knocking back the second cocktail as quickly as the first. 'Nice?'

'It was... interesting.'

Rose frowned. 'He doesn't usually drink like this.'

'It's been a tough day,' David said. 'I've spent an hour at the police station trying to remember my exact whereabouts for the past week, because the local constabulary suspect me of moonlighting as a highwayman. No idea what put that in their heads, other than someone has it in for the Elliott family and I'm their best fit.'

'But you're the *vicar!*' Rose spluttered.

'Yet not above suspicion. The police are interviewing anyone with a grudge against the Elliott family. It wasn't hard to work out because there was a whole line of people waiting to go into the interview room after me, including faces I recognised from the security depot where Dad worked, all those years ago.'

Rose glanced nervously at Milla, and then lowered her voice. 'You did make it clear that Dad was forced into helping those men?'

'We don't know that.'

'They threatened you! What was Dad supposed to do?'

'It wasn't like that.' David stared unhappily into his empty glass. 'No one was going to hurt me. They wouldn't have harmed a kid.'

'How else were they going to make Dad do what they wanted?'

'Apparently you remember that night better than me.'

'The police are only interviewing you because they have to be seen to be doing something and they don't have a clue. They've been interviewing everyone at the hospital – that's where I work,' she told Milla. 'Someone stole a *corpse*, can you believe it? They broke into the mortuary, stole the body of a woman, chopped her head off and left her beside the village pond. Now they think one of us is responsible. Bloody idiots.'

No sympathy for the victim, Milla noticed, and the only person allowed to call Ben an idiot was herself.

Wait a moment...

One of *us*? She'd thought Rose was a nurse!

'Do you work in the mortuary?'

The hum of conversation around them quietened.

'Yes,' Rose said. 'I'm an anatomical pathology technician. That means I help carry out post-mortems, collect tissue samples and specimens, remove organs...'

Remove heads?

Did Ben know what Rose did for a living – and, more

importantly, *where* she did it? The police had questioned David, but had they thought to look at his sister, Rose? Why not? Because she was a woman?

Nearby guests edged closer, eager to hear more.

Milla could work this to her advantage.

She assumed a suitably awed expression. 'Do you help solve crimes?'

'That would be the remit of the forensic pathologist, Caroline Warner, but yes, I help her too.'

'It must be *fascinating* work.'

'It can also be mundane. I clean equipment, I record findings, I sterilise instruments; routine things like that.'

'It sounds so interesting!'

'My brother wanted me to be a *florist*.' Rose poked David's shoulder and he rolled his eyes good-naturedly. 'But I like working alone and I'm inherently nosy. I love a puzzle!'

'You could have been a detective...'

Rose laughed. 'I'd have made a very good detective – better than the current ones!'

David frowned but there was murmured agreement behind him.

More people had drawn closer, hanging on her every word.

'The police still haven't found that highwayman,' Rose added, slightly louder. Playing to her audience? 'How hard could it be? It makes you wonder what they do all day.'

Despite deliberately steering the conversation in this direction, Milla found her fingernails curling into her palms. How dare she? Ben worked harder than anyone she knew. When was the last time he'd taken leave?

Concentrate!

The last person to have seen Lorcan after he'd left The Drop was an unknown woman.

Could she have been Rose?

How had Sorcha described her?

'*He made friends with a woman. Dark hair, blue eyes, my height. Very much like me, but not me.*'

Rose was tall and had blue eyes. Her hair was red but anyone could wear a wig.

Milla itched to call Ben, but would he even answer his phone?

Harriet, then?

She had to tell *someone*!

Rose couldn't be allowed to get away with this.

Someone else spoke, an elderly gentleman that Milla didn't recognise. 'The detective in charge, he's one of the Elliotts, isn't he? Even though he calls himself something else.'

'That's right,' the woman beside him said. 'His father died in prison. What were the police thinking, making the son of a man like that an *inspector*?'

'When you come down to it,' the older gentleman was saying, 'the police are all a bunch of crooks.'

Gritting her teeth, Milla turned back to Rose and changed her scowl into her sweetest smile.

'If the police are interviewing everyone who has a grudge against the Elliott family, won't that include you, Rose?'

The other woman shifted, her gaze darting towards the door. 'I've never met any of the Elliott family.'

'Didn't I hear you say that your father helped plan the robbery on the security depot?'

'No,' Rose glared at David. 'My darling brother said that.'

'Weren't you there that night, taken hostage with David? You said the Elliott brothers murdered your father.' *One more, below the belt.* 'Did they kill him in front of you?'

Milla waited, let others draw the conclusion.

If anyone had a grudge against the Elliott family, it might be...

You could have heard a dust mote hit the ground, let alone the proverbial pin.

A buzz of excited whispers broke out.

'The police said the manager was in on it. He was her father.'

'Do you think...?'

'Could she be...?'

Could she be *what*? Milla willed. Come on, someone say it!

Was she going to have to say it for them?

Rose Griffiths was the highwayman.

On the other side of the room, Granny Brianna was frowning. She knew something was up, that trouble was brewing, and she'd guessed Milla was somehow at the root of it.

David shook his head. 'That's unfair, Milla. Rose was ten years old. She suffered enough trauma that night without witnessing our father's death.'

He was the only one who thought so. The other guests were drawing away, as though guilt was somehow contagious, creating a circle of shame with the three of them in the centre.

While David had been completely honest about his father's criminal past, even to the point of including it in his inspirational school talks, Rose, apparently, wanted to keep it a secret.

A secret Milla had just announced to the world.

For a moment Rose stood completely still, hearing the whispers but not reacting, her pretty face as white as death.

Then she turned and fled.

The guests began talking again, louder this time, not bothering to be discreet, dredging up all the old gossip about the Elliott and Griffiths families.

David wasn't listening. He stared worriedly after his sister, and then pushed his way through the crowd to follow her.

Milla hesitated. Could Rose *really* be the highwayman? She was tall (although everyone was tall from Milla's point of view) but slight. Milla couldn't imagine her on a horse, swinging a broadsword.

Had she made a terrible mistake?

She took out her phone and sent Ben a text.

> Have you interviewed Rose Griffiths? She's
> David's sister and works in the mortuary at the
> hospital.

It failed to send.

Hartfell, in the middle of the forest, had no phone signal, despite being owned by one of the richest men in the country. She felt like stamping her foot.

Instead, she walked back through into the main hall, waving her phone about, opening the front door and going down the stone steps. The phone beeped a 'sent' notification before she reached the bottom.

She waited, staring at the phone, willing a response, muttering, 'Come on, Ben...' but there was no reply.

'Rose doesn't like anyone knowing,' a voice behind her said.

David was leaning against the wall, half-hidden by a holly tree in a large slate pot. She must have walked right past him – and now he knew she was in contact with Ben.

'I'm sorry,' she lied, sliding her phone back into her pocket. 'You're so open about your family history. I assumed Rose was the same. She seemed happy enough to talk about it earlier.'

David pushed away from the wall and came down the two steps to stand beside her.

'Rose appears to be confident, but the reality is she's very shy and suffers from social anxiety – another reason I suspect she chose pathology over floristry.'

'I didn't mean to upset her.'

'Yes, you did. She was bad-mouthing Ben Taylor, who I guess is your boyfriend? It was your way of getting revenge.'

How petty that made her sound, but at least he missed out the part about publicly accusing Rose of attempted murder.

David sighed. 'Unfortunately, Rose appears to have forgotten that she gave me a lift here tonight.'

That's why he was standing on the doorstep. 'You're stranded?'

'I was about to call an Uber.'

He'd lived in a city for too long. 'I don't think Ubers have made it as far as Raven's Edge, and I'm pretty sure we only have one taxi in the entire village. Why don't I give you a lift home?'

'You've been drinking,' was his dry response.

'I don't drink alcohol. I only took the glass to humour my grandmother.'

'Then, yes. If it's not too much trouble, I would love a lift to the church. I left my car parked in The Square. I was planning to catch up on some work this evening.'

'You're going to write a sermon after knocking back two double gins?'

'The church accounts, actually.'

'I'm saying nothing.'

'That would be lovely,' he said, 'because I'm starting to get a really bad headache and I'm pretty sure I know what caused it.'

THIRTY

David was silent on the drive back to Raven's Edge, staring out of the window, his fingers tapping on the arm rest. Milla knew better than to engage him in conversation. She'd done enough damage this evening. She'd outed his sister as the daughter of a criminal and implied Rose had attacked Ben with a sword. Pretty good going, even for her.

Would the gossip spread from the party to the village?

Undoubtedly.

What if Rose *wasn't* the highwayman?

It didn't bear thinking about.

Ben hadn't replied to her message, although any response would be incredibly awkward with David sitting right next to her.

She pulled into the lay-by beside the church, behind David's blue estate car. She hoped he wasn't planning on driving it this evening.

'Thanks for the lift.' He fumbled for the door handle without even glancing at her. 'I'll see you around.'

Very likely, because she lived right opposite the church. She didn't point that out though. Instead, she did a U-turn and

parked down the alley beside her house, and was about to get
out when something moved in the shadows ahead of her.

Was someone there? The alley didn't lead anywhere except
for a six-foot fence and the forest that grew right up against it.

Could it be Drake? Wanting to make another point?

She got out of the car. 'Hey, Drake? You really need to get
over yourself!'

The reply was a steady clop, clop, clop.

That sound alone was enough to send a cold shiver through
her.

The *highwayman*? That was *impossible*!

There was no way Rose had the time to return home,
change her clothes, and paint her face in that intricate skull
design Milla had seen on TV. Yet here was the reality right in
front of her, a horse emerging from the shadows, moving slowly,
purposefully, and directly towards her, the rider entirely in
black.

Her first instinct was to run, but she was on the wrong side
of her car and, even if she could make it to her front door, it was
locked and would take too long to open, leaving her exposed.

What if she moved into the gap between her car and the
wall of her house? He'd find it hard to reach her there, unless he
dismounted – or climbed on top of her car and attacked her
from above.

Why did she *always* have to imagine the worst-case
scenario?

Slowly, carefully, without taking her eyes from the shadowy
figure, she slid behind her car and into the gap, stabbing 999 on
her phone.

'Emergency. Which service?'

She was too distracted by the highwayman to answer.

'Do you need police, fire or ambulance?'

Milla lifted the phone to her mouth. 'Police. The Square.
Raven's Edge. There's a man with a sword—'

She screamed as the highwayman swung said sword in her direction, smashing it into the window of her car and shattering it.

'Ma'am? Are you OK? We're sending assistance. They should be with you shortly. Please stay on the line.'

The highwayman was now between her and her front door. 'I'm not going anywhere—' She screamed again as the blade slashed in her direction. 'But hurry!'

Crouching behind the car, she heard the horse walk up the alleyway and into The Square. She risked a peep through the shattered rear window. Did he think she wasn't worth his time? That was fine by her.

Hardly daring to believe her luck, she eased out from her hiding place and ran to her front door, her key already in her hand... and then remembered David. Was he outside the church? Walking through the graveyard, unaware of the danger coming up behind him?

Again, her head helpfully ran through a series of possible scenarios, none of them good.

Damn, damn, damn. She could hardly leave him on his own.

Giving the door a frustrated kick, she ran to the corner of the alley and peered into The Square, in time to see the highwayman riding towards David. As she'd guessed, David was retrieving a box from the boot of his car, completely oblivious to what was happening behind him.

The moonlight glinted on the sword as the highwayman lifted it high.

'David!'

He turned his head, frowning as he saw the horse coming towards him.

Why didn't he move? Didn't he know the danger he was in? Was he in shock?

Milla patted her pockets for any kind of a weapon and came up with nothing but her phone. She ran forward and threw it.

Everything happened in slow motion.

David staggered back against the car parked in front of his own. The alarm went off, screeching shrilly into the night, and Milla's phone hit the flank of the horse.

It reared in fright, almost throwing the highwayman, who had to struggle to control it.

He was a good rider, she'd give him that, except now she'd drawn his attention, she realised exactly how vulnerable she was standing on her own in the centre of The Square with no weapon and now no phone.

Gradually, she became aware of soft, murmuring voices. Her fellow residents had emerged to see what all the noise was about.

Yet now he had an engaged audience, the highwayman swung around and rode back down the alley, passing Milla as he went. She wished she'd kept her phone; she could have taken a photo. He wore the same clothes as last time but, instead of the black and white skull make-up, there was a black feathered mask covering the top half of his face.

The mask would save time on the face painting, but wasn't that the same one Lorcan had worn on the cover of his *Raven King* album?

Which meant...

No, it couldn't be.

'*Lorcan?*'

The highwayman glanced back and laughed, disappearing back into the shadows. It would have been a neat vanishing trick, except now they all knew there was a route through Fliss and Elvira's garden into the forest.

David ran over to her. 'Did he hurt you? Are you OK?'

'I'm fine.'

'Was it a prank like last time? Did he film it?'

'*He* didn't need to.' She pointed to the residents around the edge of The Square, their phones raised as though watching a free show. 'He has them to do it for him – creating an event designed purely to humiliate us.'

'You think we've been targeted deliberately?' David paled and took out his own phone. 'I'm calling the police.'

'Ask for DI Taylor or DS March. Tell them the high-wayman is heading towards the farmhouse.'

David keyed in 999 and then held out his phone. 'Can't you tell them?'

'No, because I won't be here.' She scooped up her own phone and ran down the alley, ignoring the familiar shout of 'Milla!' behind her.

Milla ran through the forest on fury and adrenalin. It took two trips over tree roots to remember to turn on the torch on her phone, which had miraculously survived being thrown across The Square with only one crack across the screen.

She'd accidently cut off the emergency services when her phone had hit the road, but the signal was non-existent in the forest anyway. At no point could she see the black horse in front of her but she didn't need to. Whoever was on its back, they were returning to the farmhouse – because that was the only place this path led – joining with the path to Meg's Pond and on to the coastal road.

Twenty minutes later and she was standing outside the Elliott Farmhouse. There was no sign of a horse and the only light shone in the kitchen window. Milla shouldered open the back door, which wasn't locked, and barged into the kitchen. She wasn't sure what she expected to see, but it certainly wasn't Lorcan wearing yellow joggers and an old *Raven King* tour T-shirt, sitting on a bar stool and eating pepperoni pizza straight out of the box.

'Hi, Milla! Is everything OK?'

'No, everything is *not* OK. How dare you scare everyone with your stupid pranks, just to get publicity for your album?'

'What album? I've not written a thing. Not one song, despite spending hours on the bloody thing... Wait, "scare everyone"? What do you think I've done?'

'Where's the horse?'

'What horse? Milla, you're not making any sense!'

'Is it in the stables? Give me the key.'

As she strode towards him and flung her hand out, something large and black flew from the top of a cupboard and landed on the counter between them. A raven, all flapping wings and rusty croaks, waddled towards her, snapping its beak.

'Whoa!' She took a step back. 'What the *hell*...?'

Lorcan stroked the bird's back, firmly soothing the feathers. 'Calm down, Eddie. It's only Milla. She won't hurt you.'

Eddie?

'You keep a raven... as a *pet*?'

'Eddie's a wild bird. He comes and goes as he pleases.'

If the raven hadn't hopped onto his shoulder, she might have believed him.

'Eddie, this is my friend Milla. Milla, this is Eddie. I expect you both to play nice.'

The raven eyed her beadily.

The feeling was mutual.

'Let's start again,' Lorcan said. 'Milla, I'm assuming the highwayman made another appearance in the village?'

'You attacked David!'

'The vicar? Is he OK?'

'He's fine, no thanks to you.'

'It wasn't *me*. I've been here all evening. I ordered a pizza.' He indicated the box. 'It arrived less than five minutes ago. It's still warm. Check it and see. Would you like a slice?'

She glanced at the box. 'You could have reheated it.'

Although he didn't look like a man who'd ridden from Raven's Edge, stabled a horse, changed his clothes and reheated a pizza.

'OK, so you're working with Rose. Where is she?'

Lorcan peeled off a slither of pepperoni and held it up for the bird. 'Rose who?'

'The vicar's sister!'

'Oh, yes. I remember her. Redhead. The two of them came to visit the day I moved in. I was looking for somewhere to have dinner that night, and Rose recommended The Drop.'

'I bet she did. Did you meet her there?'

'No, I met someone else.'

'Who?'

He grimaced. 'That's the problem. The police want to know and I can't remember.'

Sure he couldn't.

In the distance, a toilet flushed.

'Rose?'

'No, not Rose! Someone else.' Lorcan sighed. 'Ironic, really. Since I moved to Raven's Edge for the peace and quiet, all I've done is entertain visitors.'

The door opened. Milla took a step back, clenching her phone, although the chance of her hitting an intended target twice in one evening was probably remote.

A man the same age as Ben walked through the door, wearing a suit. He looked very much like... a detective?

'Hi, Pete,' Lorcan said, 'this is Milla. Milla, this is DC Pete Kershaw from Calahurst Police Station. He's been tasked with keeping me safe, along with DC Freddie Kuang. I thought they might be getting cold in their car outside, so I invited them in for pizza. I'm assuming you can't have a beer, Pete, as you're on duty? How about a cola?' He pushed a can towards him.

'Great,' Pete said, walking up to the counter. 'Is mine the barbecue chicken?'

It was as though she'd strayed into a parallel universe. She looked again at the counter. Saw three pizza boxes, a pack of garlic bread and another box of chicken pieces – far too much for one person.

'I saw him, Lorcan,' she said. 'He was coming here. This is the only place that path leads to.'

Apart from Meg's Pond, but why would the highwayman go there?

'What path?' Another stranger in a suit had joined them. 'Ooh, is that my meat feast? Brilliant!'

'There's an alley beside my house, opposite the church in the village,' she said. 'It's a dead end, but in the old days, it must have been a road that led here.'

'That makes sense,' Lorcan nodded. 'I've always said the farmhouse would have been an important place when it was originally built, perhaps even a manor house.'

'The highwayman *must* be here. I don't understand where he's gone. Come on, Lorcan! Help me! Where would you hide a horse? I mean, the obvious place is the stables…'

The three men froze, and then exchanged glances.

'Ben thought the highwayman was using the stables,' Lorcan said slowly. 'One night he turned up to search it, but didn't find anything.'

'The highwayman must be here now, and you two,' – she glared at the DCs – 'are supposed to be guarding the house!'

'We're guarding *him*,' Pete pointed to Lorcan. '*Not* the house.'

'I'm calling it in.' Freddie pulled out his phone.

'Meanwhile,' Milla said, 'don't either of you care that he's getting away?'

'Our job is to keep Mr Black safe.'

She spun on her heel. 'Luckily it's not my job.'

'Miss?' Pete ran after her. 'I strongly advise you to stay indoors.'

Milla paid him no attention whatsoever, wrenching open the back door and stepping into the night.

It was impossible to run diagonally from the house because the new garden had been landscaped in an Elizabethan style, with silly little gravel paths in a starburst pattern, lined with box hedging. She couldn't take a short cut, due to the shrubs, and was forced to take the long way around. As she arrived at the stables, the door opened and a man in black came out, a feathered mask in one hand and a sword in the other.

For a moment they stared at each other, equally shocked.

'Oh, hell,' he said, and sprinted right towards the orchard, presumably hoping he'd lose Milla amongst the long grass and trees.

Bother that. She hurled herself at him, wrapping her arms around his waist and bringing him down.

There was a satisfying crunch as he hit the gravel path, swearing volubly, but before she could do anything else, someone dragged her off him and held her back.

'Let me go!' She heard a grunt as she elbowed her captor in the ribs.

Followed by, 'For goodness' sake, Milla! I'm trying to help you!'

'*Ben?*'

Harriet and Pete hauled the highwayman to his feet, wrenching his hands behind his back to cuff him.

Ben released Milla, who promptly darted forward and yanked at the highwayman's ponytail. He swore and pulled away from her – leaving his hair in her hand and him in a weird skullcap thing.

He'd been wearing a wig.

Ben stared at him in disbelief. '*Rose Griffiths?*'

'Told you so,' said Milla.

Benedict untied the horse and led it across the yard towards the stables, its hooves clattering over the cobblestones and echoing back to him.

It was so, so quiet.

And yet... could he hear voices?

He stopped and shh-ed the horse, which nudged his shoulder and then his pocket, seeking treats.

Half-hidden by the chestnut tree in the centre of the yard was a patch of illuminated cobblestones. He led the horse towards it and then looked up.

The stable door was open and the light flooded through.

Had Uncle Liam returned? But why the stables, rather than the house?

Benedict was tempted to tie the horse to the tree and leave, but his grandfather would never have forgiven him, so he crept towards the stables, as quietly as he could leading a horse that weighed nearly half a ton, pausing on the threshold.

The horse nudged his shoulder, pushing him forward.

The carriage house was in darkness but the stables were fully lit and, at the far end, four men were arguing violently. Three were wearing black – highwaymen costumes, similar to the ones he and his cousins had worn earlier that day. None wore masks but, although they had their backs to him, he recognised his father and two uncles.

Who else in Raven's Edge had that height and distinctive blond hair?

The fourth man was sitting on an upturned barrel, head in his hands. 'You bastard, Liam,' he muttered. 'You utter bastard.'

'You still going on about that? Seriously, man. Grow a pair.'

The horse shoved Benedict again, apparently eager to be home, but he ducked into the darkness of the carriage house and allowed the horse to wander into a stall, its hooves muffled by the straw. The men were now shouting so loudly they didn't notice, not even when Benedict tripped over a crate and crashed painfully onto his knees.

In his grandfather's time the carriage house had been crammed with boxes that wouldn't fit in the attic, but one of the first things Liam had done was chuck everything into a skip. So where had these crates come from?

Benedict lifted the lid of the nearest, then dropped it just as quickly.

Cash? Wads and wads of cash?

He took another look.

What the...?

He picked one up. Ran his finger over the coloured plastic. How much was in one of these? And there were crates of the stuff!

He did the maths.

Millions?

Where had it come from?

The horse whinnied, perhaps indignant about finding its trough empty, and kicked the stall.

His uncles turned as one.

'Who's there?' Liam shouted. 'Show yourself!'

Not bloody likely.

Benedict dropped the money and ran, closing and locking the stable door behind him, and pocketing the key.

THIRTY-ONE

Harriet knew she should never judge by appearances (Ben had nagged her about it often enough), but Rose Griffiths was so good at playing innocent even she was starting to believe they'd make a mistake arresting her.

Was it her looks? Her pretty face? She was stunning; there was no doubt about it, and she'd behaved impeccably from the moment she'd been arrested. She'd thanked Ash for holding open a door, Sam for a cardboard cup of that horrible coffee from the machine, which she'd sipped without the slightest grimace. She'd even thanked the custody sergeant when he'd booked her in and relieved her of the feathered mask. They'd found a bunch of keys in her pocket, which Harriet had snagged back at the farmhouse, but no phone, unfortunately. Now Rose was sitting on the other side of the table in the interview room, her hands neatly placed on her lap, the only expression on her face polite interest, as though she were at some vicarage tea party.

She'd also declined a solicitor. 'I'm sure that won't be necessary, Detective Inspector,' she said to Ben, ignoring Harriet completely. 'Once we've had our chat, you'll realise this is a big misunderstanding.'

She beamed at them both.

Harriet gave Ben the side eye, but he seemed as baffled by Rose's behaviour as she was.

They began the interview. Harriet started the audio and visual, introduced herself and Ben, read the caution, and asked Rose to confirm her name and date of birth.

'Rose Griffiths, no middle name, and I was born on the 26th of June, which was why I was called "Rose", because when my mother brought me home from hospital the garden was full of pink roses. They were her favourite flower. She took it as a sign.'

Another talkative one. Interesting that she made no mention of her father, Michael Griffiths, although not unexpected.

'I'm twenty-five years old,' Rose added.

Five years younger than her brother, the vicar, and the same age as Harriet herself, although she seemed far younger, sweeter, almost innocent.

Harriet mentally shook herself. She was here to interview *Rose*, an anatomical pathology technician. Even if her hobbies did include watching Disney films and collecting Barbie dolls (Harriet hadn't got far enough to ask and it was hardly relevant), there was no way this woman was as blameless as she was presenting herself.

Presenting. Was that it?

Was Rose Griffiths a skilled actress?

It was something to check on. Someone with an interest in the theatre was more likely to have access to the highwayman costume she'd been wearing when they'd brought her in, and the retro red party dress Raquel's body had been dressed in, not to mention the sword, which Ben said was far too shiny to be an antique.

'What do you think of our coffee?' Harriet asked her.

(Number Two in the *Idiot's Guide to Interviewing Suspects*. Put them at their ease. Pretend to be nice.)

'Truthfully?' Rose said. 'A little bitter...' She winked at Ben, who looked as though he'd quite like the ground to swallow him whole.

OK, she was telling the truth.

Although they could have done without the wink.

'We need a new coffee machine,' Ben said. He hadn't quite worked out why Harriet was taking this approach to the interview but seemed happy to play along.

'Miss Griffiths,' she said, 'are you aware of why you are here?'

A tiny frown marred that perfect forehead. 'I'm not *entirely* sure, so I may have this wrong, but I do believe it's because I was rehearsing for the carnival, and Camilla Graham mistook me for the highwayman who's been terrorising the village. Understandable really. I don't blame her at all.'

'*Terrorising the village?* I'm not sure I'd go that far. What do you think, DI Taylor?'

Ben did not disappoint. 'The highwayman thing?' He shrugged. 'Just a prank. Silly juvenile behaviour.'

Rose's blue eyes darkened. 'I thought you seemed particularly terrified, Detective Inspector,' she said sweetly. 'The highwayman almost chopped your head off with that big sword of his.'

Ben shrugged. 'It wasn't much more than a toy. Wouldn't even cut paper.'

'It seemed quite sharp to me!'

'Why would you say that? Did you see it happen? Were you one of our witnesses?' He pretended to leaf through his notes.

'I saw the video on the news.'

Good point.

'It's difficult to cut a head off cleanly,' Harriet said, coming to his rescue. 'The blade has to be very sharp and the person wielding it, very strong.'

'This is all very interesting,' Rose said, 'although slightly macabre. I'm sorry to disappoint you, but I'm not that strong.' She lifted one arm in a classic 'strongman' pose.

She appeared perfectly toned to Harriet. She certainly hadn't obtained those biceps from lounging around in front of the television.

'Fortunately, a surgical saw will do it every time,' Harriet said. 'You work as an anatomical pathology technician in the mortuary at Norchester General, don't you?'

Rose raised her hand. 'Let me stop you there, if I may? I know where you're going with this, and I'm sorry to disappoint you, because you've obviously done lots of research, and good for you, but I was not responsible for the disappearance of Raquel Marsh's body from the mortuary. I've been interviewed by your colleagues, at least twice, and Caroline Warner, the forensic pathologist, will personally vouch for me.'

Name-dropper. Was that a dig at Ben? Did Rose know Caroline was his ex-wife?

They were jumping too far ahead and in danger of losing control of the dialogue.

Rose, the sweet and innocent, was running rings around them.

'Miss Griffiths.' Ben sighed. Even he sounded as though he was losing his cool. 'Why were you at Ravenswood House, dressed as a highwayman?'

'Ravenswood House?' Rose frowned again. 'Where's that?'

Did she know the house by its original name?

'Formerly known as the Elliott Farmhouse,' Harriet said.

'Oh, yes,' she said. 'I know where you mean. I was rehearsing for the carnival.'

'Do you have a part to play?'

'Yes, in the torchlight procession, later in the evening.

Although they've not trusted me with a flaming torch,' she laughed, self-deprecatingly, 'but I'm sure it'll be great fun.'

The torchlight procession was one of the highlights of the carnival. About thirty people from the local riding schools escorted the main procession through the village for a second time, carrying real flaming torches. It was supposed to represent Matthew Elliott's trip to the gallows, or something like that, but if one thought about it, it didn't make sense. Why would his escort also be dressed as highwaymen?

'Why choose the farmhouse to rehearse?'

'That was an accident,' Rose said. 'I thought it'd be amusing to follow one of the bridleways through the forest but unfortunately I got lost. The signage is appalling, as I'm sure you know. I was supposed to come out at Meg's Pond, but must have taken a wrong turning. I was lucky not to end up in Port Rell!'

It was plausible. Even Harriet didn't know every pathway through the forest and where they all led.

'Do you enjoy horse-riding?' Harriet asked.

'Yes. It's a fabulous stress-buster.'

'You ride a lot?'

'Every weekend.'

'Do you own a horse?'

'I would *love* to own a horse – isn't that every little girl's dream? – but I live with my brother, David, at the vicarage – he's the vicar for St Francis. It's a small, modern house with certainly no room for a horse!'

'Which riding stables do you use?'

Rose mentioned one of the ones they'd visited following the first appearance of the highwayman.

'Do you always ask for the same horse?'

Rose hesitated and then said, 'No, as I sometimes arrive with very little notice, I take whichever horse is available. I have my favourites, of course.'

'The horse you were with tonight, he was *beautiful*.'

'Isn't he? That was Raffy. He's a sweetheart.'

'Such an unusual colour though. Is it rare?'

'No, not really, although the truly black horses are not as common as others.'

'Great aesthetic though,' Harriet said. 'Particularly if you're playing the part of a highwayman recently risen from the grave. Very Gothic. No face paint though? Perhaps there wasn't time? You attended a cocktail party at Hartfell earlier in the evening?'

'At Brianna Graham's personal invitation. She's a lovely woman.'

Brianna Graham! Harriet almost slapped the table in delight. *That* was who Rose was imitating! She had the gracious, slightly patronising tone down pat. A *very* skilled actress.

'I could hardly be in two places at once,' Rose said. 'Could I, Detective Inspector?'

Had she actually *fluttered* her *eyelashes* at Ben? Did she expect him to jump in and save her from Harriet's questions?

Disgusted, Harriet flipped back through her notes. 'Black horse, black clothes, black mask... I *love* the feathers on that mask. Are they real? Is the mask Venetian? I've been invited to Brianna's Masquerade Ball tomorrow and I'm still not happy with my costume. I'd love a mask like that. I expect it's too late now, it wouldn't arrive in time, but where did you get it from?'

Rose hesitated. 'Online.'

'A theatrical website?'

'I can't remember.'

'Perhaps if you looked at your bank statement? It might jog your memory? Do you have an app on your phone? Where is your phone, by the way?'

'At home,' Rose said bluntly. 'Wouldn't it be more fun for you to find your own mask? To be original?'

'I wouldn't buy one *exactly* the same...' Harriet said.

'It was a very long time ago.' Rose's fingers began curling and uncurling in her lap, perhaps wishing they were around

Harriet's throat. 'It might not have been online. It might have been from a car boot sale or something like that. Well, anywhere really!'

Why, of all their questions, had that been the one to rattle her?

'Is that right? Because I wondered if you'd borrowed the mask?' Harriet held up her phone to show Rose a photo she'd seen far too much of over the past week. A man in black, wearing the exact same feathered mask. 'You know, from your friend Lorcan Black? It was his house you were found at after all...'

'I don't know Lorcan Black,' Rose said, far too quickly. 'I mean, I've heard of him, obviously, but never met him.' She didn't fidget, her hands remained still in her lap, and her gaze never left Harriet's.

A sure sign of a liar, Harriet had always thought, especially one who set too much store by body language.

'Haven't you?' Harriet said, in a very I'm-the-cat-you're-the-mouse-get-over-it kind of way. 'Why are both the keys to his house *and* his stables on your keyring?' In a move worthy of the closing scene in any television soap opera, she tossed them onto the table.

Talk your way out of that, Rose Griffiths.

THIRTY-TWO

Ben watched the keys skitter across the plastic. *Were* those the keys to Lorcan's house or was Harriet bluffing? Why hadn't she warned him what she was planning to do?

Hadn't she *trusted* him?

Because if those were Lorcan's keys...

Could his cousin have been guilty all along?

As soon as Rose saw her keys slide over the table, her expression switched to neutral. 'I'm not saying another word without my solicitor.'

'I expect that's for the best,' Harriet said cheerfully, her fingers closing over the keys and sliding them back into an evidence bag. 'Do you have one in mind or would you like me to give you a list of the ones we have on call?'

'Olivia Greenwich-Fitzpatrick.'

'Good choice.'

Ben wasn't surprised. Olivia Greenwich-Fitzpatrick was the most expensive solicitor in the King's Forest District for a reason. She was good.

He'd be interested to know how Rose could afford her though.

Ben closed the interview as someone knocked on the door.

'Did you put the sign up?' he asked Harriet. He was still peeved she hadn't warned him about her stunt with the keys.

'Yes.' She busied herself gathering her notebook and files, so Ben went to open the door himself.

Sam was on the other side. 'Sorry to interrupt. Something came up. The DCI needs you at Green Acres Livery Yard.'

Ben slid through the door, closing it behind him, so Rose wouldn't hear what was said.

'It's Anthony Elliott. He's been murdered. Well, butchered, really.' Sam silently drew his finger across his throat.

A 'click' made them both glance around. The door hadn't shut properly and, as it swung open again, Ben's eyes inadvertently met Rose's.

She'd overheard. There was no faking that look of horror.

Rose knew Anthony Elliott, Rose *liked* Anthony Elliott, and now Ben knew exactly where Rose had obtained her distinctive black horse.

He'd walked into a bona fide nightmare. They had found the highwayman. They had caught her red-handed, the case was closed, and there should have been congratulations all round. Now *another* body had been found. Could it be a copycat? Or, as an insidious voice whispered in his head, had the highwayman been Lorcan all along?

The familiar smell of horse hit him as soon as he got out of Sam's car, which took him right back to the days when the Elliott Farmhouse had been a riding stables. Sam parked beside the house, meaning they had a short walk to reach the yard, an impressive modern complex with stabling for over thirty horses living in better accommodation than he'd seen for some people. The horses were clearly unsettled by the noise and the lights, despite the staff's efforts to calm them. If they began to cause problems, for themselves as well as his colleagues, he'd have to see about getting them moved.

There was police tape across the entrance to the main yard. He and Sam suited up before walking through a gate and across the central courtyard. Each stall opened directly onto the yard, but there was also a tack room, feed and bedding stores, changing facilities, accommodation for the staff as well as a recreational area.

As they crossed the yard, Sam briefed him.

Anthony Elliott's body had been found in the recreation area used only by the staff. Did that mean Anthony had known his killer? There was more tape across the door leading to the staff kitchen and Caroline met them on the threshold.

'What do we have?' Ben asked, hearing the robotic tone of his voice. Was he in shock? Anthony was his uncle, even if he'd never had much to do with him. Why had the DCI asked for Ben, rather than Harriet? Had Cameron assumed that the family relationship might give him more of an insight?

'White male, mid-fifties, preliminarily identified as Anthony Philip Elliott,' Caroline said. 'Early indications are that he died as a result to a stab wound directly to the heart, but you will see that there are defensive wounds to the hands, and cuts, lacerations and abrasions to the face.'

Ben must have appeared confused, because Caroline elaborated, 'The victim was in a fist fight and then he was stabbed. The head was removed after death but not... cleanly.'

Ben's stomach dropped and he hadn't even got past the tape. 'Time of death?'

'Very recent. Within the last couple of hours.'

It couldn't have been Rose. There was no better alibi than being safely locked up in police custody.

'Any sign of a murder weapon?'

'Not my remit, but I don't believe so.'

He hardly liked to ask, but, 'Any idea what it could have

been?'

At this point Caroline would usually tell him to wait for the post-mortem, but this time she sighed and said, 'A long knife... Possibly... a sword.'

'A sword,' he repeated flatly.

They *had* the highwayman, they *had* the sword. This wasn't possible.

'Thank you,' he said, and moved forward, lifting the tape to pass beneath it.

She stepped in front of him, speaking in a low tone to avoid her colleagues overhearing. 'Ben, are you sure you're up to this?'

'I'm fine.'

Was he? Certainly, he'd witnessed this level of bloodshed regularly while in the Met. Not so much since his return south.

'Anthony was your uncle,' Caroline said. 'The DCI shouldn't have asked you to attend. It's not fair on you.'

'I hardly knew Anthony.' Even his uncle's name felt strange on his lips. 'I've never been close to that side of my family. DCI Cameron is the Senior Investigating Officer, not me. I thought he was here?'

Where *was* the boss?

'He's been called away,' Sam muttered.

'There you go,' Ben said. 'You're stuck with me.'

'Benedict...' she said softly.

The kindness in her voice unsettled him. He preferred it when they were fighting. That way he knew where he was and who he was.

And he certainly wasn't Benedict Elliott.

'My name is *Ben*,' he said, gently pushing her arm away and ducking beneath the tape.

On the other side of the door, Ben took care to breathe through his mouth and mentally distance himself from what he was seeing. There were signs of a messy fight. Bar stools overturned, mugs smashed, coffee pooling on the white tiled floor. A riding crop lay on the floor, a numbered yellow triangle beside it, drawing his attention to others leading away from it, following the progression of the fight. The grey, shaker-style cabinets were closed. A knife block on the counter was undisturbed.

The murderer had brought their own weapon with them.

It had been premeditated. Murder, not manslaughter. His uncle had not gone quietly and, hopefully, the murderer hadn't been left unscathed either, which might help with his identity.

Ben followed the markers into a cosy seating area. He could see his uncle's feet emerging from the other side of a large leather couch. He was still wearing riding boots.

The buzzing inside Ben's head grew louder.

Breathe.

That didn't work.

He tried again.

A DI couldn't faint like a rookie.

He needed a distraction. Tried to remember each of his male relatives in turn, none of whom he'd liked apart from his grandfather. They'd had nothing in common either. Ben was 'bookish' and had never cared much for horses. Terrence Elliott despised 'over-educated twits' and was *obsessed* by horses. Of all his sons, Anthony had been the most like him. Arrogant, but occasionally kind.

He hadn't deserved to die like this.

Had Anthony been happy to meet his killer, assuming he was a prospective client? It would explain why he'd been wearing riding boots so late in the evening.

'Dakota is in the office,' Sam said, oblivious to the chaos surrounding them. 'The DCI asked her to check through Mr Elliott's appointments for today.'

Good idea, but would the killer have booked an appointment in his real name?

No, but learning the alias might be useful.

'Let me know what she discovers.'

'Will do.' Sam wandered off, careful to use the designated squares as stepping stones.

Ben surveyed the scene again. The CSIs worked around him, very careful not to make eye contact. Did *everyone* know Anthony was his uncle?

His uncle had been deliberately targeted. The police hadn't released any information about Rose's arrest, so either the murderer was working with her – Lorcan? David? Someone else? – or they'd taken the opportunity to blame the high-wayman for a killing that was personal to them.

Yet another person with a grudge against the Elliott family?

The kitchen floor, the seating area, the counter top... they were all littered with forensic markers, and he could see more leading around the couch. There was no getting out of it; he had to get on with it.

Another deep breath.

Follow the yellow brick road...

Ben stepped around the couch, careful to stay on the designated areas. His uncle lay on a red rug, which disguised the blood, but the flecks on the surrounding white tiles made up for it. What idiot had decided that a white tiled floor in a working stables was a good idea?

Ben recalled the crime scene at Meg's Pond. How Raquel had been placed neatly at the water's edge, her beautiful dress arranged with barely a crease. He compared that scene to this, where Anthony lay sprawled on the ground.

Breathe.

A memory from his childhood forced itself into his mind, of Anthony showing him how to groom a horse while Liam argued with someone in the yard, of slipping him a fiver with a wink 'For work well done'.

Ben turned away, swallowing back the emotion that threat-ened to engulf him.

The nearest CSI regarded him warily. 'Sir? Are you all right?'

'I'm fine,' he snapped. 'Just checking out the...'

They both stared at the large leather couch.

'...sofa,' he said, rather lamely. There were little forensic markers here too, bright against the black leather, although the cushions were a creamy colour, he noticed, and also flecked with blood, particularly the one at the end.

Ben pointed to the cushion. 'What caused that rectangular stain?'

'We're not entirely sure, sir. There are other similar marks throughout the scene. Put together, we're considering a theory that it might be a partial imprint of the murder weapon. It *is* only a theory though.'

Surely they couldn't be that lucky?

Ben leant over, as far as he dared without falling off the square he stood on.

Within the stain was a pattern of shapes, almost like lettering.

'Does that look like writing to you?'

'We haven't had time to follow it up, sir. The word isn't complete, but it might be "Sheffield" – the place of manufacture?'

'No,' he said. 'No, no, no.'

'Sir?' Sam was calling him from the doorway. 'Dakota has a name for you.'

Ben sighed. 'Matthew Elliott?'

'Well, a "Mr E Matthew", but how did you know?'

Ben glanced again at the cushion and the almost illegible swirling letters that only made sense when read backwards.

STORTFORD

'Just a wild guess.'

The yard between the stables and the house was horribly exposed with nowhere to hide; it was impossible to make it across to the woodland track unobserved.

Benedict had a split second to choose.

He ran left, through the gap in the hedge and into the orchard.

This slowed him down considerably.

In his grandfather's day, the grass had been cut regularly and the apples gathered in early October before they had the chance to fall.

Liam obviously hadn't set foot here in the two years since he'd inherited.

The long grass slowed Benedict down. His feet squelched through the rotten fruit.

He heard nothing behind him, no warning at all, until he was grabbed and spun around, something hard and metallic gouging into his forehead.

It was the stranger he'd seen in the stables.

'You're one of them,' the man said. 'Another bloody Elliott.'

Benedict was too terrified to speak or even to nod his head.

His attention slid to the thing that had cracked his head.

A gun?

He tried to pull away but the man yanked him closer. The movement caused something heavy to swing in his coat pocket, smacking into his hip. He put his hand in there, remembering what it was, his fingers closing over the metal.

'I suppose this is a double-cross,' the man said, bending so his face was inches from Benedict's, a move calculated to intimidate. 'What's it to be? You kill me and bury me in the orchard, taking my share of the cash. Is that it?'

'No, I—' Benedict cringed back but the man pulled him closer.

'How about I kill you, you snivelling weasel, and bury you in the orchard?'

There was a deafening bang.

The pain in his ears was excruciating.

He stumbled as the man released him, watching him fall away feeling no emotion at all. The man's eyeballs rolled back as he hit the ground, the blood welling out just above his heart.

Was he dead?

Ben took his grandfather's pistol from his pocket, the one that wasn't supposed to work, and stared at it. What had he done?

He'd forgotten he was wearing his highwayman mask until Uncle Liam appeared at his side and ripped it off.

'Bloody hell, Benedict!'

He wanted to answer. He wanted to explain how the man had threatened to kill him. But somehow his mouth wouldn't say the words. It was like a horrible, horrible dream.

The body on the ground groaned.

Liam gave Benedict a shove. 'Run, lad. Go through the forest and don't look back. And don't you dare *say a word about what you've seen tonight.'*

Benedict ran. Slipping, sliding and falling into the mud, walking headfirst into branches, the twigs ripping at his hair and digging into his skin, running faster as he heard a second shot behind him, and then a third, finally sobbing with relief when he saw the shimmer of moonlight on Meg's Pond and knew he'd reached the village.

And then he threw up.

THIRTY-THREE

By the time Ben and Sam returned to the station, Harriet had gone home and Rose had been sent back to the custody suite to wait for her solicitor to arrange bail. Even the duty sergeant eyed them askance when they walked in. 'Shouldn't you two have knocked off by now?'

'If only the bad guys worked eight 'til eight...' Sam sighed, but then he knew he was going home.

Before Sam left, Ben asked him to call Olivia Greenwich-Fitzpatrick back. Rose was returned to Interview Room #2, sleepily rubbing her eyes, shortly joined by an uncharacteristically dishevelled Harriet. It was now past midnight and everyone was happy to drink the coffee from the machine, disgusting or not.

Harriet handed out copies of Rose's statement from earlier that night, which she'd already signed, although Ben noticed Rose's hand was shaking as she took it from Harriet.

'Thank you for all coming back,' he said.

'I assume you have a good reason to be conducting this interview so late?' Olivia said frostily.

'A very good reason.' He pointed to the machine. 'If I may?'

Olivia nodded curtly.

Ben did the usual and then held up Rose's statement. 'Miss Griffiths, this is the statement you gave to DS March and myself a few hours ago. I am now giving you the chance to change this statement in light of what's happened.'

'What *has* happened?' Olivia asked.

'He's dead, isn't he?' Rose said. 'I heard you talking to that other detective, the one with the short brown hair. Anthony Elliott has been killed – had his head chopped off. I saw the move the detective made, his finger across his throat. It's true, isn't it?'

Ben didn't answer. Give an interviewee enough rope and...

Rose collapsed over the desk, weeping. 'It's my fault,' she wailed. 'It's all my fault.'

Olivia looked unimpressed.

Harriet huffed, reached behind for a box of tissues and batted them across the desk towards Rose.

'Are you admitting to killing Anthony Elliott?' Ben asked.

Rose lifted her head. 'Anthony helped me,' she hiccupped, 'and now someone's copied my idea and killed him.'

My idea?

He could work with that.

Harriet grimaced and pushed the tissues a little closer.

Rose took a handful and buried her face in them.

'You don't have to say anything,' Olivia reminded Rose. 'We can talk this through in private. You are entitled to—'

Rose ignored her. 'He was such a dear, sweet man.' She blew her nose noisily. 'He was like a father to me. My own died, as you know, killed by those murdering thugs that robbed the security depot.'

Ben refrained from pointing out that Anthony was *also* one of those murdering thugs.

Harriet reached for the waste-paper basket and dropped it on the floor beside Rose's feet.

'After my father died, we were stony broke,' Rose said. 'His life insurance wouldn't pay up because we had no proof that he was dead and he was suspected of taking part in the robbery. The bank took our house back. Mum had to get a job in one of the gift shops. We had no money. It was super-embarrassing.'

'*Embarrassing?*' She'd been only ten, he supposed.

'No one *liked* us anymore. Everyone believed Dad was guilty. None of my friends would come round to play. Then Uncle Anthony let us stay in one of his houses for free.'

'Houses?' Ben knew his uncle had owned a nightclub. It had run into financial problems, which is why he'd agreed to take part in the robbery. Like Ben's father.

'Anthony Elliott owned a portfolio of rental properties,' Harriet said. 'Drew took everything over when his father went into prison but it sounds as though Anthony was still pulling the strings.'

Ben doubted that. Drew Elliott never did anything he didn't want to and had always been far smarter than Anthony.

'After about a year, we went to live with my grandfather in Norchester,' Rose said, 'but Anthony Elliott still sent David and me money on our birthdays and Christmas, and he paid for us to go to university.'

Anthony or Drew? It would have been a significant sum. Ben and Harriet exchanged glances. Where had Anthony obtained the money from? Had he managed to keep some of the money from the robbery? Or had Drew paid for everything in his father's name, out of guilt?

'Did Anthony pay for your house too?' Harriet asked.

'No, we live in the vicarage and that's provided by the diocese.'

'Did he loan you the horse?'

Rose hung her head. 'Yes, he gave me the horse last birthday. His name's Raffy. I stable him at Green Acres.'

'Let me guess,' Harriet said. 'For free?'

'Yes.'

'Did he know you were using Raffy to play at highwaymen?'

'I think so. Raffy is fairly distinctive. I didn't tell him what I was doing and he never said anything. Perhaps he *didn't* know?'

Harriet leant towards Ben, speaking in an undertone. 'That fits in with my interview with Anthony yesterday. He was genuinely shocked when he heard what had happened to Lorcan.'

So Anthony was fine with Rose riding around the countryside brandishing a sword, but not so keen when it endangered a member of his own family?

Rose raised her head to look Ben directly in the eyes. 'I didn't kill him! He was good to me. Why would I do that?'

'Why stage the prank on Lorcan? Rather over-the-top, wasn't it? Steal a corpse, set up Lorcan by leaving him in the church—'

'You do not have to answer that,' Olivia said.

Rose's eyes didn't leave his own. 'I wanted revenge on the men who kidnapped my father, forced him to take part in that robbery, and then killed him. My father's dead, while the Elliotts are all successful. You're a police inspector, Greg owns a dive centre, Drew's rich and Lorcan's famous. I wanted to even things up a bit. Embarrass you, humiliate you.' Her lips twisted. 'You've got to admit it worked! You even made national television.'

Beside her, Olivia winced.

Did Rose realise what she'd casually admitted?

'I didn't mean for anyone to get hurt,' she said. 'It was only a bit of fun. The body I placed beside Meg's Pond was already dead.'

'You admit to stealing the corpse of Raquel Marsh from the mortuary at Norchester General Hospital?'

'I work as an APT. It took you long enough to connect the dots.'

'For the record?'

She leant toward the machine, the spark of defiance back in her eyes. 'Yes, I admit to stealing the corpse of Raquel Marsh. I admit to everything – but I didn't kill Anthony. I would never to do that.'

'Everything' was a bit too wide a description.

'Why did you steal the corpse?'

'I'd worked out that Lorcan Black was really Liam Elliott's son, William. It was obvious from his songs and the artwork on his website. Everything is about Raven's Edge and the various legends – Magik Meg, the Raven Queen, Matthew Elliott – He lifted it wholesale. I'm amazed no one else noticed.'

Perhaps they had, but not thought anything of it. Musicians, writers, artists – they all took inspiration from something.

'I couldn't believe my luck when Lorcan moved into the Elliott Farmhouse, right here in my village. He was asking David for dinner recommendations – like *he'd* know – so I told Lorcan about The Drop. He mentioned that his Uncle Charlie used to work there. It seemed like fate.'

'Lorcan agreed to meet you at The Drop?'

Lorcan had already known who she was? There had been no mystery woman. He'd been protecting her.

'David was doing one of his "Welcome to the Neighbour-hood" visits and I tagged along, because who wouldn't want to meet a real life rock star?' Rose rolled her eyes.

Ben felt very sorry for that brother of hers.

'You suggested Lorcan meet you for dinner?'

'I might have hinted that I'd be there, but I didn't go as myself.'

'You wore the wig.'

'Yes, and knowing when he'd be there meant I could get everything ready.'

'Steal the body and the blood from the hospital?'

Olivia opened her mouth, sighed, and shut it again.

Rose nodded. 'I find life so much less stressful when everything is organised properly, don't you?'

'You must have had help? A colleague at the mortuary?'

'One of the other APTs called Lee. He's such a sweetheart. Madly in love with me. Will do anything I say. He shifted everything into position while I went to find Lorcan.'

'Who was waiting for you at The Drop, right where you wanted him to be?'

'Uh huh.'

'Then you sedated him?'

Rose held up her hand. 'Let me stop you there, Detective Inspector. Lorcan was already drunk when I arrived. It was nothing to do with me.'

'You took advantage though,' Harriet said.

'I wasn't going to let an opportunity like that pass me by. I called Lee, who met me outside the pub. We helped Lorcan to the car and then drove him to the church, and asked him to pose on Lady Miranda's grave – recreate his *Deadly Sin* album cover, which he was perfectly happy to do – that man is such an arse.'

That man was desperate to make a friend.

'Is that when you stole his keys?'

'Yes, he was practically unconscious.'

Unconscious? After all those sedatives and alcohol, they were lucky he hadn't died.

'What happened then?'

Rose shrugged. 'We took a photo of him and left.'

Ben was speechless. Of all the cold-hearted, callous...

Poor, poor Lorcan.

Rose sat back, particularly pleased with herself. Was she expecting praise?

'It was you we saw coming out of the church the morning Raquel's body was found,' he said.

'That's right. I wanted you to find Lorcan on the tomb before he woke up. You were taking far too long at the pond, so I stood outside the church and screamed. It worked a treat. You were falling over yourselves to rescue me.'

She'd manipulated all of them – and was so *smug* about it.

Ben didn't trust himself to speak.

He ended the interview and left Harriet reeling off the charges – stealing a corpse, desecrating a corpse, assault with a deadly weapon, etc – while he headed up to the evidence room to take another look at the sword they'd seized when they'd arrested Rose. He didn't have to take it out of the PVC tube it had been sealed in to see it was only a modern replica: heavy and well-made, and sharp enough to cut a chunk out of a wooden door, but still a fake.

So who had the original?

THIRTY-FOUR

31st October

It was 5.00 am by the time Ben finished at the police station. He'd received a text from DCI Cameron several hours ago, reminding him to go home and sleep. Instead, he drove in the opposite direction, past The Witch's Brew, skirting the edge of the moor, and then back along the coastal road to the Elliott Farmhouse.

He arrived there in much the same time it would have taken him to walk through the forest. As usual, the farmhouse was eerily quiet. How many centuries had it stood here, lording it over the encroaching trees? How many generations of Elliotts had resided here before Lorcan?

He walked up the front path and rang the doorbell. He didn't expect Lorcan to be awake at such an early hour, but his cousin answered the door, fully dressed in yellow joggers and a *Raven King* tour T-shirt, accessorised with Eddie on his shoulder.

Wild bird, my arse.

'Hi, Benny-Boy. Come on in.'

'You don't seem surprised to see me.' Ben stepped into the gloomy hall. 'You do know it's only 5.30 am?'

'Is it?' Lorcan walked away, ducking into the sitting room. 'I've completely lost track since I stopped taking my pills. I kind of like it. I don't feel so dopey, but my internal clock has completely gone to pot and I'm basically nocturnal.' He pointed to the open box on the table. 'Pizza?'

The curling pepperoni and congealed cheese were not appetising.

'Dinner or breakfast?' Ben asked.

'No idea.' Lorcan took a slice. 'I'm listening to my body and my body wants pizza.'

Eddie croaked, as though in agreement, and flew down onto the open box, digging his beak into a slice of pepperoni.

'So does Eddie.'

Ben fancied a slice even less now.

'Sit down,' Lorcan said, oblivious to the piles of screwed-up paper littering the sofa and a guitar on the remaining chair. 'I was working on a new song.'

Ben cleared a space and gingerly sat on the edge of the sofa. 'I'm sorry to interrupt.'

'It's OK. I had to have a break. It wasn't going well.' Lorcan flopped back into the only empty chair and pulled the guitar onto his lap. 'I need some kind of inspiration. I feel like I'm looking into a deep, dark well of nothing.'

You and me both, Ben thought.

Lorcan hugged the guitar against him, as though its weight were comforting. Was this normal behaviour for a musician? Or, between them, had the Elliott family truly screwed him up?

'What can I do for you?' Lorcan asked. 'I'm assuming this isn't a social call. Have you come to arrest me?'

'What for?'

'I don't know.' A rueful smile. 'What have you got?'

'Have Drew or Greg been in touch?'

'No, should they have?'

'I'm sorry to tell you this, but Anthony Elliott died last night. He was murdered.'

Lorcan stared at him. 'By Rose? I don't believe it. She's not capable.'

Rose Griffiths would be capable of anything she put her mind to, but in this instance, 'No, not Rose. She was responsible for the pranks – the headless body, and you left on that tomb covered in blood. Rose was also the one who chased me around The Square with a sword. But Anthony... Well, that was something different.'

'How did he die?'

'I can't tell you that at the moment.'

'I think I can guess. Poor Uncle Anthony.' Lorcan stared down at his guitar, drawing circles on the wood with his finger. 'I always liked him. One year, he was the only person who remembered my birthday.'

Was that true? What a horrible childhood Lorcan must have had, yet no one had noticed – just complained what a nuisance he was.

'Have you been in contact with Anthony since you came back to Raven's Edge?'

'I've not met any of my family, apart from you. I've not had the chance.'

He didn't sound resentful at all. Wasn't this why he'd returned to Raven's Edge? To reconnect with his family? He'd travelled all this way, yet his family carried on ignoring him.

'I'm sure they'll be in touch with you soon,' Ben said, making a mental note to ask Lorcan out for a drink when he was no longer under suspicion.

'No, they won't.' Lorcan didn't sound bitter. 'Poor guys. Their dad's just died. They'll have other things on their mind.'

'There was something else,' Ben said. 'It might be important to our investigation. Do you remember the night of the robbery?

It was the same night as the carnival. We met in the village, the four of us, dressed as highwaymen. Later, you stole Matthew Elliott's sword from the museum.'

'Borrowed,' Lorcan said primly. 'The curator said I could have it.'

'The last I saw of the sword, it was leaning against the wall in your bedroom. Did you take it with you to Ireland?'

'No, I thought Dad would go mad if he saw it, so I hid it under the floorboards.'

'Here, at the farm?'

'Yes, in my old bedroom. There were loose boards beneath the window. I often hid things there that I didn't want him to find. Cigarettes, beer; that kind of thing.'

It was too good to be true. 'Is the sword still there?'

'No, it's gone.'

'Damn.'

'It was one of the first things I checked when I came back to Raven's Edge. Although the floorboards are original, they were taken up during the renovation to replace the wiring and install plumbing – that bedroom is now my ensuite bathroom. I wasn't here at the time. I did wonder if one of the workmen took it, but I can't go around randomly accusing people. I've checked to see if someone was selling it online but, so far, nothing.'

Could the sword have become covered in dust and debris? It might easily have been missed. What if he put in a request for all the floorboards to be taken up, in case Lorcan had forgotten exactly where he'd hidden it? It had been fifteen years ago. Perhaps he'd made a mistake?

Knowing how house-proud Lorcan was, that could take some convincing.

'May I see where you hid the sword?'

'Don't you need a warrant for that?'

'I...'

Lorcan smirked. 'That was a joke. You should have seen your face. Sure, I'll fetch a chisel and hammer right now.'

Was that another joke? Did he keep them lying around?

Apparently so, because his cousin was back within minutes. They went upstairs, Eddie flapping from stag head to stag head ahead of them.

'That's the hole where he gets in.' Lorcan pointed out a tiny square gap in the end gable of the house. 'I think it's an owl hole.'

'They were only built into barns, to control mice. This is a house.'

'It's a house *now*,' Lorcan said. 'It could have been a barn once.'

Unlikely, because the style was all wrong, but he went with the more diplomatic, 'Perhaps a long time ago?'

'I believe the original house was further into the forest. That would make more sense, wouldn't it? Why build a house so close to the cliff?'

'Why build anything close to a cliff?'

Then again, the Elliotts weren't known for behaving rationally.

Access to the ensuite was through what had once been his grandfather's bedroom. The room hadn't changed since Ben had visited with the CSIs, although there was now a dark green brocade tailcoat hanging from a peg in one of the oak beams, with a matching black waistcoat beneath it.

'What's that?'

'That is the costume I wore for my *Raven King* tour. Jonesy had it couriered from storage in London. I've been invited to Brianna Graham's Masquerade Ball.'

'By whom?' Ben heard the tightness in his voice.

'Milla – but as a friend, nothing more. I don't want to go. It's not my thing and I've got this album to finish, but I made the mistake of telling Jonesy. He thought it would be good publicity

– you know how these society parties make all the newspapers and magazines. Personally, with Anthony's death, I think it would be in bad taste *and* I'm going to look like a prat. Who goes to a fancy-dress party dressed as themselves?'

'You'll need a mask.'

'The original one went mysteriously missing recently.'

Ben had a very good idea where it might have gone, but kept it to himself.

'I have a duplicate on the wall in my studio though. I bought them in Venice, years ago. Beautiful things, real raven feathers – sorry, Eddie.'

Lorcan went into the ensuite, walking over to the window. He bent down, using the chisel to lever up one floorboard and gently wiggle it free.

'This is where I last saw the sword,' he said, placing the board to one side.

Ben used his phone to shine a light into the hole. There didn't seem to be anything there. Any debris or rubbish must have been cleared during the renovation. Damn. That meant the sword used to kill Anthony was original – and anyone could have it.

Even Lorcan?

His cousin was still chattering away. 'Do you remember Granddad once found a mummified cat in the wall behind the sitting room fireplace?'

'No, but thank you for that.'

Lorcan slid the floorboard back into place. 'The site manager said they found all sorts of things during the renovation. Old coins, bits of bone, shells, medicine bottles, a teaspoon with the family crest – I've got them in a box somewhere – but no sword.'

Someone must have known the sword was here before the renovation – and used it to kill Anthony, hoping to blame the highwayman, not realising Rose had already been arrested.

It was so simple, yet so bloody hard.

Find the sword, find the murderer.

Now he was right back at square one.

On the way home, Ben called in at The Witch's Brew for a full English breakfast. Fried egg, sausages, bacon, mushrooms, beans, hash brown... It seemed like a good idea at the time but he wasn't used to eating so much fried and processed food and soon felt queasy.

He was tempted to return to work, but could imagine the DCI's reaction at his less than pristine appearance, so headed home for a shower, shave and a change of clothes.

His black cat, Binx, fussed until he fed him, although the automatic feeder appeared to be working fine. He made a pot of strong coffee to try and wake himself up, switching on the local news while he drank it to see if there'd been a press release about Anthony's death.

Nothing yet, but they wouldn't be able to keep it under wraps for ever. Soon the speculation would begin and they'd be forced to release something. Gossip could be wilder and more lurid than the truth. Although, in this case...

Binx jumped onto the sofa and then settled on his lap, purring loudly, probably assuming it was film night. He stroked the cat's head, feeling calmer, then checked his watch. Could he squeeze in a nap? If he got to the station by ten, that should be OK.

He sent Harriet a message and set the alarm on his phone for 9.30 am, just in case. Would Milla be watching the carnival parade? When he'd planned to take this week off, he'd imagined taking both her and Sophie, his six-year-old daughter. They could have bought chocolate-coated apples from The Witch's Brew, studded with cashew nuts or walnuts, or caramel apples coated with sweets, or even classic toffee apples, glistening a deep, dark red. All the tea shops and coffee shops set up stalls on the high street for the carnival. It was hard to choose just one to visit. Sophie already had a historically inaccurate Magik Meg costume, glittering with sequins, but it would have been fun to dress up with Milla and go trick-or-treating as a family.

He smiled. It would have been like the old days, when he'd been a teenager, going trick-or-treating with his cousins. Peanut butter cookies from Miss Lily at The Witch's Brew, bonfire toffee from the Merriweather sisters at Practically Magic...

His eyes began to close.

It took half an hour for Benedict to stagger through the woods and along the high street, to the pub where he lived with his parents.

It was surrounded by police cars.

What should he do?

Keep walking. What choice did he have?

He limped along the road for another half hour, stepping onto the grass verge every time a car whizzed past, until he reached a pretty little cottage that looked like a gingerbread house. The lights were on and, as he approached the door, he could hear the sound of soft jazz.

He knocked.

It was opened by a sixty-something woman wearing a red satin wrap, her gunmetal-grey hair cut into a sharp bob.

'Benedict!' She looked him up and down, her mouth pursing with disapproval, pushing his hair back to see the cut on his forehead, now trickling blood into his eyes. 'Who did this to you? Was it Drew Elliott?'

'Not Drew.' His legs were shaking so hard he had to lean against the door frame. 'Someone else. Older. I don't know his name.'

'Bloody carnival. An excuse for grown men to behave like children. Come inside. I'll call your mother. It's nearly midnight. She must be out of her mind with worry.'

'No, the police are there already. Something else has happened. I... I don't know what.'

How could he tell her the truth? That he had killed a man. It would break her heart.

'The police?' Her eyes narrowed. 'That wretched man. He thinks he can sweet-talk his way out of—' She broke off, drawing a calming breath. 'I'll send your mother a text. You, upstairs.'

Every step was an effort but she pushed him in the direction of the bathroom and shone a light in his face, tutting over his wound.

'It will scar,' she said, cleaning it and sticking a dressing over it. 'Now, bath and bed.'

It was only after she'd left that he realised he still had the old pistol in his pocket.

If anyone knew he'd killed a man, he'd be sent to prison for the rest of his life.

But if someone innocent was blamed, how could he live with not owning up?

THIRTY-FIVE

Harriet had been born in Raven's Edge and had lived her entire life there. Although the family home was a large Victorian house on the other side of the bridge, she currently lived alone in a warren of rooms above the florist, Foxglove & Hemlock, the scents of countless flowers drifting through the old, cracked floorboards and eddying through the apartment: a different blend every day. She couldn't imagine living anywhere else.

Another thing she'd never imagined was the number police officers patrolling the high street as the annual carnival began. This was a rural English village. It was wrong to see their uniforms mingling with smiling painted faces as everyone watched the crowning of the Raven Queen – a representation of Magik Meg, presumably meant as a belated apology for chucking her off the bridge.

Unfortunately, when she'd grumbled about it to Sam, the DCI had overheard.

'It reassures the public,' Cameron had snapped, as though he'd already had that argument several times today. 'We've told them the highwayman business was a stunt but we're not in a position to release a statement about Anthony Elliott. You know as well as I, gossip in this village takes off like wildfire and is so much juicier than the truth.'

Yes, she'd received the message loud and clear.

Solve the case, release congratulatory statement, and *then* remove officers from the street.

She flicked back through her notes to double-check where they were at. Review crime-scene evidence, finish interviewing the staff, look at Anthony Elliott's personal life to try and work out who had the patience to wait until they had the perfect opportunity for murder. Although, judging by the mess that had been the crime scene, she'd have said that person was more an opportunist than a strategist.

Would Ben have agreed with her? She'd never know because he hadn't turned up for work, despite all the messages she'd sent him. Had he returned to the Elliott Farmhouse, to let Lorcan know he was back under suspicion?

Was he *deliberately* trying to sabotage his career? Sometimes she really couldn't understand what got into his head. Did he want to stay a detective inspector forever?

She kept her sigh silent as she turned another page. DCI Cameron might be working in Ben's office but he had the hearing of a bat. Every sigh and mutter had him asking, 'What's the problem *now*, DS March?'

The hidden camera Anthony Elliott had mentioned when she and Milla had talked to him at Green Acres had been found. Dakota had been in the conference room all night, trying to access the footage with the help of one of the guys from Tech. Anthony had only used his phone for calls and texts, and that had already proved to be a dead end.

'The murderer's out there somewhere, plotting his next move,' the DCI called out, somewhat randomly.

Was that supposed to be motivational? Harriet tried hard not to roll her eyes but knew he was becoming increasingly frustrated. Unlike Ben, the DCI was a brooder, seeing every murder as a personal chess game against an adversary. The more irritated he became, the more sarcasm tripped from his tongue, and the more he intimidated the junior officers. It was *not* helping.

Where the hell was Ben?

He'd failed to turn up to the morning briefing – almost understandable if he'd been working for most of the night – but it was lunchtime now.

Harriet's stomach was rumbling.

DCI Cameron didn't look the type to walk down to The Witch's Brew for a bacon and cheese panini. She'd bet he'd already booked himself in for some kind of fancy salad at The Drop.

Maybe she'd wait for him to leave first. She really didn't want to go to lunch with him. Apart from the brooding and the sarcasm, his immaculately styled suits always made her feel scruffy. She was certain that was Ozwald Boateng he was wearing today – at *work*! He probably didn't even own a pair of wellingtons – essential, when you never knew from one day to the next where you were likely to end up staring at a corpse – a muddy field or a pig farm.

Could Ben have had another migraine? Lack of sleep didn't help.

She hid her phone beneath her desk to send him another message.

More likely he'd swiped his phone to mute or put it on airplane mode, or turned it off completely.

She must have been grinding her teeth because now it was Sam who glanced up from his laptop. 'Are you OK?'

No she wasn't bloody OK, and even Dakota dancing into the office at that exact moment to hand her a familiar orange paper bag with a bacon and cheese panini in it, plus a large cappuccino, all from The Witch's Brew, didn't cheer her up. Now she had no excuse to leave the office and do an 'I was just passing' visit to Ben's cottage.

The DCI had despatched Ash there earlier (of all people). He'd reported back that Ben had been lying on his sofa with Binx on his lap, watching TV, apparently unwell.

Duh! Ben could have been lying there dead and Ash wouldn't have noticed!

This was another point of contention between her and DCI Cameron. He had contacted Drew, Greg and Lorcan, and suggested that they and their families be removed to a place of safety or given police protection, whichever they preferred.

'What about Ben?' Harriet had demanded. 'He's an Elliott too.'

The DCI had not bothered to hide his exasperation. 'A touch ridiculous, don't you think? A police officer guarding a police officer?'

The DCI's mood had not improved when he received a message to say Drew and Greg had impolitely told the attending officers where they could go.

Lorcan, however, appeared to have bonded with DCs Kershaw and Kuang, and was happy for one of them to remain in situ at the farmhouse, which was sad if Harriet thought about it too long. He was *famous*. Didn't he have any *friends*? Her brother, in exactly the same job, had a pack of mates on every continent.

By the end of the day they were no further along in their investigation. Harriet was unsurprised when the DCI called her and Sam into the office and told them he required two officers to work late tonight – the part about providing protection duty at Brianna Graham's Masquerade Ball came as a shock though.

Harriet stared at him. *Someone* had had far too much black coffee.

'I thought we'd stopped hiring out officers due to the need to preserve front-line staffing levels?' she said. 'And protection duty is a whole different department. I'm not risking my offi-cers' lives to protect those rich idiots.'

Sam winced at 'rich idiots' and tried to casually blend in with the bookcase.

'It could be connected with our case,' the DCI said. 'Anthony Elliott was a "rich idiot" and there'll be plenty of other "rich idiots" at the ball for our murderer to target. He's on a roll.'

She'd been a sergeant too long not to recognise politics at play. 'You mean Brianna Graham has personally requested a police presence, and the Chief Constable has rolled over and agreed?'

How lovely to be so rich you had the local law enforcement under your thumb.

Now it was Cameron's turn to sigh, and she almost felt sorry for him. 'Mrs Graham will be paying for it, don't worry.'

'OK, who do you want to send?'

'You and DC King.'

Had she heard him correctly? 'I'm a detective sergeant.'

'I'm a detective chief inspector. Your point?'

'How about sending Dakota?'

'DC Lawrence has gone above and beyond, working all night. She deserves some time off.'

Harriet didn't? Well that hurt.

'OK, how about Ash?'

Cameron didn't even bother to give an excuse. 'I thought you'd be pleased. Isn't that every girl's dream? You *shall* go to the ball?'

Sam, presumably expecting an imminent explosion, took a step towards the door.

Harriet bit her lip. That comment was incredibly sexist and, as the DCI was usually fair, she could only assume he was spoiling for an argument. Like her, he'd been stuck in this office coordinating the investigation for far too long.

Why didn't *he* go to the bloody ball?

She knew better than to suggest it though.

The sad thing was, ordinarily Harriet would have *loved* to have gone to the ball – the glamour, the fashion, the chance to sneak a peek inside Hartfell – hell, even the opportunity to go to a plain old party. When was the last time she'd done that?

Being stuck inside, she'd also missed the carnival parade but had been hoping to go with Sam to watch the fireworks, and maybe 'accidentally' bump into Misha. Now she wouldn't even get to do that! It was incredibly unfair.

A party, where one had to work, wasn't a party at all.

'How much is Mrs Graham paying?' Might as well make some money out of this. Christmas was coming up after all.

'Top rate – plus a little bit more. I made sure of that. I also negotiated extra to ensure you were both properly attired.'

She folded her arms. 'Where do you think we're going to find fancy-dress costumes this late in the day?'

Sam looked as though he'd be quite happy for someone to shoot him right now.

If Ben had been there, he'd have recognised the glint in her eye but the DCI merely shrugged and turned back to his laptop.

'DC King, stick on a suit and you can be James Bond. As for you, DS March, you're a resourceful officer, I'm sure you'll work something out.'

The thing about fancy-dress parties was that most people popped on their best frock/suit and had done with it. For a masquerade party Harriet would need a mask, but she had plenty of those lying around the place thanks to previous carnivals where dressing up as Matthew Elliott was almost de rigueur, no matter what sex you were.

However, Harriet *did* have the perfect gown. She had a wardrobe full of gowns, paid for by her brother when he wanted her to accompany him to an award ceremony, when he was unwilling to subject a new girlfriend to the spotlight of the gutter press. (Not that he was a beast or anything, but Harriet did sometimes wonder if that was why the girl in question wanted to date him in the first place.)

The dress Harriet decided to wear tonight she'd only worn once, to the Brit Awards in February. It was pale pink satin, with a tight strapless bodice and a bell-shaped skirt finishing mid-calf, meaning she could still tackle bad guys to the ground if necessary. The killer detail was the cut-out, thigh-flashing front of the skirt, revealing pink lining so dark, it was almost burgundy. The designer called it the 'foxglove dress'; her brother had nicknamed it the 'mullet dress'. There were long, pale pink gloves to match, as well as a tiny evening bag. There was no way Harriet was going to fit all her stuff inside *that* bag, so she left both gloves and bag in the bottom of the wardrobe. She also spurned heels in favour of trainers.

Well, they *were* pale pink!

Every other woman at this ball might have had all day to prepare but Harriet could put on make-up in ten minutes flat. She stepped into her dress, using a hook on a stick to zip it up at the back, and then flipped upside down to fluff up her curls. Finally, she transferred everything from her work bag to a burgundy-coloured satchel (which *almost* matched), including a taser she'd signed out from Weapons.

It was always wise to be prepared.

A blast from a horn outside told her Sam had arrived. She ran downstairs and jumped into the car. They set off at Sam-speed. In other words, 29mph.

'You look good,' Sam said, although she noticed he didn't take his eyes from the road ahead.

'Thanks, so do you. Do you have a mask?'

'Top pocket.' Daringly, he took one hand off the steering wheel to pat it.

'Taser?'

'My other pocket. I'm a cut-price James Bond with a taser instead of a PPK. It's chunky though, ruins the line of my suit.'

'Ha ha, be grateful you have pockets. I'm a woman; we're not supposed to need them.'

Once they left the village, he turned onto the road that led between the forest and the moor. The sea glittered in the distance. There was a huge grey wall on their left. Hartfell was famous for its high level of security. *No one* could access the house without the owner being aware of it. Weren't a couple of police protection officers overkill?

The main gate opened when Sam spoke into a speaker and held his warrant card in front of a camera. They followed a single-track road and ended up in a large gravel parking area, already crammed with cars. No valet parking? That was remiss. Sam picked a spot to one side, from where it might be easier to retrieve the car when the time came. Harriet slid out before he had any outdated ideas about chivalry.

Hartfell, all lopsided cubes of grey stone and obsidian glass, had been built in the centre of a man-made lake, but fortunately there was a narrow footbridge rather than some stupid boat waiting to ferry them across.

'Do you think Mr Graham pulls up the drawbridge if people annoy him?' Sam asked.

Harriet, remembering Graham Media's reputation for ruthlessness, said, 'He would probably blow it up.'

Sam was bouncing his fingertips off each other, with an accompanying 'Pow!', when the butler opened the door, and he had to hide his hands behind his back.

Harriet, trying to keep a straight face, explained who they were. In return, the butler introduced himself as 'Hodges'. He was a grey-haired gentleman, with hawkish features, and appeared to be already well into the age when anyone else would have retired. Perhaps butlers didn't retire?

Hodges stepped back to allow them entry into a large

hallway and another member of staff took them to the ballroom. Who had their own *ballroom*, for heaven's sake? There was no introduction to the famous Brianna Graham, currently holding court in a side room, a firm reminder that they were paid staff.

Cinderella, indeed. This was going to be such a long night.

'Perhaps we should split up before we get too comfortable,' she said, 'and check for possible suspects?'

'Like Cluedo?' Sam grinned. 'Brianna Graham in the ball-room with the cake slice?'

They snorted with laughter – until they entered the ball-room and saw all the costumes: medieval knights to super-villains – complete with incredibly realistic weapons. It would be easier to find a guest without one.

'Well, *they're* all on my suspect list,' Sam said.

She was beginning to see why Mrs Graham wanted to pay for security. 'You start this end; I'll go to the other. We'll meet in the middle and compare notes. Call me if you spot anyone acting suspiciously.'

'No signal,' he said. 'I've already checked.'

It got better and better.

'Don't even *think* about referencing some horror movie.'

'*Do you like scary movies?*'

'Sam...'

'*It's Halloween, everyone's entitled to one good scare.*'

'That's it, I'm going.'

'Do you even watch horror movies?' Sam sighed. 'That's always their first mistake.'

'What?'

'Splitting up.'

THIRTY-SIX

Harriet stalked around the edge of the ballroom. This was such a waste of her time, patrolling a society ballroom as though it were some dodgy part of Norchester, looking the part in her designer frock but feeling like the spectre at the feast.

The murderer had done what he'd set out to do – kill Anthony. Why hang around in Raven's Edge waiting to be caught? DCI Cameron thought they might be able to identify him (or her) by Matthew Elliott's sword, but what idiot went to a party flaunting a murder weapon? After using it to kill Anthony, the murderer would have disposed of the sword in the forest or the sea somewhere it would never be found. If she was the killer, that's what she would have done.

Harriet smirked. She would have made a very good murderer.

As she weaved between the dancers, she occasionally met Sam. They exchanged rueful smiles and shrugs, and moved past each other. She'd already recognised a large chunk of the guests, despite the masks and the costumes. Lorcan Black was holding court in one corner, wearing his Raven King outfit, chatting up a cluster of eager women, including the one who'd been crowned

Raven Queen earlier and wore a gown the same green as his tailcoat. Harriet would definitely be keeping an eye on *him*.

Harriet had spotted Milla too, in a midnight-blue ballerina-style gown, and a little black sequinned mask. She was spending her time staring hopefully at the door, ignoring the ever-revolving circle of men trying to chat her up.

Waiting for Ben?

After three hours Harriet desperately wanted to go home, but the unmasking was at midnight, meaning there was another thirty minutes to go. Hopefully, people would leave after that. The fireworks in the village were due to go off at midnight. Would the guests go outside to watch?

Actually, that wasn't a bad idea. The ballroom was unbearably warm and stuffy. The glass windows appeared designed to slide back, because someone had left one open by a few inches to let in the cool autumn air. Harriet gave it a surreptitious push, creating a gap big enough to turn sideways and slip though. The view of the garden, sparkling with fairy lights and reflected in the lake, was certainly worth suffering a few goosebumps. There were more lights looped along the balustrade. Everything was incredibly pretty.

Her breath created little puffs of condensation. Maybe it would be a mistake to stay outside too long. Her bare shoulders already felt cold. She turned to go back inside and spotted movement at the end of the decking. A man was hunched over the balustrade, his dark clothing helping him to blend into the shadows. Now he *definitely* looked shifty.

Harriet forgot she was at a party. 'Hello?' she demanded. 'Can I help you?'

She received a baleful glance in return. 'I'm fine, thank you.'

Four words, one flat reply. She had her answer, she should head back inside. Yet her detective imagination went into overdrive.

Was he ill? Had he broken up with his girlfriend? Was he

planning to jump? Not that he'd risk anything more than getting wet. The water was less than a foot below the decking and anyway, he'd be able to touch the bottom of the lake if he went in. Why lurk in the shadows unless he was trying to hide? Was he a journalist, preparing to gatecrash? He was up to no good, she could tell. What would he do if she challenged him?

He sighed. 'I'm not ill and I'm not planning to jump. The water isn't any deeper than three feet. I'd barely get wet. It would be humiliating, to say the least. I'd have to wade all the way around to the front of the house, because that's where the steps are. Oh, and I don't need to gatecrash. This is my family home.'

'I didn't say anything!'

'You didn't have to.' He pointed to her face. 'Your thoughts are fairly transparent.'

He wasn't the first person to have said so.

'I'm sorry to have disturbed you,' she said. 'I'll leave you to it.'

Whatever 'it' was. What was it with men and 'brooding'?

Contrarily, he walked over. He was younger than she'd thought: her age or a little bit older. His skin was brown and his hair black, scraped into a half-hearted ponytail. A chunk had already escaped. His clothes were plain and contemporary, and he carried no pistols or sword, but one look into those familiar pale grey eyes and she knew him immediately.

Malcolm Graham, known as 'Mal', Milla's elder brother. Hartfell was his family home, owned by their super-wealthy father, who also owned a publishing company, several newspapers, even a television production company.

For some reason Mal seemed fascinated by her feet. 'You're wearing trainers.'

Was that his killer chat-up line? 'They match my dress.'

He nodded, as though that were perfectly reasonable,

before switching his attention to the lake in an absent-minded way. 'Did you hear something?'

The last time someone had said that, it had ended with a blood-soaked body sprawled on a tomb, and she really didn't want to repeat the experience.

'No.' She stared out across the lake. 'Did you?'

'It sounded like a scream.'

In her head, she could almost hear Sam reel off another movie quote. *Be afraid... be very afraid.*

'I didn't hear anything.' She waited but there was no sound other than the muted music from the ballroom.

Muted? Wonderful. To make her evening complete, someone had closed the window and locked her out.

Harriet saw a long walk around the outside of the house in her future.

Could she go home now please?

'I don't think it's anything to worry about,' she said. 'Lots of people scream when they're having fun.'

'Do they?' His voice held that hint of innuendo revealing that, absolutely, he knew how to have fun.

Harriet was no longer paying attention. A movement had caught her eye: a blur snagged in the lights of the car park. Two figures, facing off. Male, female: she couldn't tell. One shoved the other against a black car. No one appeared to be having fun.

That wasn't good.

'Lovely talking with you, Mr Graham,' – *it totally wasn't* – 'but I have to go.' She walked over to the balustrade, peering into the dark. Now, how to get to the car park, other than swim?

'Follow the decking around the side of the house,' Mal said.

How did he do that?

'If you want to reach the car park, follow the decking,' he repeated, perhaps thinking she hadn't understood. 'It'll be quicker than going through the house.'

'Thank you.' She slid her satchel over her head and around

to her back and began running, picking up speed as the automatic lighting popped on to show her way.

She arrived at the front door quicker than she'd anticipated but it was closed and there was no sign of Hodges. Crossing the footbridge, she arrived at the car park in less than a minute.

It was empty. How strange.

Where had they gone? If they'd returned to the house, she'd have passed them on the bridge. Had they headed into the garden?

That was all she needed, to trip over a copulating couple in the dark, but what if it was the murderer choosing another victim?

That was not logical. Anthony's murder had been spur-of-the-moment, opportunistic, she was sure of it, but perhaps she should call for Sam to be on the safe side?

She took out her phone. No signal.

'I can see why you wear trainers, if this is what you do at parties. I hadn't realised my company was so disagreeable.'

Harriet let out an involuntary shriek and almost dropped her phone.

Mal had *followed* her?

'Sorry,' she snapped, 'but I'm working. Your grandmother hired me—'

'I know who you are, DS March, I thought you might need help with whatever sent you sprinting off into the night. The scream, right?'

'I don't *need* any help—'

'Yet here I am.' He pointed to a black Peugeot 208. 'That's my sister's car.' He circled it warily, peering through the window and checking the doors. 'The doors are unlocked and she has a flat tyre. Why hasn't she changed it or called out our father's mechanic?'

The family had their own *mechanic*?

Before she could say something contentious, Harriet

glimpsed something glittering in the gravel and bent to pick it up.

This was not good...

'Maybe your sister didn't get the chance.' Harriet held out her hand to show him the silver chain coiled on her palm. 'If I know one thing about Milla, she never goes anywhere without her charm bracelet.'

Benedict decided to wait until the fuss about the robbery had died down. It might take a couple of days, but he could go to the police station and admit everything. He'd take his grandmother with him, she'd be more than a match for any police officer, and he'd seen enough television shows to know it was essential to have a good lawyer.

First, he needed to hide the old Luger pistol before his grandmother found it and came to all the right conclusions. It had to be somewhere outside, where she wouldn't find it during one of her cleaning blitzes.

Ignoring the bath, he tiptoed down the passage into his bedroom, shoving open the window and climbing onto the sill. Within grabbing distance was a walnut tree and built into the fork was a tree house. It had been created by his grandfather for an eight-year-old (Benedict's mother), not a gangling fifteen-year-old, so scrambling inside proved to be a tight squeeze.

Could he hide the pistol in here? No, sod's law meant his grandmother would take it into her head to clean that out too, saying he was too old for a tree house. He'd have to bury it in the garden.

He took a tin of old coins from a shelf, and had just emptied it to stick the pistol and key inside, when a vehicle pulled up outside the cottage. He couldn't see it, but he recognised his mother's car by the blare of pop music and her high heels on the drive.

He didn't have much time.

Dropping through the hole in the floor, he landed on the soft earth below. It would have to be here. He crouched and swiftly dug a shallow hole with his bare hands, shoved in the box, kicked over the soil, and swung himself back up to the tree house. A quick balancing act across to his bedroom window – his grandmother would have a heart attack if she could see him – before jumping into bed and pulling the covers over his head. Noticing *his fingers had left muddy marks on the duvet cover, he swore, folding it over to hide them.*

As his breathing calmed, he heard his mother's muffled voice from the sitting room below. 'The police had a tip-off and Charlie was caught trying to hide the money in the basement – something even he couldn't charm his way out of.'

'Will you stand by him?'

His mother laughed bitterly. 'He's used up all his last chances. Starting tomorrow, I'm changing our surname back to Taylor. I don't want to hear the name Elliott ever again.'

Benedict drifted off to sleep.

Would he like to change his name to Ben Taylor?

Yes, why not? It was dull, anonymous... and absolutely perfect.

THIRTY-SEVEN

Ben dreamt he'd killed a man – shot him with an ancient pistol, without even taking it out of his pocket. He'd buried the evidence in an old tin box beneath a walnut tree, stamping down the dirt until it was level, kicking stones and leaves over the disturbed earth to hide it.

He awoke, heart pounding and gasping for breath as though he'd been the one buried in a box beneath the soil.

He was slumped sideways on the sofa, his neck, bent at an awkward angle, cracking as he shifted upright. Binx had disappeared from his lap, perhaps in search of more scintillating conversation or, more likely, food. The television was halfway through an old Bette Midler film, *Hocus Pocus*, the scene where a zombie chased children through a graveyard.

He frowned. In his dream, *he'd* been the one who was chased. There'd been a horse and a sword, a pile of cash and that old Luger pistol.

His heart picked up speed again, thudding uncomfortably in his chest as he recalled his panic. If the police found that pistol, they'd know he was the murderer. He should get rid of it, bury it in the garden beneath the old walnut tree. Anywhere else could be dug up for flowers or vegetables. No one would dig beneath a tree.

He ran to the back door but it was locked and there was no sign of the key. The raven must have it – but where was the raven? In a panic he rattled the door and a face appeared at the glass window: pale-skinned with hollow eyes, dark-blond hair and a beard that needed trimming.

Ben lurched back. His father?

But Charlie Elliott was *dead*...

He took another look.

A beard?

Charlie had been clean-shaven. One of the reasons Ben had grown a beard in the first place. Why would he want to look like his father?

He blinked and this time saw himself.

He slumped back against the door. What was *wrong* with him? Burying a *gun*? What gun? He didn't have a *gun*. What the hell had given him the idea that he did?

He returned to the sitting room and switched on the light, his heart slowing to a more regular rhythm. He'd worked all day and night, and fallen asleep on the sofa still wearing his suit. No wonder he was having hallucinations. He'd been so tired.

His hand froze over the light switch. Why was it dark?

What time was it?

His phone was face-up on the coffee table, flashing a multitude of notifications. He snatched it up.

9.30?

Please let that be 9.30 am.

But if it was dark...

Oh, *damn*.

With fifty-seven notifications iced on top.

Four messages from Harriet, the last one reading:

> No sweat, boss. Take the day off. We're doing
> fine without you.

Seven messages from the boss, including: #1:

> Where are you?

#4:

> Are you sick?

#7:

> You'd better be sick.

One from Sam:

> The boss is not happy. He's sending Ash round.
> Where are you???

Ash: #1:

> I've been knocking on your door but you're not
> answering. I can see you watching TV, are you
> sick?

#2:

> I'll tell the boss you're sick.

There was a text from Caroline, but that was about childcare not the murder case, and a message from Sophie, with a short video of her rabbit eating a carrot, which he watched three times and found oddly calming.

He scrolled further down.

Three missed calls from Milla but no messages. Had she been after a partner for her grandmother's ball? Maybe not –

the last call had been less than two minutes ago. Perhaps that was what had woken him? Was she in some kind of trouble?

Milla was *always* in trouble, almost as though she deliberately sought it out, but he returned her call anyway, leaving a message on her voicemail when she didn't answer. Hopefully she was having such a good time at her grandmother's ball she hadn't heard the phone ring.

But not *too* good a time.

His stomach rumbled, distracting him enough to head into the kitchen for coffee and toast, where he nearly tripped over a disgruntled Binx. Should he go to work? To do what, exactly? Everyone would have gone home. It would make more sense to wait until tomorrow and head in for the morning briefing.

If he still had a job.

Instead of waiting for the toast to pop, he walked around the cottage, drawing curtains and pulling down the blinds, ending up in his study. It overlooked the back of the house, including Sophie's vegetable patch and the hutch where the rabbit lived when Sophie was staying with him. There was some rickety garden furniture that he didn't have time to use, and the old walnut tree with Sophie's tree house wedged in it. The tree was as old as the cottage, according to his late grandmother, but the tree house had been built for his mother.

Ben paused, one curtain drawn, his hand bunching the fabric.

The tree house had been in his dream. He'd climbed through the window of the bedroom that was now Sophie's, and into the tree house before dropping into the garden. For a child it was the perfect escape route, but in the dream he'd been concealing something. A box? Yes, a tin box. He'd buried it beneath the tree in the middle of the night.

He rubbed his hand over his face. What the hell had *that* been about? Usually his dreams were a series of random events, generated by whatever had happened that day or the film he'd watched before bed.

This dream had been different.

He'd been talking with Lorcan about their past. Had *that* triggered it?

Today had been the carnival – and the anniversary of his father and uncles robbing that security depot. He'd tried so hard to forget it; had it forced its way into his subconscious?

Part of the dream seemed familiar. He did remember going to the carnival with his cousins, all four of them dressed as high-waymen, as they did every year. Greg had disappeared into the woods with a girl he fancied, Drew had escaped to the pub, and Ben had been lumbered with babysitting Will/Lorcan, returning him home on the horse he'd 'borrowed' from Liam's riding stables.

What had happened then?

He'd tied the horse to a drainpipe, tucked Will/Lorcan up in bed, given him a glass of water and gone home. That was how he remembered it, he'd no cause to believe any different, but now?

If he examined the memory too closely he knew he'd never leave a horse tied up outdoors overnight, particularly after a ride. He'd have taken the animal into the stables, removed the tack, given him water and groomed him at the very least.

Had he really gone into the stables? Why couldn't he remember?

It was like a chunk of his memory had been wiped, from when he'd taken Will/Lorcan back to the Elliott Farmhouse, to waking up at his grandmother's cottage and the immense relief he'd felt at being told over breakfast that his parents were getting divorced. Wasn't that what happened with memories? One always recalled moments of strong emotion.

Why would he forget an encounter with a gun?

With increasing unease he recalled the disturbing image he

thought he'd seen in Lorcan's stables, that of a redheaded stranger arguing with his uncle.

'*You bastard, Liam. You utter bastard.*'

'*You still going on about that? Seriously, man. Grow a pair.*'

Had that happened? Was it a flashback?

The same redheaded stranger had been in his dream, threatening him.

Ben ran his finger over his forehead, feeling the little dip in the flesh, knowing it was the tiny, semi-circular scar he'd had forever. He'd assumed he'd gouged it while climbing a tree or falling off his bike, but in his dream there had been that sharp pain when the stranger had hit him.

If he'd seen a man killed – if *he'd* killed a man – surely he'd remember?

Unless he hadn't wanted to?

He'd done enough courses on mental health. He knew all the phrases: *Post-traumatic stress, dissociative amnesia, forgotten trauma from childhood...*

He rubbed his finger over the scar, as though he could rub the dream away.

'*Who did this to you? Was it Drew Elliott?*'

He could almost see his grandmother beside him, as she cleaned and dressed the cut.

Had he gone to sleep that night and woken with a complete 'reset'?

There would be one way to settle this.

He went out to the garden shed, grabbed a shovel and headed to the walnut tree.

Picking a likely spot, he began digging.

He didn't have to dig for very long. Two stabs with the shovel and it hit something hard and metal. He bent to smooth away the earth, uncovering something rusty and tightly packed into the soil. He attempted to loosen it, but had to use the shovel again, digging around until he could lever it out.

The lid sprung open before he could pick it up.

Wedged into the little tin box were two items: an ornate key, which he recognised as the original key to the stables at the Elliott Farmhouse.

And his grandfather's old Luger pistol.

THIRTY-EIGHT

DCI Cameron lived in an apartment in an exclusive block right by the marina in Calahurst. Ben had never understood why. As far as he knew, Doug Cameron had no interest in sailing or any other water sports. In fact, the thought of him looking anything less than pristine in his designer suits was faintly ludicrous.

Ben flashed his warrant card to get past the doorman and headed up to the top floor. As far as he knew, the DCI didn't have a significant other. It didn't mean he wasn't alone though, which could be awkward, but when the door opened it was by Cameron himself, stylish as ever in black trousers and a cashmere sweater. In his hand he held a glass of red wine. In the background, Ben could hear Etta James singing about stormy weather. How curious that they both liked the same kind of music.

'Hi,' Ben said. 'I'm sorry to bother you at home, but—'

Cameron sighed. 'I'm not sure where I should start, Benedict. I assume you received all my messages?'

'Most of them, sir. I'm sorry, I overslept.'

'Overslept? An entire *day*? That's the one you're going with?'

'Yes, sir. I'm sorry.'

The DCI sighed again. 'I suppose you'd better come in. I assume this is important?'

'Yes, sir.'

Cameron walked into the apartment, leaving Ben to follow and close the door behind him. Immediately his feet sank into the lush charcoal-coloured carpet. Should he take off his shoes? In the end he kept them on, walking into Cameron's sitting room, where the DCI was already sitting in what appeared to be his favourite chair next to an expensive-looking music system. The television was switched off but a book had been left on the arm of the chair, a leather bookmark peeking out of the top. No turned-down corners or broken spines for DCI Cameron.

Cameron waved a hand in the direction of the sofa. 'Sit.'

Ben did as he was told. His seat looked straight at the wall opposite, which was entirely made of glass. It was too dark to see the River Hurst and the forest beyond, but if he could look down, he'd be able to see the sparkling lights of the marina below. It was a fabulous location – if you liked apartment blocks. Ben thought he preferred his cottage, even if it did look like a gingerbread house and made strange creaking noises in the night.

'What's in the tin?' Cameron asked.

Ben had almost forgotten why he was there – and that he was nursing an old biscuit tin on his lap, which was probably flaking mud and rust onto Cameron's immaculate carpet.

He placed it carefully on the coffee table instead, hoping it wouldn't scratch the wood.

'I know who killed Michael Griffiths,' he said.

'I'd be impressed – if we were actually investigating that man's death.'

Ben flipped open the lid.

Cameron leant forward, eyebrows rising when he saw what

was inside: an old pistol and an ornate key. 'Is that the murder
weapon?'

'Yes, it's an old World War Two pistol. It belonged to my
grandfather. We thought it didn't work – that's not an excuse,
by the way.'

Over ten years in the police and it ended here, igno-
miniously.

Cameron took a sip of his wine, regarding Ben with coal-
black eyes and a slightly bemused expression. 'I assume there's a
big revelation coming?'

'What? Oh, yes, sorry. *I* killed Michael Griffiths.'

For a moment Cameron stared at him, as though waiting for
a punchline, and then he closed his eyes and pinched the bridge
of his nose.

Ben went on to explain about his dream, and how he'd
assumed it was a hallucination caused by tiredness, until he
decided he might as well dig beneath the walnut tree to find out
the truth one way or another.

'I found that,' he said, indicating the box. 'It's the murder
weapon. I used it to kill Michael Griffiths. I'll resign from the
Force, of course.'

If he hadn't known better, he'd have assumed Cameron was
glaring at him.

'What the hell for?'

Hadn't he been paying attention? 'I'm a murderer.'

'Sounds like self-defence to me,' Cameron shrugged. 'You
were... what? Fifteen years old? Someone points a gun at you,
tells you he's going to kill you and bury you, of course you're
going to shoot him. I'd have shot the man too.'

'We need to find the body.'

'*Why?*'

'To close the case – closure for the family too.'

'The Griffiths family were better off without him, from
what I've heard, but in principle, all right. Not right now

though. We have enough to worry about and the man's been dead for fifteen years. He's not going anywhere.'

'Could I have a team to dig up the grounds of the Elliott Farmhouse? I suspect Michael's buried there, possibly in the orchard.'

'Don't you know? Oh, I see. You weren't the one who buried him.'

Too late, Ben realised he'd indicated his Uncle Liam was an accessory, but surely Liam was dead too? No one could vanish without trace for fifteen years. Unless he'd jumped off the Irish ferry? But the Irish had a record of him arriving in Dublin...

'I'm not digging up a pop star's garden on one of your hunches, Benedict. This is low priority, even if I did have the budget and the manpower. We're flat out at the moment, as you would know if you'd bothered to turn up to the briefing. I have both Raven's Edge and Calahurst working all hours. I've even borrowed manpower from Norchester. I'm not the Chief Constable's favourite person right now. We still haven't released a press statement about Anthony's murder. I had to deploy officers to patrol the carnival because everyone's on edge. Even Brianna Graham demanded a couple of officers for her bloody masquerade ball. At least she's paying top rate.'

'She did? Who did you send?'

'DS March and DC King.'

'Good choice.' Although Harriet would have been furious to be assigned protection duty. They truly were short-staffed.

'You know, Lorcan Black is incredibly enthusiastic about archaeology; if we phrase it properly, we could make it sound like—'

'*No*, Benedict. Archaeologists take a completely different approach, as you are aware. It wouldn't be fair and, more importantly, it wouldn't be legal.' He was pinching his nose again. 'Let's conclude this case and I'll see about a cadaver dog.

They're pretty damned effective. They can scent a body that's decades old.'

'The orchard would be a good place to start.'

'Then it's a pity it's still there and not beneath a housing estate, like a good chunk of the rest of the district.'

'The body would have been found.'

'Exactly. It wouldn't be coming back to bite us on the arse now, figuratively speaking.' Cameron regarded him speculatively. 'You look done in, lad. Sleep it off. I'll see you tomorrow at the briefing and we'll go over the Anthony Elliott case again. Somehow it's linked to your family, I know it.'

Ben managed not to make any remarks about hunches, said his thanks and his goodbyes, and took the stairs rather than the lift to the ground floor, hoping to give himself time to think. Instead, the missed calls from Milla popped into his head and he called her again.

No reply, not even voicemail.

Now he *was* worried. Had something happened?

He could call Harriet, who was also at the ball, but he really didn't want to go over why he'd been absent from work, so he called Milla's brother instead. If he was at the ball, the call might also go to voicemail, but Mal picked up on the second ring. The line kept breaking up, but Ben heard a distinct, 'I'm so glad it's you,' although that was hardly reassuring.

'What's happened?' he demanded.

'Milla's gone missing,' he heard Mal say between crackles. 'She was here... car park... Hartfell.' *Crackle, crackle.* 'No sign of her.'

'Where's she gone?'

'We think...' *crackle, crackle,* '...forest.'

'Milla's always walking through the forest and it doesn't matter if it's day or night, sunshine or sleet—' His heart flipped, remembering she would have been wearing a ballgown. Why the hell *had* she gone into the forest? 'What are you not telling me?'

'We heard a scream, saw a couple of people struggling...' The line became suddenly clear, enough to hear the pain shadowing Mal's voice. 'And Harriet found her charm bracelet...'

Michael had been shot.

That hadn't been part of the plan.

Damn, it hurt...

Michael heard himself groan, and then someone else spoke.

'Run, lad. Go through the forest and don't look back.'

Liam. The reason he was flat on his back amongst a pile of rotting apples, probably bleeding out, instead of watching Disney films with his kids. Bloody Liam.

What would Liam do now? Finish him off?

Not if he had anything to do with it.

The kid had shot him in the shoulder. If he was lucky, the bullet had been slowed by his thick sweater and not hit any bones. Still bad, but with less chance of any complications – provided he could get to a hospital very soon.

Now, how to get away from Liam?

In Michael's hand, the gun he'd threatened the boy with.

The gun, ironically, that he'd taken from Liam when he'd run from the stables to chase after that boy.

Michael opened his eyes.

Liam wasn't even watching him.

'Hey,' he said, slightly peeved.

Liam started and swung round, looking up before remembering to look down.

Michael took great satisfaction in shooting him.

Liam collapsed to his knees, looking shocked.

Bye, bye, Liam.

To be on the safe side, Michael shot him again.

Would Charlie and Anthony hear the shots and come running?

Nah, they'd be in the stables, counting out their money, blithely unaware there was now one less person to share it with.

What should he do with the body?

He was tempted to leave it, although hiding it would buy him more time. There was no way he was going to spend hours *digging a hole to bury it though. He didn't have a shovel for a start.*

What he needed was some kind of inspiration.

And there, in the far corner of the orchard, was another of those tumbledown outbuildings that littered the farm. He could hide the body inside. But as he dragged Liam through a decorated stone arch, he had a better idea. Leaving the body lying against the wall, he went back outside and shoved against the crumbling stones with his good shoulder.

It took two attempts but the wall collapsed inward, leaving Michael coughing in a cloud of dust and the body buried beneath a pile of rubble.

If Liam Elliott hadn't been dead before, he certainly was now.

THIRTY-NINE

One hour earlier

The ball was no fun without Ben.

As a teenager, Milla had seen photos in the celebrity magazines of parties like this. Beautiful people, exquisitely dressed, drinking champagne cocktails and having a great time. Now she was living that life, why did she feel so utterly miserable?

She'd chatted with Kat and her husband about how this year had been the best yet for The Witch's Brew. Fliss Merriweather had admired her vintage Dior gown (prima ballerina-style midnight-blue chiffon over ivory silk organza), on loan from Granny Brianna, before being distracted by a handsome waiter and wandering off. Fliss's sister, Elvira, hadn't lingered, muttering something about having to 'save the poor man'. There was no sign of Sorcha, thank goodness, but then The Drop would be open until very late.

Milla had almost resorted to asking Lorcan to dance, but he was having far too much fun on the other side of the dance floor, chatting with woman after woman, who'd all recognised him despite his Venetian feathered mask. As he was wearing his

Raven King costume – dark green tailcoat and black breeches, with a sword glinting at his side – he was hard to miss. He'd come to the party dressed as himself, and she couldn't even tease him about it because he hadn't looked in her direction once.

She leant against the wall, sipping at a non-alcoholic cocktail, watching everyone else having a fabulous time, and wondered how soon she could leave.

David Griffiths was also leaning against the wall, a few feet away. He'd spurned any kind of costume or mask, and was completely dressed in black apart from his clerical collar – more goth than Lorcan tonight.

'We look like a couple of bookends,' she said, but he didn't smile. When it became obvious he wasn't going to reply, she asked, 'How are you doing?'

'As well as can be expected, with my sister in jail.' He left out the part where it was entirely Milla's fault, but she received the underlying message anyway.

She walked over to him. 'Haven't they released Rose yet?'

David regarded her uncertainly, as though she'd asked a trick question. 'Not since Anthony Elliott was murdered, no.'

Her stomach went into freefall. 'Anthony's *dead*? I was speaking with him only yesterday.' He'd seemed like a kind-hearted man and had reminded her of Ben. A bit dodgy but, in her experience, people like that were often more trustworthy than the honest ones.

'He was killed with a sword,' David added rather too brutally. 'At least they can't pin that on Rose, because she was in custody at the time, but understandably the police are twitchy. I expect they think it's a copycat.'

Milla lowered her drink. 'That's... horrible.'

David shrugged. 'With his background, I suppose he made a lot of enemies over the years.'

'The security depot robbery? That was fifteen years ago and

he's served his time. What happened to not casting the first stone, Reverend Griffiths?'

Even in the dim lighting, she could see his pale cheeks turning pink.

'You're right, that wasn't kind. I'm upset about my sister, but that's no excuse. I've no idea why I'm here. A party is the last place I want to be, but I needed to get out of the house.'

'Ditto.' Milla raised her glass. 'This is non-alcoholic but I'm sure I can find you one with alcohol in.'

'No, thank you. I'm still suffering from yesterday's cocktails. I'm going to call it a night.'

'Good idea, but do you think you could distract my grandmother while I sneak out too? Because Ben's not here, she's been trying to match-make all evening.'

He gave her a bemused half-smile. 'You too? So far I've been introduced to the curator of the museum, a waitress from The Drop, a barista from The Witch's Brew—'

'Ruby's nice – and you might get free cookies – that's not a euphemism.'

'I'll bear that in mind.'

'We'd better not leave together though. That would make my grandmother's day.'

'I know; I'm on distraction duty. Goodbye, Milla. I'm sure I'll see you again.'

As her house was directly opposite his church, it would be hard for him to avoid her.

She didn't want to remind him of that though.

'Goodbye, David.'

Milla slipped out of the ballroom and crossed the hall, saying goodbye to Hodges, who admonished her for not having the patience to wait for her coat.

'I have a car. I won't be cold and it's not raining.' She stepped through the door before he could object, gave him a quick wave and walked briskly over the footbridge, only slumping when the shadows engulfed her and she was out of his sight.

She should never have come. She should have stayed at home with a mug of hot chocolate, binge-watched television, and wallowed in her misery.

It wasn't too late to do that now.

She called Ben again, but it went straight to voicemail. As she couldn't think what to say, she didn't say anything.

'Home, hot chocolate, TV,' she promised herself.

It would have been an excellent plan – if her car hadn't had a flat tyre.

She stared at it in disbelief. She'd had the glass in the rear window replaced this morning, the wing mirror replaced last week, now this? It was as though the car were cursed.

She kicked it and swore beneath her breath, which, unsurprisingly, did not make any difference. She had a spare in the boot, as well as a jack, but hadn't a clue how to go about changing it. She didn't want to risk spoiling her dress either.

'And this is why I don't wear dresses,' she told the sky.

'Can I help?'

She spun around, assuming David had followed her to cadge another lift to the village. Instead, it was Lorcan, still wearing that sinister feathered mask that hid three quarters of his face. How could he even *see* in that thing? If she hadn't known who it was beneath the feathers, she might have felt intimidated.

'I can drive you home,' he said.

He'd re-dyed his hair. It was now sleek, shiny and very black, tied neatly at the nape of his neck, although the damp weather was starting to make the ends curl and frizz.

'That's a kind offer but not necessary, thank you.' She had a ton of options. She could stay the night in her own room back at the house, or call a taxi. David owed her a lift, if he'd brought his car. She could even walk through the woods. What did she care if it was night or day? The villagers might mutter about ghosts and restless spirits, but there was nothing in that forest that frightened her.

'I insist,' he said.

She laughed. This was Lorcan, after all.

'*Insist?* Are you drunk? Don't be an idiot.'

His lips tightened.

The unexpected change in expression made her pause. Lorcan, it seemed, had mislaid his sense of humour.

She opened her car door, to check if she'd left anything she might need inside.

He slammed it shut. 'I'm trying to be helpful, girl.'

Whoa! *Girl?*

Now the words were wrong.

The *voice* was wrong.

Why hadn't she noticed that?

Lorcan spoke softly, his conversation peppered with wry, self-deprecating jokes. Like Ben, he had no noticeable accent, and would often use twelve words when three would have done, and still keep talking after that. In fact, it was hard to get him to shut up. So why was he silent now?

'That's very kind of you, but this is my family home. I can stay here tonight.'

No way was she going to admit to her plan to walk through the forest.

He leant against the car, crowding her. 'You're the kind of girl who likes to have a good time. Why not have a good time with me?'

'Has that line ever worked for you? And get off my car.' She pushed him away, knocking him off balance. This was her family home, her territory; she didn't have to put up with this. She could walk away, back to the house, and she was damn well going to.

He caught her wrist, slowly pulling her towards him, a

crude display of strength. 'We haven't finished our conversation, darling.'

'Lorcan!' She tried to shake him off. 'Why are you being such an—'

Because he wasn't Lorcan. His tone was sharper, rougher, the timbre not so deep but oh, it was familiar, his name dancing out of reach.

She stared into those mocking eyes, trying to see behind the mask. Blue eyes, but that didn't make any difference. Lorcan often wore coloured contact lenses.

'Who the hell are you?'

'You don't remember me? You're breaking my heart.'

It was the kind of thing Drake might have said, but he wasn't Drake either.

She yanked her wrist from his grip. 'I really can't be doing with this,' she said, hearing a tart echo of Granny Brianna in her voice.

Before she could cross the bridge, he stepped in front of her.

She ground her teeth. Why did some men have such a problem with being told 'no'?

'Not good enough for you?' he growled. 'This time last year you were pouting those pretty lips at me, desperate to win my approval. Now you've come into all this money, no one's good enough for you, not even my boy.'

My boy?

We have a winner.

'Jonesy.' Who else would have access to Lorcan's stage costumes? He'd dyed his grey hair black. Had that been to deliberately deceive? Chilled, she remembered those women hanging on his every word at the party, some younger than her. They believed they'd caught the attention of a handsome young singer. Instead, they were being chatted up by *this* old man. Ugh!

'We're past that now, you stuck-up bitch. It's "Mr Jones" to you.'

She almost laughed but that would have been a mistake. She'd been quiet too long: he'd become more assured.

'What's *wrong* with you?' He must have been drinking or worse. Alcohol, along with the mask he was wearing, had added another arrogant layer to that cocky self-confidence he'd always had. He was the kind of man she hated. A man who thought he could do anything and say anything, because he was rich.

Fortunately, she didn't have to put up with *that* anymore.

She shoved him again, hard.

Already unsteady, he stumbled back, almost tripping over his sword, clutching at the bridge balustrade for support.

Why hadn't she remembered that Lorcan's Raven King costume didn't come with a sword? She'd listened to the album many times, and watched Lorcan perform in character on stage. Lorcan's Raven King, as far as she could remember (unlike the Welsh deity), had been a shape-shifting sorcerer, not a warrior or a knight, or anyone who would need a sword.

It was old though, pitted and scratched, with a curling inscription down the side.

David had told her about such a sword, a stolen one that had belonged to that famous highwayman. The legend was that he'd engraved the name of his enemy along the edge of the blade.

Stortford.

'Nice sword,' she said.

He glanced down, confused by the change in subject.

'How old is it?'

'Why would I know?'

'It's your sword, isn't it? Do you have provenance? If not, I know several people who would be *very* interested in that sword and how you came by it.'

'Would they?'

It was the wrong thing to say. She knew that immediately. She'd done it again. Her mouth had run away with her, because she always needed to prove she was cleverer than the other person. She *had* to have the last word. *Damn*. What had David said? Anthony Elliott had been killed by a sword? She was smart enough to solve his murder but not smart enough to keep quiet about it. Now she was about to become victim number two.

Jonesy smiled in a way she really didn't like. 'You're not going to tell anyone about the sword, are you?'

'Nope, I won't breathe a word. Promise.'

If he believed that, he'd be the one believing in fairy tales.

He was blocking the way across the bridge, so she turned to run back to the car park.

He yanked her back.

She stamped on his foot and he laughed.

'You'll have to do better than that, girl.'

'Help!' she screamed defiantly into his face. 'Someone *help* me!'

'No one is going to hear you. It's too bloody cold for anyone else to be outside.' He pulled her closer, an imitation of a lover's embrace. 'Just us. Nice and cosy like.'

His first mistake.

Drake would not have been stupid enough to do that.

Drake could have told him what would follow if you pulled an unwilling woman too close to vulnerable parts of your body.

She slammed the side of her hand into the most vulnerable part of Jonesy and, as he buckled over in pain, she fled into the forest.

FORTY

As Milla ran through the trees, brambles snatched and snagged at her dress with eager little claws, the sequins ripping away in an iridescent shower. The same sequins she'd left scattered throughout the forest like a trail of glittering breadcrumbs, leading him straight to her.

It wasn't the first time she'd been pursued with such single-minded intent, nor the first time she'd ended up slamming against a tree to hide. It was the first time she'd done it wearing a ballgown, however, and she cursed profusely as she tried to squash the mass of frothy petticoats behind her legs to recreate herself as small, unobtrusive and, most hard of all for her: silent.

Had her breathing always been this loud?

As she shivered in the dark, it was hard to believe that beyond the woods life went on as normal. She could hear fireworks signalling the end of the carnival and, from one of the pubs in the village, a chorus of 'Bad Moon Rising' fading in and out on the breeze.

Wasn't that appropriate? Music to be murdered by.

Here in the forest there was no sound at all. No scuffling of leaves, no cracking of twigs, no creatures of the night. Nothing to prove she wasn't entirely alone. Yet she knew he was there, waiting for her to make one tiny mistake, to reveal exactly where she was hidden, just as she waited for his.

And *there* it was.

A soft, gentle swish. The sound a slender, whippy branch might make if pulled back and released too carelessly.

She didn't stop to think. She didn't stop to wonder why she should have heard him at all when until now he'd been silent. She shoved away from the tree, ducking beneath the mass of branches before they could hook into her hair and yank her back, and stumbled onto the track leading into the village – facing the wrong direction. Facing him.

He didn't bother to grab her, merely grinned, his teeth flashing white in the moonlight.

'Do you quit?' he asked.

She spun away, hitching up that damned ballgown and sprinting towards the village. Not bothering to be clever about it this time, just running as fast as she could. She was so, so close. She could see the lights of cars moving along the road and hear the music, louder now – and his footsteps behind her, hard and hollow, gaining distance with every stride.

Considering his age, he was the faster runner. Why didn't he catch her and have done with it?

Because he was playing with her.

Her life, her *death*, was a game to him.

One she was determined he wouldn't win.

The trees dropped back, revealing an expanse of silvery water, and she stopped when she should have kept going. Her feet slid from under her and she fell hard onto her knees, into the mud, inches from the water's edge. Her reflection, pale-faced and hollow-eyed, stared back... and then merged with his.

Did he expect her to scream? To beg and plead for her life? *Never.*

His gaze met hers in the still water of the pond, yet he said nothing.

'Go on,' she said. 'Do it.'

(Not for a moment believing that he would.)

Until she heard the scrape of metal upon metal as he unsheathed the blade.

She still had time. It *wasn't* over. It couldn't end like this. It *wouldn't* end like this.

She dug her fingers into the mud, never taking her eyes from his reflection, waiting for that chance, that break in concentration when he thought he'd won.

One small chance.

Please give me that chance.

It was all she needed.

'You're right about the sword,' he said. 'It belonged to that highwayman, Matthew Whatshisname. Lorcan stole it from the museum and hid it beneath the floorboards in his bedroom at the farmhouse. It's been there ever since.'

A flicker of hope. He'd paused to *gloat*?

She watched his reflection as he admired the sword, turning it this way and that, making it glint in the moonlight. 'Maybe I'll take it back to the States, or maybe I'll stay here in the village and hang it on my wall. I fancy your dad's house. Do you think he'd sell it to me?'

She blocked out the taunt. She'd got what she wanted. He'd been distracted by his own cleverness, just as she had earlier, and he'd made a fatal error.

She scooped up a handful of mud and threw it into his face.

Her mistake was to wait to see if it reached its target.

The mud splattered his face and he cursed, rubbing his eyes with his sleeve. He didn't drop the sword but this was an opportunity that wouldn't come again.

'Bitch!' he roared. 'I'm going to end you!'

Run, her head told her. *Run…*

To replay the last twenty minutes? Allow him to find another victim, perhaps someone less willing than her to take risks? But how did you disarm a man with a sword?

You didn't. You ran like hell, and now she'd missed that opportunity. The pond was behind her, Jonesy was in front of her. There wasn't anywhere to go.

'Maybe I won't kill you right away,' he said. 'Maybe we can have some fun first?'

'Drop dead.'

'You talk too much.' He lifted the sword, there was a sound like a firecracker, and he paused, surprised.

Then he collapsed onto the grass without another word.

Had he had a heart attack or was this another trick?

She leant towards his body. There were two copper wires protruding from his back. She traced them back into a yellow plastic gun, held by a woman in a pale pink ballgown, standing next to her brother Mal.

'Harriet?'

'I thought you might need assistance,' Harriet said, in her usual no-nonsense way. 'I'm sorry I'm late. It's bloody impossible to find your way through that forest in the dark. I would have become completely lost if it hadn't been for Mr Graham.'

'You... *Tasered Jonesy*?'

'He *was* threatening to chop your head off. We are clear on that, right? Because I do have to have a good reason for firing one of these off and I don't want to get into trouble.'

Mal gave Milla a hug. 'Are you OK? When we found your bracelet in the car park...' He shook his head, unable to finish the sentence.

'I'm OK. A bit shaken, I suppose. Thank goodness you turned up when you did.'

Because she didn't like to think about what would have happened if they hadn't.

Mal fastened the charm bracelet back onto her wrist. 'Do you want to come back to Hartfell?'

'I think I'll just go home.'

Jonesy groaned.

Harriet pointed the taser and there was that firecracker sound again.

He twitched. Milla almost felt sorry for him.

'I hope you've got handcuffs in that bag,' Mal said to Harriet, 'because you can't keep tasering him forever, and that guy has "runner" written all over him.'

Jonesy scrambled to his feet.

'And there you go.' With the minimum of effort, Mal grabbed him by his collar, swung him around and dealt a deft punch that knocked him out.

'Do you mind?' Harriet grumbled. 'I had everything under control.'

'Sure you did.'

'I'm not having some man come along and take credit—'

'A "thank you" would be nice.'

'We have rules and regulations we're supposed to adhere to, one of which is that we're not allowed to knock out the bad guys. That's called "assault".'

'Tasering them isn't?'

'It's perfectly legal, although I do have to account for every time I take the taser out of the holster. We're only allowed to use reasonable force to effect an arrest, as I said. It has to be done *properly*, according to the *law*.'

'You're welcome,' Mal said, as Ben and Sam ran into the clearing. 'I need a drink. I'm off to see if any of the pubs are still open. If you need rescuing again, Sergeant March, do me a favour? Call someone else.'

Michael staggered back to the farmhouse, feeling weaker by the minute. He felt cold and shivery, and blood was soaking his sweater and dripping on the ground, despite his effort to stop the bleeding with a handkerchief.

The stables were in darkness, so he walked right up to the farmhouse and shoved open the door. On the other side, Liam's wife was brandishing a large kitchen knife with a shaking hand.

He regarded her warily. 'Hi, Dina.'

'Where's Liam?'

'Dead.'

'Thank goodness for that!' She dropped the knife, exclaimed over his bloodstained clothing and shoved him into a chair. 'What happened?'

He collapsed heavily into the seat, the kitchen doing a couple of laps without him. 'I've been shot.' He didn't elaborate. Who wanted to admit to being shot by a kid? 'You're going to have to treat it.'

'I'm a nurse practitioner, not a surgeon. I only know the theory. Is the bullet still in there?' She pulled off his makeshift padding and grimaced. 'You got off lightly. The bullet went in at an angle.'

Lightly? 'We have a ferry to catch. Just dig the thing out, stop the bleeding and I'll be fine.'

'Until the infection kills you.' She took a first-aid box from the cupboard and began cleaning the wound. 'This will help but you're going to need antibiotics.'

'Got any?'

'Sure, the surgery dishes them out like sweeties. Honestly, Michael! What do you think? The only antibiotics around here are for the horses!'

'Same thing.'

'No, they're not, but I expect they'll have to do.' She worked in silence for a few minutes and then, 'I was so worried you'd be caught. Did you get the money?'

He could hardly think straight with the pain. 'Everything went according to plan.' Liam's *plan*. Michael would never see his children again, but Dina wouldn't care about that. Dina didn't care about anything other than herself. Right now she thought herself in love with him but after that? 'We'll take the lorry,' he said. 'Grab your belongings and stash them in the crates on top of the money. Pretend we're doing a removal. You'll have to do it. I don't have the strength. And I'll need Liam's passport and his new ID.'

'You don't look anything like him!'

'Does anyone look like their passport photo? When we're ready to leave, wake up Will, and I'll tip off the police about Charlie and Anthony. That should give us a head start. They think we're going to Spain.'

Dina frowned. 'Why do we need to take Will?'

Was she serious? 'You can't leave him here on his own. The poor kid's only eleven years old.'

'He'll be fine. Charlie's wife will take him. She's always been a sucker for kids.'

This *was* the woman he was planning to spend the rest of his life with?

'We're taking Will,' he said. After all, wouldn't that be the best revenge?

If he couldn't have his own family, he'd have Liam's.

Liam's kid, Liam's wife, Liam's money, Liam's life.

FORTY-ONE

Ben began the interview. 'What should I call you?'

'How about "sir"?'

Jonesy's solicitor cleared his throat. 'I believe he meant your birth name, Mr Jones,' and then muttered something beneath his breath that must have been some kind of admonishment because Jonesy sighed and said,

'Michael Caradoc Jones. I never liked it. The only ones who ever called me Michael were the wife and her family, and the people round here. My parents called me Caradoc. My mates call me Jonesy.'

'You took your wife's surname when you married?'

'She didn't fancy "Jones" and it made no odds to me.'

'You had a string of convictions to your name when you left London in the early 90s. A new name, a new start?'

'If you say so.'

'You're good at new starts, aren't you, Mr Jones? From a petty thief to the son-in-law of a vicar; to a robber; to a successful musician; a manager; a murderer. Did I miss anything out?'

'Are you judging me, Mr Detective Inspector? Last time I

saw you, you were a snivelling kid way over his head. Made me laugh when you turned up at my hotel to interview me. You didn't recognise me, but I knew you all right.' He slid his shirt from his shoulder to reveal a wicked-looking starburst scar, and winked at Harriet. 'Your boss shot me, did you know that? Left me for dead.'

Harriet, who had already been briefed, said, 'You were holding a gun to his head at the time, Mr Jones. I'd call it self-defence.'

Jonesy rolled his eyes. 'Bloody police. You all stick together.'

'He was fifteen years old!'

'He was as tall as me!'

'Why did you kill Liam Elliott?' Ben asked.

'Ha! You're not pinning that one on me. Where's your evidence? You're telling me you have DNA after fifteen years?'

Ben seriously hoped so but it would take weeks to find out. Jonesy had been bleeding when he'd left Liam in the orchard. With any luck, some of that blood would have transferred itself to Liam's clothing when Jonesy buried his body. Cotton clothing would have rotted but, whatever the material, finding a viable sample was also going to depend on exposure to fifteen years of weather conditions.

'You'd be surprised,' he said. 'How about Anthony Elliott? Why did you kill him?'

Jonesy sat back in his chair, far too confident. 'You have nothing to link me to him. Do you take me for a fool?'

'We have the murder weapon, evidence of said murder weapon left at the scene, and you were caught trying to kill Camilla Graham with it.'

'You don't want to believe anything that girl says. She's a liar.'

'You were also caught on camera at Green Acres—'

'Where's that?' scoffed Jonesy.

'Anthony Elliott's livery yard.'

'I don't believe it. Some grainy footage on one of those nanny-cam jobs? Could be anyone! Good luck taking that to court.'

Harriet took out her phone, which had been set up for just this moment, and tapped 'play'.

The secret camera Anthony had set up to catch a coffee pod thief had filmed the last moments of him fighting for his life. 'Grainy footage' was not a problem. It was rather *too* clear.

Jones turned pale. His solicitor went green, swallowed and looked away from the screen. Ben knew how he felt. Not many in the earlier briefing had been able to watch the film to its conclusion.

'Damn,' Jonesy said, a last attempt at bravado. 'I guess you got me.'

'Would you care to revise your statement?' Harriet asked politely.

'I wanted my life back. It was that simple.'

'After all these years?'

'I came to England a few months ago to meet with record company execs about the recording of Lorcan's new album, which had already been put back twice. His original label dropped him after the last album bombed, but his sales were still good in the UK. I figured I'd check out this precious farm-house of his at the same time.' He sighed. 'It brought back memories, not all of them bad. I saw my son – David – in the street outside the church. I said "hello" but even though he smiled, he didn't recognise me. Why would he? A raddled old geezer like me? Damn, that hurt.'

Ben almost felt sorry for him. What must it be like, not to be recognised by your own child?

'I took a walk around the village,' Jonesy said. 'It's a nice place, better than I remembered. I even went for a pint at old Charlie's place. The prices have gone up since my day!'

'It's a restaurant now,' Ben said, 'owned by Anthony's son, Drew.'

'Yeah? He always was a sharp one. After that, I drove out to the farmhouse. It was in bad shape. The roof had gone; some of the floorboards were rotten. When I went into Lorcan's old room I could see the sword glinting through a gap right away. I'm amazed no one had spotted it before me. If I hadn't taken it, someone else would have. I took it back to London, to an old mate of mine, to get it restored. Thought I'd give it to Lorcan as a Christmas present. He's mad on family history. I didn't know he'd stolen it from the museum.'

'What happened then?'

'I went back to New York and thought nothing of it, until Lorcan was arrested and the highwayman showed up on telly waving a sword about. That gave me the idea.'

'To kill the only person left who could not only identify you, but testify that you took part in the robbery.' There was a twisted logic to it. Anthony Elliott was standing between Jonesy and his much-longed-for happy ending – a reunion with his children.

Jonesy laughed bitterly. 'My own kid didn't recognise me, you didn't either, but Anthony did – immediately. Lucky I had the sword, so I took care of him. I thought I could blame it on the highwayman – except you'd already got the bloke.'

'Woman,' Harriet said. 'Rose Griffiths.'

'I didn't know it was my own daughter! Too much like her old man, that was her problem. Bloody hell! What a mess! I should have stayed in New York. Why the hell did Lorcan want to return?'

'He wanted to find his roots,' Ben said. 'He wanted to meet with his real family.'

'Real family! No one cared about that poor kid except me; don't try to tell me any different.'

Jonesy had a point; Ben had to grant him that.

'Strange though,' Jonesy said, 'that you became a police officer when your dad was a robber.'

Did he think he was the first person to have made that observation?

'Greg too,' Ben said. 'He was a detective sergeant in the Met before he moved back to Port Rell.'

'So the crooks' kids went straight, eh? Even my David became a bloody vicar!' Jonesy's laugh was bitter. 'I believe that's what they call "irony", son.'

FORTY-TWO

Liam Elliott was cremated with the minimum of fuss. A cadaver dog found his body under the rubble of a partially ruined outbuilding in one corner of the orchard. It was Harriet who noticed the ornate doorway and unusual shape as it was cleared. Lorcan paid for the county archaeologist to attend, and it was confirmed that the building was the missing chapel of Ravenswood House – the last resting place of the famous highwayman, Matthew Elliott.

The funeral for Anthony Elliott took place at St Francis's Church in Raven's Edge, two weeks later. Drew Elliott had spared no expense. The hearse had driven past each of Anthony's businesses, starting in Norchester with The Crooked Cat nightclub and ending with Green Acres, where it was joined by a fleet of black limousines for the final trip to the church.

Milla, sitting halfway down the church with her grandmother, was surprised to see Ben walk in as one of the pallbearers, along with his cousins, Drew, Greg and Lorcan. In one of those strange paradoxes, David was conducting the service. Granny Brianna had already told Milla that Anthony had left his entire estate to a charity that supported victims of crime.

Drew was going to match that amount, and had asked for donations rather than flowers.

Ben went to sit with the rest of the Elliott family at the front of the church, so there was no chance for her to talk to him, not that it would have been appropriate. When the family filed out for the interment, many of the other mourners began to leave. Granny Brianna stopped to talk to her friend Mrs Lancaster, a neighbour of Ben's. They'd chat forever, given half a chance, so Milla carried on alone towards the lych-gate, intending to skip the wake and head on home.

Instead, she found Ben leaning against one pillar, looking very pale, and Harriet saying, 'Are you sure you don't want a paracetamol? You look *terrible.*'

'You're always saying I look terrible...'

Both of them straightened shiftily as Milla approached.

'Hello,' she said, with a polite, Granny Brianna-ish smile.

'Hi,' Harriet replied. 'It's good to see you. I hope you're feeling better after your ordeal, and now I'm going to make a tactful withdrawal to allow you two to sort out your sh... er, problems without an audience. Goodbye!'

She walked off in the direction of the police station and didn't look back.

Tactful *was* a good place to start.

'I'm sorry for your loss,' Milla said. 'Are you OK?'

'Yes,' he grimaced. 'Anthony's death hit me harder than I thought it would. It brought back a lot of trauma from my childhood that I'd blanked out, but I've been able to reconnect with my family. Although Drew persists in calling me 'Benny Dickhead', as though we're still twelve.'

There was an awkward pause.

'I'm sorry I've not been in touch,' he said.

For two bloody weeks. Yes, I noticed.

'I've been busy with this case,' he added. 'I've not been

sleeping much either.' His migraines had always been worse after a sleepless night. 'I should have sent you a message.'

Yes, you should.

'It's been hard, finding out that I wasn't the person I thought I was.'

'That you were the one who shot Jonesy? Yes, I heard about that. It sounds as though it was self-defence. You were only a kid.'

'I'd completely wiped it from my memory. I went to bed and the next day it was as though it had never happened.'

'Shock will do that.' It had happened to her, the night her uncle had been killed. She'd lost several days afterwards. Post-traumatic stress syndrome.

'I'm sorry for the things I said about trust. I'd like us to get back together.' His words came out in a rush. 'I still care about you, a lot. It's just...'

Just?

Was he about to do it *again*?

'Please don't give me another lecture about the importance of trust,' she said. 'I *know* I should have trusted you and I apologise for that. I should have contacted you as soon as I walked into Lorcan's bedroom and found that head. I've made a complete mess of everything, including your investigation. I'm sorry. We rushed into this relationship and now we're paying the price. We should have tried to be friends first.'

'*Friends?*'

'We'll agree to be friends,' she repeated, 'and see what develops from there.'

'OK, friends.' She didn't miss the flash of pain in his green eyes. 'If that's what you want.'

She'd hurt his feelings? Well, good! At least it proved he had some.

'Maybe take a few more weeks and then go on a non-date date?' she suggested.

'A non-date date?'

'Because we still like each other?'

Didn't they?

Almost reluctantly, the corner of his mouth twitched. 'Yes,' he said. 'We do.'

The distant hum of the mourners grew louder as the funeral ended and everyone began making their way to the cars.

Milla sighed. 'Well, goodbye, Ben,' she said. 'You know where I live.'

'Take care, Milla. I'll be in touch about the... non-date date.'

It was adorable that he thought that decision was up to him. She turned, so he couldn't see her smile, crossing The Square and walking up to her front door as everyone began to climb into the waiting cars.

Determined not to watch him leave, she unlocked her door and went inside.

'Hello, Princess. How did it go?'

Drake was sitting in her favourite chair by the window. He'd been there some time, judging from the empty coffee mug in front of him, and had a perfect view of the lych-gate.

Meaning he'd had a ringside seat to her conversation with Ben.

Confirmed when he asked, far too casually, 'Did you break his heart?'

She rather thought Ben had broken hers.

'Get lost, Drake. I'm not in the mood.' She dropped her bag on the couch and went to switch on the kettle. Perhaps she should have gone to the wake. There was sure to have been alcohol, and this *must* count as a moment of severe stress.

She began opening and closing cupboards, in case there was a bottle of something, forgotten at the back, but all she could find was soy sauce.

Then Drake was behind her, gently taking the bottle from her hand and placing it back on the counter. 'Remember my offer? Come and work for me. It'll be better than sitting here all day, feeling sorry for yourself.'

'Who says I'm feeling sorry for myself?'

Yet what was the alternative? Spend her days in her little-old-lady cottage, watching life pass her by through that window, where she could already see the tail-lights of Ben's car as it went in the direction of the bridge and, presumably, the car park of The Drop.

If Ben came back, it would have to be his choice, but she wasn't going to change.

She wouldn't change for anyone.

And she was so heartily tired of pretending to be good.

'There's a new case I've taken on,' Drake said. 'You might be interested?'

'No, I wouldn't.'

'Perfect for your skill set. Let me tell you about it. Big old house with a locked room in the attic that no one can get into.'

'Have they tried a sledgehammer?'

He winced. 'Maybe something more subtle? It's Grade 1 listed and owned by a pillar of the community. I'll let you know his name once you've agreed to take it on, although you might be able to work it out for yourself. He's recently re-married, but under a cloud because his previous wife disappeared in myste-rious circumstances.'

Despite everything, Milla burst out laughing. 'Drake, that's the plot of *Bluebeard*!'

That grin of his was far too wide.

'Trust you to spoil my fun. Come on, Camilla. Come work for me.'

She hesitated for far too long before saying, 'No.'

'Doughnuts on Fridays, remember? Are you sure you're not tempted? Just a little bit...?

A LETTER FROM THE AUTHOR

Dear reader,

Thank you so much for reading this book. I do hope you enjoyed it. I have lots more mysteries planned for Ben, Harriet and their team to solve. If you'd like to be the first to hear about new releases and bonus content, you can click on the link below to sign up. Don't miss out!

www.stormpublishing.co/louise-marley

If you have enjoyed this book and could spare a few moments to leave a review that would be hugely appreciated. Even a short review can make all the difference in encouraging a reader to discover my books for the first time. Thank you so much!

When I was asked to write a second Raven's Edge story, I had thought I would continue the fairy tale themes of the first book. However, it wasn't until I'd almost finished that I realised the story was a homage to those Gothic movies made by Hammer House of Horror, even though I've always been a wimp when it comes to scary films! I spend a lot of time hiding behind my fingers, especially when I suspect a jump shock might be coming up!

Tim Burton has always been someone I admire, especially his version of *Sleepy Hollow*, which is a lot more fun than the original book – sorry Mr Irving! And I've always loved ghost stories, especially the ones with headless horsemen and ghostly highwaymen.

Halloween is one of my favourite festivals, so it was fun to write a story set at this time of the year. The inspiration for the carnival in Raven's Edge was one that used to take place in the Hampshire village of Titchfield, close to where I grew up. It was a family tradition that we would walk down to The Square and watch it every year, then visit the funfair afterwards. My grandmother would make her famous (rock hard!) 'bonfire toffee' as a treat and, because she came from the North of England, would carve us a turnip Jack-o'-Lantern instead of a pumpkin. Now those things are *proper* scary!

I had such fun writing this story. I do hope you've enjoyed reading it!

Thank you for being part of this journey with me. Would you like to know what Milla does next? And what Harriet's father did to be called a hero? Will she ever pluck up courage to ask Misha out on a date? Do stay in touch. I have so many new stories planned!

You can contact me at louise@louisemarley.co.uk. I'd love to hear from you!

Louise x

louisemarley.co.uk
Bluesky: bsky.app/profile/louisemarley.bsky.social
Threads: www.threads.net/@louisemarleywrites
Blog: louisemarleywrites.blogspot.com

facebook.com/LouiseMarleyAuthor

x.com/louisemarley

instagram.com/louisemarleywrites

ACKNOWLEDGEMENTS

Lots of love to my family for having to put up with the many moods of a writer and being kind enough to reassure me that *of course* I haven't forgotten how to write. I'm sorry I made you watch *Sleepy Hollow* so many times, and forced you to eat all those takeaways when I didn't have time to cook. I'll buy broccoli to make up for it. My treat. Also, a big hug for my husband for helping Milla get out of yet *another* fix.

Huge thanks to Kathryn Taussig for her unerring ability to pick up on my plot holes and being such an inspiring editor. Her brilliant advice and encouragement has helped me breathe life into the very unusual village of Raven's Edge. Also, to Oliver Rhodes and the fabulous team at Storm for all the hard work that goes on behind the scenes. I'll say it again: I'm *very* fortunate to work with some of the loveliest people in publishing!

Big thanks to my writing buddies, Novelistas Ink, for cheering me on from the sidelines. I don't know what I'd do without their unwavering support. Special mention to Trisha Ashley and Juliet Greenwood for the caffeine-fuelled, brainstorming sessions at various cafés and garden centres throughout North Wales, and to Lottie Cardew, who always messages me when I've gone too quiet during mammoth writing sessions.

Last but definitely not least, a big hug to my lovely readers for all your support, the shares on social media, the kind-hearted messages, and the wonderful reviews. You never fail to brighten my day!

Printed in Great Britain
by Amazon

42922324R00212